The Island of Missing Trees

The Island of Missing Trees

ELIF SHAFAK

VIKING

an imprint of

PENGUIN BOOKS

VIKING

UK | USA | Canada | Ireland | Australia
India | New Zealand | South Africa

Viking is part of the Penguin Random House group of companies
whose addresses can be found at global.penguinrandomhouse.com.

First published 2021

010

Copyright © Elif Shafak, 2021
Illustrations copyright © Josie Staveley-Taylor, 2021

Set in 11/13 pt Dante MT Std
Typeset by Jouve (UK), Milton Keynes
Printed and bound in Great Britain by Clays Ltd, Elcograf S.p.A.

The authorized representative in the EEA is Penguin Random House Ireland,
Morrison Chambers, 32 Nassau Street, Dublin D02 YH68

A CIP catalogue record for this book is available from the British Library

HARDBACK ISBN: 978-0-241-43499-4
TRADE PAPERBACK ISBN: 978-0-241-43500-7

www.greenpenguin.co.uk

To immigrants and exiles everywhere,
the uprooted, the re-rooted, the rootless,

And to the trees we left behind,
rooted in our memories . . .

Anyone who hasn't been in the Chilean forest doesn't know this planet. I have come out of that landscape, that mud, that silence, to roam, to go singing through the world.

– Pablo Neruda, *Memoirs*

It will have blood: They say blood will have blood. Stones have been known to move and trees to speak . . .

– William Shakespeare, *Macbeth*

Contents

Island

Once upon a memory, at the far end of the Mediterranean Sea, there lay an island so beautiful and blue that the many travellers, pilgrims, crusaders and merchants who fell in love with it either wanted never to leave or tried to tow it with hemp ropes all the way back to their own countries.

Legends, perhaps.

But legends are there to tell us what history has forgotten.

It has been many years since I fled that place on board a plane, inside a suitcase made of soft black leather, never to return. I have since adopted another land, England, where I have grown and thrived, but not a single day passes that I do not yearn to be back. Home. Motherland.

It must still be there where I left it, rising and sinking with the waves that break and foam upon its rugged coastline. At the crossroads of three continents – Europe, Africa, Asia – and the Levant, that vast and impenetrable region, vanished entirely from the maps of today.

A map is a two-dimensional representation with arbitrary symbols and incised lines that decide who is to be our enemy and who is to be our friend, who deserves our love and who deserves our hatred and who, our sheer indifference.

Cartography is another name for stories told by winners.

For stories told by those who have lost, there isn't one.

Here is how I remember it: golden beaches, turquoise waters, lucid skies. Every year sea turtles would come ashore to lay their eggs in the powdery sand. The late-afternoon wind brought along the scent of gardenia, cyclamen, lavender, honeysuckle. Branching ropes of wisteria climbed up whitewashed walls, aspiring to reach the clouds, hopeful in the way only dreamers are. When the night kissed your skin, as it always did, you could smell the jasmine on its breath. The moon, here closer to earth, hung bright and gentle over the rooftops, casting a vivid glow on the narrow alleys and cobblestoned streets. And yet shadows found a way to creep through the light. Whispers of distrust and conspiracy rippled in the dark. For the island was riven into two pieces – the north and the south. A different language, a different script, a different memory prevailed in each, and when they prayed, the islanders, it was seldom to the same god.

The capital was split by a partition which sliced right through it like a slash to the heart. Along the demarcation line – the frontier – were dilapidated houses riddled with bullet holes, empty courtyards scarred with grenade bursts, boarded stores gone to ruin, ornamented gates hanging at angles from broken hinges, luxury cars from another era rusting away under layers of dust . . . Roads were blocked by coils of barbed wire, piles of sandbags, barrels full of concrete, anti-tank ditches and watchtowers. Streets ended abruptly, like unfinished thoughts, unresolved feelings.

Soldiers stood guard with machine guns, when they were not making the rounds; young, bored, lonesome men from various corners of the world who had known little about the island and its complex history until they found themselves posted to this unfamiliar environment. Walls were plastered with official signs in bold colours and capital letters:

NO ENTRY BEYOND THIS POINT

KEEP AWAY, RESTRICTED AREA!

NO PHOTOGRAPHS, NO FILMING ALLOWED

Then, further along the barricade, an illicit addition in chalk scribbled on a barrel by a passer-by:

WELCOME TO NO MAN'S LAND

The partition that tore through Cyprus from one end to the other, a buffer zone patrolled by United Nations troops, was about one hundred and ten miles long, and as wide as four miles in places while merely a few yards in others. It traversed all kinds of landscapes – abandoned villages, coastal hinterlands, wetlands, fallow lands, pine forests, fertile plains, copper mines and archaeological sites – meandering in its course like the ghost of some ancient river. But it was here, across and around the capital, that it became more visible, tangible, and thus haunting.

Nicosia, the only divided capital in the world.

It sounded almost a positive thing when described that way; something special about it, if not unique, a sense of defying gravity, like the single grain of sand moving skywards in an hourglass just upended. But, in reality, Nicosia was no exception, one more name added to the list of segregated places and separated communities, those consigned to history and those yet to come. At this moment, though, it stood as a peculiarity. The last divided city in Europe.

My home town.

There are many things that a border – even one as clear-cut and well guarded as this – cannot prevent from crossing. The Etesian wind, for instance, the softly named but surprisingly strong *meltemi* or *meltem*. The butterflies, grasshoppers and lizards. The snails, too, painfully slow though they are. Occasionally, a birthday balloon that escapes a child's grip drifts in the sky, strays into the other side – enemy territory.

Then, the birds. Blue herons, black-headed buntings, honey buzzards, yellow wagtails, willow warblers, masked shrikes and, my favourites, golden orioles. All the way from the northern hemisphere, migrating mostly during the night, darkness gathering at the tips of their wings and etching red circles around their eyes, they stop here midway in their long journey, before continuing to Africa. The island for them is a resting place, a lacuna in the tale, an in-between-ness.

There is a hill in Nicosia where birds of all plumages come to forage and feed. It is thick with overgrown brambles, stinging nettles and clumps of heather. In the midst of this dense vegetation is an old well with a pulley that creaks at the slightest tug and a metal bucket tied to a rope, frayed and algae-covered from disuse. Deep inside it is always pitch-black and freezing cold, even in the fierce midday sun beating down directly overhead. The well is a hungry mouth, awaiting its next meal. It eats up every ray of light, every trace of heat, holding each mote in its elongated stone throat.

If you ever find yourself in the area and if, led by curiosity or instinct, you lean over the edge and peer down, waiting for your eyes to adjust, you may catch a glint below, like the fleeting gleam from the scales of a fish before it disappears back into the water. Do not let that deceive you, though. There are no fish down there. No snakes. No scorpions. No spiders dangling from silken threads. The glint does not come from a living being, but from an antique pocket watch – eighteen-carat gold encased with mother of pearl, engraved with lines from a poem:

> *Arriving there is what you are destined for,*
> *But do not hurry the journey at all . . .*

And there on the back are two letters, or more precisely, the same letter written twice:

Y & Y

The well is thirty-four feet deep and four feet wide. It is constructed of gently curved ashlar stone descending in identical horizontal courses all the way down to the mute and musty waters below. Trapped at the bottom are two men. The owners of a popular tavern. Both of slender build and medium height with large, jutting ears which they used to joke about. Both born and bred on this island, and in their forties when they were kidnapped, beaten and murdered. They have been thrown into this shaft after being chained first to each other, then to a three-litre olive oil tin filled with concrete to ensure they will never surface again. The pocket watch that one of them wore on the day of their abduction has stopped at exactly eight minutes to midnight.

Time is a songbird, and just like any other songbird it can be taken captive. It can be held prisoner in a cage and for even longer than you might think possible. But time cannot be kept in check in perpetuity.

No captivity is forever.

Some day the water will rust away the metal and the chains will snap, and the concrete's rigid heart will soften as even the most rigid hearts tend to do with the passing of the years. Only then will the two corpses, finally free, swim towards the chink of sky overhead, shimmering in the refracted sunlight; they will ascend towards that blissful blue, at first slowly, then fast and frantic, like pearl divers gasping for air.

Sooner or later, this old, dilapidated well on that lonely, beautiful island at the far end of the Mediterranean Sea will collapse in on itself and its secret will rise to the surface, as every secret is bound to do in the end.

PART ONE

How to Bury a Tree

A Girl Named Island

England, late 2010s

It was the last lesson of the year at Brook Hill Secondary School in north London. Year 11 classroom. History lesson. Only fifteen minutes before the bell, and the students were getting restless, eager for the Christmas holidays to start. All the students, that is, except for one.

Ada Kazantzakis, aged sixteen, sat with a quiet intensity in her usual seat by the window at the back of the classroom. Her hair, the colour of burnished mahogany, was gathered in a low-slung ponytail; her delicate features were drawn and tight, and her large, doe-brown eyes seemed to betray a lack of sleep the night before. She was neither looking forward to the festive season nor feeling any excitement at the prospect of snowfall. Every now and then she cast furtive glances outside, though her expression remained mostly unchanged.

Around midday it had hailed; milky-white, frozen pellets shredding the last of the leaves in the trees, hammering the bicycle shed roof, bouncing off the ground in a wild tap dance. Now it had fallen quiet, but anyone could see the weather had turned decisively worse. A storm was on its way. This morning the radio had announced that, within no more than forty-eight hours, Britain would be hit by a polar vortex bringing in record-breaking lows, icy rains and blizzards. Water shortages, power cuts and burst mains were expected to paralyse large swathes of England and Scotland as well as parts of northern Europe. People had been stockpiling – canned fish, baked beans, bags of pasta, toilet paper – as if getting ready for a siege.

All day long the students had been carrying on about the

9

storm, worried for their holiday plans and travel arrangements. Not Ada, though. She had neither family gatherings nor exotic destinations lined up. Her father did not intend to go anywhere. He had work to do. He always had work to do. Her father was an incurable workaholic – anyone who knew him would testify to that – but ever since her mother had died, he had retreated into his research like a burrowing animal hiding in its tunnel for safety and warmth.

Somewhere in the course of her young life, Ada had understood that he was very different from other fathers, but she still found it hard to take kindly to his obsession with plants. Everyone else's fathers worked in offices, shops or government departments, wore matching suits, white shirts and polished black shoes, whereas hers was usually clad in a waterproof jacket, a pair of olive or brown moleskin trousers, rugged boots. Instead of a briefcase he had a shoulder bag that carried miscellaneous items like his hand lens, dissecting kit, plant press, compass and notebooks. Other fathers endlessly prattled on about business and retirement plans but hers was more interested in the toxic effects of pesticides on seed germination or ecological damage from logging. He spoke about the impact of deforestation with a passion his counterparts reserved for fluctuations in their personal stock portfolios; not only spoke but wrote about it too. An evolutionary ecologist and botanist, he had published twelve books. One of them was called *The Mysterious Kingdom: How Fungi Shaped Our Past, Changes Our Future*. Another one of his monographs was about hornworts, liverworts and mosses. The cover depicted a stone bridge over a creek bubbling around rocks coated in velvety green. Right above the dreamlike image was the gilded title: *A Field Guide to Common Bryophytes of Europe*. Underneath, his name was printed in capital letters: KOSTAS KAZANTZAKIS.

Ada had no idea what kind of people would read the sort of books her father wrote, but she hadn't dared mention them to anyone at school. She had no intention of giving her classmates yet another reason to conclude that she – and her family – were weird.

No matter the time of day, her father seemed to prefer the company of trees to the company of humans. He had always been this way, but when her mother was alive, she could temper his eccentricities, possibly because she, too, had her own peculiar ways. Since her death, Ada had felt her father drifting away from her, or perhaps it was she who had been drifting away from him – it was hard to tell who was evading whom in a house engulfed in a miasma of grief. So they would be at home, the two of them, not only for the duration of the storm but the entire Christmas season. Ada hoped her father had remembered to go shopping.

Her eyes slid down to her notebook. On the open page, at the bottom, she had sketched a butterfly. Slowly, she traced the wings, so brittle, easily breakable.

'Hey, you got any gum?'

Snapping out of her reverie, Ada turned aside. She liked sitting at the back of the classroom but that meant being paired off with Emma-Rose, who had the annoying habit of cracking her knuckles, chewing one piece of gum after another although it was not allowed at school, and a tendency to go on about matters that were of no interest to anyone else.

'No, sorry.' Ada shook her head and glanced nervously at the teacher.

'History is a most fascinating subject,' Mrs Walcott was now saying, her brogues planted firmly behind her desk, as though she needed a barricade from behind which to teach her students, all twenty-nine of them. 'Without understanding our past, how can we hope to shape our future?'

'Oh, I can't stand her,' Emma-Rose muttered under her breath.

Ada did not comment. She wasn't sure whether Emma-Rose had meant her or the teacher. If the former, she had nothing to say in her own defence. If the latter, she wasn't going to join in the vilification. She liked Mrs Walcott, who, though well meaning, clearly had difficulty keeping discipline in the classroom. Ada had heard that the woman had lost her husband a few years back. She had pictured in her mind, more than a few times, what her teacher's daily life must be like: how she dragged her round body out of bed in the mornings, rushed to take a shower before the hot water ran out, rummaged in the wardrobe for a suitable dress hardly different from yesterday's suitable dress, whipped up breakfast for her twins before dropping them off at the nursery, her face flushed, her tone apologetic. She had also imagined her teacher touching herself at night, her hands drawing circles under her cotton nightie, and at times inviting in men who would leave wet footprints on the carpet and a sourness in her soul.

Ada had no idea whether her thoughts corresponded with reality, but she suspected so. It was her talent, perhaps her only one. She could detect other people's sadnesses the way one animal could smell another of its kind a mile away.

'All right, class, one final note before you go!' Mrs Walcott said with a clap of her hands. 'We'll be studying migration and generational change next term. It's a nice fun project before we knuckle down and get on with GCSE revision. In preparation, I want you to interview an elderly relative during the holidays. Ideally, your grandparents, but it could just as well be another family member. Ask them questions about what it was like when they were young and come up with a four-to-five-page essay.'

A chorus of unhappy sighs rippled across the room.

'Make sure your writing is supported by historical facts,' Mrs Walcott said, ignoring the reaction. 'I want to see solid research backed up by evidence, not speculation.'

More sighs and groans followed.

'Oh, don't forget to check if there are any heirlooms around – an antique ring, a wedding dress, a set of vintage china, a handmade quilt, a box of letters or family recipes, any memorabilia that has been passed down.'

Ada dropped her gaze. She had never met her relatives on either side. She knew they lived in Cyprus somewhere but that was about the extent of her knowledge. What kind of people were they? How did they spend their days? Would they recognize her if they passed by on the street or bumped into each other at the supermarket? The only close relation she had heard of was a certain aunt, Meryem, who sent cheerful postcards of sunny beaches and wildflower pastures that jarred with her complete lack of presence in their lives.

If her relatives remained a mystery, Cyprus was a bigger one. She had seen pictures on the internet, but she had not once travelled to the place after which she was named.

In her mother's language, her name meant 'island'. When she was younger she had assumed it referred to Great Britain, the only island she had ever known, only later coming to the realization that it was, in fact, another isle, far away, and the reason was that she was conceived over there. The discovery had left her with a sense of confusion, if not discomfort. Firstly, because it reminded her that her parents had had sex, something she never wanted to think about; secondly, because it attached her, in an inevitable way, to a place that hitherto had existed only in her imagination. Since then she had added her own name to the collection of non-English words she carried in her pockets, words which, though curious and colourful, still felt distant and unfamiliar enough to remain impenetrable, like perfect pebbles you picked up on a beach and brought home but then didn't know what to do with. She had quite a few of them by now. Some idioms too. And songs, merry tunes. But that was about it. Her parents had not taught her their native languages, preferring to communicate solely in English at home. Ada could speak neither her father's Greek nor her mother's Turkish.

Growing up, each time she had enquired about why they had not yet been to Cyprus to meet their relatives, or why their relatives had not come over to England to visit them, both her father and her mother had given her a whole host of excuses. The time just wasn't right; there was too much work to be done or too many expenses to take care of . . . Slowly, a suspicion had taken root inside her: maybe her parents' marriage had not been approved by the families. In that case, she surmised, nor was she, the product of this marriage, really *approved*. Yet for as long as she was able to, Ada had retained the hopeful belief that if any of her extended family were to spend time with her and her parents, they would forgive them for whatever it was that they had not been forgiven for.

Since her mother's death, however, Ada had stopped asking questions about her next of kin. If they were the kind of people who would not attend the funeral of one of their own, they were hardly likely to have any love for the child of the deceased – a girl they had never laid eyes on.

'While you conduct your interview, do not judge the older generation,' said Mrs Walcott. 'Listen carefully, try to see things through their eyes. And make sure to record the entire conversation.'

Jason, sitting in the front row, interjected. 'So if we interview a Nazi criminal, shall we be nice to them?'

Mrs Walcott sighed. 'Well, that's a bit of an extreme example. No, I don't expect you to be nice to that sort of person.'

Jason grinned, as if he had scored a point.

'Miss!' Emma-Rose chimed in. 'We've got an antique violin at home, would that count as an heirloom?'

'Sure, if it's something that's belonged to your family for generations.'

'Oh, yes, we've had it for so long.' Emma-Rose beamed. 'My mother says it was made in Vienna in the nineteenth century. Or was it the eighteenth? Anyway, it's very valuable, but we're not selling it.'

Zafaar put his hand up. 'We've got a hope chest that belonged to my granny. She brought it with her from Punjab. Would that do?'

Ada felt her heart give a little thud, not even hearing the teacher's response or the rest of the conversation. Her whole frame went rigid as she tried not to look at Zafaar, lest her face give away her feelings.

The month before, the two of them had unexpectedly been paired up for a science project – assembling a device to measure how many calories different types of food contained. After days of trying to coordinate a meeting and failing, she had given up and done most of the research herself, finding articles, buying the kit, building the calorimeter. They had both received an A at the end. A tiny smile forming at the corner of his mouth, Zafaar had thanked her with an awkwardness that could have been a guilty conscience, but which might equally have been indifference. It was the last time they had spoken.

Ada had never kissed a boy. All the girls in her year had *something* to tell – real or imaginary – when they gathered in the changing rooms before and after PE, but not her. This absolute silence of hers had not gone unnoticed, provoking much ribbing and ridicule. Once, she had found a porn magazine inside her school bag, slipped in by unknown hands, she was certain, to freak her out. All day long she had agonized that a teacher might spot it and inform her father. Not that she was scared of her father the way she knew some other students were of theirs. It wasn't fear that she felt. Not even guilt, after having decided to keep the magazine. That wasn't the reason why she had not told him about the incident – or about other incidents. She had stopped sharing things with her father ever since she sensed, on some primal level, that she needed to protect him from more pain.

If her mother were alive, Ada might have shown her the magazine. They might have looked at it together, giggling. They might have talked, cradling mugs of hot chocolate in their hands, breathing in the steam that rose towards their faces. Her mother had understood unruly thoughts, naughty thoughts, *the dark side of the moon*. She once said, half jokingly, that she was too rebellious to be a good mum, too motherly to be a good rebel. Only now, after she was gone, did Ada acknowledge that, despite everything, she was a good mum – and a good rebel. It had been exactly eleven months and eight days since her death. This would be the first Christmas she would spend without her.

'What do you think, Ada?' Mrs Walcott asked suddenly. 'Would you agree with that?'

Having gone back to her drawing, it took Ada another beat to shift her gaze from the butterfly and realize that the teacher was looking at her. She blushed up to her hairline. Her back tensed as if her body had sensed a danger she was yet to comprehend. When she found her voice, it came out so shaky, she wasn't sure she had spoken at all.

'Pardon?'

'I was asking whether you think Jason is right.'

'Sorry, miss . . . right about what?'

A suppressed titter rose.

'We were talking about family heirlooms,' said Mrs Walcott with a tired smile. 'Zafaar mentioned his grandma's hope chest. Then Jason said, why is it always women who cling to these souvenirs and knick-knacks from the past? And I wanted to know whether you agree with that statement.'

Ada swallowed drily. Her pulse thudded in her temples. Silence, thick and glutinous, trickled into the space around her. She imagined it spreading out like dark ink on to crocheted white doilies – like the ones she had once found in the drawer of her mother's dressing table. Neatly cut into obsessively small pieces, destroyed, they had been placed between layers of tissue paper, as if her mother could neither keep them as they were, nor bring herself to throw them away.

'Any thoughts?' said Mrs Walcott, her voice tender but insistent.

Slowly and without thinking why, Ada stood up, scraping the chair noisily against the flagstone floor. She cleared her throat, though she had absolutely no idea what to say. Her mind had gone blank. On the open page in front of her the butterfly, alarmed and desperate to flee, took to the air, even though its wings, unfinished and blurred at the edges, were hardly strong enough.

'I . . . I don't think it's always women. My father does it too.'

'He does?' asked Mrs Walcott. 'How exactly?'

Now all her classmates were staring at her, waiting for her to say something that would make sense. Some had a gentle pity in their eyes, others crude indifference, which she much preferred. She felt unmoored by their collective expectation, pressure building in her ears as if she were sinking underwater.

'Can you give us an example?' said Mrs Walcott. 'What does your father collect?'

'Uhm, my father . . .' Ada said in a drawl and paused.

What could she tell them about him? That he forgot to eat or even speak sometimes, letting whole days go by without consuming proper food or uttering a full sentence, or that, if only he could, he would probably spend the rest of his life in the back garden or, better yet, in a forest somewhere, his hands plunged in the soil, surrounded by bacteria, fungi and all those plants, growing and decaying by the minute? What could she tell them about her father that would make them understand what he was like when she herself had a hard time recognizing him any more?

Instead, she said a single word. 'Plants.'

'Plants . . .' echoed Mrs Walcott, her face twisted with incomprehension.

'My father is fond of them,' Ada added in a rush, instantly regretting her choice of words.

'Oh, how cute . . . he fancies flowers!' Jason commented in a syrupy tone.

Laughter rippled through the classroom, no longer constrained. Ada noticed even her friend Ed was avoiding her gaze, pretending to read something in his textbook, his shoulders slumped and his head down. She then searched for Zafaar and found his bright, black eyes that rarely saw her now studying her with a curiosity that bordered on concern.

'Well, that's lovely,' said Mrs Walcott. 'But can you think of an object he cares about? Something that has emotional value.'

In that moment there was nothing Ada wanted more than to find the right words. Why were they hiding from her? Her stomach constricted with a stab of pain, so sharp that for a few seconds she thought she couldn't breathe, let alone talk. And yet she did, and when she did, she heard herself say, 'He spends a lot of time with his trees.'

Mrs Walcott gave a half-nod, her smile fading from her lips.

'Especially this fig tree, I think that's his favourite.'

'All right then, you may sit down now,' said Mrs Walcott.

But Ada did not comply. The pain, having darted towards her ribcage, was searching for a way out. Her chest tightened, as though squeezed by invisible hands. She felt disorientated, the room swaying slightly under her feet.

'God, she's so cringey!' someone whispered loud enough for her to hear.

Ada clenched her eyes shut, feeling the burn of the comment, a raw scorch mark on her flesh. But nothing they did or said could be worse than her hatred for herself just then. What was wrong with her? Why could she not answer a simple question like everyone else?

As a child she had loved turning in circles on the Turkish carpet to make herself dizzy and drop to the floor, from where she would watch the world spin round and round. She could still remember the hand-woven patterns of the carpet dissolving in a thousand sparks, the colours blending into each other, scarlet into green, saffron into white. But what she experienced right now was a different kind of dizziness. She had the sense of entering a trap, a door locking behind her, the click of a latch falling into place. She felt paralysed.

So many times in the past she had suspected that she carried within a sadness that was not quite her own. In science class they had learned that everyone inherited one chromosome from their mother and one from their father – long threads of DNA with thousands of genes that built billions of neurons and trillions of connections between them. All that genetic information passed from parents to offspring – survival, growth, reproduction, the colour of your hair, the shape of your nose, whether you had freckles or sneezed in sunlight – everything was in there. But none of that answered the one question burning in her mind: was it also possible to inherit something as intangible and immeasurable as sorrow?

'You may sit down,' repeated Mrs Walcott.

Still she did not move.

'Ada . . . did you not hear what I said?'

Remaining upright, she tried to choke back the fear that filled her throat, clogged her nostrils. It reminded her of the taste of the sea under a harsh, beating sun. She touched it with the tip of her tongue. It wasn't the salty sea brine after all, it was warm blood. She had been biting the inside of her cheek.

Her eyes slid towards the window, beyond which the storm was approaching. She noticed in the slate-grey sky, amidst banks of clouds, a sliver of crimson bleeding into the horizon, like an old wound that had never quite healed.

'Please sit down,' came the teacher's voice.

And, once again, she did not comply.

Later, much later, when the worst had already happened and she was alone in her bed at night, unable to fall asleep, listening to her father, also sleepless, pacing the house, Ada Kazantzakis would revisit this moment, this fissure in time, when she could have done as she was told and returned to her seat, remaining more or less invisible to everyone in the classroom, unnoticed but also undisturbed; she could have kept things the way they had been, if only she could have stopped herself from doing what she did next.

Fig Tree

This afternoon, as storm clouds descended over London and the world turned the colour of melancholy, Kostas Kazantzakis buried me in the garden. In the back garden, that is. Normally I liked it here, among the lush camellias, sweetly fragrant honeysuckles and witch hazels with their spidery flowers, but this was no normal day. I tried to cheer up and see the bright side of things. Not that it helped. I was nervous, filled with apprehension. I had never been buried before.

Kostas had been toiling outside in the cold since the early hours. A light sheen of sweat had formed on his brow and it glistened every time he forced the steel edge of the spade into solid earth. Behind him extended the shadows of the wooden trellises that in summer were covered with climbing roses and clematis vines, but were now no more than a see-through barrier separating our garden from the neighbour's terrace. Slowly accumulating beside his leather boots, alongside the silvery trail left by a snail, was a pile of soil, clammy and crumbling to the touch. His breath clouded in front of his face, his shoulders were taut inside his navy parka – the one he had bought from a vintage shop on Portobello Road – and his knuckles were red and raw, slightly bleeding, but he didn't seem to notice.

I was cold and, though I did not want to admit it to myself, frightened. I wished I could have shared my worries with him. But even if I could have spoken, he was too distracted to hear me, absorbed in his own thoughts as he kept digging without so much as a glance in my direction. When he was done, he would put the spade aside, look at me with those sage-green eyes that I knew had seen things both pleasant and painful, and push me down into the hollow ground.

Only days to Christmas, and all around the neighbourhood sparkled fairy lights and metallic tinsels. Inflatable Santas and reindeer with plastic smiles. Bright, blinking garlands dangled from shop awnings and stars twinkled in house windows, offering furtive peeks into other people's lives, which always seemed less complicated somehow, more exciting – happier.

Inside the hedge a whitethroat began to sing – swift, scratchy notes. I wondered what a North African warbler was doing in our garden at this time of the year. Why hadn't it left for warmer places with all the others that must now be on their way south, and who, if they made a slight change in their flight path, might just as well head towards Cyprus and visit my motherland.

I knew they got lost occasionally, passerine birds. Rarely, yet it happened. And at times they just could not make the journey any more, year in year out, the same but never the same, miles of emptiness rolling out in all directions, and so they stayed, even though it meant hunger and cold and, too often, death.

It had been a long winter already. So unlike last year's mild weather, with its overcast skies, scattered showers, muddy tracks, a cascade of gloom and grey. Nothing out of the ordinary for dear old England. But this year, since early autumn, the climate had been erratic. At night we heard the howling of the gale and it brought to mind things untamed and unbidden, things within each of us that we were not yet ready to face, let alone comprehend. Many mornings when we woke up, we found the roads glazed with ice and blades of grass stiffened like shards of emerald. There were thousands of homeless people sleeping rough on the streets of London and not enough shelters for even a quarter of them.

Tonight was set to be the coldest night of the year so far. Already the air, as if composed of splinters of glass, pierced everything it touched. That is why Kostas was rushing, bent on completing his task before the ground turned to stone.

Storm Hera – that's what they had called the impending cyclone. Not George or Olivia or Charlie or Matilda this time, but a mythological name. They said it was going to be the worst in centuries – worse than the Great Storm of 1703, which had torn the tiles from rooftops, stripped ladies of their whalebone corsets, gentlemen of their powdered wigs, and beggars of the rags on their backs; wrecked timber-framed mansions and mud-built slums alike; smashed sailing ships as if they were paper boats and blown all the sewage floating down the Thames on to the riverbanks.

Stories, perhaps, but I believed in them. Just as I believed in legends, and the underlying truths they tried to convey.

I told myself that if everything went according to plan, I would only be buried for three months, maybe even less. When the daffodils bloomed along the footpaths and the bluebells carpeted the woods, and the whole of nature was animated again, I would be unburied. Bolt upright and wide awake. But, hard as I tried, I could not hold on to that sliver of hope while the winter, fierce and unrelenting, felt as if it were here to stay. I had never been good at optimism anyway. It must have been in my DNA. I was descended from a long line of pessimists. So I did what I often did: I began to imagine all the ways in which things could go wrong. What if this year spring did not arrive and I remained under the earth – forever? Or what if spring did make an appearance at long last, but Kostas Kazantzakis forgot to dig me up?

A gust of wind swept past, cutting into me like a serrated knife.

Kostas must have noticed for he stopped digging. 'Look at you! You're freezing, poor thing.'

He cared about me, always had. In the past, whenever the weather turned frigid, he took precautions to keep me alive. I remember one chilly afternoon in January he set up windbreaks all around me and wrapped me with layer upon layer of burlap to reduce moisture loss. Another time he covered me with mulch.

He placed heat lamps in the garden to provide warmth through-out the night and, most crucially, before the crack of dawn, the darkest hour of the day and often the coldest. That is when most of us fall into a sleep we never wake up from – the homeless on the streets, and us . . .

. . . fig trees.

I am a *Ficus carica*, known as the edible common fig, though I can assure you there's nothing common about me. I am a proud member of the great mulberry family of Moraceae from the kingdom of Plantae. Originating in Asia Minor, I can be found across a vast geography from California to Portugal and Leba-non, from the shores of the Black Sea to the hills of Afghanistan and the valleys of India.

Burying fig trees in trenches underground during the harshest winters and unearthing them in spring is a curious if well-established tradition. Italians settled in sub-zero towns in America and Canada are familiar with it. So are Spaniards, Portuguese, Maltese, Greeks, Lebanese, Egyptians, Tunisians, Moroccans, Algerians, Israelis, Palestinians, Iranians, Kurds, Turks, Jordan-ians, Syrians, Sephardic Jews . . . and us Cypriots.

Maybe not the young so much these days, but the elderly are no stranger to the custom. The ones who first migrated from the milder climes of the Mediterranean to the blustery cities and conurbations across the West. The ones who, after all these years, still dream up ingenious ways to smuggle across borders their favourite smelly cheese, smoked pastrami, stuffed sheep intes-tines, frozen *manti*, homemade tahini, carob syrup, *karidaki glyko*, cow stomach soup, spleen sausage, tuna eyeballs, rams' testicles . . . even though they might, if only they searched, find at least some of these delicacies in the 'international food' section of supermar-kets in their adopted countries. But they would claim it is not the same taste.

First-generation immigrants are a species all their own. They wear a lot of beige, grey or brown. Colours that do not stand out. Colours that whisper, never shout. There is a tendency to formality in their mannerisms, a wish to be treated with dignity. They move with a slight ungainliness, not quite at ease in their surroundings. Both eternally grateful for the chances life has given them and scarred by what it has snatched away, always out of place, separated from others by some unspoken experience, like survivors of a car accident.

First-generation immigrants talk to their trees all the time – when there are no other people nearby, that is. They confide in us, describing their dreams and aspirations, including those they have left behind, like wisps of wool caught on barbed wire during fence crossings. But for the most part, they simply enjoy our company, chatting to us as though to old, long-missed friends. They are caring and tender towards their plants, especially those they have brought along with them from lost motherlands. They know, deep within, that when you save a fig tree from a storm, it is someone's memory you are saving.

Classroom

'Ada, please sit down,' Mrs Walcott said one more time, tension lending a hard edge to her voice.

But once again Ada did not move. It wasn't that she hadn't heard the teacher. She understood perfectly what was being asked of her and she had no intention of defying it, but in that moment she just couldn't make her body obey her mind. At the corner of her vision she glimpsed a hovering dot – the butterfly she had sketched in her notebook was fluttering around the classroom. She watched it with unease, worried that someone else might see it, though a small, separate part of her knew they wouldn't.

Steering a zigzag course, the butterfly settled on the teacher's shoulder and hopped on to one of her dangling silver earrings, shaped like chandeliers. Just as quickly, it took off and wheeled towards Jason, alighting on his slim shoulders, wriggling under his shirt. Now Ada could picture in her mind's eye the bruises hidden beneath Jason's vest, most of them old and faded, but one fairly large and fresh. A glaring colour – raw purple. This boy, who was always cracking jokes and oozing confidence at school, was beaten by his own father at home. She gasped. Pain, there was so much pain everywhere and in everyone. The only difference was between those who managed to hide it and those who no longer could.

'Ada?' Mrs Walcott said, louder.

'Maybe she's deaf!' one of the students quipped.

'Or retarded!'

'We do not use such words in the classroom,' Mrs Walcott said, without convincing anyone. Her gaze focused back on Ada, confusion and concern passing in turn across her broad face. 'Is something wrong?'

Rooted to the spot, Ada did not say a word.

'If there is something you want to tell me, you can do that after class. Why don't we talk later?'

Still Ada did not comply. Her limbs, acting of their own volition, refused to respond. She remembered her father telling her that in extremely cold temperatures some birds, like the black-capped chickadee, entered short periods of torpor just so they could save energy for the worst weather. That's exactly how she felt right now, collapsed into some kind of inertia so that she could brace herself for what was coming.

Sit down, you idiot, you're embarrassing yourself!

Was it another student who had whispered these words or a spiteful voice inside her own head? She would never know. Her mouth drawn into a tight line, her jaw clenched, she clutched the edge of her desk, desperate to hold on to something, worried that if she let go she might lose her balance and fall down. With each inhale, panic churned and rolled in her lungs, seeped into her every nerve and cell, and no sooner did she open her mouth again than it spilled out and gushed forth, an underground stream eager to break loose from its confines. A sound both familiar and too strange to be her own surged from somewhere inside her – loud, hoarse, raw, wrong.

She screamed.

So unpredicted and forceful and impossibly high-pitched was her voice that the other students fell quiet. Mrs Walcott stood still, her hands pressed to her chest, the creases around her eyes deepening. In all her years of teaching she had never seen anything like this.

Four seconds passed, eight, ten, twelve . . . The clock on the wall inched its way forward painfully slowly. Time warped and leaned into itself, like dry, charred timber.

Now Mrs Walcott was by her side, trying to talk to her. Ada could feel her teacher's fingers on her arm and knew the woman was saying something but she could not make out the words as she kept screaming. Fifteen seconds passed. Eighteen, twenty, twenty-three . . .

Her voice was a flying carpet that lifted her up and carried her against her will. She had the sense that she was floating, observing everything from a lamp in the ceiling, except it didn't feel like she was high above, more like she was outside, a sense of falling out of herself, not part of this moment, nor of this world.

She recalled a sermon she had once listened to, maybe in a church, maybe in a mosque, for at different stages of her childhood she had visited both, though not for long. *When the soul departs the body, it ascends towards the firmament, and on its way there it stops to watch all that lies below, unaffected, unmoved, untouched by pain.* Was it Bishop Vasilios who said that or Imam Mahmoud? Silver icons, beeswax candles, paintings with faces of the saints and apostles, the angel Gabriel with one wing open and the other folded, a worn copy of the Orthodox Bible, the pages thumbed, the spine strained . . . silk prayer mats, amber rosaries, a book of *hadiths*, a weathered volume of *Islamic Interpretation of Dreams*, consulted after each dream and each nightmare . . . Both men had tried to persuade Ada to choose their religion, take their side. It seemed to her, more and more, that in the end she had chosen emptiness. Nothingness. A weightless shell that still hedged her in, kept her apart from others. Yet as she went on screaming in the last hour of the last day of school, she felt something almost transcendental, as if she were not, and had never been, confined to the limits of her body.

Thirty seconds passed. An eternity.

Her voice cracked but persisted. There was something profoundly humiliating yet equally electrifying about hearing yourself scream – breaking off, breaking away, uncontrolled, unfettered, without knowing how far it would carry you, this untamed force that rose from inside. It was an animal thing. A wilderness thing. Nothing about her belonged to her previous self in that moment. Above all her voice. This could have been the high shriek of a hawk, the soul-haunting howl of a wolf, the rasping cry of a red fox at midnight. It could have been any of them, but not the scream of a sixteen-year-old schoolgirl.

The other students, eyes widened in astonishment and disbelief, stared at Ada, spellbound by this display of insanity. Some of them had cocked their heads to the side as if trying to fathom how such an unsettling shriek could ever have come from so timid a girl. Ada sensed their fear and, for once, it felt good not to be the one who was frightened. At the blurred edge of her vision they all gathered, indistinguishable with their baffled faces and matching gestures, a paper chain of identical bodies. She was no part of this chain. She was no part of anything. In her unbroken loneliness, she was complete. Never had she felt so exposed, yet so powerful.

Forty seconds passed.

And still Ada Kazantzakis continued to scream, and her rage, if this was indeed rage, propelled itself forward, a fast-burning fuel, with no signs of abating. Her skin had turned a mottled scarlet, the base of her throat was scraped raw and throbbing with pain, the veins on her neck pulsed with the rush of blood, and her hands remained open in front of her, though by now they grasped nothing. A vision of her mother crossed her mind just then and, for the first time since her death, thinking of her did not bring tears to her eyes.

The bell went.

Outside the classroom, multiplying down the corridors, hurried footsteps, animated exchanges. Excitement. Laughter. A brief commotion. The beginning of the Christmas holidays.

Inside the classroom, Ada's madness was so captivating a spectacle that no one dared to move.

Fifty-two seconds passed – almost but not quite a minute – and her voice gave out, leaving her throat dry and hollow inside like a parched reed. Her shoulders sank, her knees trembled and her face began to stir as if waking from a disturbed sleep. She fell quiet. Just as suddenly as she had started, she stopped.

'What the hell was that?' Jason muttered out loud, but no one offered an answer.

Without looking at anyone, Ada collapsed back on to her

chair, breathless and drained of energy, a puppet whose strings had snapped onstage in the middle of a play; all of which Emma-Rose would describe later on in exaggerated detail. But, for now, even Emma-Rose was silent.

'Are you okay?' Mrs Walcott, her face etched with shock, asked again, only this time Ada heard her.

As banks of clouds gathered in the distant sky and a shadow fell on the walls as though from the wings of a giant bird in flight, Ada Kazantzakis closed her eyes. A sound reverberated inside her head, a heavy, steady rhythm – *crack-crack-crack* – and all she could think of in that instant was that somewhere outside this class-room, far beyond her reach, someone's bones were breaking.

Fig Tree

'When you are buried, I'll come and talk to you every day,' Kostas said as he drove the spade into the ground. He bore down on the handle and lifted up a clod of soil, tossing it on to the growing mound beside him. 'You won't feel lonely.'

I wish I could have told him that loneliness is a human invention. Trees are never lonely. Humans think they know with certainty where their being ends and someone else's starts. With their roots tangled and caught up underground, linked to fungi and bacteria, trees harbour no such illusions. For us, everything is interconnected.

Even so, I was glad to learn Kostas was planning to visit me frequently. I tilted my branches towards him in appreciation. He was standing so close now I caught the scent of his cologne – sandalwood, bergamot, ambergris. I had memorized every detail of his handsome face – high, smooth forehead, prominent, slender and sharply tipped nose, clear eyes shaded by eyelashes that curled like half-moons . . . the crisp waviness of his hair, still abundant, still dark, though silvered here and there, and greying at the temples.

This year, love, not unlike the unusual winter, had crept up on me, so gradual and subtle in its intensity that by the time I realized what was happening it was already too late to guard myself. I was stupidly, pointlessly besotted with a man who would never think of me in an intimate way. It embarrassed me, this sudden neediness that had come over me, this deep yearning for what I could not have. I reminded myself that life was not a trade agreement, a calculated give-and-take, and not every affection needed to be returned in kind, but the truth was I just couldn't stop wondering what would happen if Kostas Kazantzakis were to reciprocate some day – if a human were to fall in love with a tree.

I know what you are thinking. How could I, an ordinary *Ficus carica*, possibly be in love with a *Homo sapiens*? I get it, I'm no beauty. Never been more than plain-looking. I'm no *sakura*, the dazzling Japanese cherry tree with its winsome pink blossoms extending in four directions, all glitz and glamour and swagger. I'm no sugar maple, aglow in stunning shades of ruby red, saffron orange and golden yellow, blessed with perfectly shaped leaves, a total seductress. And I am certainly no wisteria, that exquisitely sculptured purple femme fatale. Nor am I the evergreen gardenia with its intoxicating perfume and glossy, verdant foliage or the bougainvillea with its magenta splendour climbing up and spilling over adobe walls under the baking sun. Or the dove tree, which keeps you waiting for so long and then offers the most enchanting, romantic flower bracts that flap in the breeze like scented handkerchiefs.

I don't have any of their charms, I admit. If you were to pass me on the street, you probably wouldn't give me another glance. But I'd like to believe I'm attractive in my own disarming way. What I lack in beauty and popularity, I make up for in mystery and inner strength.

Throughout history I have seduced into my canopy droves of birds, bats, bees, butterflies, ants, mice, monkeys, dinosaurs . . . and also a certain confused couple, wandering around aimlessly in the Garden of Eden, a glazed look in their eyes. Make no mistake: that was no apple. It is high time someone corrected this gross misunderstanding. Adam and Eve yielded to the allure of a fig, the fruit of temptation, desire and passion, not some crunchy apple. I don't mean to belittle a fellow plant, but what chance does a bland apple have next to a luscious fig that still today, aeons after the original sin, tastes like lost paradise?

With all due respect to believers, it makes no sense to assume that the first man and the first woman were tempted to sin by eating some plain old apple and that, finding themselves naked, shivering and mortified, and despite fearing God would catch them at any moment, they nonetheless took a stroll through the enchanted garden until they stumbled across a fig tree and decided to wrap themselves in its leaves. It's an interesting story, but something doesn't add up here, and I know what it is: me! Because it was me all along – the tree of good and bad, light and dark, life and death, love and heartbreak.

Adam and Eve shared a tender, ripe, deliciously alluring, aromatic fig, splitting it open right down the middle, and as the fleshy opulent sweetness dissolved on their tongues they began to see the universe around them in a completely new light because that is what happens to those who attain knowledge and wisdom. Then they covered themselves with the leaves of the tree they happened to be standing under. As for the apple, I am sorry, it didn't even feature.

Look into each religion and creed, and you will find me there, present in every creation story, bearing witness to the ways of the humans and their endless wars, combining my DNA in so many new forms that today I can be found on almost every continent across the world. Of lovers and admirers, I have had plenty. Some have even gone crazy for me, crazy enough to forget everything else and stay with me until the end of their brief lives, like my little fig wasps.

Even so, I understand, none of that makes me entitled to love a human being and hope to be loved back. Not a very sensible thing to do, I admit, to fall for someone who is not of your kind, someone who will only complicate your life, disrupt your routine and mess with your sense of stability and rootedness. But, then again, anyone who expects love to be sensible has perhaps never loved.

'You'll be warm under the ground, Ficus. It's going to be okay,' said Kostas.

After all these years in London, he still spoke English with a palpable Greek accent. It was reassuringly familiar to me, his raspy *r*, sibilant *h*, blurred *sh*, truncated vowels, the cadence quickening when he felt excited and retreating when thoughtful or unsure of himself. I recognized every twist and turn of his voice as it rippled and rolled, washing over me like clear water.

He said, 'It won't be for long anyway – just a few weeks.'

I was used to him talking to me, but never as much as he did today. I wondered if, deep down, the winter storm might have triggered feelings of guilt in him. It was he, after all, who had brought me to this sunless country from Cyprus, hidden inside a black leather suitcase. I was, if truth be told, smuggled on to the European continent.

At Heathrow airport, as Kostas pulled the suitcase past the gaze of a burly customs officer, I tensed, expecting him to be stopped and searched any second. His wife, meanwhile, walked ahead of us, her stride brisk, purposeful and impatient as always. Defne was pregnant with Ada at the time, though they did not yet know it. They thought they were bringing only me into England, unaware that they were also bringing their unborn child.

When the Arrivals doors opened wide, Kostas exclaimed, unable to control the excitement in his voice, 'We're here, we made it! Welcome to your new home.'

Was he talking to his wife or was he talking to me? I'd like to think it was the latter. Either way, that was more than sixteen years ago. I have never been back to Cyprus since.

I still carry the island with me, though. The places where we were born are the shape of our lives, even when we are away from them. Especially then. Now and again in my sleep I find myself in Nicosia, standing under a familiar sun, my shadow falling against the rocks, reaching towards the prickly broom bushes that burst with blossoms, each as perfect and bright as the golden coins in a children's fable.

Of the past we left behind I remember everything. Coastlines etched in the sandy terrain like creases in a palm waiting to be read, the chorus of cicadas against the rising heat, bees buzzing over lavender fields, butterflies stretching their wings at the first promise of light ... many may try, but no one does optimism better than butterflies.

People assume it's a matter of personality, the difference between optimists and pessimists. But I believe it all comes down to an inability to forget. The greater your powers of retention, the slimmer your chances at optimism. And I'm not claiming that butterflies have no recollection of things. They have, surely. A moth can recall what it learned as a caterpillar. But me and my kind, we are afflicted with everlasting memory – and by that, I don't mean years or decades. I mean centuries.

It is a curse, an enduring memory. When elderly Cypriot women wish ill upon someone, they don't ask for anything blatantly bad to befall them. They don't pray for lightning bolts, unforeseen accidents or sudden reversals of fortune. They simply say,

> *May you never be able to forget.*
> *May you go to your grave still remembering.*

So I guess it is in my genes, this melancholy I can never quite shake off. Carved with an invisible knife into my arborescent skin.

'Okay, this should be good enough,' Kostas said as he examined the trench, seeming satisfied with its length and depth.

He stretched out his aching back and wiped the mud off his hands with a handkerchief that he pulled from his pocket.

'I need to prune you a bit, it'll be easier that way.'

Grabbing a pair of clippers, he trimmed my wayward lateral branches, his moves deft, practised. With the help of a nylon rope, he encircled me, fastening my thicker branches together. Carefully, he tightened the bundle and made a square knot, loose enough to avoid damage but snug enough for me to fit in the trench.

'I'm almost done,' he said. 'Need to hurry up. That storm is not far off!'

But I knew him well enough to sense that the looming storm was not the only reason why he was in such a rush to bury me. He wanted to finish the task before his daughter came home from school. He did not want young Ada to witness another burial.

The day his wife fell into a coma from which she never woke, grief settled on this house like a vulture that would not leave until it had gorged itself on every last trace of lightness and joy. For months after Defne was gone, and still every now and then, usually before midnight, Kostas would come to the garden and sit by my side, wrapped in a thin blanket, his eyes red and raw, his moves listless as if he had been dredged against his will from the bottom of a lake. He never cried inside the house, not wishing his daughter to see his suffering.

On such nights I felt so much love and affection for him that it hurt. It was in those moments that the difference between the two of us pained me the most. How I lamented that I could not turn my branches into arms to embrace him, my twigs into fingers to caress him, my leaves into a thousand tongues to whisper back his words, and my trunk into a heart to take him in.

'Right, that's all done,' Kostas said, surveying his surroundings. 'I'm now going to push you down.'

There was a tenderness to his face and a soft glimmer in his eyes, reflecting the slowly setting sun far in the west.

'Some of your roots will break, but don't worry,' Kostas said. 'The ones remaining will be more than enough to keep you alive.'

Trying to maintain my composure, trying not to panic, I sent a quick warning down below, informing my subterranean limbs that in a few seconds many of them would die. Just as swiftly they responded in hundreds of minute signals telling me that they knew what was coming. They were ready.

With a sharp intake of breath, Kostas bent forward and shoved me down towards the hole in the ground. I didn't budge, at first. Placing his palms against my trunk, he tried harder this time, the pressure careful and balanced but equally firm, constant.

'You'll be fine. Trust me, darling Ficus,' he said dotingly.

The gentleness in his tone enfolded me and held me tight in place; even a single word of endearment from him had a gravity of its own that drew me back to him.

Slowly, all my fears and doubts abandoned me, floating away like wisps of mist. I knew in that instant that he would unearth me at the first sight of snowdrops peeping their heads out of the ground or golden orioles winging their way back through the blue skies. I knew as I knew myself that I would see Kostas Kazantzakis again, and it would still be there, behind his beautiful eyes, engraved in his soul, this searing sadness that had settled on him since he had lost his wife. How I wished he could love me the way he had loved her.

Farewell, Kostaki, till spring, then . . .

A look of wonder passed across his face, so rapid and fleeting that for a second it seemed he might have heard me. A recognition, almost. It was there, then gone.

Grabbing me tighter, Kostas gave one last forceful thrust downwards. The world tilted, the sky tipped and dipped, the low leaden clouds and the clods of earth merged into one muddy morass.

I braced myself for the fall as I heard my roots strain and snap, one by one. A strange, muffled *crack-crack-crack* rose from the ground beneath. If I were human, it would have been the sound of my bones breaking.

Night

Standing by her bedroom window, her forehead pressed against the glass pane, Ada watched her father in the garden spookily illuminated by the light of two lanterns, his back turned to her as he raked dry leaves over raw earth. Since they had returned home together this evening, he had been out there, working in the cold. He said when he received the call from school he had left the fig tree lying unattended, whatever that meant. Another one of her father's foibles, she supposed. He said he urgently had to cover the tree now, promising he would be done in a few minutes, but minutes had stretched to almost an hour and he was still out there.

Her mind kept returning to the events of the afternoon. Shame was a serpent coiled inside her stomach. It bit her again and again. She still could not believe what she had done. There, in front of the entire class, screaming her head off like that! What had got into her? Mrs Walcott's face – ashen, terrified. That expression must have been contagious, for Ada had then seen it on the faces of the other teachers when they were each apprised of what had transpired. Her insides constricted as she remembered the moment she was summoned to the headmaster's office. By then all the other students had left, the building echoing like an empty shell.

They had treated her kindly but with visible concern, both worried for her and deeply puzzled by her behaviour. Until today, they had probably regarded her as one of the introverts, neither shy nor quiet, just not exactly fond of putting herself forward. A contemplative girl who had always preferred to live in her own mind but had become all the more distant and withdrawn since her mother's loss. Now they were not sure what to make of her.

They had immediately called her father, and he had rushed there straight away, without even changing out of his gardening clothes, his boots mud-caked, a small leaf caught in his hair. The headmaster had had a private talk with him while Ada waited out in the corridor, sitting on a bench, bouncing her leg.

On the way back her father had kept asking her questions, trying to comprehend why she had done such a thing, but his persistence had only made Ada quieter. As soon as they got home, she had retreated into her bedroom, her father into his garden.

Her eyes filled with tears as she concluded that she would have to change schools now. There was no other way. In the meantime, would the headmaster issue her a detention or something? If he did, it would be the least of Ada's worries. No punishment he could come up with would be as horrifying as the looks the other students were sure to give her when the new term started. From now on, no boy would ever want to date her. No girl would invite her to her birthday party or shopping trip. From now on, the labels *weirdo* and *psycho* would stick to her, tattooed on her skin, and every time she walked into the classroom, that's what everyone would see first. Even the thought of it made her feel sick, a weight inside her gut like damp sand.

Having worked herself up into a frenzy, Ada couldn't stay alone in her room any longer. She walked out, passing down the hall, the walls decorated with framed sketches and family photos of holidays, birthdays, picnics, wedding anniversaries . . . snapshots of blissful moments, bright and glowing but long gone, like dead stars pulsing the last of their light.

Crossing the living room, Ada opened the sliding door that led into the back garden. Instantly, the wind charged in, ruffling the pages of the books on the table, scattering sheets of paper across the floor. She picked them up and glanced at the one on top of the pile, recognizing her father's neat handwriting: *How to Bury a Fig Tree in Ten Steps*. It was a list with detailed instructions and rudimentary images. Her father – unlike her mother – had never been good at drawing.

As soon as Ada stepped out into the garden, the bitterness of the cold made her wince. Immersed in her own concerns, she hadn't given Storm Hera much thought, but now it felt all too real. A musty, sour smell hovered in the air – of rotting leaves, damp stone and wet wood burning.

She trod purposefully along the stony path, the gravel crunching under her slippers – fluffy fur, open back, cream-white. She should have changed into her boots, but it was too late for that. Her eyes were fixed on her father, merely a few feet ahead. Many a night Ada had watched him from her bedroom window, in the same spot by the fig tree, as darkness gathered around him like crows about carrion. A slumped outline against the inky sky, stricken with grief. Not even once had she gone outside, sensing that he would not want to be seen by her in that state.

'Dad?' Her voice sounded shaky to her ears.

He did not hear her. Ada drew closer, only now noticing there was something different about the garden, a change she couldn't immediately grasp. As she scanned the area, she drew breath, realizing what it was: the fig tree wasn't there.

'Dad!'

Kostas spun round. His face lit up upon seeing her. 'Sweetheart, you shouldn't have come out without a jacket.' His gaze slid to her feet. 'No boots? Ada *mou*, you're going to catch cold.'

'I'm okay. Where did the fig go?'

'Oh, she's here, underneath.' Kostas gestured down towards some sheets of plywood he had laid carefully over the ground by his feet.

Ada came closer, staring at the partly covered trench with curious eyes. When this morning at breakfast her father had mentioned he was planning to bury the fig tree, she hadn't really paid attention, not quite understanding what he meant by that. Now she muttered, 'Wow, so you really did it!'

'I had to. I was worried she might suffer dieback.'

'What is that?'

'It's how trees die in an extreme climate. Sometimes it's the frost that does the damage or the repeated freezing and thawing. Then they are gone.' Kostas crouched and tossed an armful of mulch over the plywood, patting it down with his bare hands.

'Dad?'

'Hmm?'

'Why do you always talk about the tree as if it were a woman?'

'Well, she's . . . it's a female.'

'How do you know that?'

Kostas stood up, taking a moment to respond. 'Some species are dioecious – that means each tree is distinctly female or male. Willow, poplar, yew, mulberry, aspen, juniper, holly . . . they are all like that. But many others are monoecious, they bear both male and female flowers on the same tree. Oak, cypress, pine, birch, hazel, cedar, chestnut . . .'

'And figs are female?'

'Figs are complicated,' said Kostas. 'About half of them are monoecious, the other half dioecious. There are cultivated varieties of fig and then there is the "wild caprifig" in the Mediterranean that produces inedible fruit, which is usually fed to goats. Our *Ficus carica* is female, and she's a parthenocarpic variety – that means she can make fruit on her own, without needing a male tree nearby.'

He stopped, conscious of having said more than he had intended, worried that he might have lost her, the way he always seemed to be doing these days. The wind picked up, rustling the shrubs. 'I don't want you to catch cold, love. Go back inside. I'll join you in a few minutes.'

'That's what you said an hour ago,' Ada said with a shrug. 'I'm fine. Can't I stay and give you a hand?'

'Sure, if you want to.'

He tried not to show his surprise at her offer of help. Ever since Defne's death, it seemed to him, father and daughter had been stuck on a pendulum of emotions. Whenever he asked her about school and her friends, she shut down, and only opened up a little when he retreated into his work. More and more he noticed that in order to have her move a step closer, he had to

40

take a step away first. It reminded him of how, when she was little, they would go to the playground every weekend, holding hands. It was a charming place with obstacle courses and lots of wooden equipment, though Ada barely paid them any attention – she was only interested in the swing. Each time Kostas pushed her on the swing, watching her fly away from him, up into the air, laughing and kicking her legs, Ada would shout, 'Higher, Daddy, higher!' Struggling with the fear that she might flip over or the metal chains might break off, he would push her harder, and then, as the swing came back, he would have to move out of the way to make space for her. And so it still was, this back and forth, with the father ceding space to his daughter so she could have her freedom. Except, in those earlier days, they'd had so much to tell each other that they would talk constantly; this awkward, painful silence had not yet lodged itself between them.

'So what do I need to do?' asked Ada when she realized he wasn't issuing instructions.

'Right. We need to cover the trench with soil and leaves – and some straw I've got here.'

'I can do that,' she said.

Side by side, they began to work: he, focused and conscientious; she, distracted and slow.

Somewhere in the distance an ambulance siren ripped through the stillness of the night. Down the road, a dog barked. Then silence returned, save for the loose gate in front of the house, banging on its hinges every now and then.

'Does it hurt?' Ada said, so quietly it was almost a murmur.

'What?'

'When you bury a tree, does it feel pain?'

Kostas lifted his chin, the line of his jaw tightening. 'There are two ways of answering that. The scientific consensus is that trees are not sentient in the way most people use the word . . .'

'But you don't seem to agree?'

'Well, I think there's still so much we don't know, we're only just beginning to discover the language of trees. But we can tell

41

with certainty that they can hear, smell, communicate – and they can definitely remember. They can sense water, light, danger. They can send signals to other plants and help each other. They're much more alive than most people realize.'

Especially our Ficus carica. *If you only knew how special she is,* Kostas wanted to add, but stopped himself.

Under the faint glitter of the garden lanterns, Ada studied her father's face. He had aged visibly these past months. Half-circles had formed under his eyes, pale crescents. Pain had resculpted his countenance, adding new planes and angles. She looked away, and asked, 'But why do you always talk to the fig?'

'Do I?'

'Yes, you do, all the time. I've heard you before. Why do you do that?'

'Well, she's a good listener.'

'Come on, Dad! I'm serious. Do you have any idea how crazy that sounds? What if someone hears you? They're going to think you're off your head.'

Kostas smiled. It crossed his mind that maybe one of the most telling differences between the young and the old lay in this detail. As you aged you cared less and less about what others thought of you, and only then could you be more free.

'Don't worry, Ada *mou*, I don't talk to trees with other people around.'

'Yeah, but still . . . one of these days you're going to get caught,' she said as she scattered a handful of dry leaves over the trench. 'And I'm sorry but what are we doing here anyway? If a neighbour sees us, they're going to think we're burying a body. They might call the police!'

Kostas lowered his eyes, his smile replaced by something uncertain.

'Honestly, Dad, I don't want to hurt your feelings, but your fig gives me the creeps. There's something strange about it, I can tell. Sometimes I feel like it – *she* – is listening to us. Spying on us.

Crazy, I know, but that's how I feel. I mean, is that even possible? Can trees listen to what we are saying?'

A momentary look of unease flickered across Kostas's face before he said, 'No, love. You mustn't worry about such things. Trees may be remarkable creatures, but I wouldn't take it that far.'

'Okay, good.' She stepped aside and silently watched him work for a while. 'So how long are you planning to keep her buried?'

'A few months. I'll dig her up as soon as the weather is warm enough.'

Ada whistled. 'A few months is so long. You sure she can survive?'

'She'll be all right,' said Kostas. 'She's been through a lot, our *Ficus carica* – your mum always called her a warrior.'

He paused, as if worried he might have said too much. Quickly, he spread a tarpaulin over the trench and placed stones on the four corners to make sure it didn't shift in the wind.

'I think we're done here.' He dusted off his hands. 'Thanks for helping, love. I appreciate it.'

They walked back into the house together; the wind had tangled their hair. And even though Ada knew there was no way the fig tree, latched on to earth with its remaining roots, could get out of that hole and follow them, just before she closed the door she could not help stealing a glance over her shoulder towards the dark, cold ground, and when she did, she felt a chill crawl up her spine.

Fig Tree

'Your fig gives me the creeps,' she says. And why does she say that? Because she suspects there might be more to me than meets the eye. Well, there is indeed, but that doesn't mean I am *creepy*.

Humans! After observing them for so long, I have arrived at a bleak conclusion: they do not really want to know more about plants. They do not want to ascertain whether we may be capable of volition, altruism and kinship. Interesting as they consider these questions at some abstract level, they'd rather leave them unexplored, unanswered. They find it easier, I guess, to assume that trees, having no brain in the conventional sense, can only experience the most rudimentary existence.

Well . . . no species is obliged to like another species, that's for sure. But if you are going to claim, as humans do, to be superior to all life forms, past and present, then you must gain an understanding of the oldest living organisms on earth who were here long before you arrived and will still be here after you have gone.

My guess is humans deliberately avoid learning more about us, maybe because they sense, at some primordial level, that what they find out might be unsettling. Would they wish to know, for instance, that trees can adapt and change their behaviour with purpose, and if this is true, perhaps one does not necessarily depend on a brain for intelligence? Would they be pleased to discover that by sending signals through a network of latticed fungi buried in the soil, trees can warn their neighbours about dangers ahead – an approaching predator or pathogenic bugs – and such stress signals have escalated lately, due to deforestation, forest degradation and droughts, all of them caused directly by humans? Or that the climbing wood vine *Boquila trifoliolata* can alter its leaves to mimic the shape or colour of those of its supporting

44

plant, prompting scientists to wonder if the vine has some kind of visual capability? Or that a tree's rings do not only reveal its age, but also the traumas it has endured, including wildfires, and thus, carved deep in each circle, is a near-death experience, an unhealed scar? Or that the smell of a freshly mown lawn, that scent humans associate with cleanliness and restoration and all things new and zestful, is in fact another distress signal issued by grass to warn other flora and ask for help? Or that plants can recognize their kith and kin and feel you touching them, and some, like the Venus flytrap, can even count? Or that trees in the forest can tell when deer are about to eat them, and they defend themselves by infusing their leaves with a type of salicylic acid that helps the production of tannins, which their enemies detest, thus ingeniously repelling them? Or that, until not that long ago, there was an acacia in the Sahara desert – 'the loneliest tree in the world', they called it – there at the crossroads of ancient caravan routes, and this miracle of a creature, by spreading its roots far and deep, survived on its own despite the extreme heat and lack of water, until a drunk driver knocked it down? Or that many plants, when threatened, attacked or cut, can produce ethylene, which works like a type of anaesthetic, and this chemical release has been described by researchers as akin to hearing stressed plants screaming?

Most arboreal suffering is caused by humankind.

Trees in urban areas grow faster than trees in rural areas. We also tend to die sooner.

Would people really like to know these things? I don't think so. Frankly, I am not even sure they see us.

Humans walk by us every day, they sit and sleep, smoke and picnic in our shade, they pluck our leaves and gorge themselves on our fruit, they break our branches, riding them like horses as children or using them to birch others into submission when they become older and crueller, they carve their lover's name on our trunks and vow eternal love, they weave necklaces out of our needles and paint our flowers into art, they split us into logs to heat their homes and sometimes they chop us down just because we obstruct their view, they make cradles, wine corks, chewing gum and rustic furniture, and produce the most spellbinding music out of us, and they turn us into books in which they lose themselves on cold winter nights, they use our wood to manufacture coffins in which they end their lives, buried six feet under with us, and they even compose romantic poems to us, calling us the link between earth and sky, and yet still they do not see us.

I believe one reason why humans find it hard to understand plants is because, in order to connect with something other than themselves and genuinely care about it, they need to interact with a face, an image that mirrors theirs as closely as possible. The more visible an animal's eyes, the more sympathy it will receive from humankind.

Cats, dogs, horses, owls, bunny rabbits, pygmy monkeys, even those toothless ostriches that swallow pebbles like berries, they all get their fair share of affection. But snakes, rats, hyenas, spiders, scorpions, sea urchins, not so much . . . Creatures with the smallest eyes or none at all do not stand a chance. But, then again, nor do trees.

Trees might not have eyes but we have vision. I respond to light. I detect ultraviolet and infrared and electromagnetic waves. If I weren't buried now, I could tell next time she was nearby whether Ada was wearing her blue coat or her red one.

I adore light. I need it not only to process water and carbon dioxide into sugars, grow and germinate, I also need it to feel safe and secure. A plant always bends towards light. Having figured this out about us, humans use the knowledge to trick and manipulate us for their own ends. Flower farmers turn on the lamps in the middle of the night, deceiving chrysanthemums into blossoming when they shouldn't. With a bit of light you can make us do so much. With a promise of love . . .

46

'A few months is so long . . .' I heard Ada say. She doesn't know that we measure time differently.

Human-time is linear, a neat continuum from a past that is supposed to be over and done with towards a future deemed to be untouched, untarnished. Every day has to be a brand-new day, filled with fresh events, every love utterly different from the previous one. The human species' appetite for novelty is insatiable and I'm not sure it does them much good.

Arboreal-time is cyclical, recurrent, perennial; the past and the future breathe within this moment, and the present does not necessarily flow in one direction; instead it draws circles within circles, like the rings you find when you cut us down.

Arboreal-time is equivalent to story-time – and, like a story, a tree does not grow in perfectly straight lines, flawless curves or exact right angles, but bends and twists and bifurcates into fantastical shapes, throwing out branches of wonder and arcs of invention.

They are incompatible, human-time and tree-time.

How to Bury a Fig Tree in Ten Steps

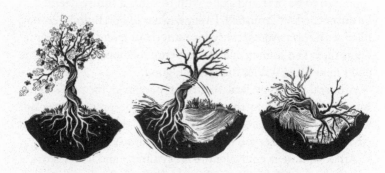

1. Wait until a severe frost or winter storm causes the tree to drop its leaves.
2. Dig a trench in front of your tree before the ground freezes over. Make sure it is long enough and wide enough to fit the whole tree in comfortably.
3. Prune back any lateral branches and taller vertical shoots.
4. With the help of a hemp rope, fasten the remaining vertical branches, taking care not to bind them too tightly.
5. Dig around the front and back of the tree to about a foot deep. You may need to use a spade or hoe to sever the roots but do not touch the ones at the sides as it's important not to cut through all the roots. Make sure the central root ball is intact and can be easily pivoted into the trench.
6. Carefully bend the tree downwards. Continue to push until the tree is lying horizontally inside the trench (branches may snap and pop, capillary roots may break, but the largest roots will survive).
7. Fill the trench with organic matter, such as dry leaves, straw, green manure or wood mulch. The tree needs to be covered

with at least one foot of soil. You may then use boards for
further insulation.

8. Place strips of plywood on top of your tree, leaving gaps for
   air and water to circulate.
9. Cover everything with porous fabric or tarp, weighed down
   with a couple of inches of topsoil or stones placed at the
   edges so that the wind doesn't carry it away.
10. Say some soothing words to your fig tree, trust in her and
    wait for spring.

Stranger

The following day the mercury had dropped so low that, despite waking early, Ada was reluctant to get out from under her duvet. She could have spent the whole morning dozing and reading, had the landline not started ringing. Loud, persistent. She jumped out of bed, seized by an irrational fear that it might be the headmaster calling again even though it was a weekend, keen to tell her father what kind of punishment he had deemed fitting.

Her heart quickened with each step she took down the hall. Midway to the kitchen, she stopped, hearing her father pick up the receiver.

'Hello?' Kostas answered. 'Oh, hi . . . hello. I was planning to call you today.' Something new had entered his voice. A spark of anticipation.

Pressing her back against the wall, Ada tried to work out who he might be talking to. She had a feeling it was a woman on the other end of the line. It could be anyone, of course – a colleague, a childhood friend, even someone he had met in a supermarket queue, though he wasn't one for striking up easy friendships. There were other possibilities, too, however unlikely, but she was not ready to consider them.

'Yes, by all means, the invitation is still open,' Kostas carried on. 'You can come whenever you'd like.'

Taking a deep breath, Ada mulled over his words. Her father rarely entertained guests, not since her mother's death, and when he did it was usually colleagues. This sounded like something else.

'I'm glad you managed to get on a plane – many flights were called off.' His tone switched to a low murmur as he added, softly, 'It's just, I haven't had a chance to tell her yet.'

Ada felt her cheeks burn. A pall of gloom settled on her as she realized this could only mean one thing: her father had a secret girlfriend. How long had this been going on? When exactly had it started – right after her mother's death, or maybe even before? It must be a serious relationship, otherwise he would not be bringing her into this house where her mother's memory was everywhere.

Cautiously, she peered through the kitchen door.

Her father was sitting at the end of the table, eyes cast down, fidgeting with the telephone cord. He looked slightly nervous.

'No, no! Definitely not! You mustn't go to a hotel. I insist,' Kostas continued. 'Pity you arrived in such terrible weather. I'd have loved to show you around. Yes, you should come straight from the airport. It's fine, really. I just need a bit of time to talk to her.'

After her father hung up the phone, Ada counted up to forty and walked into the kitchen. She poured herself a bowl of cereal and splashed in some milk.

'So, who was that?' she asked, even though she had initially decided to pretend not to have heard the conversation.

With a tilt of his head, Kostas gestured towards the nearest chair. 'Ada *mou*, please take a seat. I have something important to tell you.'

Not a good sign, Ada thought to herself, even as she did what she was told.

Kostas glanced down at his mug, the coffee gone cold. Still, he took a swig. 'That was your aunt.'

'Who?'

'Your mum's sister, Meryem. You used to love the postcards she would send us, remember?'

And although Ada had read those postcards countless times ever since she was a little girl, she would not acknowledge it now. She straightened her back and asked, 'What about her?'

'Meryem is in London. She flew in from Cyprus and she'd like to visit us.'

Her dark lashes brushing her cheek, Ada blinked. 'Why?'

'Sweetheart, she wants to see us – but, primarily, she wants to meet you. I told her she could stay with us for a few days – well, a bit longer. I thought it'd be good for you to get to know each other.'

Ada plunked her spoon into the bowl, a trickle of milk spilling from the sides. Slowly, she stirred the cereal around, remaining outwardly composed.

'So you don't have a girlfriend?'

Kostas's face shifted. 'Is that what you were thinking?'

Ada shrugged.

Reaching over the table, Kostas took his daughter's hand and gave it a gentle squeeze. 'I don't have a girlfriend and I'm not looking for one. I'm sorry, I should have told you about Meryem before. She gave me a call last week. She said she was planning to visit but wasn't sure she could make it. So many flights were cancelled, frankly, I thought she'd have to delay her plans. I was going to talk to you this weekend.'

'If she was so eager to visit us, why didn't she come to Mum's funeral?'

Kostas sat back, the lines in his face chiselled by the overhead light. 'Look, I know you're upset – and you've every right to be. But why don't you listen to what your aunt's got to say? Maybe she can answer that question herself.'

'I don't understand why you are being nice to this woman. Why do you have to invite her to our house? If you're so keen to see her, you can have coffee with her somewhere.'

'Sweetheart, I have known Meryem since I was a boy. She's your mum's only sister. She's family.'

'Family?' Ada scoffed. 'She's a total stranger to me.'

'Okay, I understand. My suggestion is let her come; if you like her, you'll be glad you've met her. And if you don't like her, you'll be glad you haven't met her before. Either way, you have nothing to lose.'

Ada shook her head. 'That's a strange approach, Dad.'

Kostas stood up and walked to the sink, a weariness in his eyes that he could not disguise. Pouring away the remaining coffee, he washed the mug. Outside, by the spot where the fig tree was buried, a bullfinch was pecking at the feeder, seeming in no hurry, as if it sensed there would always be food in this garden.

'Okay, love,' Kostas conceded as he returned to the table. 'I don't want you to feel pressured. If you're not comfortable, that's totally fine. I'll meet Meryem separately. After staying with us, she was planning to visit an old friend. I guess she can go there straight away. She'll understand, don't worry.'

Ada blew her cheeks out, then released the air slowly. All the words that she had prepared to say now felt useless. A new kind of anger came over her then. She did not want her father to give up so easily. She was tired of seeing him lose all his battles against her, whether trivial or consequential, retreating to his corner each time like a wounded animal.

Her anger softened into sorrow, and sorrow into resignation, and resignation into a sense of numbness, swelling thickly, filling the emptiness inside. In the end, what difference did it make whether her aunt came to visit them for a few days? It would all be as fleeting and pointless as the postcards she had sent them in the past. Granted, it would be annoying to have a stranger wandering around the house, but perhaps her presence would, in some little way, conceal this pitiful gulf widening between her father and herself.

'You know what, I really don't care,' Ada said. 'Do as you like. Let her come. Just don't expect me to play along, all right? She's your guest, not mine.'

Fig Tree

Meryem! Here in London. How bizarre. It has been so long since I last heard her husky voice in Cyprus.

I guess now is the time I need to tell you something important about myself: I am not what you think I am – a young, delicate fig tree planted in a garden somewhere in north London. I am that, and much more. Or perhaps I should say, in one life I have lived several, which is another way of saying, I am old.

I was born and raised in Nicosia, once upon a time. Those who knew me back then couldn't help breaking into a smile, a tender glint in their eyes. I was treasured and loved to such a degree that they had named a whole tavern after me. And what a tavern that was, the best for many miles! The brass sign over the entrance read:

THE HAPPY FIG

It was inside this celebrated eating house and watering hole – crowded, rowdy, joyous and hospitable – that I spread my roots and grew up through a cavity in the roof that was specifically opened for me.

Every visitor to Cyprus wanted to dine here – and taste its famous stuffed courgette flowers followed by chicken souvlaki, cooked over open-air charcoal – if they were so lucky as to find a table. In this very spot was offered the best food, the best music, the best wine and the best dessert, speciality of the house – oven-roasted figs with honey and aniseed ice cream. But there was something else to the place, too, so said its regular customers: it made one forget, even if for just a few hours, the world outside and its immoderate sorrows.

54

I was tall, robust, self-confident and, surprisingly for my age, still laden with rich, sweet figs, each giving off a perfumed scent. During the day I enjoyed listening to the clatter of plates, the chatter of customers, the singing of musicians – songs in Greek and Turkish, songs about love, betrayal and heartbreak. At night I slept the untroubled sleep of those who have never had a reason to doubt that tomorrow would be better than yesterday. Until it all abruptly came to an end.

Long after the island was partitioned and the tavern fell into disrepair, Kostas Kazantzakis took a cutting from one of my branches and put it in his suitcase. I guess I will always be grateful to him for doing that, otherwise nothing of me might have remained. Because I was dying, you see, the tree that I was in Cyprus. But the cutting that was also me survived. A teeny thing – ten inches long, no wider than a pinky finger. That little cutting grew into a clone, genetically identical. And from this clone I sprouted forth in my new home in London. The pattern of my branches would not be exactly the same, but we were similar in every other detail, who I was in Cyprus and who I would become in England. The only difference was that I was no longer a happy tree.

In order for me to survive the long journey from Nicosia to London, Kostas carefully wrapped me in layers of damp sacking before tucking me at the bottom of his suitcase. It was a risk, he knew. The English climate was not warm enough for me to thrive, let alone bear edible fruit. He took the risk. I did not fail him.

I liked my new home in London. I worked hard to fit in, to belong. From time to time, I missed my fig wasps, but fortunately, for the past several thousand years of evolution, there have been parthenocarpic fig trees and I am one of those who have no need of pollination. Despite all this, it would take me seven years to be able to yield fruit again. Because that is what migrations and relocations do to us: when you leave your home for unknown shores, you don't simply carry on as before; a part of you dies inside so that another part can start all over again.

Today, when other trees ask me how old I am, I find it hard to give a definite answer. I was ninety-six years old the last time I remember myself in a tavern in Cyprus. I, who grew from a cutting planted in England, am now slightly over sixteen.

Do you always have to calculate how old someone is by adding up the months and years with simple, straightforward arithmetic – or are there instances in which it is actually wiser to offset passages of time in order to arrive at the correct total number? And what about our ancestors – can they, too, continue to exist through us? Is that why, when you meet some individuals – just as with some trees – you can't help feeling that they must be much older than their chronological age?

Where do you start someone's story when every life has more than one thread and what we call birth is not the only beginning, nor is death exactly an end?

Garden

Saturday evening, Ada had just finished a bottle of Diet Coke and Kostas his last coffee of the day when the sound of the doorbell tore through the house.

Ada flinched. 'Could that be her? Already?'

'I'll get it,' Kostas said, glancing apologetically at his daughter as he left the room.

Ada dropped her hands on her lap, examining her fingernails, all chewed to the quick. She picked at the cuticle on her right thumb, pulling slowly. Seconds later, voices wafted in from the hallway.

'Hey, Meryem, you're here! Good to see you.'

'Kostas, my goodness, look at you!'

'And you . . . but you haven't changed a bit.'

'Ah, that's such a huge lie, but you know what, at my age, I'll take whatever I can.'

Kostas laughed. 'And I'll take your suitcases.'

'Thank you, they're a bit heavy, I'm afraid. Sorry, I know I should have called earlier in the week to confirm I was coming. Things got terribly hectic. I didn't think I could find a flight until the last moment, I even had a bit of a quarrel with the travel agency –'

'It's fine,' Kostas said, his tone gentle. 'I'm glad you are here.'

'Me too . . . I'm so happy to be here, finally.'

Listening, Ada sat up straight, surprised by the touch of intimacy in their exchange. She pulled at the cuticle harder. A bright red pool appeared between her flesh and thumbnail. Quickly, she sucked it away.

In a little while a woman walked in, bundled in a fuzzy taupe overcoat with a hood that made her round face appear rounder and her olive skin warmer. Her eyes were shifting hazel with specks of copper, set slightly apart under thinly plucked eyebrows; her hair fell to her shoulders in auburn, wavy ripples. Her nose was undoubtedly her most prominent feature – strong, angular. In her left nostril shone the tiniest crystal stud. Ada studied their guest, concluding that she looked nothing like her mother.

'Oh, wow – this must be Ada!'

Chewing the inside of her cheek, Ada stood up. 'Hi.'

'My goodness, I was expecting to see a little girl, but I found a young lady!'

Ada extended a cautious hand, but the woman had already lurched towards her in one quick movement and pulled her into her embrace, her bosom, large and soft, bumping up against Ada's chin. Her cheeks were cold from the wind and she smelled like a mixture of rosewater and lemon cologne.

'Let me look at you!' Meryem disentangled her arms and held Ada by the shoulders. 'Oh, you're so beautiful, just like your mother! More than your photos.'

Ada took a step back, freeing herself from the woman's embrace. 'You have photos of me?'

'Of course, hundreds! Your mum would send them to me. I keep them in albums. I even have tiny clay footprints of your baby feet, so cute!'

With her left hand, Ada grabbed her bleeding thumb, which had begun to throb – a steady, pulsating beat.

Just then Kostas entered the room, carrying three large suitcases, each a shade of pink and imprinted with the face of Marilyn Monroe.

'Oh, bless you. Please don't bother, just drop them,' Meryem said in a fluster.

'No problem,' said Kostas. 'Your room is ready if you'd like to rest first. Or we could have a cup of tea. Either way. Maybe you're hungry?'

Collapsing into the nearest armchair, Meryem shrugged off

her coat, her many bracelets and rings jingling. A gold necklace glinted at her neck, threaded with an evil eye bead, blue and unblinking.

'I'm full, thank you – it's teensy portions all that airline food, but it bloats you up like a puffer fish. So nothing for me, please. But I'll always have a cup of tea – without milk, though. Why do the English do that? I've never understood.'

'Sure.' Kostas put the suitcases on the floor and headed towards the kitchen.

Suddenly finding herself alone with this boisterous stranger, Ada felt her shoulders tense.

'Now tell me, which school do you go to?' Meryem asked, her voice chiming like silver bells. 'What is your favourite subject?'

'Sorry, I better go and help my father,' Ada said and bolted from the room without waiting for a response.

In the kitchen she found her father filling the kettle.

'So?' Ada whispered as she approached the worktop.

'So?' echoed Kostas.

'Aren't you going to ask why she's here? There must be a reason. I bet it's something to do with money. Maybe my grandparents died, there's some dispute over inheritance and she wants to get my mother's share.'

'Ada *mou*, take it easy, don't jump to conclusions.'

'Then ask her, Dad!'

'I will, sweetheart. We will. Together. Patience,' Kostas said as he placed the kettle on the stove. He arranged teacups on a tray and opened a packet of biscuits, realizing they were running out. He had forgotten to go shopping.

'I don't like her,' Ada said, chewing her lower lip. 'She's totally over the top. Did you hear what she said about my baby foot-prints? So annoying. You can't just barge into the house of

59

someone you've never met and straight away expect to be all lovey-dovey.'

'Listen, why don't you make the tea? The teapot is ready, just add water. Okay?'

'Fine,' Ada said with a sigh.

'I'll go and chat with her. Take your time. No pressure. You can join us whenever you want.'

'Do I have to?'

'Come on, Aditsa, let's give her a chance. Your mum loved her sister. Do this for her.'

As she waited for the water to boil, alone in the kitchen, Ada leaned back against the worktop, thinking.

You're so beautiful, her aunt had said. *Just like your mother.*

Ada remembered a drowsy afternoon the summer before last. Beds of petunias and marigolds painted the garden a rich orange and purple, and death had yet to touch the house. She and her mother sat on reclining chairs, their feet bare, their legs hot in the sun. Her mother was biting on the end of a pencil, solving a crossword puzzle. Sipping lemonade by her side, Ada was writing a school essay on Greek deities, but she was finding it hard to concentrate.

'Mum, is it true that Aphrodite was the prettiest goddess of all the Olympians?'

Brushing a strand of hair out of her eyes, Defne glanced at her. 'She was pretty, yeah, but was she nice, that's another question.'

'Oh! She was mean?'

'Well, she could be a bitch, excuse my language. She was no supporter of women. Her feminism score was pitiful, if you ask me.'

Ada giggled. 'You speak as if you know her.'

'Of course I do! We all come from the same island. She was born in Cyprus, from the foam of Paphos.'

'Didn't know that. So she's the goddess of beauty and love?'

'Yup, that's her. Desire and pleasure too – and procreation. Although some of that was attributed to her later, through Venus, her Roman incarnation. The earlier Aphrodite was more subversive and selfish. Under that beautiful face was a bully who tried to control women.'

'How?'

'Well, there was this young, brilliant girl called Polyphonte. Clever, headstrong. She looked at her mother and she looked at her aunt and she decided she wanted a different life for herself. No marriage, no husband, no possessions, no domestic obligations, thank you very much! Instead she would travel the world until she found what she was looking for. And if she couldn't find it, then she would go and join Artemis as a virgin priestess. That was her plan. When Aphrodite heard about this, she was incandescent with rage. You know what she did to Polyphonte? She drove her to madness. Poor girl lost her mind.'

'Why would a goddess do that?'

'Excellent question. In all the myths and fairy tales, a woman who breaks social conventions is always punished. And usually the punishment is psychological, mental. Classic, isn't it? Remember Mr Rochester's first wife in *Jane Eyre*? Polyphonte is our Mediterranean version of a deranged female, except we didn't lock her up in the attic, we fed her to a bear. An uncivilized end for a woman who didn't want to be part of civilization.'

Ada tried to smile but something inside prevented her.

'Anyway, that's Aphrodite for you,' Defne said. 'Not a friend of women. But yes, pretty!'

When Ada returned to the living room carrying a tray laden with teapot, porcelain cups and a plate of shortbread biscuits, she was surprised to find it empty.

Setting the tray on the coffee table, she glanced around. 'Dad?'

The door to the guest room stood ajar. Her aunt was not there, just her suitcases, thrown on the bed.

Ada checked the study and the other rooms, but her father and aunt were nowhere to be seen. Only when she returned to the living room did she notice that, behind the thick curtains, the French windows on to the garden were unlocked. She pushed them open and stepped out.

Cold. It was piercingly cold and dimly lit. One of the lanterns must have gone off. A pale glimmer from the sliver-moon fell on the stone path. As her eyes adjusted to the shadows around, she made out two shapes nearby. Her father and her aunt were there, under the falling sleet, despite the approaching storm, standing side by side where the fig tree was buried. So peculiar was the sight of their silhouettes huddled together against the night that Ada recoiled.

'Dad? What are you doing?' she said, but the wind snatched her voice away.

She took a step closer, then another. She could see them clearly now. Her father held himself upright, his arms crossed, his head slightly inclined to one side, not speaking. Her aunt was carrying in her arms a pile of stones she must have collected from the garden, her lips moving in a prayer, her words coming fast and tumbling into each other in a breathless plea. What could she be saying?

When done, the woman began placing the stones on the ground, stacking them up into little towers, one upon another. The rhythmic sound reminded Ada of the gentle lapping of the waves against the side of a boat.

And then, Ada heard a melody – deep, raw, plangent. She leaned forward almost despite herself. Her aunt was singing. A low, keening voice. A dirge in a language she could not understand but the sadness of which she did not doubt.

Ada stopped moving, not daring to disturb whatever it was

they were doing. She waited, her hair blowing about her head, her nails digging deep into her palms, though she would not realize this until later. Half hiding in the shadows, she watched the two adults by the buried fig tree, drawn to the strangeness of their behaviour but equally detached from them, as if witnessing someone else's dream.

Fig Tree

It was a ritual for the dead. An ancient rite to guide to safety the spirit of a loved one, so that it would not wander off in the vast recesses of the ether. As a rule, the ceremony ought to be performed *under* a fig tree, but – given my current position – I guess it had to be above this time.

From where I lay, I listened to the low, resonant, steady *rap-rap-rap*, stone laid on stone, rising like a column to support the vault of heaven. Those who believe in such things say the sound represents the footsteps of a lost soul treading across the Bridge of Siraat, thinner than a strand of hair, sharper than a sword, straddling precariously the void between this world and the next. At every step, the soul jettisons yet another one of its innumerable burdens, until finally it lets go of everything, including all the pain stored within.

Fig trees, those who know us will tell you, have long been regarded as sacred. In many cultures spirits are believed to reside inside our trunks, some good, some bad and some undecided, all invisible to the uninitiated eye. Others claim that every genus of *Ficus* is, in truth, a meeting point, a gathering place of sorts. Under, around and above us they mass, not only humans and animals, but also creatures of light and shadow. There are plenty of stories about the way the leaves of a banyan tree, a relative of mine, can all of a sudden rustle in the absence of even the slightest breeze. While other trees remain motionless, when the entire universe seems to stand still, the banyan stirs and speaks. A thickening in the air like a premonition. It is a spooky sight, should you ever see it happen.

Humans have always sensed there was something uncanny about me and my kind. That is why they come to us when in need or in trouble, and tie velvet ribbons or strips of fabric on our branches. And sometimes we help them without them even noticing. How else do you think those twin brothers Romulus and Remus would have been found by a she-wolf, had their basket, floating dangerously in the waters of the River Tiber, not got caught in the roots of a *Ficus ruminalis*? In Judaism, sitting under a fig tree has long been associated with a deep, devout study of the Torah. And, while Jesus might have held in disfavour a certain barren fig tree, let us not forget it was a poultice made of us that, upon being applied to his wound, saved Hezekiah. The Prophet Mohammed said the fig was the one tree that he wished to see in paradise – there is a *sura* with our name in the Qur'an. It was while meditating under a *Ficus religiosa* that Buddha attained enlightenment. And did I mention how King David was fond of us or how we inspired hope and new beginnings in every animal and human on board the Ark of Noah?

Anyone who seeks refuge under a fig tree, for whatever reason, has my deepest sympathy, and humans have been doing so for centuries, all the way from India to Anatolia, from Mexico to El Salvador. The Bedouin settle their disagreements in our shade, the Druze kiss our bark reverently, placing personal objects around us, praying for *ma'rifah*. Both Arabs and Jews make their wedding preparations beside us, hoping for marriages sturdy enough to weather any storms which may lie ahead. Buddhists want us to blossom near their shrines, and so do the Hindus. Kikuyu women in Kenya daub themselves with the sap of fig trees when they want to get pregnant and it is the same women who defend us bravely whenever someone tries to cut down a sacred *mugumo*.

Under our canopy, sacrificial animals are slaughtered, vows taken, rings exchanged and blood feuds settled. And some even believe that if you circle a fig tree seven times while burning incense and uttering the right words in the right order, you can change the sex attributed to you at birth. Then there are those who hammer the sharpest nails into our trunks to pass on to us whatever illness or malady assails them. This, too, we endure silently. It is not for no reason that they call us holy trees, wishing trees, accursed trees, ghostly trees, unearthly trees, eldritch trees, soul-stealing trees . . .

And it is not for no reason that Meryem insisted on holding a ritual for her dead sister under – or above – a *Ficus carica*. As she struck the stones against each other, I heard her sing – an elegy, slow and mournful, a belated keening for the funeral she had not been able to attend.

Meanwhile, I was sure my beloved Kostas kept his distance, not saying much. I didn't have to see his face to know that it must have acquired an expression of polite disapproval. As a man of science, reason and research, he would never give credence to the supernatural, yet neither would he belittle anyone who did. A scientist he might be but, first and foremost, he was an islander. He, too, was raised by a mother prone to superstition.

I once heard Defne say to Kostas, 'People from troubled islands can never be normal. We can pretend, we can even make amazing progress – but we can never really learn to feel safe. The ground that feels rock hard to others is choppy waters for our kind.'

Kostas listened to her carefully, as he always did. Throughout their marriage and long before, while they were dating, he had tried to ensure those rough waters would never swallow her, and yet in the end they had.

I don't know why that memory seeped back into me tonight as I lay buried under the ground, but I wondered if the stones Meryem placed on the cold earth were a form of comfort for her, a token of reassurance, when nothing else felt solid.

Banquet

When Ada woke up the next morning, the house was filled with unusual smells. Her aunt had prepared breakfast – or a banquet, more like it. Grilled halloumi with za'atar, baked feta with honey, sesame halva, stuffed tomatoes, green olives with fennel, bread rolls with black olive spread, fried peppers, spicy sausage, spinach börek, puff-pastry cheese straws, pomegranate molasses with tahini, hawthorn jelly, quince jam and a large pan of poached eggs with garlic yogurt were all neatly arrayed on the table.

'Oh, wow!' Ada said as she walked into the kitchen.

Meryem, chopping parsley on a wooden board at the worktop, turned towards her with a smile. She was wearing a long black skirt and a chunky grey cardigan that almost reached her knees. 'Good morning!'

'Where did all this food come from?'

'Well, I found a few things in the cupboards, and the rest I brought with me. Oh, you had to see me at the airport! I was terrified those sniffer dogs would get wind of my halva. I passed through customs with my heart in my mouth. Because they always stop people like me, don't they?' She pointed to her head. 'Dark hair, wrong passport.'

Ada sat at the end of the table, listening. She watched her aunt cut a large slice of börek and spoon out a generous portion of poached eggs and sausage on to a plate. 'For me? Thank you, but this is too much.'

'What's too much, it's nothing! An eagle doesn't feed on flies.'

If Ada found that an odd thing to say, her face revealed nothing. She glanced around. 'Where's my dad?'

Meryem pulled a chair up for herself, a glass of tea in her hand. It seemed she had also brought from Cyprus a set of tea glasses

67

and a brass samovar, which was now boiling and hissing in a corner.

'Out in the garden! He said he needed to go and talk to the tree.'

'Yeah, well, I'm not surprised,' Ada muttered under her breath as she stabbed her fork into the pastry. 'He's obsessed with that fig.'

A shadow crossed Meryem's face. 'You don't like the fig?'

'Why would I not like a *tree*? What do I care?'

'That's no ordinary tree, you know. Your mum and dad brought it all the way from Nicosia.'

Ada had not known that, and had nothing to say in return. The *Ficus carica* had always been there in the back garden, for as long as she could remember. She took a bite of börek and chewed slowly. There was no denying her aunt was a good cook, in striking contrast to her mother, who had always been uninterested in any kind of domestic life.

She pushed the plate away.

Meryem raised her eyebrows, plucked so thin they resembled a pair of pencilled arches on her ample features. 'What, that's it? You're not eating any more?'

'Sorry, I'm not a breakfast person.'

'Is that a separate group now? Aren't all people in the world breakfast people? We all wake up hungry.'

Ada shot a quick glance at her aunt. The woman had a peculiar way of talking, which she found amusing and annoying in equal parts.

'Good morning, both,' came Kostas's voice from behind. He strode into the kitchen, his cheeks webbed red from the cold, a scattering of snowflakes settled on his hair. 'What a fabulous spread.'

'Yes, but somebody's not eating,' Meryem said.

Kostas smiled at his daughter. 'Ada doesn't have much appetite in the mornings. I'm sure she'll eat later.'

'Later is not the same thing,' said Meryem. 'One must have

breakfast like a sultan, lunch like a vizier, dinner like a mendicant. Otherwise the whole order is broken.'

Ada sat back and crossed her arms. She studied this woman who had appeared in their lives out of the blue – the generous dimensions of her face, her loud and boisterous presence. 'So you haven't told us why you are here yet.'

'Ada!' said Kostas.

'What? You said I could ask.'

'It's okay. It's good that she asks.' Meryem dropped a sugar cube into her tea and stirred. When she spoke again, her voice was different. 'My mother passed away; it's been ten days exactly.'

'Mother Selma is dead?' Kostas said. 'I didn't know. I'm sorry for your loss.'

'Thank you,' said Meryem, though her eyes remained focused on Ada. 'Your granny was ninety-two years old, went in her sleep. A blessed death, as we say. I took care of the funeral, then I booked the first flight I could find.'

Ada turned to her father. 'I told you it was about inheritance.'

'What inheritance?' Meryem interjected.

Kostas shook his head. 'Ada thinks you need to sort out some paperwork, and that's why you are here.'

'Oh, I see, like a will. No, my parents were people of modest means. I don't have paperwork to discuss with you.'

'Then why are you here all of a sudden?' said Ada, her stare taking on a feverish tinge.

In the ensuing silence something passed between Meryem and Kostas, an unspoken exchange. Ada sensed this, but what it was she could not say. Fighting the urge to ask them what they were hiding from her, she held herself ramrod straight, the way her mother had taught her.

'I always wanted to come and visit you,' said Meryem after a brief pause. 'How could I not want to meet my sister's child? But I had made a promise. My father passed away fourteen years ago – you were a baby then. But until both my parents were dead, I was bound by my word.'

'What kind of promise?' Ada asked.

'That I would never see any of you, so long as my parents were alive,' Meryem replied, her breathing a little ragged. 'When my mother died, I felt free to travel.'

'I don't get it,' said Ada. 'Why would you make such a horrible promise? And what kind of a person would ask you to do that?'

'Ada *mou*, take it easy,' said Kostas gently.

Ada looked towards her father, anger illuminating her eyes. 'Come on, Dad, I'm not a child. I get it. You're Greek, Mum is Turkish, opposite tribes, blood feud. You upset some people when you got married, didn't you? So what? Nothing excuses this type of behaviour. They haven't once come to see us. Not only them. None of our relatives did on either side. They didn't attend Mum's funeral. You want to call this *family*? I'm not going to sit here, eat falafel and listen to proverbs, and pretend I'm okay with all this!'

Absent-mindedly, Meryem tipped another sugar cube into her tea, forgetting that she had already done so. She took a sip. Too sweet. She set the glass aside.

'Sorry if I'm being rude.' Ada shook her head and, in one fluid movement, pushed her chair back and stood up. 'I've got homework to do.'

After she left, an awkward silence descended on the kitchen. Meryem removed her rings, one by one, and put them back on. She muttered to herself, 'I didn't make falafel. It's not even our cuisine.'

'I'm sorry,' said Kostas. 'Ada has gone through a lot this year. It's been extremely hard for her.'

'And for you too,' Meryem said, lifting her head and directing her gaze towards him. 'But the resemblance is striking. She's . . . she's just like her mother.'

Kostas nodded with a half-smile. 'I know.'

'And she has every right to ask these questions,' Meryem said. 'How come you're not angry with me?'

'How's that going to help us? Have we not had enough of all that – anger, hatred, hurt? More than enough.'

Meryem glanced around as though she had misplaced something. Her voice dropped to a whisper when she spoke again. 'How much does Ada know?'

'Not much.'

'But she's curious. She is young and clever, she wants to learn.'

'I've told her a few things, here and there.'

'I doubt that's enough to satisfy her.'

Kostas tilted his head, the furrows in his brow deepening. 'She's a British kid. She has never even been to Cyprus. Defne was right all along. Why burden our children with our past – or the mess we've made of it? This is a new generation. A clean slate. I don't want her to be preoccupied with a history that caused us nothing but pain and distrust.'

'As you wish,' said Meryem pensively.

She dropped another sugar cube into her tea and watched it dissolve.

PART TWO

Roots

Lovers

Cyprus, 1974

An hour to midnight. The moon, bright and joyous, was a day past full. And though Defne would normally have liked that, tonight she needed the cover of darkness.

She rose from her bed, threw off her pyjamas and changed into a full blue skirt, cinched with an embroidered leather belt, and a white frilled blouse that everyone said looked good on her. She put on her earrings, not the gold ones – which were barely visible, so tiny against her earlobes – but the crystal ones that dangled to her shoulders and sparkled like stars. They made her feel more grown up and glamorous. She tied the laces of her trainers together and slung them around her neck. She had to be as quiet as the night itself.

Lifting the window sash, she eased herself up on to the sill and crouched on the ledge for a few seconds. She could hear a noise in the distance, a soft two-note call, probably an owl in pursuit of prey. She held her breath, listening. Kostas had taught her the precise sequence of their hooting: brief note, brief silence, long note, long silence. An owl Morse code just for them.

She reached for a limb of the mulberry tree and carefully pulled herself on to it. From there she climbed down, one branch at a time, as she had so often done when she was a little girl. As soon as she jumped to the ground, she looked up to see if anyone had been watching. For a split second, she thought she saw a shadow in a window. Could it be her sister? But Meryem should be asleep in her room. She had checked on her earlier.

Her stomach clenching with anxiety, Defne sneaked out of the garden. The moonlight reflected off the stone setts along the narrow street, forming rivulets of silver that shimmered in front of her as if she were coasting over water. She accelerated her steps, glancing over her shoulder every few seconds to make sure no one was following.

They usually met here late at night, at this bend in the road by an ancient olive tree. They walked around a little or sat on a wall, ensconcing themselves in the shadows, the darkness a downy shawl enveloping their nerves. Sometimes a black-crowned night heron flew overhead or a hedgehog shuffled by, nocturnal creatures as secretive as the lovers themselves.

Today she was running late. As she approached their meeting point, her breathing quickened. With no street lamps and no houses nearby, it was almost pitch-black in places. As she got closer, she squinted ahead and tried to pick out his familiar outline amidst the trees but could not see anything. Her heart tripped. He must have left. Still she kept walking, hoping.

'Defne?'

His voice gave her name a softer edge, the vowels slightly rounded. Now she discerned his silhouette. Tall, lean, unmistakable. A tiny orange glow moved in tandem with his hand.

'Is that you?' Kostas whispered.

'Yes, you silly, who else could it be?' Defne drew closer, smiling. 'I didn't know you smoked.'

'I didn't know either,' Kostas said. 'I was nervous. I nicked my brother's packet.'

'But why are you smoking, *ashkim*? Don't you know it's just a few puffs that disappear as soon as you exhale?' Seeing his stricken expression, she laughed. 'I'm kidding, it's okay. Don't mind me. Both my parents smoke. I'm used to it.'

They held hands, their fingers interlaced. Defne noticed he had put on a bit too much cologne. Clearly she wasn't the only one trying to impress. She pulled him to her and kissed him. Being a year older, she considered herself more mature.

'I was so worried you wouldn't come,' Kostas said.

'I promised, didn't I?'

'Yes, but still . . .'

'In our family we always keep our word. Father brought us up that way – both me and Meryem.'

He flicked out the last of the cigarette and crushed it under his shoe. 'So you've never broken a promise in your life?'

'No, I haven't, actually. I don't think my sister has either. I am not proud of it, it's pretty boring. Once we give our word, we have to stick to it. That's why I try not to make many promises.' She threw her head back and looked him steadily in the eye. 'But I can easily promise one thing: I will always love you, Kostas Kazantzakis.'

She could hear his heart thumping behind his ribcage. This boy who was gentle as the dew on a fresh morning and could sing the most touching ballads in a language she could not follow, this boy who could chatter excitedly about evergreen shrubs and crested hoopoes, now seemed lost for words.

She leaned forward, so close he could feel her breath upon his face. 'What about you?'

'Me? But I've already pledged myself – long ago. I know I'll never stop loving you.'

She smiled, even though her habitual cynicism didn't allow her to believe him. Neither did she allow herself to doubt him. Not tonight. She wanted to wrap herself around his words, shielding them the way you would cup your palms around a flame against the blowing wind.

'I brought you something,' Kostas said, producing a small item from his pocket, unwrapped.

It was a music box made of cherry wood with an inlaid design of brightly coloured butterflies on the lid and a key with a red silk tassel.

'Oh, it's so beautiful, thank you . . .'

She held the box close to her chest, feeling its smooth coldness. She knew he must have saved money to buy it. Carefully, she wound the key underneath, and a sweet melody spilled out. They listened until it came to an end.

'I've got something for you too.'

She took a roll of paper from her bag. A pencil sketch of him sitting on a rock, birds floating over the horizon, a set of stone-built arches extending on either side. The week before, the two of them had strolled by the old aqueduct, which once carried water down from the mountains north of the city. Although daytime was always riskier, they had spent the whole afternoon there, inhaling the smell of wild grass, and that was the moment she had wanted to capture.

He held the drawing up, inspecting it in the moonlight. 'You made me look handsome.'

'Well, it wasn't hard.'

He studied her expression, his fingers tracing the soft line of her jaw. 'You're so talented.'

They kissed, this time for longer, reaching for each other with an urgency, as though to keep themselves from falling. Yet there was also a timidity to their moves, even as every caress, every whisper, made them more tender. For it is a land without borders, a lover's body. You discover it, not at once, but step by anxious step, losing your way, your sense of direction, treading its sunlit valleys and rolling fields, finding it warm and welcoming, and then, hidden in quiet corners, running into caverns invisible and unexpected, pits where you stumble and cut yourself.

Wrapping his arms around her, Kostas laid his cheek against her head. Defne buried her face in his neck. They were both aware that, however unlikely at so late an hour, someone could see them and report back to their families. An island, large or small, was filled with eyes watching from behind every latticed window, every crack in the wall, and through every red-tailed hawk that rose high on the wind – an unblinking, raptor gaze.

Holding hands, careful to stay in the shadows, they strolled, in no rush to be anywhere. The night had turned slightly chilly. She shivered in her thin blouse. He offered her his jacket, but she refused. When he asked again, she got upset, not wanting to be treated as if she were weaker than him. She was stubborn like that.

He was seventeen, she eighteen.

Fig Tree

Here under the ground, I lie still listening to every little sound. Cut off from all sources of light – sun or moon – my circadian clock is disrupted and regular sleep eludes me. I suppose it is a bit like being jet-lagged. Day and night patterns are thrown into disarray, leaving me in a perpetual haze. I will adjust eventually, but it will take me a while.

Life below the surface is neither simple nor monotonous. The subterranean, contrary to what most people think, is bustling with activity. As you tunnel deep down, you might be surprised to see the soil take on unexpected shades. Rusty red, soft peach, warm mustard, lime green, rich turquoise ... Humans teach their children to paint the earth in one colour alone. They imagine the sky in blue, the grass in green, the sun in yellow and the earth entirely in brown. If they only knew they have rainbows under their feet.

Take a handful of soil, press it between your palms, feel its warmth, texture, mystery. There are more microorganisms in this small clod than there are people in the world. Packed with bacteria, fungi, archaea, algae and those wriggly earthworms, not to mention broken bits of ancient crockery, all working towards converting organic material into nutrients on which we plants gratefully feed and thrive, the earth is complicated, resilient, generous. Every inch of soil is the product of hard work. It takes a multitude of worms and microorganisms hundreds of years of ceaseless labour to produce even that much. Healthy, loamy dirt is more precious than diamonds and rubies, though I have never heard humans praise it that way.

A tree has a thousand ears in all directions. I can detect the munching of caterpillars as they eat holes in my leaves, the buzzing of passing bees, the chirring of a beetle's wing. I can recognize the soft gurgling of water columns breaking inside my twigs. Plants can pick up vibrations, and many flowers are shaped like bowls so as to better trap sound waves, some of which are too high for the human ear. Trees are full of songs and we are not shy to sing them.

Prostrate here in the midst of winter, I seek refuge in arboreal dreams. I don't ever get bored but there is so much I miss already – the slivers of light from the stars, the beauty of the moon against the night sky, perfect and delicately mottled like a robin's egg, the aroma of coffee spilling from the house every morning . . . and most of all, Ada and Kostas.

I miss Cyprus too. Maybe because of the frigid climate, I can't help harking back to my days in the sun. I might have become a British tree, but some days it still takes me a moment to fathom where I am, on which island exactly. Memories come rushing back upon me, and if I listen intently I can still hear the songs of meadowlarks and sparrows, the whistling of warblers and wigeons, the birds of Cyprus, calling my name.

Shelter

Cyprus, 1974

The next time they met, Defne seemed uneasy, a flame of apprehension burning in her dark eyes.

'The other night, on the way back, I ran into my uncle,' she said. 'He asked me what I was doing out so late. I had to scramble to find an excuse.'

'What did you say?' Kostas asked.

'I said my sister was feeling poorly, I had to go to the pharmacist. But guess what, he bumped into Meryem the next morning! He asked her if she was feeling better, and Meryem, bless her, played along. Then she came home and questioned me. I had to tell her, Kostas. My sister knows about us now.'

'Can you trust her?'

'I can,' Defne replied without skipping a beat. 'But if my uncle had spoken to my parents, it'd have been a different story. We can't keep meeting like this.'

Kostas ran his fingers through his hair. 'I've been thinking about it for a while. I've been looking for a safe place.'

'There is none!'

'Well, there is one, actually.'

'Where?'

'It's a tavern.' He watched her eyes widen, then narrow. 'I know what you're going to say, but listen. This place is nearly empty during the day. The customers start dropping in no earlier than sunset. Before that, it's only the staff. And even in the evenings, if we manage to meet in a back room, and leave through the kitchen door, it's safer than being out on the streets. In a tavern everyone's in their own world anyway.'

Defne bit her bottom lip, turning the idea in her head. 'Which one?'

'The Happy Fig.'

'Oh!' Her face brightened. 'Never been there, but I've heard lots of things about it.'

'My mum sells them stuff every week. I take them carob jam, *melitzanaki glyko*.'

She smiled, knowing how close he was to his mother and how dearly he loved her. 'Do you know the owner?'

'It's two guys that own the place. They are very nice people – complete opposites, though. One is incurably chatty, always telling some story or joke. The other is quiet. It takes a while to get to know him.'

Defne nodded, although she wasn't fully listening. In that second, all the dread she had been carrying within had lifted and she felt light again, bold. She touched his lips, which were slightly chapped, sun-roughened. He must have been biting them, just like she did.

'What makes you think they'll help us?' she asked.

'I've a feeling they won't say no to me. I've been observing these guys for so long. They are honest and hardworking, they mind their own business. Imagine, they meet all sorts of people, but never gossip about anyone. I like that about them.'

'Fine. Let's give it a try,' said Defne. 'But if it doesn't work, we'll have to find another way.'

He smiled, relief coursing through his veins. This he never told her, but he feared she might one day suggest that it had become too dangerous for them to see each other, this secret too heavy to hold, that they should break up before things got out of hand. Every time he felt this fear, he gently pushed it down into a place in the basement of his soul where he kept all uncontrolled and painful thoughts. He tucked it next to the memories of his father.

Fig Tree

Before you meet me in the tavern, I must tell you a few more things about myself and my motherland.

I came into this world in 1878, the year that Sultan Abdul Hamid II, sitting on his gilded throne in Istanbul, made a secret agreement with Queen Victoria, sitting on her gilded throne in London. The Ottoman Empire agreed to cede the administration of our island to the British Empire in exchange for protection against Russian aggression. The same year the British Prime Minister, Benjamin Disraeli, called my motherland 'the key to Western Asia', and added, 'in taking it the move is not Mediterranean, but Indian'. The island, though without much economic value in his eyes, was ideally placed for lucrative trade routes.

A few weeks later the Union Jack was hoisted over Nicosia. After the First World War, during which the Ottoman Empire and the British Empire became adversaries, the British annexed Cyprus and thus we became a Crown Colony.

I remember the day they arrived, Her Majesty's troops, tired and thirsty from the long journey, and slightly confused as to who exactly were to be their colonial subjects. The English, though themselves islanders at heart, have never quite known where to place our island inside their minds. One minute we seemed reassuringly familiar to their eyes, the next minute strangely exotic and oriental.

On that fateful day, Sir Garnet Wolseley, the first High Commissioner, showed up on our shores with a large force of soldiers wearing thick uniforms – English pattern trousers and red woollen tunics. The thermometer showed 110 degrees Fahrenheit. They camped at Larnaca, near the Salt Lake, carrying single bell tents that did little to protect them against the scorching sun. In his letters to his wife, Wolseley would later complain: 'It was a very unwise move sending these British regiments here during the hot weather.' But what disappointed him the most was the arid landscape: 'Where are the forests we thought Cyprus was covered with?'

'Good question,' we trees conceded. Life was not easy for us. Swarms of locusts had plagued the island for too long, arriving in dense, dark clouds, devouring all things green. Forests had been decimated, cleared for vineyards, cultivation and fuelwood, and at times deliberately destroyed in endless vendettas. Constant logging, multiple fires and sheer ignorance were all responsible for our disappearance, not to mention the blatant neglect of the previous administration. But so were wars, of which we had already had too many throughout the centuries. Conquerors from the East, conquerors from the West: Hittites, Egyptians, Phoenicians, Assyrians, Greeks, Persians, Macedonians, Romans, Byzantines, Arabs, Franks, Genoese, Venetians, Ottomans, Turks, British . . .

We were there when violent attacks against Britons began to unfold in the name of enosis – union with Greece – and the first bombs went off in the early 1950s. We were there when the British Institute on Metaxas Square, and the library inside, *the finest English library in the Middle East*, was set on fire by protesting youths, and all those books and manuscripts made of our flesh were burned to ash. By 1955 things had deteriorated so badly that a State of Emergency was proclaimed. The local florists and flower farms, whose businesses had seen a dramatic decline perhaps because no one felt entitled to beauty when fear and chaos reigned, now made most of their money from fashioning wreaths for the funerals of the Gordon Highlanders and other Britons killed in the conflict.

By 1958, the Greek nationalist organization known as EOKA had banned all English lettering across the island. English street names were crossed out and daubed with paint. Soon Turkish names would be expunged too. Then the Turkish nationalist organization known as TMT started erasing Greek names. And there came a point when the streets in my home town were left nameless, only wet paint over wet paint, like watercolour washes that slowly fade into nothingness.

And we trees watched, waited and witnessed.

Tavern

Cyprus, 1974

The Happy Fig was a popular hang-out frequented by Greeks, Turks, Armenians, Maronites, UN soldiers and visitors to the island who quickly fell in step with the local ways. It was run by two partners, a Greek Cypriot and a Turkish Cypriot, both in their forties. Yiorgos and Yusuf had opened the place in 1955 with money borrowed from families and friends, and kept their business afloat, even managed to thrive, despite the tensions and troubles besetting the island on all sides.

The entrance of the tavern was partially covered with twisting vines of honeysuckle. Inside, solid blackened beams ran the length and breadth of the ceiling, from which hung garlands of garlic, onion, drying herbs, chilli peppers and cured sausages. There were twenty-two tables with mismatched chairs, a carved wooden bar with oak stools, and a charcoal grill at the back from which the smell of flatbread wafted daily, along with the enticing aromas of cooking meats. With more tables out on the patio, the tavern was packed every night.

It was a place with history and small miracles of its own. In here, stories of triumphs and travails were shared, long-standing accounts squared, laughter and tears combined, admissions and promises made, sins and secrets confessed. Between its walls, strangers turned into friends, friends into lovers; old flames rekindled, broken hearts mended or shattered once again. Many a baby on the island had been conceived after a merry evening in the tavern. The Happy Fig had touched people's lives in so many unknown ways.

When Defne, following Kostas, walked in for the first time,

she knew none of this. Tucking a lock of hair behind her ear, she eyed her surroundings curiously. The place seemed to have been decorated by someone who clearly worshipped the colour blue. The entrance was bright azure, with dangling evil eye beads and horseshoes nailed up. The chequered tablecloths were navy and white, the curtains a vivid sapphire, the tiles on the walls adorned with patterns in aquamarine, and even the wide, languid ceiling fans were of a similar hue. Two columns were crammed with framed photos of the celebrities who had visited the restaurant over the years: singers, actresses, TV stars, footballers, fashion designers, journalists, boxing champions . . .

Defne was surprised to see a parrot perched high up on a cabinet, absorbed in eating a biscuit, a short-tailed exotic bird with a yellow head and bright green plumage. But it was what she found at the centre of the tavern that immediately caught her attention. Nestling in the middle of the dining area, growing through a cavity in the roof, was a tree.

'A fig!' An expression of delighted surprise crossed her features. 'Is that real?'

'Oh, you bet it is,' came a voice from behind them.

Turning round, Defne saw two men of medium height and build, standing side by side. One of them, with close-cut hair and a silver crucifix around his neck, doffed an imaginary cap in her direction. 'You should see this tree at night-time, with all the lights on. It looks electrified, magical! This is no ordinary tree – more than ninety years old, but she still bears the sweetest figs in the whole town.'

The other man, probably of similar age, had a well-groomed moustache and a clean-shaven chin marked by a pronounced cleft; his hair fell in long tresses to his shoulders. He gestured towards Kostas and said, 'So this is the f-f-friend you were telling us about.'

Kostas smiled. 'Yes, this is Defne.'

'Oh, she's T-T-Turkish?' said the man, his face changing. 'You didn't say.'

'Why?' Defne asked instantly and, when she didn't get a response right away, her gaze hardened. 'Do you have a problem with that?'

The first man chimed in, 'Hey, don't get upset! Yusuf himself is Turkish. He didn't mean anything, he just speaks slowly. If you rush him, you're going to make him stutter.'

Pursing his lips in an attempt not to smile, Yusuf nodded in agreement. He leaned towards his friend and murmured something inaudible in his ear, which made him chuckle.

'Yusuf is asking, does she always get angry this easily?'

'Oh, she does,' said Kostas with a grin.

'God help us, then!' said the first man. He took Defne's hand and squeezed it gently as he said, 'My name is Yiorgos, by the way. The tree doesn't have a name. The parrot is called Chico. Now I must warn you about him. Don't be surprised if he lands on your shoulder and tries to snatch your food. Terribly spoiled, that bird! We think he must have lived in a palace or somewhere before he found us. Anyway, welcome to our humble place.'

'Thank you,' said Defne, slightly embarrassed by her outburst.

'Now you two follow me.'

He ushered them to a room at the back where they kept boxes of potatoes, baskets of apples and onions, harvests from local orchards and casks of beer. There was a small table in a corner with two chairs, prepared well ahead of their arrival, and a green velvet curtain at the entrance that could be pulled for privacy.

'Not very luxurious, I'm afraid,' said Yiorgos. 'But at least no one will disturb you youngsters here. You can talk as much as you want.'

'This is great, thank you,' said Kostas.

'So what shall we bring you to eat?'

'Oh, we don't want anything.' Kostas fingered the few coins in his pocket. 'Just water.'

'Yes,' said Defne firmly. 'We are fine with water.'

She had barely finished speaking when a waiter appeared, carrying a tray laden with stuffed vine leaves, shrimp saganaki, chicken souvlaki with tzatziki sauce, moussaka, pitta bread and a jug of water.

'Yusuf sent you these, on the house,' said the waiter. 'He asked me to tell you to eat!'

A minute later, finally alone in the room, for the first time in months not having to worry about who might see them and inform their families, Kostas and Defne looked at each other and began to laugh. An incredulous laughter, the kind of effervescent lightness that only comes after constant distress and fear.

They ate slowly, savouring every morsel. They talked incessantly, making the most of what language could offer, as if they didn't trust words would still be available come tomorrow. Meanwhile, the smells and sounds inside the premises intensified. Shadows from the candlelight on the table played across the whitewashed walls. Every time the door to the tavern opened, and a new draught of wind fluttered the curtains, the same shadows danced a little dance just for them.

They heard customers arrive. The sounds of cutlery, idle chatter. Then a plate smashing, followed by a woman's laughter. Someone began to sing in English.

> *So kiss me and smile for me,*
> *Tell me that you'll wait for me . . .*

Others joined in. A spontaneous, loud, rowdy chorus. They were British soldiers, many of them just out of school, their voices rising and falling, hanging on to each other for support and camaraderie, a sense of home, belonging. Young men trapped in a zone of conflict, stuck on an island where they did not speak the languages, nor really understand the subtleties of the political landscape; servicemen fulfilling orders, knowing one of them might not make it to tomorrow.

Two hours later, Yusuf opened the kitchen door and quietly let them out.

'C-c-come back. We don't always get young lovers here, you'll b-bring us luck.'

As they stepped into the evening breeze, they smiled at their host, suddenly shy. Young lovers! They had never thought of themselves in those terms, but now that someone had said it out loud, of course, they knew, that's exactly what they were.

Fig Tree

And that's how she came into my life – Defne.

It was a quiet afternoon. I was dozing off inside the tavern, enjoying a moment of calm before the evening rush, when the door opened and they strode in, slipping from the bright glare of sunlight into the cool shade.

'A fig! Is that real?'

That's what I remember Defne saying as soon as her eyes landed on me. The surprise on her face was unmistakable.

I perked up, curious to know the person who had made this remark. Vanity, perhaps, but I have always been interested in what humans see – or fail to see – in us.

I remember Yiorgos saying something about how I looked electrified at night. He used the word 'magical'. I was pleased to hear that. It was true. In the evenings, when the staff turned on the lamps and lit the candles placed at various corners, a golden light reflected off my bark, glowing through my leaves. My branches stretched out confidently, as if everything around here was an extension of me, not only the trestle tables and wooden chairs, but also the paintings on the walls, the strings of garlic hanging from the ceiling, the waiters scooting back and forth, the customers who came from diverse parts of the world, even Chico flying around in a blaze of colours, all of it happening under my supervision.

I had nothing to worry about back then. My figs were juicy, plentiful, soft to the touch, and my leaves were strong and spotlessly green, the newer ones larger than the older, a sign of healthy growth. Such was my allure that I even uplifted the customers' mood. The furrows in their foreheads relaxed, the edges in their tones smoothed out. Perhaps what they said about happiness was true, after all: it was contagious. In a tavern named The Happy Fig, with a blooming tree at the centre, it was hard not to feel hopeful.

I know I should not be saying this, I know it is wrong of me, unloving and ungrateful, but since that fateful afternoon many years ago there have been more than a few times when I've regretted meeting Defne and I wished she had never crossed our threshold. Maybe then our beautiful tavern would not have been consumed by flames, destroyed. Maybe I would still be that same happy tree.

Loneliness

London, late 2010s

The storm hit London in earnest in the small hours of the night. The sky, dark as a jackdaw's breast, weighed down upon the city with all its load of steeled intensity. Bolts of lightning flashed overhead, expanding out in neon branches and shoots, like some ghostly forest that had been uprooted and swept away.

Alone in her room with the lights turned off save for a reading lamp by her side, Ada lay still in bed, the duvet pulled up to her chin, listening to the thunder and thinking, worrying. As scary as it had been to scream in front of her classmates, there was something she found even scarier: the realization that it could happen again.

During the day, distracted by her aunt's presence, she had somehow banished the incident from her mind, but now it all came rushing back to her. Mrs Walcott's expression, the students' jibes, the confusion on Zafaar's face. That gnawing sensation in her stomach. There must be something wrong with her, she reckoned. Something wrong in her head. Maybe she, too, had what her mother had, the thing they never talked about.

She thought she would not be able to fall asleep, yet she did. A shallow, fitful sleep in the middle of which she opened her eyes, unsure what had woken her. It was raining hard outside, the world engulfed in a torrential downpour. The hawthorn tree in front of her bedroom brushed against the window with each gust of wind, as if wanting to tell her something through the glazing.

A car drove by down the road; it must have been an emergency, out in this weather, its headlights sweeping over the blinds so that for a passing moment every item in the room came alive, rising out of the dark. Silhouettes sprang up like characters in a shadow play. And just as quickly, they disappeared. She remembered, as she had done countless times these past months, her mother's touch, her mother's face, her mother's voice. Grief spooled itself around her entire being, tightening its grip on her like a coil of rope.

Slowly, she sat up in bed. How she yearned for a sign! For the truth was, no matter how frightened or sceptical she might be of ghosts or spirits or all those invisible creatures she suspected her aunt believed in, there was a part of her that hoped if she could only find a door to another dimension, or allow that dimension to reveal itself, she might see her mother one more time.

Ada waited. Her body went still, even as her heart thudded wildly against her chest. Nothing happened. No supernatural signs, no unearthly mysteries. She took a rugged breath, disorientated. The door she had been looking for, if there was one, remained closed.

She thought about the fig tree then, buried all alone in the garden, its remaining roots dangling by its side. Her eyes slid towards the void stretching beyond the window. In that instant she had the strangest feeling that the tree was awake too, tuned into her every movement, listening to every creak in the house, waiting, just like her, waiting without knowing for what.

Ada got out of bed and turned on the lights. Sitting in front of the vanity mirror, she studied her nose, which she always thought was too big, her chin, which she feared was too prominent, her wavy hair, which she fought hard to flatten . . . She remembered a day not that long ago when she had been watching her mother work on a painting in her studio.

'When I finish this, I'm going to do a new portrait of you, Adacim.'

Ever since she was a baby, her mother had drawn pictures of her; the house was full of portraits, some in the brightest colours, others in monochrome.

But that afternoon, for the first time, Ada had refused. 'I don't want it.'

Putting her brush aside, her mother levelled her gaze at her. 'Why not, love?'

'I don't like my pictures.'

Her mother was silent for a moment. A look akin to hurt flickered across her face, and then she asked, 'What's his name?'

'Whose name?'

'The boy . . . or the girl . . . what's the name of the idiot who made you feel this way?'

Ada felt her cheeks burn and for a split second she almost told her mother about Zafaar. But she kept quiet.

'Listen to me, Ada Kazantzakis! The women of Cyprus, whether of the north or the south, are beautiful. How can we not be? We are related to Aphrodite – and while she was a bitch, there's no denying she was a stunner.'

'Mum, be serious.' Ada let out a long whistle.

'Hey, I am serious. And I want you to understand a fundamental rule about love. You see, there are two kinds: the surface and the deep water. Now, Aphrodite emerged from foam, remember? Foam love is a nice feeling, but just as superficial. When it's gone, it's gone, nothing remains. Always aim for the kind of love that comes from the deep.'

'I'm not in love!'

'Fine, but when you are, just remember, foam love is interested in foam beauty. Sea love seeks sea beauty. And you, my heart, deserve sea love, the strong and profound and enchanting type.'

Grabbing her brush back, her mother had added, 'As for that boy – or girl – whose name I don't know, if he doesn't see how special you are, he doesn't deserve a speck of your attention.'

Now, as she sat in front of the mirror inspecting her face as if looking for faults in a freshly plastered surface, Ada realized she had never asked her mother if the love between her parents had been of the first or the second kind. But then, of course, she knew. She knew in her gut that she was the child of the type of love that rose from the bottom of the ocean, from a blue so dark it was almost black.

Ada took out her phone, having lost interest in the mirror and what she saw there. Despite her father's warnings not to use technology at night, which he claimed delayed circadian rhythms, she liked to browse the web when she couldn't get to sleep. As soon as she turned on her mobile a message pinged. An unknown number.

Check this out, surprise!!!

A claw of anxiety dug into her chest as she hesitated for a second over whether or not to click on the link attached to the message. Then she pressed 'play'.

It was an awful, awful video. Somebody had filmed her in history class while she was screaming. It must have been one of her classmates, bringing in a phone illicitly. Her stomach dropped and yet she managed to watch it till the end. There she was, her profile a faint blaze against the light from the window but still identifiable, her voice rising to a deafening, disturbing pitch.

A stab of shame lanced through her, sliced into her self-esteem. It was terrifying enough that she had done something so shocking and unexpected, yet to find out that it had been recorded without her knowledge was beyond mortifying. Her mind started to spin as panic took hold of her, the taste of acid in her mouth. It was horrible to witness your own insanity being displayed for all to see.

Her hand trembling, she visited a video-sharing network.

Whoever had recorded this had already posted it publicly – just as she feared. Underneath, people had been making comments.

Wow, what a freak!

She's clearly faking it.

Some people will do anything for attention.

What's her problem? someone had asked, and someone else had replied, *Maybe she saw herself in the mirror!*

And so it went on, words of contempt, ridicule; reams of sexual jokes and dirty remarks. There were pictures and emojis too. A copy of Munch's painting, the screaming figure in the foreground replaced with some crazy-looking girl.

Ada gripped her phone tight, shaking. She paced the room like a caged animal, her nerves more tautly drawn with each step. This humiliating video would be on the internet forever, her whole life. Who could she ask for help? The headmaster? A teacher? Write a letter to the tech company – as if they would care? There was nothing she or anyone could do, not even her father. She was all alone.

She slumped into her bed and pulled her legs towards her chest. Quietly rocking her body, she started to cry.

Fig Tree

Towards midnight, I picked up an odd sound. Alarmed, I tensed. But it turned out it was my old friend the hawthorn tree, a native species, a gentle hermaphrodite, sending signals through roots and fungi, asking how I was doing. It touched me, his/her kindness, the sheer simplicity of it. For kindness always is – direct, naive, effortless.

Under and above the ground, we trees communicate all the time. We share not only water and nutrients, but also essential information. Although we have to compete for resources sometimes, we are good at protecting and supporting each other. The life of a tree, no matter how peaceful it may seem on the outside, is full of danger: squirrels that strip our bark, caterpillars that invade and destroy our leaves, bonfires in the vicinity, loggers with chainsaws . . . Defoliated by the wind, scorched by the sun, attacked by insects, threatened by wildfires, we have to work together. Even when we might seem stand-offish, growing away from others or at the edge of forests, we still remain connected across entire swathes of land, sending chemical signals through the air and across our shared mycorrhizal networks. Humans and animals can wander around for miles on end in search of food or shelter or a mate, adapting to environmental changes, but we have to do all that and more while rooted to the spot.

The dilemma between optimism and pessimism is more than a theoretical debate for us. It is integral to our evolution. Take a closer look at a shade plant. Despite the meagre light in its environment, if it remains optimistic, the plant will produce thicker leaves to let chloroplast volume increase. If it is not so hopeful about the future, not expecting the circumstances to change any time soon, it will keep its leaves at a minimum thickness.

A tree knows that life is all about self-learning. Under stress we make new combinations of DNA, new genetic variations. Not only stressed plants but also their offspring do this, even if they themselves might not have undergone any similar environmental or physical trauma. You might call it transgenerational memory. At the end of the day, we all remember for the same reason we try to forget: to survive in a world that neither understands nor values us.

Where there is trauma, look for the signs, for there are always signs. Cracks that appear in our trunks, splits that won't heal, leaves that display autumn colours in spring, bark that peels like unmoulted skin. But no matter what kind of trouble it may be going through, a tree always knows that it is linked to endless life forms – from honey fungus, the largest living thing, down to the smallest bacteria and archaea – and that its existence is not an isolated happenstance but intrinsic to a wider community. Even trees of different species show solidarity with one another regardless of their differences, which is more than you can say for so many humans.

It was the hawthorn tree that informed me young Ada was not doing well. I was filled with immense sadness then. For I felt connected to her, even if she might not think much of me. We had grown together in this house, a baby and a sapling.

Words Fly

Cyprus, 1974

Thursday afternoon, Kostas walked into The Happy Fig, whistling a tune he had picked up on the radio, 'Bennie and the Jets'. These days it was hard to listen to anything without it being interrupted by breaking news of a terror attack somewhere on the island or a report on the escalating political tensions, and he kept humming the melody as though to prolong it, to stay inside another realm of lightness and beauty.

It was still early in the day so there were no customers around. In the kitchen the chef was alone, a basket of figs and a bowl of whipped cream in front of him, his hand on his chin. He didn't lift his head to see who had come in, so absorbed was he in his work.

Yiorgos was behind the counter wiping glasses, a white cloth slung over his shoulder.

'Yassou,' said Kostas. 'What's the chef doing?'

'Oh, don't bother him,' said Yiorgos. 'He's practising the dessert Defne was telling us about. Her father's recipe, remember? We are planning to add it to the menu.'

'That's great.' Kostas looked around. 'And where is Yusuf?'

Yiorgos gestured with his chin towards the patio at the back. 'Out there, watering the plants. He sings to them, did you know?'

'Really?'

'He does, and every day he chats to the fig tree. I swear to God! The number of times I have caught him . . . The funny thing is, when he talks to humans he stutters and mumbles his words, but when he talks to plants, he has such a silver tongue – the most eloquent man I've heard.'

'How extraordinary!'

'Yeah, well. Maybe I need to turn myself into a cactus to make him say more than two words to me,' said Yiorgos and chuckled. He took another glass from the rack, wiped it gently and glanced at Kostas, his gaze sharp. 'Your mother was here earlier.'

Kostas paled. 'She was?'

'Yes, she was asking about you.'

'Why? She knows I come to see you. She's the one who sends me here to sell things.'

'Yes, but she was asking whether you visit at other times too, and if so, what might be the reason.'

Their eyes met for a second.

'My guess is someone saw you leaving this place with Defne. On an island, words fly faster than a falcon – you know that.'

'What did you tell her?'

'I told her you are a good lad and that both Yusuf and I are proud of you. I said you sometimes stop by in the evenings to lend us a hand, that's all. I told her she shouldn't worry.'

Kostas lowered his head. 'Thank you.'

'Look . . .' Yiorgos tossed the cloth aside and placed his palms on the counter. 'I understand. Yusuf understands. But there are many in Cyprus who never will. You two must be careful. I don't need to tell you things are bad. From now on, always go out separately through the back door. Do not walk out together. You can't risk being seen by a single customer.'

'What about the staff?' asked Kostas.

'My staff are reliable. I trust them. No problem there.'

Kostas gave a tight shake of his head. 'But are you sure it's okay for us to keep coming here? I don't want to cause you any trouble.'

'No trouble for us, *palikari mou*, don't you worry about that,' said Yiorgos. His face flushed with a new thought, perhaps a memory. 'But I hope you don't mind me saying this: when we are young, we think love is forever.'

Kostas felt a chill slide down his spine, a sinister tide rippling under his skin. 'I'm sorry if that's been your experience, but it's different with us. Our love is forever.'

Yiorgos said nothing. Only a young person would make such a claim and only the old would recognize its false promise.

At that second the door opened and Defne strode in, wearing a fern-green dress hemmed with silver thread, her eyes burning bright. The parrot, Chico, excited by the sight of her, began to rustle his wings and squawk her name, 'Dapnee! Dapnee! Kiss-kiss!'

'That's cheeky!' Defne said on an outrush of breath, then turned to the others, her spirited expression instantly dispelling the mood in the room. '*Yassou!*'

Walking towards her, Kostas broke into a smile, despite the anxiety beginning to gnaw away at him.

THE HAPPY FIG
MENU

*Our cuisine is a mixture of the many cultures who have inhabited
this heavenly island throughout the centuries. Our food is fresh,
our wine is old and our recipes timeless.
We are a family here – a family that gives, shares, listens, sings, laughs, cries,
forgives and, most importantly, appreciates good food.
Enjoy!*

Y & Y

Appetizers
Baba Ghanoush with Tahini
Yellow Split Pea Fava (served on flatbread)
Stuffed Bell Peppers (*Dolmadakia/Dolma*)
Stuffed Courgette Flowers with a Surprise Inside
Minced Meat and Rice Wrapped in Vine Leaves

Soups
Crushed Sour Wheat Soup (*Trahanas/Tarhana*)
Hungry Fisherman's Soup

Salads
Cypriot Village Salad
Watermelon and Pomegranate Salad with Whipped Feta
Grilled Halloumi Salad with Orange and Mint

Chef's Specials
Meatballs in Yogurt Sauce (*Keftedes/Köfte*)
Slow-roasted Pork with Wild Oregano
Golden Fried Fillets of Plaice
Shrimp Saganaki

Grilled Lamb with Onions, Stuffed into the Lining
of a Lamb's Stomach
Oven-baked Spicy Moussaka
Artichoke Stew with Mussels, Potatoes and Saffron
Chicken Souvlaki Wraps (served with chips and tzatziki)

Desserts

Oven-roasted Figs with Honey and Aniseed Ice Cream (secret recipe
smuggled in by one of our favourite customers)
Good Old-fashioned Rice Pudding (no secrets here)
Crispy Honey Puffs (*Loukoumades/Lokma*)
Nomadic Baklava (Greek/Turkish/Armenian/Lebanese/Syrian/
Moroccan/Algerian/Jordanian/Israeli/Palestinian/Egyptian/
Tunisian/Libyan/Iraqi . . . Did we forget anyone? If so, please add)

Liqueurs

See Our Exquisite Wine Menu!

Hot Drinks

Cosmopolitan Coffee Roasted with Cardamom
Mediterranean Mountain Tea
Carob Tea with Dandelion Root
Naughty Hot Chocolate with Whipped Cream and Vodka

To Sober Up

Tripe Soup with Garlic, Vinegar, Dried Lime, Seven Spices and Herbs
(the oldest cure for hangovers across the Levant)

Saints

Cyprus, 1974

His mother was deeply religious. Kostas could not remember a time when she was not, but as years went by religion had become all the more manifest in their lives. Up the white-painted walls, along wooden shelves, in nooks studded with drops of candle wax, clusters of icons stood guard, staring from an unknown world, silently watching.

'Never forget, the saints are always with you,' Panagiota said. 'Our eyes only notice what's in front of us, but it's different with holy men. They see everything. So, if you do something in secret, *levendi mou*, they'd know it immediately. You could fool me, but you could never fool the saints.'

As a young boy, Kostas had spent many an idle hour mulling over the optical structure of the eyes of holy men. He imagined they must have 360-degree vision, not unlike dragonflies, though he did not expect his mother to approve that thought. He himself would have been thrilled to have dragonfly qualities – how spectacular it would be to hover in the air like a helicopter, a flight so unique it had inspired scientists and engineers worldwide.

Some of the most lucid memories from his childhood involved sitting by a peat fire in the kitchen, watching his mother cook, a sheen of perspiration slowly forming across her forehead. She was always working, and her hands would testify to that, the skin rough with calluses, the knuckles raw from harsh detergents.

His father had died when he was only three years old, of lung disease from prolonged exposure to asbestos. Black death from white dust. The mineral, extracted from the eastern slopes of the Troödos, was exported in large amounts from Cyprus. Across the island, mining companies unearthed iron, copper, cobalt, silver, pyrite, chrome and gold-bearing umbers. International firms made huge profits while in the mines, mills and manufacturing plants local workers were poisoned, little by little.

It would take Kostas years to find out that the wives and children of asbestos workers suffered from secondary exposure to the toxic substance. Especially the wives. A creeping, gradual demise without any diagnosis, let alone compensation. They knew nothing of this back then. They weren't aware that the cancer that had started to tear through Panagiota's cells had stemmed from washing her husband's overalls every day and holding him in bed at night, inhaling the white asbestos powder settled in his hair. Panagiota was sick, though people who didn't know her well would not have guessed, watching her forever rushing from one task to the next.

Kostas barely remembered anything of his father. He knew that his elder brother had many memories of him, and his younger brother, a newborn back then, had absolutely none. But he, the middle one, was left with a layer of fog, a frustrating illusion that if he could only part the cloud with his hands, he might find his father's face in there, the pieces no longer missing, finally complete.

Panagiota had not married again, raising the three boys on her own. With no other income since her husband passed away, she had turned to selling homemade goods to local shop owners and, over the years, she had built up her own business. The real revenues came from carob liquor, a feisty drink that burned the throat and settled warmly in the bloodstream like a friendly campfire, and every so often her brother, who lived in London, sent her some money.

Strong and resilient, Panagiota was both loving and strict. She believed malicious spirits were everywhere, preying on their innocent victims. The tar that stuck to your shoes, the mud that clung to your tyres, the dust that got into your lungs, the scent of hyacinth that tickled your nose and even the mastic flavour that lingered on your tongue could well turn out to be tainted with the breath of unholy spirits. To keep them at bay, one had to be vigilant. Still they sneaked into people's homes through the slits in the doors, the cracks in the windows, the doubts in the human soul.

It helped to burn olive leaves and Panagiota did this regularly, the odour sharp and faintly suffocating and so pervasive that, after a while, it singed itself into your skin. She would also light charcoal since the devil was known to hate its smoke. Making the sign of the cross over and again, she would tread softly about the house, her lips locked in prayer, her fingers clutching a silver-plated *kapnistiri*. Each time Kostas left the house, and upon each return, he had to cross himself, always with his right hand, his good hand.

Whenever Kostas felt unwell or could not sleep, Panagiota would suspect the working of an evil eye. To undo the damage, she performed a *xematiasma*, setting him on a stool in front of her, a glass of water in one hand, a spoon of olive oil in the other. How often had he watched those golden drops fall into the water, waiting to see whether they would pool or spread so that she could assess the strength of the curse? Afterwards, she would tell him to drink the water, now heavy with incantations, and he would do so, draining it down to the last gulp, hoping to be freed of whatever malady it was that had seized him unawares.

When he was younger, Kostas would often slip out and sit under a tree on quiet afternoons, immersed in a book as he nibbled on a slice of bread spread with thick yogurt and a sprinkle of sugar. With all-encompassing curiosity he would study a moss-covered log, inhale the aromas of garlic mustard and pokeweed, listen to a beetle munch its way through a leaf, and he would marvel at his mother's fear of this world so full of wonders.

Rules were what gave life a structure and rules had to be obeyed. Salt and eggs and bread must not leave a house after sunset. If they did, they would never return. To spill olive oil was a particularly bad omen. Should this happen, you had to knock over a glass of red wine to balance things out. When digging the ground, you should never put the shovel on your shoulder because then someone might die. Equally important was refraining from counting the number of warts on your body (they would multiply) or the coins in your pockets (they would disappear). Of all the days of the week, Tuesday was the most unpropitious. One should never get married on a Tuesday or embark on a journey or give birth if it could be avoided.

Panagiota explained that it was a Tuesday in May, centuries ago, when the Ottomans captured the queen of cities, Constantinople. It happened after a statue of the Virgin Mary, carried to a shelter to evade the tumult of the ongoing siege, tumbled down, shattering into pieces so small it could never be put back together again. It was a sign, but people didn't recognize it in time. Panagiota said one should always look out for signs. An owl hooting in the dark, a broom falling on its own, a moth flying into your face – none of these boded well. She believed some trees were Christian, others Mohammedan, yet others heathen, and you had to make sure you had the right ones planted in your garden.

She was especially wary about three things: sitting under a walnut tree, because it would give you nightmares; planting a *koutsoupia*, the Judas tree, because Judas had hanged himself from its branch after betraying the Son of God; and cutting down a mastic tree, which was known to have cried twice in its long history, once when the Romans tortured a Christian martyr and, the second time, when the Ottoman Turks conquered and settled in Cyprus.

Whenever his mother said such things, Kostas felt his heart constrict. He loved all trees, without exception, and as for the days of the week, as far as he was concerned they were divided into two kinds only: the ones he spent with Defne and the ones he spent missing her.

Once or twice he had tried, but then swiftly changed his mind. He knew he could never tell his mother that he was in love with a Turkish Muslim girl.

The Castle

London, late 2010s

All morning, watching the storm working itself into a tempest, Ada stayed in her room. She skipped breakfast and lunch, snacking on a packet of popcorn she found in her school bag. Her father checked on her twice, but each time she sent him away under the pretext of doing GCSE coursework.

Later in the afternoon, there was a knock. Sharp, insistent. Opening the door, Ada found her aunt.

'When are you going to come out?' Meryem asked, the gleam of her evil eye bead necklace catching the light from the ceiling.

'Sorry, I've got things to do . . . *homework*,' said Ada, emphasizing the last word, which she knew had a calming effect on grown-ups. Once you uttered it, they always left you alone.

Except it did not seem to work on her aunt. If anything, she seemed upset. 'Why would English schools do this? Look at you, locked up in your room like a prisoner at such a young age. Come, forget about homework. Let's go and cook!'

'I cannot *forget about* homework, you are supposed to encourage me to study,' Ada said. 'And besides, I don't know how to cook.'

'That's fine, I'll teach you.'

'I don't even like it.'

Meryem's hazel eyes were inscrutable. 'That can't be true. Come, give it a try. You know what they say, if you find a happy village, look for the cook.'

'Sorry,' said Ada flatly. 'I really need to go.'

Slowly, she closed the door, leaving her aunt standing in the hall with her accessories and proverbs, fading like yet another family photo on the wall.

The year she started primary school, Ada caught the school bus back home every afternoon. It stopped at the end of her road. Always arriving at the house around the same time, she would find her mother waiting for her in front of the garden gate, her eyes locked on nothing in particular, the tip of a slipper tapping against the fence, as if to a melody only she could hear. Rain or snow, Defne would be there, outside. But one day in mid-June, she wasn't.

Ada got off the bus, carefully balancing on her palms the artwork she had made in class. She had built a castle out of yogurt pots, lolly sticks and egg cartons. The towers were cardboard tubes, painted vivid orange. The surrounding moat, rendered in chocolate wrappers, glowed in the setting sun like quicksilver. It had taken her a whole afternoon to complete the piece, which she was eager to show her parents.

No sooner had she entered the house than Ada paused, arrested in her tracks by a song playing in the background, way, way too loud.

'Mum?'

She found her mother in her parents' bedroom sitting on a bench by the window, cupping her chin in her hand. Her face was pale, almost translucent, as if drained of blood.

'Mum, you all right?'

'Hmm?' She spun round, blinking fast. She seemed confused. 'Sweetheart, you're here. What time is it?' Her voice sounded indistinct, slurred. 'Here already . . . ?'

'The bus dropped me off.'

'Oh, darling, I'm sorry. I just sat here for a moment. I must have lost track of time.'

Ada could not take her gaze off her mother's eyes – swollen, red-rimmed. Gently, she set the castle on the floor. 'Were you crying?'

'No . . . just a bit. Today is a special day. It's a sad anniversary.'

Ada drew closer.

'I had two dear friends. Yusuf and Yiorgos. They used to run this lovely place, a restaurant. Oh, the food was amazing! You could fill your stomach just with those delicious smells.' Defne turned towards the window, the light from the sun falling on her shoulders like a gold thread shawl.

'What happened to them?'

'Poof!' Her mother snapped her fingers like a magician who had just pulled off an elaborate trick. 'They disappeared.'

For a moment neither of them said a word. Into the silence Defne nodded, resigned. 'So many went missing in Cyprus back then. Their loved ones would wait, hoping they were alive, held captive somewhere. Those were horrible years.' She thrust her chin into the air, pressed her lips together so hard they took on a sickly pallor. 'People on both sides of the island suffered – and people on both sides would hate it if you said that aloud.'

'Why?'

'Because the past is a dark, distorted mirror. You look at it, you only see your own pain. There is no room in there for someone else's pain.' Noticing the confusion on Ada's face, Defne tried to smile – a smile as thin as a scar.

'So did they have ice cream in this place?' Ada asked the first thing that came to mind.

'Oh, you bet. They had fabulous desserts but my favourite was oven-roasted figs with honey and aniseed ice cream. It was an unusual mixture of flavours – sweet, pungent, just a bit tart.' Defne paused. 'Did I ever tell you about your grandpa? He was a chef, did you know that?'

Ada shook her head.

'He was the head chef at a famous hotel – the Ledra Palace. Every night they had great dinner parties. My father used to make this dessert for the guests. He had learned it from an Italian chef. But I knew how it was done, and I told Yusuf and Yiorgos. They loved it so much they added it to their menu too. I was proud but also afraid that my father would get wind of it. I was worried about a stupid pudding! So naive, the things that trouble us in our youth.' Defne winked as if imparting a secret. 'You know, I never cook. I used to once. I stopped.'

A new song started in the background. Ada tried to pick up the words in Turkish – and failed.

'I'd better go and wash my face,' said Defne and rose to her feet. As she did so she nearly lost her balance and lurched forward, managing to right herself at the last second.

Ada heard the cracking sound of yogurt pots crushed underfoot.

'Good God, what did I just do?' Defne bent over, picking up the crumpled cardboard tubes. 'Was this yours?'

Ada didn't say anything, fearing that if she opened her mouth, she might burst into tears.

'Was it your schoolwork? I'm sorry, darling. What was it?'

Ada managed to say, 'A castle.'

'Oh, sweetheart.'

As Defne pulled her into her embrace, Ada felt her whole body tense. She hunched as though crushed by something invisible for which she had no name. In that moment she detected the smell of alcohol on her mother's breath. It didn't resemble the wine her parents ordered when they all went to a nice restaurant or the champagne they popped when they celebrated with friends. It was different – acrid, metallic.

It smelled sad.

Later in the afternoon, Ada left her room, feeling hungry, and shambled her way towards the kitchen. Her aunt was there, washing dishes in the sink, her wrists deep in water, watching what looked like a Turkish soap opera on her phone.

'Hi.'

'Uh?' Meryem jumped. 'You scared me!' She lifted her hand and pushed her thumb up into the roof of her mouth.

Ada studied her quizzically. 'Is that what you do when you're scared?'

'Of course,' said Meryem. 'What do the English do?'

Ada shrugged.

'Your father's checking on the fig tree again,' said Meryem as she turned off her phone. 'Out there in the storm! I told him it's too cold to go out, the wind is bestial, but he didn't listen.'

Ada opened the fridge and pulled out a bottle of milk. Grabbing her favourite cereal, she poured some into to bowl.

Frowning, Meryem watched. 'Don't tell me you're going to eat that bachelor's dish?'

'I like cereal.'

'You do? They all smell like chewing gum to me. Grains are not supposed to be like that. There's something wrong with them.'

Ada pulled up a chair and started eating, though she was now hyper-aware that the cereal had a funny sweet air about it. 'So did you learn how to cook from your father? He was a chef, wasn't he?'

Meryem stood still. 'You have heard about Baba?'

'Mum told me – once. She wasn't sober, if you must know. Otherwise, she never spoke about Cyprus. No one does in this house.'

Returning to her washing-up, Meryem was silent for a moment. She rinsed a mug, placed it upside down on the draining board and asked cautiously, 'What do you want to learn?'

'Everything,' replied Ada. 'I'm sick and tired of being treated like a child.'

'Everything,' echoed Meryem. 'But no one knows that. Neither me, nor your father . . . we only grasp bits and pieces, each of us, and sometimes your bits and pieces do not match mine and then what's the use of talking about the past, it'll only offend everyone. You know what they say, keep the tongue in your mouth a prisoner. Wisdom consists of ten parts: nine parts of silence, one part of words.'

Ada folded her arms. 'I disagree. One must always speak up, no matter what. I don't understand what you're all so afraid of. And besides, I've been reading about it myself. I know there was a lot of hostility and violence between Greeks and Turks. Brits were involved too – we can't ignore colonialism. It's obvious. I don't get why my father is so hush-hush like all this is some kind of secret. He doesn't seem to realize that everything's on the internet. People my age aren't afraid to ask questions. The world has changed.'

Meryem pulled the plug out, watching the water gurgle down the plughole in restless circles. She wiped her hands on her apron and smiled a smile that did not quite reach her eyes. 'Has the world changed that much? I hope you are right.'

Holding the trampled artwork in her palms like an injured bird, her mother had talked about Cyprus that afternoon, telling her things she had never mentioned before.

'I was born near Kyrenia, my love. I know of a castle, just like the one you built, except mine was high upon rocks. They say it inspired Disney. Remember *Snow White*? The wicked queen's home surrounded by wild bushes and terrifying cliffs?'

Ada nodded.

'This castle was named after a saint from Palestine – Saint Hilarion. He was a hermit.'

'What's that?'

'A hermit hides away from the world. He is not a misanthrope, let's clarify that. A hermit does not hate human beings, he likes them actually, he just doesn't want to mingle with them.'

Ada nodded again, though as far as she was concerned nothing was clarified.

'Saint Hilarion was a traveller. He went to Egypt, Syria, Sicily, Dalmatia . . . then he arrived in Cyprus. He helped the poor, fed the hungry, healed the sick. He had one big mission: to stay away from temptation.'

'What's temptation?'

'It's like when I give you a chocolate bar and ask you not to eat it until the next day, and you put it in the drawer, but then you open the drawer, just to check if it's still there, and you think, "Why can't I take a bite?" And you end up scoffing all of it. That's temptation.'

'And the saint didn't like that?'

'No, he was no fan of chocolate. Saint Hilarion was determined to rid Cyprus of all demons. He stomped up and down the valleys, slaying goblins, knocking off hell-bound beasts, until one day, he came to Kyrenia and climbed up the rocks to take a good look at the island. He thought his job was pretty much done and he could sail away to another port. Pleased with himself, he observed his surroundings, the villages in the distance sleeping peacefully, thanks to his hard work. But then he heard a voice: "Oh, Hilarion, son of Gaza, lost wanderer . . . Are you sure you've stamped out all the infernal fiends?"

' "Of course I have," the saint replied, feeling a bit smug. "If there are any left, show me, God, and I'll vanquish them instantly."

'The voice said, "What about those within? Did you kill them too?" And that's when the saint realized, he had destroyed demons as far as the eye could see, but not those inside. And you know what he did?'

'What?'

'So as not to hear the immoral, unholy voices inside his head, Saint Hilarion poured melted wax into his ears. Horrible, isn't it? Never do such a thing! He destroyed his hearing and refused to come down the mountain. A year went by, then another, and the saint started to think that, content though he was in his silence, there were some sounds he missed: the rustling of leaves, the babbling of a brook, the pitter-patter of rain and especially the chirping of birds. The animals, seeing his sadness, kept bringing him all kinds of shiny objects to cheer him up. Rings, necklaces, earrings, diamonds . . . But the saint didn't care about riches. He dug a pit and buried all of them. That's why people who walk up to the castle today secretly search for treasure.'

'Did you and Daddy go there?'

'Yes, *canim*. We even stayed overnight. We promised ourselves, despite what our families and relatives might say, we'd get married, and if we ever had a child we'd name the baby after our island. If a boy, a Greek name – Nisos. If a girl, a Turkish name – Ada. We didn't know back then this also meant we would never return.'

'Did you find any treasure?' Ada asked, just because she hoped she could change the conversation to a more cheerful topic.

'No, but we found something better, something priceless. You!'

Only later would Ada understand what she meant by that. Her father and mother had spent the night near the castle and that was where she was conceived, in the place where, centuries ago, a lonely saint waged a losing battle against his own demons.

Fig Tree

In the year 1974, Kostas Kazantzakis visited The Happy Fig often – both to secretly meet with Defne and to bring us the delicacies his mother prepared at home.

I remember a balmy afternoon, the two owners of the tavern standing on either side of me, chatting with Kostas.

'Tell your mum her carob liquor was divine! Bring us more,' Yiorgos said.

'He's not asking f-f-for the c-customers,' interjected Yusuf, his dark eyes twinkling. 'It's all f-for himself.'

'And what's wrong with that?' protested Yiorgos. 'Liquor is the nectar of the gods.'

'That's honey, n-not liquor.' Yusuf shook his head. He was a teetotaller, the only one in this tavern.

'Honey, milk, wine . . . if this diet was good enough for mighty Zeus, it must be good enough for me.' Yiorgos winked at Kostas. 'And *pastelli*, please. We urgently need more.'

Recently, Kostas had started selling his mother's sesame bars. Panagiota followed the ancient recipe, with a slight modern twist. The secret was in the quality of the honey, and the touch of lavender she added for its distinctive fragrance and earthy taste.

As he headed to the door, Kostas smiled. 'I'll tell my mother – she'll be delighted. We've five carob trees. Still can't keep up with the demand.'

When I heard him say this, I have to confess I felt a bit jealous. Why such praise for those chewy carobs with their leathery shells and yellowish pulp? They are not that special.

True, carob trees are worldly-wise, they have been around for more than four thousand years. They are called *keration*, 'horn', in Greek; *keciboynuzu*, 'horn of the goat', in Turkish (at least that's one thing Greeks and Turks can agree on). With sturdy branches, thick, rough bark and extremely hard seeds, shielded by an impermeable hull, they can survive the driest climates. If you wish to know just how tough they are, go watch them at harvest time. Humans have the strangest way of collecting carobs, smacking at the pods with sticks, fibre nets spread wide underneath. It's a violent scene.

So yes, carobs are strong. I give them credit for that. But, unlike us figs, they are devoid of emotion. They are cold, pragmatic and lacking in soul. There is a perfectionism to them that gets on my nerves. Their seeds are almost always identical in weight and size, so uniform that in the olden times merchants used them to weigh gold – that's where the word 'carat' comes from. It used to be the most important crop of this island, its main agricultural export. So you see where I'm coming from: there is a bit of a competition between carobs and figs.

Figs are sensual, soft, mysterious, emotional, lyrical, spiritual, self-contained and introverted. Carobs like things to be unsentimental, material, practical, measurable. Ask them about matters of the heart and you will get no response. Not even a flutter. If a carob tree were to tell this story, I can assure you it would have been very different to mine.

There is a carob tree in Nicosia with two bullets lodged inside its trunk. They have learned to live together, fused into a single being, metal and plant. Unbeknownst to Kostas, his mother visited this tree from time to time and tied votive offerings to its branches, applied balm to its injuries, kissed its wounded bark.

It was the year 1956. Kostas was not born yet, but I was alive and well. Those were terrible times. Every day at dusk, Nicosia was placed under curfew. The radio transmitted news of bloody assaults on soldiers and civilians alike. Many British expatriates, among them writers, poets and artists, were leaving the island that was their home, no longer feeling safe. Some, like Lawrence Durrell, had started carrying a pistol to defend themselves. In the month of November alone, Black November they called it, there had been 416 terror attacks – bombs, shootings, ambushes and point-blank executions. The victims were Britons, Turks, and Greeks who did not agree with the aims or the methods of EOKA.

We trees also suffered, though no one took notice. That was the year entire forests caught fire during hunts for the insurgent groups hiding in the mountains. Pines, cedars, conifers . . . they all burned down to stumps. Around the same time, the first barrier was erected between the Greek and Turkish communities in Nicosia – a barbed-wire fence with iron posts and gates that could be swiftly shut if and when violence erupted. A large prickly pear cactus, finding itself trapped by this unexpected obstacle, would keep growing nevertheless, extending its green arms through the wire mesh, twisting and bending as the steel cut into its flesh.

That day, the sun had just begun its descent and the curfew was about to start. The few locals out on the streets were rushing home, keen not to be caught by patrolling soldiers. Except for a man with sunken cheeks and green eyes the colour of a mountain river. He seemed to be in no hurry, smoking placidly as he made his way along the road, his gaze fixed on the ground. Behind the thin veil of tobacco his face was drawn, pale. This man was Kostas's grandfather. His name, too, was Kostas.

A few minutes later a group of British soldiers turned the corner. They usually patrolled in groups of four but this time it was five of them.

One of the soldiers, spotting the figure ahead, checked his watch and then shouted in Greek, '*Stamata!*'

But the man neither stopped nor slowed down. If anything, he seemed to be walking faster now.

'Halt!' another soldier ordered in English. 'Hey, you! Stop! I'm warning you.'

Still the suspect didn't flinch, just kept walking.

'*Dur!*' The soldiers yelled in Turkish this time. '*Dur dedim!*'

By now the man had reached the end of the street, where an old carob tree loomed over a broken fence. He took a drag from his cigarette and held the smoke in. His mouth was stretched thin and wide, and in that second it looked as if he were smiling, mocking the soldiers trailing him.

'*Stamata!*' One last warning.

The soldiers opened fire.

Panagiota's father fell by the carob tree, his head hitting the base of the trunk. A muffled sound escaped him, then the thinnest stream of blood. It all happened too fast. One second he was holding his breath and the next he was on the ground, riddled with bullets from multiple firearms, two of which whizzed past him and pierced the carob tree.

When the soldiers approached the fallen man to empty his pockets, they found no gun or any kind of weapon. They looked for a pulse, but there was none. The family was notified the next morning, his children informed that their father had openly defied orders, despite repeated warnings.

Only then was the truth revealed: Kostas Eliopoulos, aged fifty-one, was born deaf. He had not heard any of the words shouted in his direction, whether in Greek, Turkish or English. Panagiota, who was newly married back then, would never forget, never forgive. When she gave birth to her first son, she was set on christening him after her slain father, but her husband was adamant that their first child should take the forename of his own father instead. So when their second son came along, Panagiota would not take 'no' for an answer. Kostas Kazantzakis, then, was named after his grandfather, a deaf, innocent man, killed beneath a carob tree.

As much as I dislike carobs and their rivalry, I therefore have to include them in our tale. Just as all trees perennially communicate, compete and cooperate, both above and below the ground, so too do stories germinate, grow and come into bloom upon each other's invisible roots.

Music Box

London, late 2010s

On the second morning of the storm, the entire city grew dark, as if night had finally won its eternal battle against day. A sharp sleet serrated the air, and just when it felt it would go on forever, it receded, giving way to a blizzard from the north.

Cooped up in the house, the three of them sat in the living room, watching the news. Heavy rain had caused rivers to break their banks and thousands of homes and businesses had been flooded across the country. There had been landslides in the Lake District. A block of flats on a busy street in London had its entire roof ripped off by the gale, crushing several cars, injuring people. Fallen trees blocked roads and train tracks. Weather reports warned that the worst was yet to come, asking people to stay indoors unless strictly necessary.

When they turned off the TV, Meryem sighed audibly, shaking her head. 'Signs of the Apocalypse, that's how I feel. I worry the end is near for humanity.'

'It's climate change,' said Ada, without lifting her gaze from her phone. 'Not a revengeful God. We are doing this to ourselves. We are going to see more floods and hurricanes if we don't act now. No one is going to save us. Soon it'll be too late for coral reefs, monarch butterflies.'

Kostas, listening carefully, nodded. He was about to say something but held back, wanting to give Ada the chance to bond with her aunt.

Meryem slapped her forehead. 'Oh, yes, butterflies! Now I remember. Where's my mind? I forgot to give you something important. Come with me. It's in my room – somewhere!'

But Ada had already lost interest in the conversation, having seen another cruel comment posted under her video. It took her a few seconds to understand what her aunt was asking.

'Go on, love.' Kostas gestured with his chin, encouraging.

Reluctantly, Ada stood up. By now her video had been shared so many times it had gone viral. Complete strangers were commenting on her behaviour as if they had always known her. Memes, cartoons. Not all were bad, though. There were messages of support too, many of them, in fact. A woman in Iceland had recorded herself against a magnificent landscape, screaming at the top of her voice as a geyser went off in the background. Underneath was a hashtag that Ada noticed many others had also been using: #doyouhearmenow.

Not knowing what to make of any of this, but sorely in need of a break from her own trammelled thoughts, Ada tucked the mobile into her pocket and followed her aunt.

When she walked into the guest room, Ada almost didn't recognize the place. Against the lilac-painted walls and pastel-green furniture that her mother had carefully chosen, her aunt's suitcases lay open like gored, bleeding animals, clothes, shoes and accessories scattered everywhere.

'Sorry for the mess, *canim*,' said Meryem.

'It's okay.'

'I blame the menopause. All my life I've tidied up after my sister, my husband, my parents. Even when I'd go to a restaurant, I'd clean up the table so the waiter wouldn't think badly of us. Because it's *ayip*. Are you familiar with that word? It means "shame". It's the word of my life. *Don't wear short skirts. Sit with your legs together. Don't laugh out loud. Girls don't do that. Girls don't do this. It's ayip.* I was always tidy and organized but lately something happened. I don't want to clean up any more. I'm just not going to bother.'

Startled by the soliloquy, Ada gave a half-shrug. 'I don't mind.'

'Good. Come, sit.'

Shoving aside a pile of necklaces, Meryem cleared a small patch on the bed. Ada perched there, staring in wonder at the jumble of objects on every side.

'Oh, look what I found,' said Meryem as she pulled out a box of Turkish delight from under a pile of clothes and opened it. 'I've been wondering where they were. I brought five of these. Here, take it.'

'No, thanks. I don't have much of a sweet tooth,' Ada said, slightly disappointed that the important thing her aunt had meant to give her turned out to be confectionery.

'Really? I thought everyone had a sweet tooth.' Meryem popped a *lokum* into her mouth and sucked on it thoughtfully. 'You are so skinny. You don't need to diet.'

'I'm not on a diet!'

'Okay, just saying.'

Sighing, Ada leaned forward and selected a *lokum*. It had been some time since she had tasted one. The smell of rosewater and the gummy, sticky texture reminded her of things from way back, things she thought she had long forgotten.

When Ada was seven years old, she had seen a velvet box just like this one next to her mother's bed. Expecting to find a treat, she had opened it without a thought. Inside, in various colours and sizes, there were only pills. It had seemed wrong somehow, all those tablets and capsules hiding in such a pretty container. She had felt a sudden clench, a sick feeling in the pit of her stomach. From that day on, every now and then she had checked the box, noticing its contents dwindle fast, only to be renewed. At no point had she found the courage to ask her mother why she kept the box on her bedside table or why she was taking so much medicine every day.

Swallowing down her *lokum*, Ada eyed the clothes heaped on the carpet. A coral beaded jacket, an electric-blue dress with puffy organza sleeves, a leopard-print ruffled blouse, a pistachio-green skirt out of a fabric so shiny you could see your reflection . . .

'Wow, you really go for colour!'

'I want to,' Meryem said, glancing down at the dress she had put on today – charcoal, plain, loose-fitting. 'All my life I have worn blacks, browns and greys. Your mum would make fun of my taste. She'd say I must be the only teenage girl who dressed like a widow. I don't think I was the only one, but she had a point.'

'What about all these clothes, then, aren't they yours?'

'They are! I've been buying them ever since I signed the divorce papers. But I've never worn them. I just kept them in the wardrobe with their tags on. When I decided to come to London, I said to myself, "This is your chance, Meryem. No one knows you in England, no one is going to say it's *ayip*. If you won't do it now, when will you ever do it?" So I brought them all with me.'

'But then why aren't you wearing them?'

Meryem's cheeks flushed pink. 'I can't. They are too over the top for my age, don't you think? People would laugh at me. You know what they say: eat according to your own taste, dress according to others'.'

'There is a storm outside, we are stuck in the house! Who's going to laugh at you? And besides, who cares?'

No sooner had she pointed this out than Ada faltered, feeling the weight of her mobile phone in her pocket, its cold polished surface and all the vicious words it contained. She almost told her aunt that she should care less about what others thought, that people could be mean, and whether they mocked you or not should not matter at all. But she couldn't say any of this, when she didn't believe it herself.

Biting the tender inside of her cheek, Ada lifted her gaze. Across from her the wardrobe was open and, inside, she saw the only item that had been neatly arranged on a hanger: a long, fluffy fur coat.

'That thing is fake, I hope.'

'What thing?' Meryem swung round. 'Oh, that? It's one hundred per cent rabbit!'

'That's awful. Killing animals for their fur is appalling.'

'We eat rabbit stew in Cyprus,' said Meryem quietly. 'It's really good with chopped garlic, pearl onions. I also add a cinnamon stick.'

'I don't eat rabbits. You shouldn't either.'

'I didn't buy it, if that helps,' said Meryem. 'It was a present – from my husband. He got this coat for me in London, 1983, just before the new year. Osman gives me a call. He says, "I've a surprise for you!" Then he turns up with a fur. In Cyprus! In the sweltering heat. I always suspected he bought it for someone else but changed his mind. Maybe a mistress who lived somewhere cold. He used to travel a lot – for "business". He always had an excuse – if a cat wants to eat her kittens, she'll say they look like mice. He was the same way. Anyway, Osman purchased this from Harrods, I bet it cost him a pretty penny. In those days it was okay to wear fur. I mean, I know it's not okay, but even Margaret Thatcher did. It was the same day the IRA bombed Harrods. My husband could have died – a foolish tourist looking for a present for his mistress which he ended up giving to his wife.'

Ada was silent.

Meryem walked to the wardrobe and caressed her coat absent-mindedly, tracing the edge of the collar with the back of her hand. 'I didn't know what to do with this. It had too much history, you know? I've never worn it. Why would I need it in Nicosia? But again, when I decided to come and see you, and heard about this winter storm, I thought, this is it! This is my moment. Finally, I'm going to wear it!'

'What happened to your husband?' asked Ada cautiously.

'Ex-husband. I need to get used to calling him that. Anyway, he left me. He married a younger woman. Half his age. She is pregnant. Due any day. They are having a boy. He's over the moon.'

'You don't have children?'

'We tried . . . for years we tried, but nothing worked.' Meryem stirred as if from sleep, her face sombre. 'Again, I'm forgetting. I brought you something.' She dug into a suitcase and threw aside a few scarves and stockings, fishing out a gift box. 'Ah, there it is! Take, take. This is for you.'

Ada put her hand out for the present thrust in her direction and slowly tore away the wrapping paper. Inside was a music box made of varnished cherry wood with butterflies on the lid.

'Your mum loved butterflies,' said Meryem.

Turning the key with its jaunty red silk tassel, Ada unlocked the box. Music trilled out, the last notes of a song she didn't recognize. In a hidden compartment she found a fossil. An ammonite with intricately shaped suture lines.

'Defne kept this box under her bed,' said Meryem. 'I don't know where she got it from, she never told me. After she ran away with your father, my mother was so angry at Defne she threw out all her belongings. But I managed to hide this away safely. I thought you should have it.'

Ada closed her fingers around the fossil, both unyielding and strangely delicate against her palm. In her other hand she held the music box. 'Thank you.'

She stood up to leave, then stopped. 'I think you should wear the clothes. Except the fur, I mean. All the others, they'd look good on you.'

Meryem smiled, her face a palimpsest of shifting emotions, and for the first time since her aunt arrived, Ada felt the distance between them closing just a little.

Fig Tree

If families resemble trees, as they say, arborescent structures with entangled roots and individual branches jutting out at awkward angles, family traumas are like thick, translucent resin dripping from a cut in the bark. They trickle down generations.

They ooze down slowly, a flow so slight as to be imperceptible, moving across time and space, until they find a crack in which to settle and coagulate. The path of an inherited trauma is random; you never know who might get it, but someone will. Among children growing up under the same roof, some are affected by it more than others. Have you ever met a pair of siblings who have had more or less the same opportunities, and yet one is more melancholic and reclusive? It happens. Sometimes family trauma skips a generation altogether and redoubles its hold on the following one. You may encounter grandchildren who silently shoulder the hurts and sufferings of their grandparents.

Divided islands are covered in tree resin which, though encrusted round the edges, is still liquid deep inside, still dripping like blood. I have always wondered if this is why islanders, just like sailors in olden times, are strangely prone to superstitions. We haven't healed from the last storm, that time when the skies came crashing down and the world drained of all colour, we haven't forgotten the charred and tangled wreckage floating around, and we carry within us a primeval fear that the next storm might not be far off.

This is why, with amulets and herbs, susurrations and salts, we try to appease the gods or the wandering spirits, impossibly capricious though they are. Cypriots, women and men, young and old, of the north and of the south, equally dread the evil eye, whether they call it *mati* or *nazar*. They string blue glass beads on necklaces and bracelets, hang them at the entrance of their homes, stick them to the dashboards of their cars, tie them to the cradles of their newborns, even secretly pin them to their underwear, and, still not satisfied, they spit in the air, summoning all the protection they can get. Cypriots also spit when they see a healthy baby or a happy couple; take a better job or earn extra cash; they do so when ecstatic, distraught or bewildered. On our island, members of either community, convinced that destiny is fickle and no joy is here to last, will keep spitting into the breeze without ever thinking that in that very moment, people on the other side, the opposite tribe, might be doing the same thing for exactly the same reason.

Nothing brings the island's women closer than pregnancy. On this issue, there are no borders. I have always believed they are another nation altogether, pregnant women of the world. They follow the same unwritten rules, and at night, when they go to bed, similar worries and fears spool in their minds. During those nine months both Greek Cypriot and Turkish Cypriot women will not hand a knife to another person or leave a pair of scissors open on the table; they will not glance at hairy animals or those deemed ugly, or yawn open-mouthed lest a spirit sneaks in. When their babies are born, they will abstain from trimming their fingernails or cutting their hair for months. And when after forty days they show their babies to friends and relatives, the same women will secretly pinch them to make them cry – a precaution against the evil eye.

We are scared of happiness, you see. From a tender age we have been taught that in the air, in the Etesian wind, an uncanny exchange is at work, so that for every morsel of contentment there will follow a morsel of suffering, for every peal of laughter there is a drop of tear ready to roll, because that is the way of this strange world, and hence we try not to look too happy, even on days when we might feel so inside.

Both Turkish and Greek children are taught to show respect if they see a piece of bread on the pavement. It is sacred, every crumb. Muslim kids pick it up and touch it to their foreheads with the same reverence they would kiss the hands of their elders on the holy days of Eid. Christian kids take the slice and make the sign of the cross, putting their hands over their hearts, treating it like it was the Communion bread made from pure wheat flour and of two layers, one for heaven, one for earth. Gestures, too, mirror each other, as though reflected in a dark pool of water.

While religions clash to have the final say, and nationalisms teach a sense of superiority and exclusiveness, superstitions on either side of the border coexist in rare harmony.

Brothers

Cyprus, 1968/1974

One evening, when he was eleven years old, Kostas was sitting at the kitchen table by the open window, as was his wont, his head buried in a book. Whereas his brothers preferred to spend their time in the bedroom they all shared, he liked being here, reading or studying while watching his mother work. This was his favourite spot in the house, with the steam rising from the pots on the stove, the dishrags dangling from a string swaying in the breeze and, above his head, hanging from rafters, stalks of dried herbs and woven baskets.

Tonight Panagiota was preserving songbirds. Opening their breasts with her thumbs, she stuffed them with salt and spices, softly singing to herself. Every now and then Kostas flicked a glance at his mother, her face sculpted by the light of an oil lamp. There was a pungent tang of vinegar in the air, so strong it filled their nostrils.

A wave of nausea overcame Kostas as the taste of brine burned the back of his throat. He pushed aside the book he had been reading. Hard as he tried, he could not tear his gaze from the rows of tiny maroon hearts arranged on the wooden worktop or from the gutted warblers in glass jars, their beaks half open. Quietly, he began to cry.

'What happened, *paidi mou*?' Panagiota wiped her hands on her apron, ran towards him. 'Are you sick? Does your stomach hurt?'

Kostas shook his head, struggling to speak.

'Tell me, did someone say something, my love?'

His throat thickened as he gestured to the worktop. 'Don't do that, Mama. Don't want to eat them any more.'

Startled, she stared at him. 'But we eat animals – cows, pigs, chickens, fish. Otherwise we'll starve.'

He couldn't think of a good answer to that and he didn't pretend to have one. Instead he muttered, 'These are songbirds.'

She raised her eyebrows, a shadow falling across her face and then disappearing. She seemed to be about to say something else but changed her mind. With a sigh, she tousled his hair. 'All right, if it upsets you so much . . .'

But in that moment when the world spun in slow circuits, Kostas caught a gleam in his mother's eyes, full of compassion and apprehension. He sensed what she was thinking. He knew his mother found him too sensitive, too sentimental, and somehow more difficult to understand than her other sons.

The three brothers were very different from one another, and as the years had gone by those differences had only deepened. As much as he loved books, Kostas did not wish to be a poet, a thinker, like his older brother. Michalis lived inside language, always searching long and hard for the precise word, as if meanings were something that needed to be chased and hunted down. He called himself a Marxist, a syndicalist, an anti-capitalist – labels that tangled up in his mother's mind like bougainvillea climbing a wall. He said working-class people of all countries would some day unite to overthrow their common oppressor, the rich, and on that account, a Greek peasant and a Turkish peasant were not enemies but simply comrades.

Michalis did not approve of EOKA or any kind of nationalism for that matter. He made no secret of his views, openly criticizing the blue-painted signs that by now had started to appear on almost every wall in the neighbourhood – *Long Live* ENOSIS, *Death to Traitors* . . .

If Kostas was not like his older brother, neither did he resemble his younger brother. Andreas, a tall, lithe boy with large brown eyes and a shy smile, had changed profoundly in the course of just a few months. He spoke of Grivas, the leader of EOKA-B, who had died recently in hiding, as if he were a saint, calling him Digenis, after the legendary Byzantine hero. Andreas said he was ready to swear an oath on the Bible to liberate Cyprus from enemies – both Brits and Turks – and to this end, he was willing to kill or die. But because he had a tendency to voice whatever came to mind, and because he was the youngest in the family, always loved and pampered, they never quite believed he really meant any of it.

The three brothers, although once very close, nowadays lived under the same roof with minimal intersection between their worlds. They rarely quarrelled, assenting to Panagiota's rules, tiptoeing around each other's truths.

This was their life, until one morning in March, in plain daylight, Michalis was murdered. He was shot on the street, a book under his arm, the poem he was reading still marked. The gunman's identity was never revealed. Some said it was the Turkish nationalists that had targeted him for being Christian and Greek; others said it was the Greek nationalists that hated him for being a vocal critic. And though it was never officially proved who had done it, Andreas, through his own sources, was convinced he had discovered the truth. Kostas saw the flame of revenge catch in his younger brother's soul, burning stronger every day. Then, one night, Andreas did not come home, his bed untouched.

They never spoke about it, but Panagiota and Kostas both knew Andreas had left to join EOKA-B's ranks. Since then they had heard no news of him and had no idea whether he was alive or dead. Now it was only Kostas and his mother left in this house that had shrunk and darkened at the edges, curling into itself like a letter saved from the flames.

At night, when the moon shone high above the lemon trees and there was a shiver in the air, of insects invisible to the eye or fairies sent to earth in exile, Kostas would sometimes catch his mother staring at him with a pained expression. He could not help but wonder whether, despite her generous, loving heart, she ever asked herself or the saints she trusted so much why it was her most eloquent, passionate son who had been murdered and why it was her most adventurous, idealistic son who had abandoned home, leaving behind this diffident, distracted middle son she could never quite fathom.

Fig Tree

I once heard an English journalist who dined at The Happy Fig say that politicians in Europe and America were trying to get their heads around the situation on our island. In the aftermath of the Suez Crisis, there were protests in London, somewhere called Trafalgar Square. People carried banners that said, 'Law Not War'. Now when I look back, I realize youngsters hadn't yet started to chant, 'Love Not War'. That would come later.

The same journalist explained to his tablemates that over there in England, in the House of Commons where all important decisions were made, members of parliament were discussing 'the Cyprus problem'. He said that, in his experience, it never bode well for a country, or a community, once it was branded as 'a problem' and that was what our island had become now in the eyes of the entire world, 'an international crisis'.

Even so, back then, experts believed it was just 'paper agitation', the tension and violence that seized our land; they said it was a storm in a teacup and it would be over soon. There was no need to fear mayhem and bloodshed because how could there be a civil war on such a pretty, picturesque island of blooming flowers and rolling hills? 'Cultivated' was the word they used repeatedly. These politicians and pundits seemed to assume that civilized humans could not slaughter each other, not against an idyllic backdrop of verdant hills and golden beaches: 'There is no need to do anything about it. The Cypriots are . . . civilized people. They will never do anything violent or drastic.'

Only a few weeks after these statements were uttered in the British parliament, four hundred separate attacks had been staged across Cyprus. British, Turkish, Greek blood was spilled, and the earth absorbed it all, as it always does.

In 1960 Cyprus gained independence from the United Kingdom. No more a Crown Colony. That was a hopeful year, it felt like a new beginning, with some sort of calm reigning between the Greeks and the Turks. A permanent peace suddenly seemed possible, within reach, like a glowing, fuzzy peach hanging from a drooping branch, there at your fingertips. A new government was formed with members drawn from both sides. Finally, they were working together, Christians and Muslims. In those days, people who believed the different communities could live in amity and harmony as equal citizens often alluded to a native bird as their emblem: a type of partridge, the chukar, that built its nests on both sides of the island, heedless of divisions. That, for a while, became an apt symbol for unity.

It wasn't to last long. Political and spiritual leaders who reached out to the other side were silenced, shunned and intimidated – and some were targeted and killed by extremists on their own side.

It is a small, charming creature, the chukar, with black stripes wrapping around its body. It likes to perch on rocks, and when it sings, it does so in shy, scratchy notes, as though learning to chirp for the first time. If you listen closely, you can hear it say *chukar-chukar-chukar*. The only bird that tenderly trills out its own name.

Their numbers have dwindled significantly today for they have been hunted relentlessly all over the island – north and south alike.

Baklava

London, late 2010s

In the evening, Meryem threw herself into making her favourite dessert – baklava. She ground a whole jar of pistachios, the noise of the food processor so loud it drowned out the howling of the blizzard outside. She prepared the dough from scratch, patting and pounding it between her palms, before covering it and putting it aside for a little 'nap'.

Ada, meanwhile, watched her aunt from where she sat at the end of the table. Her history notebook lay open in front of her. Not exactly to study, but to finish the butterfly she had left incomplete on the last day of school, just before she had started screaming.

'Look at you! You're such a good student,' chirruped Meryem, flicking a sidelong glance at her niece as she opened the food processor and scooped the contents out on to a plate. 'I'm so happy you're doing your homework next to me.'

'Well, I didn't have much of a choice, did I?' Ada said wearily. 'You kept knocking on the door, asking me to come out.'

Meryem giggled. 'Of course I did. Otherwise you were going to spend the entire holidays in your bedroom. Not healthy.'

'And that baklava is?' Ada couldn't help asking.

'It sure is! Food is the heart of a culture,' replied Meryem. 'You don't know your ancestors' cuisine, you don't know who you are.'

'Well, everybody makes baklava. You can buy it in supermarkets.'

'Everyone makes baklava, true, but not everyone succeeds. We Turks make it crispy with roasted pistachios. That's the right way. Greeks use raw walnuts – God knows who gave them that idea, it just ruins the taste.'

Amused, Ada rested her chin on the tip of her index finger.

Though smiling still, a shadow crossed Meryem's face. She didn't have the heart to tell Ada that for a fleeting moment she had seen Defne in that gesture, so painfully familiar.

Ada said, 'You make it sound as if we should judge a culture not by its literature or philosophy or democracy, just by its baklava.'

'Uhm, yes.'

Ada rolled her eyes.

'You did that thing again.'

'What thing?'

'That teenage thing you keep doing with your eyes.'

'Well, technically, I *am* a teenager.'

'I know,' said Meryem. 'And in this country that's a privilege. The next best thing to being royal. Even better. Privilege minus paparazzi.'

Ada straightened her shoulders.

'It's not a criticism. Just stating a fact. I blame the English language. In English, thir-*teen* is teen, right? So is four-*teen*, fif-*teen*, six-*teen*, seven-*teen* . . . Where I come from, at seventeen you're usually preparing your dowry. At eighteen you're in the kitchen brewing coffee because your future husband is in the sitting room with his parents, asking for your hand in marriage. At nineteen you're serving your mother-in-law supper and if you burn it, you get an earful. Don't get me wrong, I'm not saying that's a good thing. Hell, no! All I'm saying is there are kids in the world – girls and boys – who can't enjoy their teens.'

Ada studied her aunt. 'Tell me about your ex-husband.'

'What do you want to know?'

'Did you love him? At least in the beginning?'

Meryem waved a hand, her bracelets jingling. 'Everybody is always raving on about love – all the songs, movies. I get it, it's cute, but you don't build a life on cute. No, love wasn't my priority. My parents were my priority, my community was my priority. I had responsibilities.'

'So it wasn't a marriage of love?'

'No, it wasn't. Not like your parents' marriage.'

Something new had lodged in Meryem's voice and Ada sensed it. 'Are you angry at them? Do you think they behaved irresponsibly?'

'Your parents, ah, they were reckless. But they were so young, just a bit older than you.'

Ada felt heat flush her neck. 'Wait a second. So, Mum and Dad were . . . what, high school sweethearts?'

'Schools were separate. Greek kids and Turkish kids didn't mingle that much back then, although there were mixed villages and mixed neighbourhoods, like ours. Our families knew each other. I liked Panagiota – your father's mum. Such a nice lady. But then things got really bad – we stopped speaking to each other.'

Ada looked away. 'I thought my parents met in their late thirties or something. I mean, my mum had me in her early forties. She always said it was a late pregnancy.'

'Oh, but that was afterwards. Because they broke up, you see, and then years later, they got together again. The first time, they were just kids, really. I was always covering for Defne. If our father had caught her, it'd have been a disaster! I was scared out of my wits. But your mum . . . she was unstoppable. She'd put pillows under bedcovers and slip out of the house in the middle of the night. She was brave – and foolish.' Meryem drew in a breath. 'Your mum was a free spirit. Even when she was a little girl, she had this wild, unpredictable side. If you told her not to touch fire, she'd go and build a bonfire! It's a miracle she didn't burn the house down. I was five years older than her, but even when I was her age, I was careful not to disappoint my parents, always trying to do the right thing, and you know what, Baba loved Defne the most. I'm not resentful, only stating the truth.'

Ada said, 'Did you also oppose my parents' marriage?'

Meryem dried her hands on her apron, looked at her palms as if for a clue. 'I didn't want your mother to marry a Greek, God knows I tried to stop it. But she didn't listen. And she did the right thing. Kostas was the love of her life. Your mother adored your father. They both paid a heavy price, though. You grew up with-out seeing your relatives. I'm very sorry about that.'

In the ensuing silence Ada could hear her father typing away at his computer in his room, a sound like a thousand little hammers beating. She listened for a while, then tilted her head, a determined set to her chin. 'Did you know my mum was an alcoholic?'

Meryem winced. 'Don't say such things. That's a terrible word.'

'But it's true.'

'Having a glass now and then is okay. I mean, I don't drink myself, but I don't mind if others do . . . once in a while.'

'It wasn't once in a while. My mum drank heavily.'

Meryem's face darkened, her mouth slightly open, an emptied bowl. She touched the edge of the tablecloth and picked at an invisible mote of dust, focusing entirely on the movement of her fingers.

As she watched her aunt, suddenly ill at ease and bereft of words, Ada saw for the first time the fragility of the universe the woman had built for herself with her recipes, proverbs, prayers and superstitions. It dawned on her that she might not be the only one who knew so little about the past.

Fig Tree

They call it the Green Line, the partition that cuts through Cyprus, aiming to separate Greeks from Turks, Christians from Muslims. It acquired its name not because it was marked with mile after mile of primeval forest, but simply because a British major general, setting out to draw the border on a map spread out before him, happened to use a green chinagraph pencil.

The colour was not a random choice. Blue would have been too Greek and red too Turkish. Yellow represented idealism and hope, but it could also be interpreted as cowardice or deceit. Pink, associated with youth and playfulness as well as femininity, would simply not work. Nor would purple, symbolizing ambition, luxury and power, have produced the desired result. Neither white nor black would do, they were too decisive. Whereas green, used in mapping to mark pathways, seemed less contentious, a more unifying and neutral alternative.

Green, the colour of trees.

Sometimes I wonder what would have happened if on that particular day, because of too much caffeine or a side effect of some medication he might have taken earlier or simply nerves, Major General Peter Young's hand had shaken just a trifle . . . Would the border have shifted a fraction of an inch up or down, inserting here, deleting there, and if so, might this involuntary change have affected my fate or that of my relatives? Would one more fig tree have remained on the Greek side, for instance, or an extra fig tree have been included into Turkish territory?

I try to imagine that inflection point in time. As transient as a scent on the breeze, the briefest pause, the slightest hesitation, the squeak of a chinagraph pencil on the shiny surface of the map, a trail of green leaving its irrevocable mark with everlasting consequences for the lives of generations past, present and yet to come.

History intruding on the future.

Our future . . .

PART THREE

Trunk

Heatwave

Cyprus, May 1974

It was the day a heatwave descended on Nicosia. Above the roof-tops, the sun was a glowing ball of anger; burning the old Venetian alleyways, the Genoese courtyards, the Greek gymnasiums and the Ottoman *hamams*. The shops were closed, the streets empty – save for the occasional stray cat curled up in a patch of shade, or a lethargic lizard, so still it might just as well have been an ornament on the wall.

The heat had started in the small hours of the morning, swiftly building up. Around ten o'clock, it had fully erupted into being, just after Turks and Greeks on each side of the Green Line had finished their morning coffees. Now it was past noon and the air was stiff, difficult to breathe. The roads were cracked in places, the tar melting in rivulets, the colour of charred wood. A car somewhere revved its engine, its rubber tyres struggling on the sticky asphalt. Then, silence.

By three o'clock, the heat had morphed into a feral creature, a snake bent on prey. It hissed and slithered across the pavements, poked its flaming tongue through keyholes. People inched closer to their fans, sucked harder on ice cubes and opened the windows, only to close them instantly. They might have stayed indoors the whole time had it not been for a peculiar smell that permeated the air, pungent and unbidden.

At first, the Turks suspected the smell must be coming from the Greek quarter and the Greeks assumed it must be coming from the Turkish quarter. But no one could exactly pinpoint its source. It was almost as if it had sprung from the earth.

Standing by the window, a book of poetry in his hands – an old edition of *Romiosini* that belonged to his elder brother – Kostas stared into the garden, certain he had heard a sound in the drowsy silence of the afternoon. His gaze wandered up towards the higher branches of the nearest carob tree, finding nothing unusual there. Just as he was about to turn away, he caught a flash out of the corner of his eye. Something had dropped to the ground, so fast he couldn't tell what it was. He dashed out of the house, blinded by the dappled sunshine through the leaves. He hurried towards the shadows in the distance, though he could not make them out at first against the glaring light. Only when he was close enough could he tell what he had been looking at all this time.

Bats! Dozens of fruit bats. Some strewn across the ground like rotten fruit, others dangling from the branches, hanging upside down by their feet, wrapped in their wings, as though in need of warmth. Most of them were about ten inches long, others as small as two inches. It was the pups that had first surrendered to the heat. Some so young they were still sucking milk, clamped to their mothers' nipples, they had dropped dead, unable to regulate their body temperature. Their skins dehydrated and scaling, their brains boiling inside their skulls, these clever animals had turned weak and woozy.

A tightness constricting his chest, Kostas began to run. He tripped over a wooden crate and fell, the metal edge cutting his forehead. He pulled himself up and kept running, despite the throbbing above his left eyebrow. When he reached the first bat, he dropped to his knees and picked up the tiny body, light as breath. He stood there motionless, holding the dead animal, feeling its satiny smoothness under his fingers, the final vestiges of life evaporating.

He hadn't cried when they had brought home Michalis's body, so peaceful one couldn't believe he was gone; the bullet that entered him perfectly hidden, as if ashamed of what it had done. Nor when he joined the pall-bearers carrying the casket to the church, a slight pressure weighing on the shoulder he had placed under the polished wood, the taste of silver lingering on his lips from kissing the cross, the smell of oil and dust in his nostrils. Nor when, at the cemetery, the casket was lowered into the ground amidst cries, and the only thing Kostas could offer his brother was a handful of soil.

He hadn't cried when Andreas, only sixteen, had left home to join an ideal, a dream, a terror, leaving them in a state of constant fear. Throughout all this, Kostas had not shed a tear, fully aware that his mother needed him by her side. But now, as he held a dead bat in his hands, grief became tangible, like something stitched together was tearing apart. He began to sob.

'Kostas! Where are you?' Panagiota called from the house, a tremble of concern in her voice.

'I'm here, *Mána*,' Kostas managed to say.

'Why did you dash out like that? I was worried. What are you doing?'

As she approached, her face changed from concern to confusion. 'Are you crying? Did you hurt yourself?'

Kostas showed her the bat. 'They're all dead.'

Panagiota made the sign of the cross, her lips moving in a quick prayer. 'Don't touch them. Go and wash your hands.'

Kostas did not move.

'You hear me? They carry diseases, filthy animals.' She gestured around, her confidence returning. 'You go. I'll get a shovel and put them in the rubbish.'

'No, not the rubbish,' Kostas said. 'Leave it with me – please. I'll bury them. I'll wash my hands.'

Panagiota, seeing the pain in his eyes, did not insist. But as she turned away she could not help murmuring, 'Our youngsters are slain on the streets, *moro mou*, mothers don't know where their sons are any more, in the mountains or in the graves, and you weep over a bunch of bats? Is this how I raised you?'

Kostas felt a sense of loneliness so acute it was almost tangible. After that day, he would no longer talk about fruit bats and how important they were for the trees of Cyprus, and hence for its inhabitants. In a land besieged with conflict, uncertainty and bloodshed, people took it for indifference, an insult to their pain, if you paid too much attention to anything other than human suffering. This was neither the right time nor the right place to carry on about plants and animals, nature in all its forms and glory, and that is how Kostas Kazantzakis slowly shut himself off, carving an island for himself inside an island, retreating into silence.

Fig Tree

The day the heatwave ravaged Nicosia will always be singed in my memory, etched in my trunk. When the islanders realized where the rancid smell was coming from, they set about getting rid of the carcasses. They swept the streets, cleared the orchards, sanitized the caves, checked the limestone areas and old mineshafts. Wherever they looked they found hundreds of dead bats. It scarred them, this sudden, collective death. In that mass extinction, perhaps they recognized their own mortality. Even so, based on personal experience, I can tell you one thing about humans: they will react to the disappearance of a species the way they react to everything else – by putting themselves at the centre of the universe.

Humans care more about the fate of animals they consider cute – pandas, koalas, sea otters and dolphins, too, of which we have many in Cyprus, swimming and frolicking about our shores. There is a romantic idea as to how dolphins perish, washed to the beach with their beak-like snouts and innocent smiles, as if they have come to bid humankind one last farewell. In truth, only a small number do that. When dolphins die, they sink to the bottom of the sea, as heavy as childhood fears; that's how they depart, away from prying eyes, down into the blue.

Bats are not deemed to be cute. In 1974, when they died in their thousands, I didn't see many people shedding a tear for them. Humans are strange that way, full of contradictions. It's as if they need to hate and exclude as much as they need to love and embrace. Their hearts close tightly, then open at full stretch, only to clench again, like an undecided fist.

Humans find mice and rats nasty, but hamsters and gerbils sweet. Doves signify world peace, whereas pigeons are nothing more than carriers of urban filth. They proclaim piglets charming, wild boars barely tolerable. Nutcrackers they admire, even as they avoid their noisy cousins, the crows. Dogs evoke in them a sense of fuzzy warmth, while wolves conjure up tales of horror. Butterflies they look on with favour, moths not at all. They have a soft spot for ladybirds, and yet if they were to see a soldier beetle, they would crush it on sight. Honeybees are favoured in stark contrast to wasps. Although horseshoe crabs are considered delightful, it's a different story when it comes to their distant relatives, spiders . . . I have tried to find a logic in all this, but I have come to the conclusion that there is none.

We fig trees hold bats in high regard. We know how essential they are for the entire ecosystem, and we appreciate them, with their large eyes the colour of burnt cinnamon. They help us pollinate, faithfully carrying our seeds far and wide. I consider them my friends. It broke me seeing them dropping to their deaths like fallen leaves.

That same afternoon, the islanders busy disposing of dead bats, Kostas walked from his house to The Happy Fig. I was surprised when he showed up. The tavern was closed and we were not expecting anyone, not while the heat was still beating down.

Slowly, Kostas trudged up the winding path, making his way across the gentle incline of the slope. With the tips of my branches that spread through the opening in the roof, I could observe his every move.

Upon arriving, he found the front door barred. He banged the metal knocker several times in quick succession. That is when I started to feel uneasy, seized by a foreboding.

'Yiorgos! Yusuf! You here?'

He tried again. The door was locked from inside.

Kostas walked around, his gaze anxiously darting over the bats lying on the ground. He poked a few of them gingerly with a stick, trying to see if any were alive. He tossed the stick aside and was about to leave when he stopped, detecting a whisper in the air. A male voice speaking in a low, dreamy tone.

Kostas swung about, listening. He strode towards the patio at the back, where he now realized the sound was coming from. Hopping over cases of empty bottles and olive oil tins, he approached one of the wrought-iron windows, strained up on his toes and peeked inside.

Panic now rose inside me, for I knew exactly what he was about to see.

Yusuf and Yiorgos were there on the patio, sitting side by side on a stone bench. Kostas was about to call out to them, but then stopped, his eyes spotting something that his mind couldn't immediately grasp.

The two men were smiling at each other, their hands clasped together, their fingers interlaced. Yiorgos leaned in and murmured a few words in Yusuf's ear, which made him chuckle. Although Kostas couldn't hear what he said, he knew it was in Turkish. They did that often, speaking Greek and Turkish when they were by themselves, alternating back and forth within the same conversation.

Yusuf wound his arm around Yiorgos's neck, touching the indent under his Adam's apple, pulling him closer. They kissed. Their foreheads resting together, they sat still, the sun looming huge and molten above them. There was an effortless tenderness to their movements, a blending of shades and contours, solid forms melting into pure liquid, a gentle flow that Kostas knew could exist only between long-term lovers.

Kostas took a step back. Suddenly dizzy, he swallowed hard. In his mouth was the taste of dust and sun-baked stone. As quietly as he could, he walked away, blood pounding in his ears. His thoughts fractured into more thoughts and those into newer ones, so that there was no way he could tell how he felt right now. He had spent so much time with these two men, day in, day out, and yet it had never occurred to him they could be more than business partners.

The day the heatwave descended on Nicosia and the fruit bats died in their thousands, the day Kostas Kazantzakis discovered our secret at the tavern, I watched his face grow serious, his forehead pucker in worry. He now realized that Yusuf and Yiorgos could be in greater danger than he and Defne had ever been. God knew there were enough people on this island who would hate to see a Turk and a Greek involved romantically, but the number of those people probably quadrupled if the couple in question were gay.

Hear Me

London, late 2010s

On the third day, the epicentre of the storm shifted westwards, hurtling towards London. That evening, the windows of the house rattled as the wind picked up and rain lashed against the panes. The neighbourhood suffered a blackout for the first time in years. It was hours before power was restored. Without electricity, they sat huddled together in the living room by candlelight, Kostas working on an article, Ada checking her phone every few seconds and Meryem knitting what appeared to be a scarf.

Eventually, Ada took a candle and stood up. 'I'm going to bed, feel a bit tired.'

'Everything all right?' asked Kostas.

'Yeah.' Ada nodded firmly. 'I'll just read a bit. Goodnight.'

As soon as she was in her room, she looked at her phone again. New videos had been posted on various social media. In one, a stocky girl with hair cut in a soft fringe across her eyebrows stood in front of the Brandenburg Gate in Berlin, holding a red balloon, which she let go just as she began screaming at the top of her lungs. By the time the balloon had floated out of the frame, she had still not run out of breath. In a video shot in Barcelona, a teenager screamed as he skated through a tree-lined promenade while pedestrians watched with half-curious, half-disbelieving eyes. Another clip, posted in Poland, showed a group of youngsters dressed head-to-toe in black staring at the camera, their mouths wide open, though silent. Underneath, the caption read: 'Screaming Inside'. Some people were screaming alone, others in groups. All the posts used the same hashtag: #doyouhearmenow. With each one she watched, Ada felt her sense of panic and

153

confusion deepen. She couldn't believe she had started this global craze, and she had no idea how anyone could possibly stop it.

Drawing her legs in, she wrapped her arms around them as she used to do when, as a little girl, she would ask her parents to tell her a story. Back then, her father, no matter how busy he might be, would always find the time to read to her. They would sit side by side on the bed, facing the window. He would choose the most unusual children's books; about fruit bats, African grey parrots, painted lady butterflies . . . books with insects and animals and, always, trees.

In contrast, her mother preferred to make up her own stories. She would relate tales from her imagination, threading the arc as she advanced into the plot, going back and changing things on a whim. Her themes were darker, featuring spells, hauntings and omens. But once, Ada remembered, her mother shared with her a different kind of story. Both disturbing and, strangely, hopeful.

Her mother told her that during the Second World War an infantry battalion was stationed along the cliffs overlooking the English Channel. The soldiers, weary and bedraggled, were patrolling the coast one afternoon. They knew that at any moment they could come under heavy attack from German artillery, via sea or sky. They didn't have much food left, they didn't have enough ammunition, and the further they trudged, the deeper the ground beneath their soaked and split boots sucked them in, like quicksand.

After a while one of them noticed an extraordinary sight on the horizon: billows of smoke were drifting over the Channel, of a colour so bright it seemed unearthly. Trying not to make any noise lest they alert the enemy, he signalled to his companions. Soon everyone was staring in the same direction, their faces etched at first with surprise, then sheer terror. The mysterious cloud could only be some type of poison gas, a chemical weapon, and, urged on by the wind, it was swelling straight towards them. Some of the soldiers fell on their knees, uttering prayers to a god they had long stopped believing in. Others lit cigarettes – one final pleasure. There was nothing else to do, nowhere to escape. The battalion was stationed right in the path of the deadly yellow gas.

One of the privates, instead of praying or smoking, stepped up on a rock, unbuttoned his jacket and started to count. It helped his nerves, the solidity of numbers, as he waited for death to strike. *Twenty-two, twenty-three, twenty-four* . . . He carried on, watching the golden menace draw closer, expanding and contracting. By the time he reached a hundred, he was bored with counting, and he grabbed a pair of binoculars. It was then that he saw the cloud for what it was.

'Butterflies!' he shouted at the top of his voice.

What they had thought was a mass of poisonous gas was, in fact, butterflies migrating from the European continent into England. Swarms of painted lady butterflies were crossing the Channel, slowly making for the mainland. They fluttered through the open sky, flitting and dancing in the summer light, oblivious to the cold, grey battlefront.

A few minutes later, rivers of butterflies, many thousands of them, flew over the battalion. And the soldiers, some so young they were merely boys, clapped and cheered. They laughed so hard there were tears in their eyes. No one, not even their commanders, dared to tell them to be quiet. Their hands reaching out towards the firmament, their expressions pure rapture, they jumped up and down, and those who were lucky enough felt the touch of a pair of gossamer wings on their skin, like a farewell kiss from the lovers they had left behind.

Remembering the story now, Ada closed her eyes and stayed that way until she was jolted by a knock on the door. Assuming it must be her aunt again, calling her to try whatever dish she had prepared, she yelled, 'I'm not hungry!'

Her father's voice rose from the other side of the door. 'Sweetheart, can I come in?'

Quickly, Ada hid her phone under the pillow and snatched up a book from her bedside table – *I Am Malala*.

'Sure.'

Kostas walked in, a candle in his hand. 'That's a great book you're reading.'

'Yeah, I agree.'

'Do you have a second to talk?'

Ada nodded.

He put the candle on the bedside table and sat next to her. '*Kardoula mou*, I know I've been a bit distant this past year. I've been thinking about it a lot – I'm sorry if I wasn't always there for you.'

'It's okay, Dad. I understand.'

He looked at her, a tenderness in his eyes. 'Can we discuss what happened at school?'

Her heart pushed against her ribs. 'There's nothing to tell. Believe me. I just screamed, okay? It's no big deal. I won't do it again.'

'But the headmaster said –'

'Dad, please, that man is weird.'

'We can talk about other things,' Kostas tried again. 'How did that science project go, I forgot to ask? You still working with that boy . . . what was his name, Zafaar?'

'That's right,' said Ada, a little sharply. 'We finished our project. We both got an A.'

'Fantastic. I'm proud of you, love.'

'Look, about the scream, you need to stop worrying. I felt stressed, that's all,' said Ada, and in that moment she believed every word that came out of her mouth. 'If you keep bringing this up, it's not going to help. Leave it with me. I'm working on it.'

Kostas took off his glasses, breathed on them, and slowly, carefully, cleaned them with his shirt, like he always did when he didn't know what to say and needed time to think.

Watching him, Ada felt a sudden rush of affection for her father. How easy it was to deceive parents, and even if you couldn't deceive, to keep them behind the walls of prevarications you had erected. If you really put your mind to it and were

156

careful not to leave any loose ends, you could do so for quite a while. Parents, especially those as distracted as her father, desperately needed things to run smoothly and were so inclined to believe the system they had created was working fine that they assumed a normality even when surrounded by clues to the contrary.

No sooner had she had this thought than guilt found its inevitable way up. She was not planning to tell her father about the video, it was embarrassing, and there was nothing he could do about it anyway, but maybe he should know how she felt.

'Dad, I've been meaning to talk to you about this . . . I want to switch schools.'

'What? No, Ada. You can't do that in the middle of your GCSEs. This is a good school. Your mum and I were so happy when you got in.'

Ada chewed the inside of her mouth, annoyed at the way he had brushed aside her concerns.

'Listen, if you're worried about your grades, why don't you and I study together during the holidays? I'm happy to help.'

'I don't need your help.' She looked away, disturbed by her own tone, the readiness of her anger, so close to the surface.

'Look, Aditsa,' he said, his skin sallow in the candlelight as if moulded from wax. 'I know this past year has been incredibly hard for you. I know you miss your mother –'

'Please stop!'

The sadness in her father's expression triggered a throbbing ache at the centre of her chest. She saw the helplessness in his eyes and yet she did nothing to pull him out of there. She fell quiet, trying to grasp how this could keep happening between them, this disorientating slide from affection and love into pure hurt and strife.

'Dad?'

'Yes, sweetheart?'

'Why do butterflies cross the Channel and come here? Don't they like warm climates?'

If Kostas found the question unexpected, he didn't show it. 'Yes, for a long time, scientists were puzzled. Some said it was a mistake, but the butterflies couldn't help it, they were conditioned that way. They even called it a genetic suicide.'

The word hovered in the space between them. They both pretended not to notice.

'Your mother loved butterflies,' Kostas said. His voice rose and fell, like water settling. 'Look, I'm no expert on them but I think it's plausible they plan their moves beyond their lifespan – not within one generation, but across many.'

'I like that. It also kind of explains what happened to us. You and Mum moved to this country, but we're still migrating.'

His face clouded over. 'Why do you say that? You're not going anywhere. You were born and raised here. This is where you belong. You're British – with a mixed heritage, which is a great richness.'

She clucked her tongue. 'Yeah, sure, I'm rolling in richness!'

'Why the sarcasm?' asked Kostas, sounding offended. 'We have always treated you as an independent being, not an extension of ourselves. You will build your own future and I'll support you every step of the way. Why the obsession with the past?'

'Obsession? I'm already burdened with it –'

He cut in. 'No, you are not. You are not burdened by anything. You are free.'

'That's bullshit!'

Kostas held his breath, shocked by the harsh word.

'You don't mind believing young butterflies inherit migrations from their ancestors, but when it comes to your own family, you think that's not possible.'

'I just want you to be happy,' said Kostas, a knot in his throat.

And then they were silent once again, drifting back to the painful place they both shared but could only occupy separately.

Fig Tree

I once heard Yiorgos tell Yusuf a story. It was late at night, all the customers had left, and the staff, having cleared the tables, washed the dishes and swept the kitchen, had gone home. Where only moments ago there had been laughter, music and bustle, calm reigned. Yusuf sat on the floor, his back to the window, his shadow sprawling across the dark glass. Resting his head on Yusuf's lap, Yiorgos lay staring at the ceiling, a sprig of rosemary between his lips. It was his birthday.

They had cut a cake earlier in the evening, a cherry-and-chocolate gateau prepared by the chef, but otherwise this evening was no different from any other. Neither man ever took a day off. They always worked and everything they earned, after covering expenses and rent, they divided between them.

'I've something for you,' said Yusuf, producing a small box out of his pocket.

I loved to observe the change in Yusuf when he was alone with Yiorgos. He rarely, if ever, stumbled over his words when he talked to us plants. But he also stammered noticeably less when it was just the two of them. The speech impediment that had tormented him forever almost entirely evaporated when he was with his beloved.

Yiorgos, a smile softening his chiselled features, propped himself up on his elbow. 'Hey, I thought we weren't buying each other anything this year.' Taking the box nonetheless, he glowed with the bright expectation of a child anticipating a treat and unwrapped the tissue paper.

'Oh my God!'

Dangling between his fingers from a chain was a pocket watch, gold and sparkling.

'This is beautiful, *chryso mou*, thank you. What have you done? This must have cost you a fortune.'

Yusuf smiled. 'Open it. There's a p-p-poem.'

Engraved inside the lid of the watch was a verse – the letters glinting like fireflies against the night. Yiorgos read them aloud:

> *Arriving there is what you are destined for,*
> *But do not hurry the journey at all . . .*

'Oh, it's Cavafy!' said Yiorgos. It was his favourite poet.

He turned the pocket watch over, finding there on the back two letters: *Y & Y*.

'Do you like it?' asked Yusuf.

'Like it? I love it!' said Yiorgos, his voice laden with emotion. 'I love you.'

The smile on Yusuf's face faded into something else as he threaded his fingers through Yiorgos's hair. He pulled him close and kissed him softly, the sadness in his eyes deepening. I knew what was troubling him. The day before he had found a note stuck on the door with a glob of chewing gum. A curt, cowardly message, written in broken English using letters cut out from newspapers, left unsigned, smudged with dirt and something red to give the impression of blood, and perhaps it was. He had read the note several times, the ugly words – 'sodomites', 'homos', 'sinners' – stabbing him like knives, cutting a vein close to the heart and opening a wound; not a new one, but an old wound that had never had the chance to fully heal. Ever since he was a boy he had been repeatedly picked on and ridiculed for not being man enough, *manly* enough, first by his own family, then the students and teachers at school, even perfect strangers; taunts and barbs hurled in sudden fits of rage and contempt, though whence they arose, he never understood; none of this was new, but this time it came with a threat. He had not mentioned any of it to Yiorgos, not wanting to worry him.

That night they chatted for hours, keeping me awake. I rustled

160

my branches, trying to remind them that a fig tree needed some sleep and rest. But they were too absorbed in each other to notice me. Yiorgos drank quite a bit, chasing all that wine with Panagiota's carob liquor. Although sober, somehow Yusuf sounded no less tipsy, laughing at every silly joke. They sang together, and my God, these two men, they both had terrible voices. Even Chico could sing better than them!

Close to dawn, overwrought and exhausted, I was about to fall asleep when I heard Yiorgos mutter, as though to himself, 'That poem by Cavafy . . . do you think some day we could leave Nicosia? I adore this island, don't get me wrong, but sometimes I wish we lived in a place where there was snow!'

They made plans to travel, drawing up a list of all the cities they wanted to see.

'Who are we k-k-kidding, we both know we won't leave,' Yusuf said with a spurt of emotion that was almost despair. 'Birds can go, not us.' He gestured towards Chico, sleeping in his cage under a black cloth.

Yiorgos was silent for a moment. Then he said, 'Did you know that in the olden days people couldn't understand why so many birds disappeared in winter?'

He told Yusuf how the ancient Greeks were puzzled over what happened to birds when the days turned mercurial and cold winds began to blow down from the mountains. They searched the empty skies, trying to find clues as to where they might be hiding, all those black kites, grey geese, starlings, swallows and swifts. Unaware of migration patterns, the philosophers of antiquity came up with their own explanation. Every winter, they claimed, birds metamorphosed into fish.

And the fish, he said, were happy in their new environment. Food was plentiful in the water, life less gruelling. But they could never forget where they came from and the way they used to soar above the earth, light and free. Nothing could replace that feeling. So when the longing became too much to bear, every year around springtime, the fish changed back into birds. And thus they refilled the firmament, all those black kites, grey geese, starlings, swallows and swifts.

For a while things worked fine and they were thrilled to be back home in familiar skies, until frost gathered on tree branches and they had to return once again to the waters down below, where they would feel safe but never complete, and thus it went on and on, the cycle of fish and birds, birds and fish. The cycle of belonging and exile.

It was the age-old question: whether to leave or to stay. That fateful night, Yusuf and Yiorgos chose to stay.

The Moon

Cyprus, May 1974

The next time they met at The Happy Fig, Kostas was late. Having helped his mother chop wood and stack the logs in piles by the hearth, he could not get away sooner. When finally free, he ran all the way from the house to the tavern.

Thankfully, Defne had not left. There she was in the small room behind the bar, waiting.

'I'm so sorry, love,' Kostas said as he rushed in.

Something in her expression stopped him. A hardness in her gaze. He slid into the seat next to her, catching his breath. Their knees touched under the table. She pulled herself back, almost imperceptibly.

'Hi,' she said without making eye contact.

He knew he should ask her what was wrong, why she looked so troubled, but a strange rationale seized him, as if by not pressing her to put her pain into words, he could ward it off, at least for a little while.

She broke the silence. 'My father is in the hospital.'

'Why? What happened?' He took her hand – it felt limp, lifeless in his palm.

She shook her head, her eyes welling up. 'And my uncle . . . my mother's brother. Do you remember I was telling you about him? The one who saw me one night and asked where I was going.'

'Yes, of course. What happened?'

'He's dead.'

Kostas froze.

'Yesterday, armed EOKA-B men stopped the bus my father and my uncle were on and asked all the passengers to say their names . . .

they separated males with Turkish or Muslim names. My uncle had a gun on him. They asked him to hand the gun over, he resisted. There was shouting back and forth. It happened so fast. My father tried to intervene. He threw himself forward and was shot. He is in the hospital now. The doctors say he might be paralysed from the waist down. And my uncle . . .' She started to sob. 'He was twenty-six years old. Just betrothed. I was joking with him the other day.'

Sucking in a quick breath, he faltered, struggling with words. 'I'm so sorry.' He tried to hug her, but not sure she would want that, he stopped himself, waiting, absorbing this new rift opening up between them. 'I am very sorry, Defne.'

She looked away. 'If my family find out . . . If they learn that I'm seeing a Greek boy, they'll never forgive me. It is the worst thing in their eyes.'

He paled. This was what he had been fearing all this time, a prelude to the end. His chest felt so full he feared it might burst. It took the effort of every muscle in his body to stay composed. Strange though it was, the only thing he could think of in that moment was the pincushion his mother used when sewing. That was his heart now, pierced by dozens of needles. He asked, his voice no more than a hoarse whisper, 'Are you saying we should end it? I can't bear to see you in pain. I'll do anything to stop that. Even if it means not seeing you any more. Tell me, please, will it help if I stay away?'

She raised her chin and looked him in the eye for the first time since he had arrived. 'I don't want to lose you.'

'I don't want to lose you either,' Kostas said.

Absent-mindedly, she lifted her glass to her lips. It was empty.

Kostas rose to his feet. 'I'll go and fetch some water.'

He pulled open the curtains. The tavern was packed tonight, a hazy fog of tobacco smoke hanging in the air. A group of Americans were sitting by the door, their heads eagerly bent over the plates of *meze* a waiter had set before them.

Kostas saw Yusuf standing in a corner, clad in a blue linen shirt, Chico perched on the shelf behind him, cleaning his feathers.

As their eyes met, Yusuf gave him a smile – trusting, untroubled. Kostas tried to return the gesture, his usual friendly demeanour tinged with shyness now that he knew their secret. But he could only manage to offer a lame smile in return, his heart aching with everything Defne had told him a moment before.

'You okay?' Yusuf mouthed over the noise.

Kostas gestured to the empty jug in his hand. 'Just getting some water.'

Yusuf beckoned over the nearest waiter – a tall, slim Greek man who had just become a father for the first time.

As Kostas waited for fresh water, he glanced about vacantly, his mind clouded by all that Defne had confided in him. The sounds of the tavern closed around him, like a hand around the hilt of a knife. He noticed a blonde, stout woman at one of the front tables take her mirror out of her handbag to reapply her lipstick. The colour would stay with him for years to come, a vivid red, a smudge of blood.

Even years later in London he would find himself revisiting that moment and, although everything would happen too fast, in his memory the events of that night would always play out excruciatingly slowly. A dazzling light such as he had not seen before, had not imagined possible. A terrible whistling filling his ears, followed instantly by a roaring crash, as if a thousand blunt stones were grinding against each other. And then . . . broken chairs, smashed plates, mutilated bodies and, raining on everyone and everything, the tiniest pieces of glass, which in his recollection would always be perfectly round, like droplets of water.

The floor lurched and swayed under his feet. Kostas fell backwards, pushed by a force greater than himself, the impact oddly deadened. Then silence. Pure silence, of a kind that sounded stronger than the explosion that had just shaken the entire place. He would have hit his head on a stone step but for the body lying underneath him – that of the waiter fetching him a jug of water.

It was a bomb. A homemade pipe bomb hurled from a passing motorbike into the garden, destroying the entire front wall. Five people would lose their lives at The Happy Fig that evening. Three Americans visiting the island for the first time, a Canadian soldier about to be discharged from peace-keeping duties and return home, and the young Greek waiter who had just become a father.

When Kostas stood up, he staggered, his left arm flailing. As he spun round, his eyes wide with terror, he saw the shredded curtain at the back of the room part and Defne bolt out, her face ashen. She ran towards him.

'Kostas!'

He wanted to say something but could not think of a single word of comfort. He wanted to kiss her too; amidst the human carnage it seemed such a wrong thing to do and yet perhaps the only thing he could do. Wordlessly, he hugged her, the blood of others soaked into his clothes.

Was it the American tourists or British soldiers who had been the target of the attackers? Or was it the tavern itself and the two owners? There was always a chance that it could have been a random act of violence, of which there were more and more these days. They would never know.

There was an acrid smell everywhere, of smoke, charred brick and debris. The entrance had taken the biggest hit, the wooden door wrenched off its hinges, tiles and framed photographs ripped from the walls, chairs splintered into pieces, shards of porcelain strewn about. In a corner small flames shot up from beneath an overturned table. Glass crunching under their shoes, Kostas and Defne quickly moved in opposite directions, trying to help the injured.

Later, just as the police arrived and long before the ambulance came, Yiorgos and Yusuf told them they should get out and this they did, leaving The Happy Fig across the patio at the back.

There was a full moon outside and it was the only peaceful thing they had seen all day. It shone with an impassive beauty, like a cold gem against dark velvet, not at all interested in the human pain down below.

That night, with neither of them wanting to go home just yet, they stayed together later than usual. They wandered for a while up the hill behind the tavern and sat by an old well, hidden amidst overgrown brambles and clumps of heather. Peering over the stone edge, feeling its silky moss under their fingers, they looked deep into the shaft, the water below too dark to see. They had no coins to toss, no wishes to make.

'Let me walk you home,' said Kostas. 'At least part of the way.'

'I don't want to go,' she said, rubbing the back of her neck where a shard had nicked her earlier without her noticing. 'My mother and Meryem are staying with my father at the hospital tonight.'

He pulled out a handkerchief and wiped the tears and the soot off her cheeks. She held his hand, resting her head against his palm, not letting go. He felt the warmth of her mouth, the swoop of her eyelashes on his skin. A hush in the air, the world suddenly far off.

She asked him to make love to her, and when he didn't respond immediately she leaned back and studied him, her gaze firm, with no hint of shyness.

'Are you sure?' he said, his face slightly flushed in the moon-light. It would be the first time for both of them.

She nodded tenderly.

He kissed her and said, 'I need to warn you there are stinging nettles around here.'

'I noticed.'

He took off his shirt and wrapped his right hand in it. He sifted amongst the grass, pulling as many nettles as he could, tossing them aside in clusters as he had seen his mother do so many times for her soup. When he lifted his head, he found her staring at him with a sad smile.

'Why are you looking at me like that?'

'Because I love you,' she said. 'You are a gentle soul, Kostas.'

You don't fall in love in the midst of a civil war, when you are hemmed in by carnage and by hatred on all sides. You run away, as fast as your legs can carry your fears, seeking basic survival and nothing else. With borrowed wings you take to the sky and soar away into the distance. And if you cannot leave, then you search for shelter, find a safe place where you can withdraw into yourself because now that everything else has failed, all diplomatic negotiations and political consultations, you know it can only be an eye for an eye, hurt for hurt, and it is not safe anywhere outside your own tribe.

Love is the bold affirmation of hope. You don't embrace hope when death and destruction are in command. You don't put on your best dress and tuck a flower in your hair when you are surrounded by ruins and shards. You don't lose your heart at a time when hearts are supposed to remain sealed, especially for those who are not of your religion, not of your language, not of your blood.

You don't fall in love in Cyprus in the summer of 1974. Not here, not now. And yet there they were, the two of them.

Fig Tree

When the bomb exploded, one of my branches caught fire from the sparks. Within a few seconds I was in flames. No one noticed. Not for a while. They were all in shock, frantically trying to help the injured, removing the fallen debris, unable to look at the dead bodies. There was dust and smoke everywhere, ashes swirling in the air like a flight of moths around a candle. I heard a woman crying. Not loud, barely audible, almost a muffled sound, as if too afraid to make any noise. I listened and I continued to burn.

In fire-prone regions trees develop myriad ways to protect themselves from the devastation. They surround themselves with thick, flaky bark or keep their dormant buds underground. You can find pine trees with hard, resistant cones ready to release their seeds at the first prickle of intense heat. Some other trees drop their lower branches altogether, so that flames can't easily climb up. We do all that and more to survive. But I was a fig tree living inside a cheerful tavern. I had no reason to take such precautions. My bark was thin, my branches plentiful and delicate, and I had nothing to shield me.

It was Yusuf who saw me first. He ran towards me, that kind, tongue-tied man, now flapping his arms around, sobbing.

'*Ah canim, ne oldu sana?*' – *My heart, what happened to you?* – he said over and over in Turkish, his eyes tinged with sorrow. I wanted to tell him that he wasn't stuttering. He never did when he spoke to me.

I watched Yusuf grab a tablecloth, then several more. He patted my branches, jumping and hopping like a crazy man. He brought in buckets of water from the kitchen. Now Yiorgos joined him and together they managed to put out the fire.

A part of my trunk was singed and several of my limbs were charred completely, but I was alive. I would be all right. I could recover from this horror unscathed – unlike the people who were there that night.

A Letter

Cyprus, June 1974

A few weeks after a bomb exploded in The Happy Fig, Panagiota penned a letter to her brother in London.

My dear Hristos,

Thank you for the lovely gifts you sent us last month, all of which arrived safely. Knowing that you are well and thriving in England is the biggest gift to my soul. May the grace of the Lord always guide you and your family, and surround you like a shield of steel.

I thought long and hard before writing this letter. I feel it is time as I cannot keep the fear locked up inside my heart any longer. I am worried – terrified – about Kostas. Remember, brother, I was so young when God left me a widow with three children to raise on my own. Three boys who sorely needed a father's guidance in their lives. I tried to be both parents to them. You know how tough that has been and yet I never complained. Look at me now, brother. I wonder if you will even recognize me when you see me next time. I have aged fast. My hair is no longer glossy, nor black, and when I comb it at night it falls out in clumps. My hands are as dry and rough as sandpaper, and I often talk to myself, like crazy old Eleftheria who used to chatter away to ghosts, do you remember?

In one year, I lost two sons, Hristos. Not knowing where Andreas is today, right now, whether he is captive or free, dead or alive, is no less excruciating than the day they carried the dead body of my beloved Michalis into this house. They are both gone, their beds cold and empty. I cannot bear to suffer the loss of a third child. I will lose my mind.

Every night, I ask myself, am I doing the right thing keeping Kostas by my side in Cyprus? And even if it has been the right thing so far, how long can I watch over him? He is almost a grown man. Sometimes he leaves the house and does not come back for hours on end. How can I know, with certainty, that he is well and safe?

The island is not the right place for young men any more. There is blood on the streets. Every day. No time to even wash off yesterday's blood. And this boy of mine is too sentimental. He finds a chick from a bird's nest that has met its death by a cat's claw and does not speak for days. Do you know, if he could, he would have stopped eating meat altogether? When he was eleven years old he was crying over preserved songbirds. If you think time must have made him tougher, not at all. The day of the heatwave he saw a pile of dead bats in the garden and he was devastated. I mean it, Hristos. It broke his spirit.

I'm worried he is not at all equipped to deal with the hardships of life – certainly not the hardships of our island. I have never seen anyone who feels the pain of animals so acutely. He is more interested in trees and shrubs than in his fellow compatriots. It's hardly a blessing, I'm sure you would agree. It can only be a curse.

But there is more, much more. I know he has been seeing some girl. He had been sneaking out at odd hours, coming back with a distracted look in his eyes, a flush to his cheeks. I didn't mind it at the beginning, to be honest. I pretended I didn't notice a thing, hoping it'd do him good. I thought, if he falls in love, he will stay off the streets and away from all the politics. I have had enough of pallikaria – those brave but rash youths. So I let it happen. By feigning ignorance, I let him see this girl. But that was until I found out through a neighbour, only this week, who she was. And now I am terrified.

Our Kostas is in love with a Turk! They have been meeting secretly. How far it has gone, I do not know and I cannot ask. A Christian cannot marry a Muslim, it offends the eyes of Our Lord. This girl's relatives might learn the truth any day now and then what will they do to my son? Or someone from our side might find out and then what will happen? Have we not suffered enough? I cannot be naive. You and I both know there are people from either community ready to punish them for what they have been doing. The lightest penalty under the circumstances will be gossip and slander. We will carry the shame forever. But that is not what I fear the most. What if they suffer a worse punishment? I don't even want to think about it. How can Kostas do this to me? To his older brother, God rest his soul.

I do not sleep properly any more. Nor does Kostas, it seems. I hear him pace up and down in his room every night. It cannot go on like this, the fear that something terrible is going to happen to him is crushing my spirit. I cannot breathe.

I have decided, after much consideration, to send Kostas away – to you, to London. I need not tell you, brother, what this does to my heart. I need not tell you that.

What I'm asking, begging, is for you to take him under your wing. Please do this for me. He is a fatherless boy, Hristos. He needs a paternal hand on his shoulder. He needs the help and advice of his uncle. I want him to stay away from Cyprus, stay away from this girl until he comes to his senses and realizes how foolishly, recklessly he has behaved.

If you agree, I can find a good excuse and tell him he will be travelling for only a week or so. But I want you to keep him there longer – till the end of the summer, at the very least. He is young. He will soon forget her. Maybe he can help you at the store and learn some trade? It is surely better for him than watching birds or daydreaming under carob trees all day. Take young Kostas into your home and family, please. Will you do this for me, brother? Will you keep an eye on my one remaining son? Whichever way you answer my prayer, may the grace of the Lord Jesus Christ and the love of God and the fellowship of the Holy Spirit be with you, now and always.

Your loving sister,
Panagiota

Bell Peppers

London, late 2010s

The next morning, Meryem sat at one end of the kitchen table, in front of her a bowl of cooked rice and tomato mixed with spices, and a pile of green bell peppers, washed and cored, their stems neatly cut off. When she saw Ada, she broke into a smile – one that slid away as soon as she registered Ada's expression.

'You okay?'

'I'm fine,' said Ada, without looking up.

'You know, back in Cyprus, we had a goat. Beautiful creature. Me and your mum were always petting him. We called him *Karpuz* because he loved watermelon. One morning Baba took Karpuz to the vet. He put him at the back of a truck. Stuffy, dusty. He had other things to do, so he kept Karpuz tied there the whole day. When the goat returned home, he was so stressed. He had this glazed look in his eyes.' Meryem leaned over and squinted. 'Right now, you look like Karpuz after the truck ride.'

Ada gave a little snort. 'I'm fine.'

'That's what Karpuz said.'

Breathing in slowly, Ada rolled her eyes. She could have felt upset at her aunt's nosiness but, strangely, she didn't. Instead she felt an urge to open up to her. Maybe she could confide in this woman, who was here for a little while. There was no risk in sharing a few things with her. Besides, she needed to talk to someone, hear a different voice to those churning away inside her mind.

'I don't like my school. I don't want to go there any more.'

'Oh dear,' said Meryem. 'Does your father know?'

'I tried to tell him, it didn't go that well.'

Meryem's eyebrows rose.

174

'Don't look so shaken, it's not the end of the world,' said Ada. 'I'm not abandoning my entire education to join an underground cult. I just don't like this school, that's all.'

'Listen, *canim*, I know you might get cross with me for saying this, but remember, good advice is always annoying and bad advice never is. So if what I say irritates you, take it as good advice.'

Ada narrowed her eyes.

'Good, I can see you are already irritated,' said Meryem. 'What I am trying to say is, you are young and the young are impatient. They can't wait for school to be over and life to begin. But let me tell you a secret: it already has! This is what life is. Boredom, frustration, trying to get out of things, longing for something better. Going to another school won't make things different. So you'd better stay. What is it? Are they giving you a hard time, the other kids?'

Ada drummed her fingers against the table to keep them busy. 'Well . . . I did something awful in front of the whole class. Now I'm too embarrassed to go back.'

The lines on Meryem's forehead deepened. 'What did you do?'

'I screamed . . . until I lost my voice.'

'Oh, honey, you should never raise your voice at your teacher.'

'No, no. Not at the teacher. It felt like I was screaming at everyone – *everything.*'

'Were you angry?'

Ada's shoulders dropped a little. 'That's the thing, I don't think it was anger. Maybe I'm just not well. My mum had mental health issues. So, yeah, I could have whatever my mum had. Genetic, I guess.'

Meryem stopped breathing for a second, though Ada did not seem to notice.

'My father says trees can remember – and he says sometimes young trees have some kind of "stored memory", like they know about the traumas their ancestors have gone through. That's a good thing, he says, because the saplings can adjust themselves better.'

'I don't know much about trees,' said Meryem, turning the

idea in her head. 'But girls your age should not be worrying about such things. Sorrow is to the soul what a worm is to wood.'

'You mean termite?'

'Let's say history is ugly, what's it to you?' said Meryem, continuing regardless. 'It's not your problem. My generation made a mess of things. Your generation is lucky. You don't have to wake up one day with a border in front of your house or worry about your father being gunned down on the street just because of his ethnicity or religion. How I wish I were your age now.'

Ada kept her eyes on her hands.

'Look, everyone has done something silly in their youth that they thought was beyond repair. Maybe you feel lonely right now. You think your classmates laughed at you and maybe they did, but that's human nature. If your beard is on fire, others will light their pipes on it. But my point is, you'll come out stronger. One day you'll look back and say, why was I even worried about that?'

Ada considered this, though she didn't believe a word. Perhaps that was true in the past but in this new world of technology, silly mistakes, if that's what they were, once online, stayed around forever.

'You don't understand, I screamed like a maniac, like I was possessed,' Ada said. 'The teacher was frightened, I saw it in her eyes.'

'Did you say . . . possessed?' Meryem repeated slowly.

'Yes, it was so bad I had to go and talk to the headmaster. He kept asking me questions about my *family situation*. Is it because I can't cope with my mother's death? Or is it my father? Is there something he needs to know? Am I experiencing problems at home? Oh God, he asked me so many personal questions, I wanted to leap on him and tell him to shut up.'

Fiddling with her bracelet, Meryem furrowed her brow in thought. When she looked up again, there was a sparkle in her eyes, a rosy glow to her cheeks. 'I understand now,' she said with a new intensity. 'I think I know what the problem is.'

Fig Tree

Meryem is an odd one, full of contradictions. She seeks help from trees all the time, although she doesn't seem to be aware of this. If she is scared or lonely, or wants to dispel evil spirits, she knocks on wood – an ancient ritual dating back to the days when we were regarded as sacred. Every time she has a wish she doesn't dare speak aloud, she hangs rags and ribbons on our boughs. If she is looking for something – buried treasure or some trivial item she has lost – she roves about holding a forked branch, which she calls a divining rod. Personally, I don't mind such superstitions. Some can even be helpful for us plants. The rusty nails she sticks inside flowerpots to chase away the djinn make soil alkaline. Similarly, the wood ash left from the fires she burns to remove a hex contains potassium, which can be nourishing. And as for the eggshells she spreads around in the hope of attracting good fortune, they, too, are an enriching compost. I just wonder how she continues to carry out these old rituals without realizing that they originate from a deep reverence for us trees.

There is a seven-hundred-year-old oak in the Marathasa Valley, in the Troödos Mountains. The Greeks will tell you how a group of peasants hid under it in fear as they were running away from the Ottoman Turks in the sixteenth century, barely escaping with their lives.

And there is a *Ficus carica* in Ayios Georgios Alamanos that Turks will tell you grew out of the body of a dead man, after a fig in his stomach, the last thing he ate that evening, grew into a tree. He had been taken into a cave with two others and killed with dynamite.

I listen carefully, and I find it astounding that trees, just through their presence, become a saviour for the downtrodden and a symbol of suffering for people on opposite sides.

Across history we have been a refuge to a great many. A sanctuary not only for mortal humans, but also for gods and goddesses. There is a reason why Gaia, the mother goddess of earth, turned her son into a fig tree to save him from Jupiter's thunderbolts. In various parts of the world, women thought to be cursed are married to a *Ficus carica* before they can pledge their troth to the one they truly love. Bizarre though I find all these customs, I understand where they come from. Superstitions are the shadows of fears unknown.

So when Meryem came into the garden, surprising me with her presence, and began to walk this way and that, oblivious to the cold and the storm, I had an inkling she was hatching up a plan to help Ada. And I knew she would, once again, resort to her endless reservoir of myths and beliefs.

Definition of Love

Cyprus, July 1974

The courtyard was dimly lit by the waning moon, the warm wind that had been whistling through the treetops all day long had finally exhausted itself and fallen quiet, and the night felt gentle and cool. The tang of jasmine, winding around the wrought-iron balustrade like a golden thread through homespun cloth, perfumed the air, mingling with the smells of burnt metal and gunpowder.

Defne sat on her own in the far corner of the courtyard in her house, still up at so late an hour. She huddled by the wall, where her parents would not be able to see her should they look out of the window. Pulling her knees to her chest, she rested her head on the palm of one hand. In her other hand, she held a letter, which she had read several times by now, although the words still swam impenetrably before her eyes.

Her gaze fell on the tomato vine that her sister was growing in a large clay pot. Over the past year, it had become her ally, this plant. Whenever she sneaked out at night to meet Kostas, she would secretly climb down the mulberry tree in front of her balcony, and then back up the way she came, carefully hoisting herself up and down using the pot as a step.

She hadn't seen Kostas since the night of the explosion at The Happy Fig. It had been almost impossible to go out and walk around. Every day the news had turned darker, scarier. The rumours that the military junta in Greece were plotting ways to oust the president of Cyprus, Archbishop Makarios, had now hardened into fact. The day before, the Cypriot National Guard and EOKA-B had launched a coup to overthrow the democratically elected Archbishop. The Presidential Palace in Nicosia was bombed and burned by armed forces loyal to the junta. Fights had erupted on the streets between supporters of the Archbishop and supporters of the military regime in Athens. The state radio announced that Makarios was dead. But just as people were mourning him, the Archbishop had broadcast from a makeshift radio station: 'Greek Cypriots! You know this voice. I am Makarios. I am the one you chose to be your leader. I am not dead. I am alive.' He had miraculously escaped, and no one knew his whereabouts.

Amidst the chaos, intercommunal violence had flared. Defne's parents had forbidden her to leave the house, even for basic provisions. The streets were not safe. Turks had to stick with Turks, Greeks with Greeks. Confined to the house, she had spent hours reflecting, worrying, trying to find a way to talk to Kostas.

Finally, today, when her mother had left the house to attend a neighbourhood meeting and her father had fallen asleep in his room as usual after taking his daily medication, she slipped out, despite her sister's protests. She ran all the way to The Happy Fig, looking for Yusuf and Yiorgos. Thankfully, they were both there.

Since the night of the bomb the two men had worked hard to restore the place and managed to repair most of the damage. The front wall and the door had been rebuilt, but now, though ready to reopen, they had been forced to close down due to the on-going unrest on the island. Defne found them stacking up chairs and tables in front of the tavern, wrapping padding around the kitchen equipment before stowing it in crates and boxes. When they saw her, their eyes brimmed with a warmth that was swiftly replaced with concern.

'Defne! What are you d-doing here?' Yusuf asked.

'I'm so glad I found you! I was worried you might be gone.'

'We are closing,' said Yiorgos. 'The staff have resigned. They don't want to work any more. And you shouldn't be out like this. It's dangerous. Did you not hear? British families are going home.

A chartered plane took off this morning carrying army wives and children. There is another plane tomorrow.'

Defne had heard stories about how English ladies had boarded the plane in their pastel hats and matching dresses, their suitcases packed tight. There was relief on their faces. But many were tearful, too, for they were departing an island they had come to love.

Yiorgos said, 'When Westerners run away like that it means those of us they leave behind are in deep shit.'

'Everyone in my community is extremely worried,' said Defne. 'They say there's going to be a bloodbath.'

'Let's n-not lose hope, it'll pass,' said Yusuf.

'But we are happy to see you,' said Yiorgos. 'We've something for you. A letter from Kostas.'

'Oh, good, you've seen him. How is he doing? He's okay, right? Thank God!' She plucked the envelope from his hand, pressing it close to her chest. Quickly, she opened her handbag. 'I've got something for him too. Here, take it!'

Neither Yusuf nor Yiorgos reached for her letter.

Defne felt her gut twist, tried to ignore the feeling. 'I can't stay long. Will you take this to Kostas?'

'We can't,' said Yiorgos.

'It's okay. There's no danger in you walking to his house. Please, this is very important. There's something urgent I need to tell him.'

Yusuf shifted his weight from foot to foot. 'So you d-d-don't know?'

'Don't know what?'

'He's gone,' Yiorgos said. 'Kostas left for England. We think his mother forced him; he didn't have much of a choice. He tried to reach you. He came here several times asking for you, left the envelope the last time. But we thought he had found you in the end. We thought he had told you.'

On the ground by her shoe she noticed a phalanx of ants, dragging a dead beetle. She watched them for a few seconds, unable to make sense of how she felt. It wasn't pain exactly that seized her, that would come later. It wasn't shock either, though that too would descend soon. It was as if she were gripped by an irresistible force of gravity, locking her forever to this spot and in this moment.

Lifting her chin, her eyes unfocused, she gave a curt nod. Without a word, she walked away. Behind her, Yusuf shouted her name. She did not respond.

In the distance, smoke billowed over the rooftops; parts of the city were burning. Everywhere she looked she saw men – carrying guns, stacking sandbags, men with grim expressions and boots caked in dust. Civilians, soldiers, paramilitaries. Where had all the island's women gone?

She steered towards the backstreets, drifting away from the turmoil, passing through gardens and orchards. Aimlessly, she kept going, her shadow pacing beside her. The day dimmed into evening, the world drained of colour. By the time she reached her house, hours later, her ankles and arms were scratched by brambles, like an inscription in a language she had never learned to speak.

Since then she had been silent, withdrawn, her lips curled in concentration. She had tried her best to act normal around Meryem, otherwise her sister would have started asking questions. It was not that hard, she had found, to postpone the pain. Just like she had postponed reading his letter until later in the evening.

My darling Defne,

I cannot believe I haven't been able to see you before I leave for England. I started writing this letter, stopped, and started again so many times. I wanted to tell you the news myself. But I couldn't reach you.

It is my mother. She is full of fears, impossible to reason with. She is worried that something awful will happen to me. She cried and cried and begged me to go to London. I couldn't say 'no' to her. But I won't let her do this ever again. She is sick, you know that. Her health is deteriorating. Since my father died, she has worked ceaselessly to take care of us. Michalis's death shattered her, and now with Andreas away, I am the only one she has to rely on. I could not bear seeing her like that. I could not let her down.

It is only for a short time, I promise. In London, I will stay with my uncle. There won't be a single day that I won't think about you, not a single heartbeat that I won't miss you. I will be back in two weeks, at most. I will bring you presents from England!

I didn't even get a chance to tell you what the other night meant for me. When we left the tavern . . . the moon, the smell of your hair, your hand in my hand, after all that horror when we realized we had only each other to depend on.

You know what I've been thinking since? I've been thinking that you are my country. Is that a strange thing to say? Without you, I don't have a home in this world; I am a felled tree, my roots severed all round; you can topple me with the touch of a finger.

I will return soon, I won't let this happen again. And maybe next time, one day, we will go to England together, who knows? Please think of me every day, I'll be back before you know it.

I love you.
Kostas

Defne held the letter so tight it crumpled around the edges. Her gaze fell on the tomato plant again as her eyes welled up. Kostas had once told her that long ago in Peru, where tomatoes were believed to have originated, they used to call it 'a plum thing with a navel'. Defne had liked that description. Everything in life should be evoked in such detail, she had thought, rather than being given abstract names, a random combination of letters. A bird should be 'a feathery thing with a song'. Or a car, 'a metallic thing with wheels and a horn'. An island, 'a lonely thing with water on all sides'. And love? She might have answered this question differently until today, but now she was certain love ought to be called 'a deceptive thing with heartbreak in the end'.

Kostas was gone and she had not even found a chance to tell him. She had never felt so scared of tomorrow. She was on her own now.

Foreigner

When Kostas Kazantzakis arrived in London he was greeted at the airport by his uncle and his English wife. The couple lived in a timber-framed brick house with a small square garden at the front. They had a dog, a brown-and-black-and-white collie named Zeus, who loved to eat cooked carrots and raw spaghetti straight from the box. It would take Kostas a while to get used to the food in this country. But it was the change in the weather that took him by surprise. He was not prepared for this new sky overhead, which was dimly lit most of the time, only occasionally flickering into life like a buzzing bulb with low voltage.

His uncle, who had settled for good in England, was a jovial man with an infectious laugh. He treated Kostas with kindness and, guided by a strong conviction that a young lad should be neither idle nor still, instantly put his nephew to work in the store. There Kostas learned how to stack shelves, count the stock, manage the till and keep the inventory ledger. It was hard work, but he didn't mind. He was used to being on his toes and it kept him busy, making the days away from Defne a bit more bearable.

A week after his arrival, Kostas heard the staggering news: a military force backed by the junta in Greece had overthrown Archbishop Makarios; gunfire had broken out between the supporters of Makarios and the de facto president, Nikos Sampson, appointed by the leaders of the coup d'état. Kostas and his uncle pored over all the newspapers, shocked to read about how 'bodies littered the streets and there were mass burials'. He barely slept at night, and whenever he drifted off, he plunged into disturbing dreams.

Then followed even more unthinkable events: five days after Archbishop Makarios was overthrown, heavily armed Turkish troops landed at Kyrenia, 300 tanks and 40,000 soldiers, marching steadily inland. The Greek villagers in their path were forced to run south to safety, leaving everything behind. In the maelstrom of chaos and war, the military regime in Athens collapsed. There were reports of clashes between Turkish warships and Greek warships near Paphos. But the deadliest fights were taking place in and around the capital, Nicosia.

Sick with dread, Kostas tried to find every titbit of information he could, glued to the radio to catch the latest reports. Words cloaked and blurred as much as they revealed and explained: 'invasion', said Greek sources; 'peace operation', said Turkish sources; 'intervention', said the UN. Strange concepts jumped out at him from the bulletins, pulled to the forefront of his mind. The articles spoke about 'prisoners of war', 'ethnic partition', 'population transfer' . . . He couldn't believe they were referring to a place that was as familiar to him as his own reflection in the mirror. Now, he could no longer recognize it.

His mother sent a frantic message, telling him not to come back. Through miles of traffic jams, she had managed to get out of Nicosia at the last minute, frightened and fighting for her life. Such was the shock and fear among Greek civilians, and so utterly terrifying the tales and testimonies they heard of the advancing army, that a little girl in the neighbourhood had died of a heart attack. Unable to take any personal items with her, Panagiota had sought refuge with some relatives down south. They no longer had a home. They no longer had a garden with five carob trees. Everything she had painstakingly built and lovingly tended since the day her husband had died and left her alone with three sons was taken away from her.

Despite Kostas's objections, his uncle cancelled his return ticket. He could not go back to an island in flames. Trapped in a situation over which he had no control, Kostas tried every which way he could think of to reach Defne – telegram, phone calls, letters . . . At first, he was able to talk to Yusuf and Yiorgos, but then, oddly, they too became unreachable.

After six weeks had passed with no reply from Defne, Kostas managed to get hold of Meryem through a friend who worked at the post office, and who brought her to a phone at a prearranged time. Her voice low and troubled, Meryem confirmed that their address was unchanged, their house intact. Defne was receiving his letters.

'Then why doesn't she write back?' Kostas asked.

'I'm sorry. I don't think she wants to hear from you any more.'

'I don't believe that,' Kostas said. 'I won't believe it until I hear it from her.'

A pause on the line. 'I'll tell her, Kostas.'

A week later a postcard arrived in Defne's handwriting, asking him to stop trying to contact her.

All kinds of customers came to the small grocery store: factory workers, cab drivers, security guards. Also, a middle-aged teacher who taught at a school nearby. Having previously noticed Kostas's interest in the environment and its conservation, and seeing his distress and loneliness now, this man began to lend him his books. In the evenings, with still no news of Defne, his limbs aching from the day's work, Kostas would stay up late, reading in bed until he could no longer keep his eyes open. During the day, whenever there was a break between customers, he would sit behind the till and pore over nature magazines sold at the shop. It was only when he thought or read about trees that he found some solace.

In one of those magazines he came across an article about fruit bats, explaining how and why more and more of them were dying en masse. The author predicted that, within no more than a few decades, the world would experience dangerous levels of warming. There would follow collective deaths of species, seemingly random, but deeply connected. The piece drew attention to the positive role that forests could play to slow down catastrophic ecological change. Something shifted in Kostas when he read this. Until then he hadn't known one could devote one's life to studying plants. He could do this, he sensed, and if it turned out to be a life of solitude, he could do that too.

He still sent letters to Defne. At first, he only wrote about Cyprus and asked her worried questions about how she was doing, trying to pass along words of encouragement and support, signs of love. But, little by little, he began telling her about London too: the ethnic mix of the neighbourhood, the soot-blackened public buildings, the graffiti on the walls, the neat little terraced houses and their manicured hedges, the smoke-filled pubs and the greasy fried breakfasts, the unarmed policemen on the streets, the Greek Cypriot barber shops . . .

He no longer expected an answer from her, but he kept writing anyway; he continued sending his words southwards, like releasing thousands of migrating butterflies he knew would never return.

Fig Tree

Now that you have come this far into our story, there is something else I need to share with you: I am a melancholic tree.

I can't help but compare myself with the other trees in our garden – the hawthorn, the English oak, the whitebeam, the blackthorn – all properly native to Britain. I wonder if the reason why I am more inclined to melancholia than any of them is because I am an immigrant plant and, like all immigrants, I carry with me the shadow of another land? Or is it simply because I grew up among human beings in a noisy tavern?

How they delighted in arguing, the customers at The Happy Fig! There are two subjects of which humans can never get enough, especially when they have knocked a few back: love and politics. So I have heard plenty of stories and scandals about each. Night after night, table after table, diners from all sorts of nationalities plunged into heated debates around me, their voices rising another notch with each glass, the air between them growing thicker. I listened to them with curiosity, but I have formed my own opinions.

What I tell you, therefore, I tell through the prism of my own understanding, undoubtedly. No storyteller is completely objective. But I have always tried to grasp every story through diverse angles, shifting perspectives, conflicting narratives. Truth is a rhizome – an underground plant stem with lateral shoots. You need to dig deep to reach it and, once unearthed, you have to treat it with respect.

In the early 1970s, fig trees in Cyprus were affected by a virus that killed them slowly. The symptoms were not visible at first. There was no cracking of the stems, no bleeding cankers, no mottled patterns on the leaves. Even so, something was not quite right. The fruits were dropping prematurely, they tasted sour and oozed goo like pus from a wound.

One thing I noticed back then, and have never forgotten, was that remote and seemingly lone trees were not as badly affected as those living together in close proximity. Today, I think of fanaticism – of any type – as a viral disease. Creeping in menacingly, ticking like a pendulum clock that never winds down, it takes hold of you faster when you are part of an enclosed, homogenous unit. Better to keep some distance from all collective beliefs and certainties, I always remind myself.

By the end of that interminable summer, 4,400 people were dead, thousands missing. Around 160,000 Greeks living in the north moved south, and around 50,000 Turks moved north. People became refugees in their own country. Families lost their loved ones, abandoned their homes, villages and towns; old neighbours and good friends went their separate ways, sometimes betrayed one another. It must all be written in history books, though each side will tell only their own version of things. Narratives that run counter, without ever touching, like parallel lines that never intersect.

But on an island plagued by years of ethnic violence and brutal atrocities, humans were not the only ones that suffered. So did we trees – and animals, too, experienced hardship and pain as their habitats came to disappear. It never meant anything to anyone, what happened to us.

It matters to me though and, so long as I am able to tell this story, I am going to include in it the creatures in my ecosystem – the birds, the bats, the butterflies, the honeybees, the ants, the mosquitoes and the mice – because there is one thing I have learned: wherever there is war and a painful partition, there will be no winners, human or otherwise.

PART FOUR

Branches

Proverbs

London, late 2010s

'So what exactly are you working on nowadays?' Meryem asked Kostas as she watched him walking around the house clutching his notes.

'Oh, he's going to present a paper,' Ada barged in. 'Dad's been invited to Brazil – the Earth Summit. He wants me to travel with him.'

'I'll be sharing our research for the first time,' said Kostas. 'I don't know what makes me more nervous – the judgement of the scientific community or what my daughter thinks!'

Ada smiled. 'Last year he was in Australia, studying eucalyptus trees. They're looking into how different trees respond to heat-waves and wildfires. They're trying to understand why some species survive better than others.'

She said nothing about how her father had cut his trip short, returning to London on the first flight when he received the news that her mother was in a coma.

'Oh, how exciting that you'll travel together,' said Meryem. 'Go, go, write then, finish your work, Kostas. Don't worry about us.'

Smiling, he wished them goodnight.

They listened to his footsteps tapping down the corridor and, as soon as they heard him close his door, Ada turned to her aunt. 'I'm also going to my room.'

'Wait, I've something important to tell you. I think I know why you screamed the other day.'

'You do?'

'Yes, I've been thinking about this. You said there's something wrong with you – and your mother was the same. Mental health

193

issues, as you put it. It made me sad to hear this because I know it's not true. There's nothing wrong with you. You are a bright young girl.'

'Then how do you account for what happened?'

Meryem glanced towards the corridor and dropped her voice to a confidential whisper. 'It's the djinn.'

'The what?'

'Listen, back in Cyprus, my mum would always say, "If you see a dust storm coming, take shelter, because that's when the djinn get married!"'

'I've no idea what you're talking about.'

'Patience, I'll explain. Now, the djinn are shamelessly promiscuous. Both males and females. A female djinni can have up to forty husbands. You know what that means?'

'Um, a juicy sex life?'

'It means too many weddings! But when will they celebrate, that's the key question, isn't it? They have to wait for a storm to arrive. A dust storm – or a winter storm. Hordes of djinn must be out on the streets of London right now.'

'Okay, now you're scaring me.'

'Don't be silly, nothing to fear. All I'm saying is the djinn have been waiting for this moment. They are out – dancing, drinking, having a ball. The last thing they want is to have humans underfoot. Though, technically, they are under our feet. Anyway, if you step on a djinni by mistake, they can make you do funny things. People have fits, speak gibberish or scream for no reason.'

'Are you trying to tell me that I could be possessed? Because when I said that, it was totally *metaphorical*. Don't be so literal. It wasn't serious.'

'Well, I always take the djinn seriously,' said Meryem, speaking slowly as if weighing each word. 'They are mentioned in the Qur'an. In our culture, we believe invisible creatures exist.'

'Right, I need to remind you that my father is a scientist and my mother was a scholar and an artist. We don't believe in such things in this house. We are not religious, in case you haven't noticed.'

'Oh, I know that,' said Meryem, sounding irritated. 'But this is ancient wisdom I'm talking about. It's part of our culture. Your culture. It's in your DNA.'

'Great,' Ada murmured.

'Don't you worry. God made lower branches for birds that cannot fly so well.'

'Meaning?'

'Meaning there is a cure. I've asked around a bit. I made some phone calls and I've found a really great healer. There's no harm in paying him a quick visit.'

'An exorcist?' said Ada. 'Wow! There are exorcists in London? You must be joking, right?'

'It's not a joke. We'll go and check, now that the weather is improving, it'll be perfect timing. I'm just waiting for an appointment confirmation. And if we don't like it, we'll walk out. We're not going to search for a calf under an ox.'

Ada drew in a breath, then released it slowly.

'Look, it can happen to anyone. Don't take it personally,' Meryem continued. 'I had to visit a healer myself when I was young.'

'Like when?'

'Like when I got married.'

'That's because your husband was not a nice man. An arsehole, I'm beginning to suspect.'

'Arsehole,' repeated Meryem, tasting the word with the tip of her tongue. 'I never swear.'

'Well, you should. It feels good.'

'He was not a nice man, you are right. But it didn't hurt seeing an *exorcist*. It might have helped me, actually. Listen, *cigerimin kösesi* . . .' Meryem's eyes raked the room as if searching for something she had only just remembered losing. 'What's the thing . . . when you start feeling better because you believe a treatment is working?'

'Placebo effect?'

'That's it! If you think a healer might help, he will. We just need to take action. A cheese vessel will not sail merely by words.'

'Are these real proverbs or are you making them up?'

'They are all real,' said Meryem, crossing her arms. 'So what do you say? Can we visit the djinn master?'

'Djinn master!' Ada tugged at her earlobe, considering. 'I might agree to this nonsense on one condition only. You said my mum and dad were childhood sweethearts. You said they broke up, it was over, but they met again, years later.'

'That's right.'

'Tell me how it happened. How did they start dating again?'

'Oh, he came back.' Meryem sighed. 'One morning we woke up and heard that Kostas Kazantzakis was in Nicosia. I thought Defne was over that phase of her life. Had she not suffered enough? She didn't even talk about him any more. She was a grown woman. But you know what they say, the bear knows seven songs and they are all about honey.'

'Meaning?'

'Meaning, she had never forgotten him. So I had a hunch and I tried to keep her away from him – fire and gunpowder should not come together – but I failed. It turns out I was right to feel uneasy because when they saw each other again, it was as if all those years had not passed. It was as if they were kids again. I said to Defne, why are you giving him a second chance? Don't you know a gardener in love with roses is pricked by a thousand thorns? But, once again, she didn't listen.'

A Thousand Thorns

Cyprus, early 2000s

Kostas Kazantzakis arrived in Northern Cyprus by ferry, for he did not want to fly. Although the eight-hour journey had not been particularly difficult, he felt disorientated, queasy. Seasickness, he presumed. But maybe it had nothing to do with that. Maybe his body was reacting in ways his mind was yet to comprehend. He was returning to the place of his birth for the first time in more than twenty-five years.

Clad in brown corduroy trousers, a linen shirt and a navy sports jacket, his dark, wavy hair tousled by the wind, his eyes scanned the port intently. Falling in step with the flow of passengers, he crossed the dock and walked down the ferry ramp. His fingers gripped the handrail so tightly that his knuckles turned white. With each second that passed, his unease grew. Under the harsh afternoon sun, he squinted at the signs around him, unable to make sense of the Turkish letters, so unlike the Greek alphabet. He tried to find a respite from the crowd, to no avail. Everywhere he turned there were families with children, pushing strollers or carrying babies bundled up despite the heat. He followed them, propelled by the current as though it were not solid ground under his feet but air alone.

Passport control came and went seamlessly, moving faster than he had expected. The young Turkish police officer greeted him with a curt nod, studying him intently but not unkindly. He did not ask any personal questions, which surprised Kostas. In his mind he had been running possible scenarios as to how he would be received, and a part of him had, until the last minute, feared they might not allow him into the Turkish side of the island, even with a British passport.

There was no one to pick him up and he hadn't dared to hope there would be. Dragging his suitcase, filled with more equipment than clothes, he insinuated himself into the town's bustling streets. Not liking the look of the first driver in the taxi rank, he lingered, feigning interest in the goods on a vendor's tray. *Komboloi* in Greek; *tespih* in Turkish. Red coral, green emerald, black onyx. He couldn't help buying some agate worry beads, just to have something to occupy himself with.

The driver of the next taxi seemed nice, and Kostas negotiated with him, wary of being cheated. He didn't tell the man that he could speak a bit of Turkish. The words he had picked up in his boyhood were like chipped, moth-eaten toys; he wanted to dust them off and check to make sure they worked before he attempted to put them into use.

After half an hour's drive in silence, they approached Nicosia, passing newly built houses on both sides of the road. Construction everywhere. Kostas surveyed the bright, sunlit landscape. Pine, cypress, olive and carob trees were interspersed with patches of arid earth, sun-baked and monochrome. Citrus orchards had been chopped down to make way for smart villas and apartments. He was saddened to see that this part of the island was not the verdant paradise he remembered. Cyprus was known in antiquity as 'the green island', famous for its dense, mysterious forests. The absence of trees was a powerful rebuke to the dreadful mistakes of the past.

Without asking if he minded, the driver turned on the radio. Turkish pop music poured out of the speakers. Kostas let out a breath. The upbeat melody was as familiar to him as the scars on his body, though the lyrics were a puzzle. Even so, it wasn't hard to imagine the subject – in this part of the world, all songs were about love or heartbreak.

'First time here?' the driver asked in English, glancing up at the rear-view mirror.

Kostas hesitated, but only for a second. 'Yes and no.'

'Yes? No?'

'I used to . . .' A surge of warmth rose in his chest. None of his Greek neighbours still lived around here, the houses he had known now belonged to strangers. He said, 'I was born and raised on this side of the island.'

'You Greek?'

'Yes, I am.'

The driver cocked his head. For a moment Kostas thought he saw a hard gleam flash in his eyes. To break a possible tension, he leaned forward, trying to change the subject. 'So, has the tourist season begun?'

A smile appeared on the driver's face, slow and cautious, like a closed fist opening. 'Yes, but you no tourist, brother. You are from here.'

And that simple word, *brother*, so unexpected yet reassuring, hovered in the air between them. Kostas did not say anything else; nor did the driver. It was as if they both had heard all they needed to know.

Hotel Afrodit was a whitewashed, two-storey building held tight in the bright magenta embrace of bougainvillea. A broad-shouldered and rosy-faced woman stood behind the reception desk, her head-scarf tied loosely in the traditional Muslim way. To her left, lounging in a wicker chair, a man who must have been her husband sipped tea. Behind him, the wall was crowded with a mishmash of items: Turkish flags in various sizes, prayers in Arabic script, evil eye beads, macramé plant holders and postcards from different parts of the world, posted by satisfied customers. One glance at the couple and Kostas sensed that, though the husband might nominally own the place, it was the wife who ran everything.

'Good afternoon.' He knew they were expecting him.

'Mr Kazantzakis, right? Welcome!' the woman chirped, a smile dimpling her round cheeks. 'Good journey?'

'Not bad.'

'Great time to visit Cyprus. What brings you here?'

He was expecting this question and had his answer ready, but still he paused. 'Work,' he said flatly.

'Yes, you scientist.' She elongated the last word, her English thickly accented. 'You said on the phone you work with trees, did you know all of our rooms are named after them?'

She offered him his room key in an envelope. For a second, Kostas dared not look at the name scribbled on it, half expecting it to be The Happy Fig. The hair at the back of his neck bristled as his eyes skimmed the words. His room was called 'Golden Oak'.

'That's good,' he said with a smile; he was finding it harder to keep memories at bay.

Upstairs, the room was spacious and full of light. Kostas threw himself on to the bed, only now realizing how exhausted he was. The soft covers invited him in, like a warm, scented bath, though he didn't allow himself to relax. He took a quick shower and changed into a T-shirt and jeans. Crossing the room, he opened the double doors to the balcony. Overhead, an eagle – the animal companion of Zeus – soared across a cloudless sky and glided westward, in pursuit of its next quarry. As soon as he stepped out, he caught a long-forgotten whiff in the breeze. Jasmine, pine, sun-baked stones. A smell he thought he had buried somewhere in the maze of memory. The human mind was the strangest place, both home and exile. How could it hold on to something as elusive and intangible as a scent when it was capable of erasing concrete chunks of the past, block by block?

He had to find her. This very afternoon. Come tomorrow, he might lose heart and put it off for another day or maybe two, make sure he was terribly busy, so busy that the entire week would pass in a blur and it would be time to pack again. But right now, fresh off the ferry and still riding the wave of longing that had carried him all the way here from England, he was certain he had the strength to see Defne.

All this time, he had kept collecting bits of information about her. He knew she was an archaeologist and had made a name for herself in the field. He knew she had never married, had no children. He had seen photos of her in newspapers sold at Turkish Cypriot stores in London, where she was speaking at academic conferences and seminars. But what did any of that say about the particularities of her life today? It had been impossibly long since they had last seen each other. You could not fill that big a void with those few paltry facts he had gathered, and yet they were all he had.

He didn't have her number and did not want to call the university where she worked. The friends they had in common from the past had all scattered to different corners of the world and could not be of help. But before leaving London he was able to find a contact, and that was as good a beginning as any.

He had a colleague, David, with whom he had collaborated on various projects initiated by the United Nations Environment Programme. They had gone their separate ways but kept in touch. A cheerful man with half a dozen languages under his belt, a propensity for alcohol and a distinctively sandy beard, David had been based in Cyprus for the last ten months. Upon deciding to travel to the island, Kostas had called him, hoping he could be the bridge that would take him to Defne, knowing that bridges appear in our lives only when we are ready to cross them.

Remains of Love

Cyprus, early 2000s

Kostas arrived at the bookshop where they had agreed to meet and checked his watch. With a few minutes to kill he browsed the books, some of them in English. In one section of the shop he found rows of stamps dating back to the years of his boyhood and before. Among the thousands was one issued in 1975, showing the island divided into two opposing colours, separated by a metal chain. So much symbolism packed into four square centimetres of paper.

From the souvenir shop next door, he bought an ammonite – an ancient marine shell, coiled around its secrets. Feeling its heft in his palm, he wandered around for a bit. On a poplar tree he spotted a bird – a black-headed bunting with splashes of yellow across its chest. A passerine bird. Every year, this tiny creature migrated from the pastures of Iran and the valleys of Europe to the coasts of India, and further east, traversing distances beyond the ken of many humans.

The bunting hopped back and forth along the branch, and then stopped. For a fleeting moment, in the gathering quiet, the two of them eyed each other. Kostas wondered what the bird saw in him – enemy, friend or something else? What he saw was a fascinating combination of vulnerability and resilience.

The sound of approaching footsteps jolted him out of his reverie. Alarmed, the bird took off. Turning his head, Kostas saw a tall, heavily built figure hurrying towards him.

'Kostas Kazantzakis, there you are! I'd recognize that scruffy hairdo from a mile away,' David said, his accent unmistakably British.

Kostas took a step forward, shielding his eyes against the sun. 'Hello, David, thanks for meeting me.'

As he grabbed the hand Kostas offered, David broke into a smile. 'I must admit I was surprised when you called to say you were coming. From what I remember, you didn't want to return to Cyprus. But here you are! What is it – work or homesickness?'

'Both,' Kostas replied. 'A bit of fieldwork . . . I also wanted to see my old town, some old friends . . .'

'Yes, you told me. As I said on the phone, I know Defne well. Come, I'll take you to her. It's just five minutes away. She and her team have been up since early morning. I'll explain it on the way.'

At the mention of her name, Kostas felt a cold panic grip his chest. They began to walk, picking their way along the rutted path, the hot wind searing their faces as they headed north-east.

'So tell me, what are they doing exactly – she and her team?'

'Oh, they are with the CMP,' said David. 'The Committee on Missing Persons. It's pretty intense stuff. It gets right inside your head after a while. Turks and Greeks are working together – for a change. The idea came into being in the early 1980s, but nothing could be done for a long time because the two sides couldn't agree on the toll.'

'The toll?'

'Of those who disappeared during the troubles,' David replied, slightly out of breath. 'In the end, they managed to finalize a list of 2,002 victims. The actual number is much higher, of course, but nobody wants to hear that. Anyway, it's a start. The UN is a partner, that's why I'm here, but it's the Cypriots who do the real work. I'll be around till the end of the month, then I fly to Geneva. They'll keep digging, your Defne and her friends.'

'The members, are they mostly archaeologists?'

'Only a few. They come from all professions: anthropologists, historians, geneticists, forensic specialists . . . The groups are formed and approved by the UN. We work in different locations, depending on anonymous informants, who tell us things for all sorts of reasons of their own. Then we start digging. You think this is a small island, but if you're looking for a missing person even the smallest place is impossibly big.'

'What about the locals, do they support the project?'

'The response has been mixed so far. We've many young volunteers from both sides who are eager to help, which gives you hope for humanity. The young are wise. They want peace. And the elderly, some kind of closure. It's the ones in the middle who cause trouble.'

'Our generation, you mean,' said Kostas.

'Exactly. There is a small but vocal minority who begrudge our work, either because they fear it might stir up old animosities or because they still bear them. Some of the CMP members have been threatened.'

They now approached a clearing in the woods. Kostas could hear low voices in the distance and a scraping, grating sound of shovels and picks stabbing the earth.

'There's the gang,' said David, waving a hand.

Kostas saw a group of about a dozen people, women and men, toiling under the sun, wearing straw hats and bandanas. Most of them had their faces half covered with cloth masks. Large black tarpaulins were stretched over the ground and suspended between the trees, like swaying hammocks.

His heart quickening, Kostas scanned the group, but he couldn't make out Defne among them. He had imagined this moment so many times, thinking of all sorts of ways it could go wrong, that he felt almost paralysed to be in it now. How would she react when she saw him? Would she turn and walk away?

'Hey, everyone!' David called out. 'Come and meet my friend Kostas!'

One by one, the team members stopped what they were doing and strode towards them, their steps calm, unhurried. Taking off their gloves and masks, putting their notebooks and instruments aside, they welcomed him.

Kostas greeted each person warmly, though he couldn't help stealing glances around to see where Defne might be. And then he spotted her, sitting perched on a tree limb with her legs dangling, her face impossible to read as she quietly watched him from above. Kostas noticed a spider's web between the branches beside her, and for a fleeting moment Defne and those silvery threads merged in his mind, wispy and fragile like the remnants of the bond between them.

'Oh, she does that all the time,' said David when he noticed where Kostas was looking. 'Defne loves sitting there like a bird, apparently she concentrates better when she's up a tree. That's where she writes our reports.' David raised his voice. 'Come down here!'

Smiling, Defne jumped down and walked towards them. Her wavy black hair fell to her shoulders. She wore khaki trousers and a loosely buttoned white shirt. On her feet were hiking boots. She didn't seem surprised. She seemed to have been expecting him.

'Hi, Kostas.' Her handshake was brief, giving nothing away. 'David told me you were coming. He said, a friend of mine is enquiring about you. I said, really, who? Turns out it was you.'

He was taken aback by the distance in her voice, not cold or formal, but carefully measured, guarded. The years had etched fine lines on to her face, her cheeks had thinned slightly, but it was her eyes that had changed the most: a hard glaze had settled on those big, round brown eyes. His heart constricted as he saw how beautiful she still was.

'Defne . . .'

Her name felt strange in his mouth. Worried that she might hear the thumping of his heart, he took a step aside, his gaze settling on the nearest tarpaulin. His breath tightened as he processed what the dusty, soiled, russet-stained fragments piled on it were. A split femur, a cracked thigh bone . . . they were human remains.

'We had a tip-off,' said Defne, seeing the expression on his face. 'A peasant pointed us here. Father of six, grandfather to seventeen. The man was in the late stages of Alzheimer's, didn't recognize his own wife. One morning he woke up and started uttering strange things – "There's a hill, a terebinth tree with a boulder at its foot." He drew it on a piece of paper, describing this place. The family contacted us, we came, we dug, and we found the remains just where he said we would.'

In all the times he had imagined their encounter, Kostas had never thought they would be talking about such things. He asked, 'How did the peasant know?'

'You mean, do I suspect he was the murderer?' Defne shook her head, her earrings swaying. 'Who knows? A killer or an innocent eyewitness? That's not our business. The CMP is not into that kind of investigation. If we conducted an enquiry or passed the information to the police, no one on this island would talk to us ever again. We can't afford that. Our job is to find the missing so that families can give their loved ones a proper burial.'

Kostas nodded, mulling over her words. 'Do you think there might be other graves around here?'

'Possibly. Sometimes you search for weeks on end and achieve nothing. It's frustrating. Some of the informants misremember the details, others deliberately lead us on wild goose chases. You search for victims, you encounter medieval, Roman, Hellenistic bones. Or prehistoric fossils. Did you know there were pygmy hippopotamuses in Cyprus? Pygmy elephants! Then, just when you think you are going nowhere, you find mass graves.'

Kostas glanced around him, taking in his surroundings, the grass tinted with gold under the sun, the pine trees with their dome-shaped tops. He stared into the distance as far as he could see, as though trying to recall what he had broken away from.

He asked, cautiously, 'And the missing you've found here, were they Greeks or Turks?'

'They were islanders,' she said and there was a sharp edge to her voice then. 'Islanders, like us.'

Overhearing, David interjected. 'That's the thing, my friend. You don't know until you send the bones to a lab and get a report. When you hold a skull in your hands, can you tell if it's Christian or Muslim? All that bloodshed, for what? Stupid, stupid wars.'

'We don't have much time, though,' said Defne, her voice tailing off. 'The older generation is dying, taking their secrets with them to the grave. If we don't dig now, in a decade or so there won't be anyone left to tell us the whereabouts of the missing. It's a race against time, really.'

From the shrubs in the distance came the buzzing song of cicadas. Kostas knew there were some cicada species that could sing at extremely high frequencies, and perhaps they were doing so right now. Nature was always talking, telling things, though the human ear was too limited to hear them.

'So, you two are old friends, huh?' asked David. 'Did you go to the same school or what?'

'Something like that,' said Defne, lifting her chin. 'We grew up in the same neighbourhood, haven't seen each other in years.'

'Well, I'm glad I reconnected you,' said David. 'We should all go out for dinner tonight. This calls for a celebration.'

A strong, delicious aroma filled the air. Someone was brewing coffee. The team members spread out, taking their break beneath the trees, chatting in low murmurs.

David perched on a rock, produced a silver tobacco box and started to roll a cigarette. When done, he offered it to Defne, who accepted it with a smile, without a word. She took a drag and handed it back to him. They began smoking together, passing the butt back and forth between them. Kostas looked away.

'*Kafé?*'

A tall, lithe Greek woman was serving coffee in paper cups. Thanking her, Kostas took one.

He walked towards the sole terebinth tree and sat under its shade. His mother would make bread out of its fruit and use its resin as a preservative in carob liquor. A profound sense of sorrow came over him. He had done everything he could to take care of her after she and Andreas joined him in England following the partition of the island, but it was too late. The cancer from second-hand exposure to asbestos had already metastasized. Panagiota was buried in a cemetery in London, far away from all that she had known and loved. He stood still, absorbing the smells of tobacco and coffee as memories rushed over him.

Overhead, the sun shone full and bright. In the heat Kostas thought he could hear the branches around them cracking like arthritic hands. He glanced at Defne, who had returned to work, her features drawn tight in concentration, writing down in her notebook every single thing they had unearthed so far that day.

Human remains . . . What exactly did that mean? Was it a few hard bones and soft tissue? Clothes and accessories? Things solid and compact enough to fit inside a coffin? Or was it rather the intangible – the words we send out into the ether, the dreams we keep to ourselves, the heartbeats we skip beside our lovers, the voids we try to fill and can never adequately articulate – when all was said and done, what was left of an entire life, a human being . . . and could that really be disinterred from the ground?

The sun was descending by the time the members of the CMP downed tools, the clouds on the horizon soaked in glowing amber.

They put every scrap of bone into plastic bags, which they carefully sealed and numbered. These were then placed in labelled boxes. They wrote the date and place of the excavation on each box, as well as the details of the group that had carried out the work. Every single piece of information was recorded and archived.

Wearily, they started making their way down the hill, splitting into smaller groups. Kostas walked alongside Defne towards the back, an awkward silence expanding between them.

'The families . . .' said Kostas after a while. 'How do they react when you tell them you have found their dead after so many years?'

'Gratitude, mostly. There was this old Greek woman, a talented seamstress in her youth, apparently. When we informed her that we'd found the bones of her husband she cried so much. But the next day, she comes to the lab wearing this pink frilly dress with silver shoes, silver purse. Bright red lipstick on her lips. I'll never forget. This woman who had worn nothing but black for decades, she came to pick up her husband's remains in a pink dress. She said she could finally talk to him. She said she felt like she was eighteen again, and they were dating. Can you believe it? A few bones, that was all we gave her, but she was as happy as if we had given her the world.'

Defne took out a cigarette and lit it, protecting the flame between her palms. As she exhaled a cloud of smoke, she asked, 'Want one?'

Kostas shook his head.

'And once there was this heartbreaking coincidence. We were digging at Karpas Road. The area was too large, and we had to hire a bulldozer operator. The guy began to excavate and he found a body. So he goes home and tells his grandmother, describing the clothes on the corpse. "That's my Ali," the old woman says and starts to cry. Apparently, Ali Zorba had a caravan of camels in the 1950s. He was returning from Famagusta when he was killed and buried by the road. All this time people passed by without knowing.'

Just then, David, walking a few feet ahead, turned round and called back. 'Hey, Kostas! Don't forget dinner tonight. We're going to a tavern – the best in town!'

Kostas flinched upon hearing this, his entire body clenched.

Defne noticed. 'Not the tavern you're thinking. That one is long gone. The Happy Fig is in ruins.'

'I'd like to visit it,' said Kostas, a sadness seizing his heart. 'I want to see the fig tree.'

'Not much to see, I'm afraid, although the tree must still be inside. I haven't been there in ages.'

'In England, I tried to contact them so many times. I managed to get hold of Yiorgos's relatives. They told me he was dead. They didn't share much, didn't seem to like that I was asking so many questions. I was never able to reach Yusuf – or his family. Someone said he had left Cyprus and gone to America, but I am not sure if that's true.'

'You don't know?' Defne squeezed her eyes tight shut before opening them. 'Yusuf and Yiorgos disappeared in the summer of 1974 – a few weeks after you left. They are the among the thousands of missing we are digging for.'

He slowed down, a knot in his throat. 'I . . . I didn't . . .'

'It's normal. You've been away for too long.' There was no emotion in her voice – not a trace of anger, bitterness or lament. A voice as flat as steel, and just as impenetrable.

A kind of desperation smouldering in his heart, he tried to say something, but words felt pointless. She didn't give him a chance anyway. Quickening her steps, she sprinted away to join David at the front.

Kostas lagged behind, watching the two of them walk in tandem, linking arms. When they reached a corner ahead under a street lamp, David swivelled round to wave goodbye, shouting:

'We'll be at The Wandering Khayyam, ask around and you'll find it. Don't be late, Kostas. God knows we all need a drink after today!'

Fig Tree

A tree is a memory keeper. Tangled beneath our roots, hidden inside our trunks, are the sinews of history, the ruins of wars nobody came to win, the bones of the missing.

The water sucked up through our boughs is the blood of the earth, the tears of the victims, and the ink of truths yet to be acknowledged. Humans, especially the victors who hold the pen that writes the annals of history, have a penchant for erasing as much as documenting. It remains to us plants to collect the untold, the unwanted. Like a cat that curls up on its favourite cushion, a tree wraps itself around the remnants of the past.

When Lawrence Durrell, having fallen in love with Cyprus, decided to plant cypresses behind his house and took his spade to the soil, he found skeletons in his garden. Little did he know that this was by no means unusual. All around the world, wherever there is, or has ever been, a civil war or an ethnic conflict, come to the trees for clues, because we will be the ones that sit silently in communion with human remains.

Butterflies and Bones

Cyprus, early 2000s

The Wandering Khayyam was a simple tavern with tile-topped tables, pastoral oil paintings and a wide selection of fish on ice. Kostas arrived around seven thirty, checking his watch, unsure whether he was early or late, having not been told what time to meet the others.

As soon as he walked in, he was greeted by an elegant, heavily made-up woman somewhere in her seventies, her platinum-blonde hair piled up in an intricate coil.

'You must be Kostas,' she said, stretching out her arms as if to give him a hug. 'I am Merjan. I'm from Beirut, but I've been here for so long, I consider myself an honorary Cypriot. Welcome, darling.'

'Thank you.' Kostas gave a nod, slightly thrown by this effusive reception from a stranger.

'Look at you!' Merjan said. 'You've become too English, haven't you? You need to spend more time in the Mediterranean. Get back to your roots. David says you left the island as a boy.'

Seeing the surprise on Kostas's face, she chuckled. 'My customers tell me lots of things. Come, let me take you to your friends.'

Merjan guided him to a table at the back, by the window. The place was bustling, the customers loud and boisterous, and with each step he took into the heart of the tavern, Kostas felt the hair on the back of his neck bristle. He could not help being reminded of The Happy Fig, the similarities were too obvious for him to ignore. He had never been in a place like that since, and it felt a betrayal to be here now.

Only when he tore his gaze away from his surroundings did he get a proper view of the table he would be joining. Three people sat there. Defne was wearing a teal dress, her sea of dark hair falling to her shoulders in rebellious waves. She had changed her earrings to a pair of pearl teardrops, and they caught the light, dancing in that quiet space between her ears and her chin. As Kostas reached the table, he realized a moment too late that he had been staring at Defne and no one else.

'Oh, there he is!' exclaimed David. 'Thank you for delivering him safe and sound.' Seizing Merjan's hand, he planted a kiss on it.

'No problem, darling. Now you take good care of him,' said the owner, before gliding away with a wink.

Kostas pulled out the empty chair next to David and sat down, opposite a woman with a wide forehead and hooded grey eyes behind horn-rimmed glasses. She introduced herself as Maria-Fernanda.

'We were chatting about exhumations, as you do,' said David, raising a glass of raki, of which he seemed to have already had a few.

The others were drinking wine. Kostas poured himself a glass. It tasted of tree bark, sweet plums and dark earth.

'Maria-Fernanda is from Spain,' said Defne. 'She played a big role in documenting atrocities from the Civil War era.'

'Oh, thank you, but we were not the first,' said Maria-Fernanda with a smile. 'A lot of progress was made in forensic fieldwork in Guatemala in the 1990s, thanks to the relentless efforts of human rights activists. They managed to discover a large number of mass graves where political dissidents and indigenous rural Maya communities had been buried. Then there is Argentina. Unfortunately, until the late 1980s, exhumations weren't included in conflict resolution. Such a shame.'

David turned to Kostas. 'The Nuremberg trials were a landmark. That's when people realized how random and widespread violence actually is. Neighbours turning against neighbours, friends selling out friends. Now that's a different kind of evil, one that we still haven't come to grips with as humanity. It's a difficult subject across the world – the acts of barbarity that happen off the battlefield.'

'It's hard work,' said Maria-Fernanda. 'But I always say to myself, at least we're not combing the ocean.'

'She's talking about Chile,' said Defne, glancing at Kostas. 'Thousands disappeared under Pinochet. Secret flights over the Pacific Ocean and lakes, packed with prisoners – tortured, drugged, many still alive. They tied railway tracks to the victims, hurled them from Puma helicopters, down into the waters. The officials always denied it, but there was an army report and it said they had "hidden" the bodies in the ocean. *Hidden!* Arseholes!'

'How did people find out the truth?' Kostas asked.

'Pure coincidence,' Maria-Fernanda replied. 'Or God's doing, if you believe in such things. One of the victims washed up on the beach. I'll always remember her name: Marta Ugarte. She was a teacher. Horribly beaten, tortured, raped. She, too, had been tied to a chunk of metal and thrown out of a helicopter, but somehow the wire came loose and the body surfaced. There is a picture of her taken right after she was fished out of the sea. Her eyes are open, looking straight into your soul. So that's how people woke up to the fact that there were many more buried under the waters.'

Kostas balanced his wine glass between his palms, feeling the round, flawless heft of it. He peered through the crimson liquid. Not at his companions around the table but into a part of his heart that he had kept closed for so long. He found old sorrows there, some his own, others of the land where he was born, the two inseparable now, layered and compressed like rock formations.

Lifting his head, he asked Maria-Fernanda, 'Where else have you worked?'

'Oh, all around the world. Yugoslavia. Cambodia. Rwanda . . . Last year I took part in the forensic exhumations in Iraq.'

'And how did you and Defne meet?'

Defne answered him. 'I knew about Maria-Fernanda, I wrote to her. She responded so graciously and invited me to Spain. Last summer, I got a grant and visited her. She and her team carried out three exhumations: Extremadura, Asturias, Burgos. Each time, Spanish families gave their dead a beautiful funeral. It was very touching. After I returned to Cyprus to join the CMP, we invited Maria-Fernanda to observe our methods. And here she is!'

Maria-Fernanda slid an olive into her mouth and chewed slowly. 'Defne was amazing! She came with me to talk to the families, she cried with them. I was so moved. You don't share a language, you think, and then you realize, grief is a language. We understand each other, people with troubled pasts.'

Kostas took a slow, deep breath and the room seemed to cradle him – or maybe it was her words. 'Do they ever appear in your dreams, the things you see during the day? Forgive me if it's too personal a question.'

'No, it's fine. I used to have disturbing dreams,' Maria-Fernanda said, taking off her glasses and rubbing her eyes. 'But not any more. Or perhaps I just can't remember.'

'*Injuriarum remedium est oblivio*,' said David. 'Oblivion is the remedy for injuries.'

'But we have to remember in order to heal,' Defne objected. She turned to Maria-Fernanda and said, with a tenderness in her tone, 'Tell them about Burgos.'

'Burgos was the heartland of Francoism. There were no battle lines there. That means, all the bodies we found in mass graves belonged to civilians. Most of the time the families did not want to talk about the past. They just wanted to give their loved ones a decent burial – dignity.'

Maria-Fernanda sipped her water before continuing. 'One day, I took a cab to an excavation site. I was running late. The cabbie seemed like a nice fellow – friendly, funny. After a while we passed by this place, Aranda de Duero. A charming town. And the driver looked at me in the mirror and said, "That's Red Aranda, full of troublemakers. Our guys executed many people, young and old, it had to be done." And I suddenly realized this man I had been chatting with about the weather and random stuff, this father of three, who proudly displayed photos of his family on the dashboard, was someone who supported the mass murder of civilians.'

'What did you do?' asked David.

'There wasn't much I could do. I was alone on the road with him. I didn't talk to him for the rest of the journey. Not a single word. Once we arrived, I paid his money and left without even looking at him. He understood why, of course.'

David lit a pipe and exhaled, gesturing towards Defne through the smoke. 'What would you have done in her situation?'

They all looked at Defne. In the candlelight, her eyes gleamed like burnished bronze.

She said, 'I don't mean to sound moralistic. Forgive me if I do. But I think I'd tell that bastard to stop the bloody car and let me out! I might have to hitchhike afterwards – whatever. I'd think about that later.'

Kostas studied her face, knowing she was telling the truth. In that fleeting instant, like a night traveller who makes out a distant shape when lightning flashes, he had a glimpse of the girl she once was, her rage in the face of injustice, her sense of righteousness, her passion for life.

David puffed on his pipe. 'But not everyone needs to be a warrior, my dear. Otherwise we'd never have poets, artists, scientists . . .'

'I disagree,' said Defne into her wine glass. 'There are moments in life when everyone has to become a warrior of some kind. If you are a poet, you fight with your words; if you are an artist, you fight with your paintings . . . But you can't say, "Sorry, I'm a poet, I'll pass." You don't say that when there's so much suffering, inequality, injustice.' She drained her drink and topped it up. 'What about you, Kostas? What would you have done?'

He drew in a breath, feeling the weight of her gaze. 'I don't know. Until I'm in that situation, I don't think I can really know.'

A half-smile flickered across Defne's face. 'You were always reasoned, logical. A close observer of the marvels of nature and the errors of the human race.'

There was an edge to her tone, impossible not to notice. It darkened the mood around the table.

'Hey, let's not judge each other now,' said David with a flippant

216

wave of his hand. 'I'd have probably stayed in the car for the full trip and carried on nattering with the cabbie.'

But Defne was not listening. She was looking at Kostas and only at him. And Kostas saw that behind her sudden anger were all the words that had been left unsaid between them, swirling inside her soul like unsettled flakes in a snow globe.

His eyes fell to her hands, which had changed with the years. She used to love to paint her fingernails, each polished to a pearly pink. She didn't do that any more. There was a slight unkemptness now, her nails short and uneven, the cuticles peeling. When he looked up again, he found her studying him.

His chest rising and falling with rapid breaths, Kostas leaned forward and said, 'There is another question we could consider, perhaps a more difficult one. What would we do, each of us, if we were young people in 1930s Burgos, caught up in the midst of civil war? It's easy to claim in hindsight we'd do the right thing. But, in truth, none of us knows where we would be when the fire is raging.'

The waiter arrived then with their main courses, breaking the ensuing silence: grilled lamb skewers with feta and mint, fish casserole in white wine, roasted garlic butter shrimps, seven-spice chicken and Lebanese jute leaf stew . . .

'Every time I come to Cyprus, I gain ten pounds,' said David, patting his belly. 'That's one thing Greeks and Turks can agree on.'

Kostas smiled, even though just then he was thinking they were all drinking too fast. Especially Defne.

As if she had read his thoughts, she pointed her glass towards him and said, 'Okay, then. Let's change the subject – too gloomy. So tell us, Kostas, what brought you back? Was it your beloved trees or mosses and lichens?'

It occurred to him then that, just as he had been collecting information about her all these years, she, too, had been digging into what he did for a living. She knew about his books.

Cautiously, he replied, 'Partly work. I'm looking into whether, and how, fig trees can help the loss of biodiversity across the Mediterranean.'

'Fig trees?' Maria-Fernanda raised her eyebrows.

'Yes, they support the ecosystem more than almost any other plant, I'd say. Figs feed not only humans, but also animals and insects for miles around. In Cyprus, deforestation is a serious problem. On top of that, in the fight against malaria, when they dried out the marshes in the early twentieth century, they planted lots of eucalyptus and other Australian plants. These are non-native invasive species that do enormous damage to the natural cycles here. I wish the authorities had paid more attention to local fig trees . . . Anyway, I don't want to bore you with the details of my research.' As always, Kostas worried that people would find his work dull.

'We're not bored at all,' said David. 'Carry on, tell us more. A fact about a fig tree beats a mass exhumation any day.'

'Butterflies feed on figs, don't they?' Defne chimed in. As she said this she unwrapped the leather band around her wrist, revealing a little tattoo on the inside of her arm.

'Oh, how pretty!' enthused Maria-Fernanda.

'That's a painted lady,' said Kostas, trying not to show his surprise. When he last knew her she didn't have the tiniest tattoo, anywhere. 'Every year they come from Israel and rest in Cyprus. Then some go to Turkey, others to Greece. Yet others travel from North Africa straight into Central Europe. But this year something unusual is going on. The ones that left North Africa changed their route. Nobody can say why. All I know is they're heading towards the island, and they'll join the others who normally come this way. If our assumptions are correct, we're going to see a massive migration of butterflies in the next few days. I expect them to be everywhere along the coast – the Greek side and the Turkish side. Millions of them.'

'That sounds fascinating,' said Maria-Fernanda. 'I hope they'll arrive before I leave.'

The desserts were finished, coffee had been served, but Defne had ordered a new bottle and did not seem to want to slow down.

'When I last saw you, you were neither a drinker nor a smoker,' said Kostas, a low, pulsing sensation in his temples.

The tiniest smile forming at the corners of her lips, she glanced at him, her gaze unfocused. 'A lot has changed since you left.'

'Hey, I'll join you, Defne,' said David as he signalled to the waiter for another glass of raki.

'But you don't seem to drink much,' said Maria-Fernanda to Kostas. 'You don't smoke, I have a feeling you don't lie . . . You never do anything wrong?'

Defne uttered a small sound that might have been disbelief or acknowledgement. A blush tinged her cheeks when she noticed the others looking at her.

'Well, he did once,' she said with a half-shrug. 'He left me.'

An expression of panic crossed Maria-Fernanda's face. 'Oh, I'm sorry. I didn't know you two were together.'

'I didn't know either.' David raised his hands.

'I didn't leave you!' Kostas said, realizing, too late, that he had raised his voice. 'You never even answered my letters. You told me not to contact you any more.'

The blush on her cheeks deepening, Defne waved her hand dismissively. 'Don't worry, I was kidding. It's water under the bridge.'

No one said a word for a few seconds.

'Well, here's to youth, then!' said David, raising his glass.

They all followed suit.

Defne set her drink down. 'Tell us, Kostas, do they have bones?'

'Sorry?'

'Butterflies. Do they?'

Kostas swallowed; his throat was raw. He stared at the candle, burned down to a stub.

'A butterfly's skeleton is not inside its body. They don't have a hard framework protected beneath soft tissues the way we do; in fact, their entire skin is an invisible skeleton, one might say.'

'How does that feel, I wonder,' mused Defne. 'Carrying your bones on the outside, I mean. Imagine Cyprus as a huge butterfly! Then we wouldn't have to dig the ground for our missing. We would know we are covered with them.'

No matter how many years would pass, Kostas would never forget that image. A butterfly island. Beautiful, eye-catching, adorned with a splendour of colours, trying to take off into the air and flutter freely across the Mediterranean, but weighed down, each time, by its wings encased in broken bones.

When the four of them finally left the tavern, in need of fresh air, they meandered along the serpentine streets, inhaling the aromas of jasmine and cedar. The moon was a few days from full, cloaked in a feathery tulle of cloud. As they passed by stone houses with latticed windows, they resembled cut-outs from a shadow display against the anaemic light from the street lamps.

That night, back in his hotel room, Kostas had a disturbing dream himself. He was in an anonymous town that could have been anywhere – Spain, Chile or Cyprus. Beyond the dunes rose a fig tree and, behind that, an empty street littered with what looked like detritus. He inched closer to check what it was, and only then did he discover, to his horror, that it was dying fish. Frantically, he found a bucket of water. He sprinted back and forth, trying to collect as many fish as he could, but they kept escaping from his fingers, flipping their tails, gasping for air.

In the distance he saw a group of people, staring at him. They were all wearing butterfly masks. Defne was nowhere to be seen. But when Kostas woke up in the middle of the night, his heart racing, he had no doubt she was somewhere in his dream, behind one of those masks, watching him.

Restless Mind

Cyprus, early 2000s

Early next morning, Kostas found the team at the site, already immersed in work. The committee had received another tip-off overnight, and once they were done here, they would start digging by a dried-out riverbed about forty-five miles away from Nicosia. From their exchanges, Kostas sensed that they preferred to search in backwoods and rural areas. In cities and towns, passers-by always came to watch, asking questions, making comments, some of which could be intrusive, even incendiary. If there was a find, emotions rose. Once, somebody had fainted and they'd had to attend to her. The members of the CMP would rather work alone, surrounded by nature, with trees as their only witnesses.

When they took a coffee break, Kostas and Defne sat together by a wild oleander bush, listening to the cicadas whirr in the rising heat. Defne produced a tobacco pouch and began rolling herself a cigarette. Kostas noticed she was carrying David's silver cigarette box. A knot gripped his chest as it occurred to him they might have spent the night together. During dinner he had observed, more than a few times, how David looked at her. He tried to quieten his restless mind. What right did he have to think about her love life when they had become strangers not only to each other but also to their former selves?

She inclined her head towards him, so close he could see the blue specks in her dark eyes, a bright cobalt. 'David quit smoking today.'

'He did?'

'Yes, and to prove his point he gave me his case. I'm sure he'll ask for it back by the end of the afternoon. Every few days he quits.'

Kostas couldn't help smiling then. He took a sip from his coffee and asked, 'So how long are you planning to do this?'

'For as long as necessary.'

'What does that mean? Until you find the last victim?'

'Wouldn't that be something? No, I'm not that naive. I know many on both sides will never be found.' Her gaze grew distant. 'But maybe it's not unimaginable. Think about it – when we were younger, if someone had told us the island would be partitioned along ethnic lines, and some day we would have to look for unmarked graves, we wouldn't have believed them. Now we don't believe it can ever be united again. What we think is impossible changes with every generation.'

He listened, crumbling a small clod of earth between his fingers. 'I noticed there are more women than men doing this job.'

'There are many of us – Greek and Turkish. Some excavate, others work in the lab. Then there are psychologists who go and talk to the families. Most of our volunteers are women.'

'Why do you think that is?'

'It's obvious, isn't it? What we do here has nothing to do with politics or power. Our work is about grief – and memory. And women are better than men at both.'

'Men remember too,' said Kostas. 'And men grieve too.'

'Do they?' She scanned his face, noting the catch in his voice. 'Maybe you're right. But, on average, men who lose a spouse remarry way faster than women in the same position. Women mourn, men replace.'

She tucked behind her ear a strand of hair that had come loose. He felt such a strong urge to touch her then that he had to cross his arms, as if worried they might act of their own volition. He thought of how they would meet in secret, surrounded by the vast night, the olive trees looming grey in the glimmer of the rising moon. He recalled how, one evening in the tavern, she asked him for water, and he left her alone for a minute, the night The

222

Happy Fig was bombed. The night, he now suspected, their lives had changed forever.

He glanced at the cigarette in her hand. 'But why are you smoking, *ashkim*? Don't you know it's just a few puffs that disappear as soon as you exhale?'

Defne narrowed her eyes. 'What?'

'You don't remember, do you? That's what you said to me when you saw me smoking that one time.'

He could see now in her expression that she did remember. Caught by surprise, she tried to brush it off with a laugh.

'Why did you not answer any of my letters?' asked Kostas.

A pause. 'There was nothing to write.'

Kostas swallowed down the lump in his throat. 'Someone from the past got in touch with me recently, a doctor . . .'

He studied her face, but her expression was hard to read.

'Dr Norman found my contact details after he saw my name in a newspaper. I had a new book out, there was an interview, and that's how he became aware of me. We met, we talked. He mentioned something in passing that made me realize there are things that happened in the summer of 1974 that I know nothing of. I had to come to Cyprus – to see you.'

'Dr Norman?' she said, raising an eyebrow slightly. 'What did he tell you?'

'Not much, really. But I put two and two together. He told you handed him a note and asked him to give it to me if anything went wrong. He kept that note in his pocket, but sadly lost it. He didn't know what it said because he had never read it, since it was private. Don't know whether I believe him. Now I'm trying to understand why a young woman would have to meet a gynae-cologist in the summer of 1974 – at a time when the island was in flames and there were soldiers everywhere . . . unless there was something unexpected . . . urgent . . . an unwanted pregnancy. An abortion.' He looked at her with sorrow. 'I want you to know that ever since I figured this out I feel awful. I feel guilty. I'm so sorry. I should have been with you. All these years I had no idea.'

Just then, someone in the team called her name. A new session was about to begin.

Taking a final drag, Defne dropped her cigarette and crushed it with the heel of her shoe. 'All right, let's get back to work. As I said yesterday, we were young. You make mistakes at that age. Horrible mistakes.'

A shiver went right through him. He stood up, took a step towards her but struggled to speak.

'Look,' she said. 'I don't want to talk about this. You must understand, whenever something terrible happens to a country – or an island – a chasm opens between those who go away and those who stay. I'm not saying it's easy for the people who left, I'm sure they have their own hardships, but they have no idea what it was like for the ones who stayed.'

'The ones who stayed dealt with the wounds and then the scars, and that must be extremely painful,' said Kostas. 'But for us . . . runaways, you might call us . . . we never have a chance to heal, the wounds always remain open.'

She tilted her head, considering, and then hastily said, 'Sorry, I need to work now.'

Kostas watched her walk away to join the others. He feared that was the end of it – the end of them. Clearly, she did not wish to discuss the past. She must want to keep their relationship distant, if cordial. He thought he would have to return to his research, and then to England, back to his old life, the repetitions and rhythms that suffocated him little by little, but never fast enough. And it could have been that way, if at the end of that afternoon, after hours of digging and cleaning, locks of dark hair escaping her bandana, the smooth olive skin of her forehead touched with dirt, she had not walked back towards him, and said, with perfect calm, 'So why don't I take you out this evening? Just the two of us. Unless you have other plans.'

She knew, of course, he had none.

Picnic

Cyprus, early 2000s

The sun was descending when they met again that evening. She had changed into a long white dress with tiny blue flowers stitched across the chest. The waning light caressed her face, leaving subtle tones on her cheeks like brushstrokes, sprinkling glints of copper over her chestnut hair. In her hand she carried a basket.

'We are going to walk a bit, do you mind?' asked Defne.

'I like walking.'

They passed by souvenir stores and houses with climbing roses across their facades. The whitewashed walls, once plastered with slogans, now glowed clean and lustrous on either side. Everything felt tranquil, peaceful. Islands had a way of deceiving people into believing that their serenity was eternal.

Leaving the busy pavements behind, they were soon wending their way through the outskirts of the city, eyes fixed on the pine-needled path ahead, as if marching into a stiff and parched wind. But there was only the mildest breeze this evening and the air was full of promise. Though his mind was racing, his tongue struggling to find the words he wanted to say, a kind of contentment swept over Kostas. He saw clusters of daffodil garlic, wild mustard, golden thistle, caper bush, their shoots pushing through the dry earth. He focused on the trees as he always did when he felt unmoored: olive, sour orange, myrtle, pomegranate . . . and that one over there, a carob. His mother's voice echoed in his ears: 'Who needs chocolate when you have carob trees, *agori mou*?'

He noticed that Defne not only walked fast but seemed to enjoy doing so. The women he had dated in the past had been usually averse to long treks. They were city dwellers, busy people, always in a hurry. Even those who claimed to like the idea of hiking quickly got bored. Time and again, on these outings, Kostas had found himself annoyed at his partners for not dressing appropriately – their clothes were too thin, their shoes not fit for purpose.

Now, as he tried to keep pace with Defne, he was surprised to see her charge onwards in her flat sandals. She picked her way over rutted fields and dirt roads, clumps of purple flowering heather and yellow gorse brushing and clutching at the hem of her skirt. He followed, tuned into every little sign from her – the ring of her laughter, the depth of her silence – wondering whether in some part of her heart she still loved him.

A partridge rattled from the bushes. A honey buzzard glided and floated on the thermals above, scanning for small mammals on the ground. Thousands of eyes peered from the leaves, eyes made up of tiny light detectors, discerning different wavelengths, clashing realities, reminding Kostas that the world humans saw was only one of many available.

When they reached the hill's summit, they stopped to take in the view. Old stone houses glinted in the distance, red terracotta roofs, an endless, generous sky. If ever there was a centre to this world, it had to be here. It occurred to Kostas that this must be what countless travellers, pilgrims and expats had seen and this was why they had stayed.

Defne opened the basket she had refused to let him carry. Inside was a bottle of wine, two glasses, a tub of figs and tiny sandwiches with various fillings that she had made at home.

'Hope you don't mind having a little picnic with me,' she said as she spread a blanket on the ground.

He sat next to her, smiling. It touched him that she had gone out of her way to prepare all this. As they ate, slowly, savouring every mouthful, just like they had done when they first visited The Happy Fig together, Kostas told Defne about his life in England. A knot formed in his throat when he spoke about Panagiota's death, his difficult and strained relationship with his younger brother, which had become more distant over the years, his inability to return to the island all this time as if scared of what he might encounter here or held back by a lingering spell. He did not mention that, though he had been content with the course of his work, he often felt lonely, but he had an inkling she knew this already.

'You were right. There was a pregnancy,' Defne said after listening to him in thoughtful silence. 'But it's been so long since I forbade myself to think about it that I'm not sure I want to do so now. I'd rather leave it all behind.'

He tried not to ask or say anything, only to understand, to be there for her.

Defne bit her lower lip, pulling at a thin layer of skin. 'You also asked me how long I planned to work with the CMP. I'd like to think until I find Yusuf and Yiorgos. They risked their lives for me, those two men. I don't think you were aware of that.'

'No,' Kostas said, the corners of his mouth pulling down.

'It drives me insane not knowing what happened to them. Every few days I phone the lab to see if they've found anything. There is a scientist there, Eleni – she's very kind but probably sick and tired of my calls.'

She laughed, a brittle sound. There was a sharpness and hardness to it that reminded Kostas of cracked, fractured slabs like broken tiles.

Defne said, 'I shouldn't tell you this, it's really embarrassing, but my crazy sister thinks we should visit a psychic. Meryem made an appointment with some wacky clairvoyant. Apparently, this woman helps bereaved families to find their missing – can you believe it? In Cyprus this is a profession now.'

'Do you want to go?'

'Not really,' she said as she bent down, loosened the soil and eased out a dock weed. Its long tap root trailed from her fingers. The deep, narrow cavity left in the ground resembled a bullet hole. She pushed a finger into the cavity and swallowed hard, her breath catching in her throat. 'Only if you are with me too.'

'I'll come with you.' Kostas leaned over and stroked her hair ever so softly.

Once, he believed they could rise above their circumstances, send their roots upwards into the sky, untethered and released from gravity, like trees in a dream. How he wished he could return them both to that hopeful time now.

'I'll come with you anywhere,' he said. His voice sounded different then, fuller, as if it had risen from somewhere deep inside him.

And even though he suspected that her habitual cynicism might not allow her to believe him, neither did she seem willing to doubt him, and so she retreated into that liminal space between belief and doubt – just like she had on another night in what now felt like another life.

Defne inched closer, burying her head in his neck. She did not kiss him and did not give any indication that she wanted him to kiss her, but she held him tight and her embrace was strong and genuine, and it was all he needed. It filled him, the feeling of her by his side, the pulse of her heartbeat against his skin. She touched the scar on his forehead, a scar so old he had long forgotten about it, a mark left from the day of the heatwave when he had tripped over a wooden crate, desperate to save the bats.

'I missed you,' she said.

In that moment Kostas Kazantzakis knew the island had pulled him into its orbit with a force greater than he could resist and he would not return to England any time soon, not without her by his side.

Digital Incense

London, late 2010s

The day before Christmas, her back turned to the decorated branches – a bundle of twigs Kostas had collected from the garden, spray-painted and trimmed with baubles as a festive tree alternative – Meryem sat slumped on the sofa, unusually silent and withdrawn. She kept peering at her mobile screen with the wounded expression of someone who had suffered an injustice.

'Are you still waiting to get an appointment with that exorcist?' asked Ada as she walked past.

Meryem lifted her head, only slightly. 'No, that's all done. They are expecting us this Friday.'

'Well, thanks for not telling me.' Ada flicked a glance at her aunt but the woman was too distracted to notice.

'Is everything okay?' asked Ada.

'Uhm, I lost something and now I can't find it. I hate technology!'

Ada plopped herself down on the other end of the sofa, holding a novel in her hand – one she had heard a lot about. She had got into it just the night before. Now she lifted her book up so that it hid most of her face, the eyes of Sylvia Plath looking straight into Aunt Meryem from the cover.

A minute passed, Meryem sighed.

'Do you need any help?' Ada asked.

'I'm fine,' replied Meryem curtly.

Ada buried her head in her book. For a while, neither of them spoke.

'Oh, why am I even trying? It's gone!' Meryem rubbed her temples. 'All right, give me a hand, please, but don't judge me.'

'Why should I judge you?'

'Just saying.' Meryem put her phone between them. 'I deleted an app by mistake. I think that's what happened. I'm trying to get it back but I don't want to pay all that money again. What do I do?'

'Let's see. What's it called?'

'I don't know. It has a blue thing on it.'

'That's not very helpful. What's it for, then?'

Meryem smoothed down her skirt. 'Oh, I use it to ward off the evil eye.'

Ada's eyebrows shot up. 'Seriously? There's an app for that?'

'I knew you were going to judge me.'

'I'm just trying to get my head around it.'

'Well, it's a modern world. Everyone is busy. Sometimes you're in a hurry, you don't have time to light incense. Or there is no salt to sprinkle. Or maybe you're in polite company and you can't spit. The app does all of that for you.'

'You mean it burns digital incense, sprinkles digital salt and spits in the air digitally?'

'Yes, kind of.'

Ada shook her head. 'So how much did you pay for this scam?'

'It's a subscription, every month I renew it. And I'm not telling you the amount. Whatever I say, you're going to think it's too much.'

'Of course I will. Don't you see they are taking you for a ride? You and hundreds, maybe thousands of gullible people!'

A quick search revealed dozens of similar apps, some for protection, others to bring good luck, and others to read coffee grounds, tea leaves or wine sediments. Ada found the deleted app and downloaded it again – without paying anything.

'Oh, thank you,' said Meryem, the frown lifting from her features. 'When God wants to please a poor soul, He lets him lose his donkey and helps him find it again.'

Ada traced the lines on the cover of her book, her fingertip tracking down its spine. 'Tell me about my grandmother. Was she like you? Did she fear something bad could happen any time?'

'Not really,' said Meryem, her eyes brightening with the recollection and then clouding over again. 'My mother used to say, even if the entire world goes crazy, Cypriots will remain sane. Because we washed each other's babies. We picked each other's harvests. Wars break out between strangers who don't know each other's names. Nothing bad can happen here. So, no, your grandmother was not fearful like me. She didn't see any of it coming.'

Ada studied her aunt, noticing a slight drop in her shoulders.

'You know what I was thinking? I have this history homework and maybe you could help me with it.'

'Really?' Meryem placed her hand on her chest as if flattered by an unexpected compliment. 'But will I know the answer?'

'It's not a quiz. More like an interview. I'll just ask you a few questions about where you come from, what it was like when you were a young girl, that kind of stuff.'

'I can do that, but don't you think you should ask your father?' said Meryem cautiously.

'Father doesn't tell me much about Cyprus. But you can.'

Thus saying, Ada sat back and grabbed her book again. She spoke from behind the pages of *The Bell Jar*, her voice rough and retreating.

'Otherwise, I'm not coming to that exorcist with you.'

Psychic

Cyprus, early 2000s

Two days later, as the evening prayer reverberated from the nearby mosques in Nicosia, Kostas met Defne and Meryem in front of the Büyük Han. He was surprised to see that the historical inn – built by the Ottomans as a *caravanserai*, converted by the British into a city prison – had become an arts, crafts and shopping centre. At a cafe inside the ancient courtyard they each had a glass of linden tea.

Meryem sighed as she cast Kostas a sidelong glance. She had been unusually silent since they met, but she could not hold back any longer. 'Imagine my surprise when Defne said you were back. I couldn't believe my ears! I told her to stay away from you. I'm saying the same thing to your face. Stay away from her. God knows, you make me nervous, Kostas Kazantzakis. You left her when she was pregnant –'

Eyes glittering, Defne interjected, '*Abla*, stop it. I told you not to bring that up.'

'Okay, okay.' Meryem lifted both hands in the air. 'So, Kostas, forgive me for asking, I know it's rude, but when are you returning to England? Soon, I hope.'

'*Abla!* You promised you'd be nice to him. I'm the one who invited him here.'

'Well, I *am* nice, that's my problem.' Meryem wedged a sugar cube between her teeth and sucked on it intently before speaking again. 'It was always me who covered for you two.'

Kostas nodded. 'I'll always be grateful to you for that. I'm sorry I make you nervous. I know you helped us a lot in the past.'

'Yeah and look where that got us.'

'*Abla*, for the last time!'

Meryem flapped her hand, whether to dismiss or acknowledge the remark, it was hard to tell. She straightened up. 'Now, about today's meeting, let's all agree on the rules first. The psychic we'll be visiting – Madame Margosha – is an important person. She's made quite a name for herself among the clairvoyant community. Whatever you say, don't offend her. This woman is really powerful. She has contacts everywhere, and by that I also mean contacts in the other world.'

Defne placed her elbows on the table and leaned forward. 'How do you know that? You don't know that.'

Meryem carried on heedlessly. 'She's Russian, born in Moscow. You know why she came to Cyprus? She had a dream one day. She saw an island full of unknown graves. She woke up in tears. She said to herself, "I must help these people find their loved ones." That's why she's here. Families go to her to seek help.'

'How magnanimous of her,' muttered Defne. 'And how much does she charge for each act of generosity?'

'I know you don't believe in these things – nor does Kostas – but don't forget you're doing this for your friends. You want to know what happened to Yusuf and Yiorgos, don't you? And I'm doing this for you. So you two must promise me you are not going to be disrespectful.'

'I promise,' said Kostas tenderly.

Defne opened her hands with a smile. 'I'll do my best, sis, but *I'm* making no promises.'

The psychic lived in a two-storey house with wrought-iron window grilles not far from the Green Line on a road that was known as Shakespeare Avenue under British rule. Following the partition, the Turkish authorities had renamed it Mehmet Akif Avenue, after a nationalist poet. But today most people referred to it as Dereboyu Caddesi – the Avenue by the River.

The first thing that struck them when they entered the house was the smell – not altogether unpleasant, but sharp, pervasive. A mixture of sandalwood and myrrh incense, of pan-fried fish and baked potato from lunchtime, and of rose and jasmine sprayed liberally by someone who liked their perfume on the heavy side.

With a curt greeting, the psychic's assistant – a gangly teenage boy – ushered them upstairs into a sparsely furnished room, its wooden floor dappled by the last rays of the sun shining through large, patterned-glass windows.

'I'll be back in a second, please sit down,' the boy said in heavily accented English.

Moments later, the assistant reappeared, announcing that Madame Margosha was ready to see them.

'Maybe I should go alone?' said Meryem anxiously.

Defne raised her eyebrows. 'Make up your mind. You dragged me all the way here and now you want to go in alone?'

'It's okay, you go. We'll wait,' said Kostas.

But no sooner had Meryem disappeared down the corridor than she rushed back, her cheeks flushed. 'She wants to see you both! Guess what? She right away knew we were sisters – and the age difference. She knew Kostas was Greek.'

'And you're impressed?' Defne said. 'Her assistant must have told her. He heard me call you *abla* and he heard me call Kostas by his name – his *Greek* name!'

'Whatever,' said Meryem. 'Can you hurry up? I don't want to keep her waiting.'

The room at the opposite end of the hall was well lit and spacious, though heavily cluttered with objects that looked like they had been accumulated over the course of a long, itinerant life: standard lamps with silk shades and tassels, mismatched chairs, solemn portraits on the walls, tapestries and hangings, credenzas piled with leather-bound books and scrolls, statues of angels and saints, porcelain dolls with glazed eyes, crystal vases, silver candlesticks, incense burners, pewter goblets, china figurines . . .

In the centre of this bric-a-brac stood a willowy blonde woman with prominent cheekbones. Everything about her was neat and angular. Slowly blinking her grey-blue eyes, the colour of a frozen lake, she nodded towards them. Around her neck she wore a pink pearl pendant, the size of a quail's egg. Each time she moved it reflected the light.

'Welcome! Take a seat. Good to see you three together.'

Meryem perched on a chair, while Defne and Kostas chose stools close to the door. Madame Margosha herself sat in a capacious armchair behind a walnut desk.

'So, what brings you here – love or loss? Usually it's one or the other.'

Meryem cleared her throat. 'My sister here, and Kostas there, they had two good friends years ago. Yiorgos and Yusuf. Both men went missing in the summer of 1974. Their bodies have never been found. We want to know what happened to them. And if they are dead, we want to find their graves so that their families can give them a proper burial. This is why we need your help.'

Madame Margosha steepled her fingers together, turning her gaze slowly from Meryem to Defne and from Defne to Kostas.

'So you are here because of loss. But something tells me you are also here because of love.'

Pursing her lips, Defne crossed her legs, then recrossed them.

'Is everything okay?' asked the psychic.

'Yes – no . . . Isn't this kind of obvious?' said Defne. 'I mean, hasn't everyone lost something and isn't everyone looking for love?'

Meryem slid to the edge of her chair. 'Sorry, Madame Margosha, please don't mind my sister.'

'It's fine,' said the psychic, focusing on Defne. 'I like a woman who speaks her mind. Actually, I'll tell you what. I won't charge you anything if you are not satisfied at the end of this session. But if you are satisfied, I'll charge you double my fee.'

'But we can't –' Meryem tried to intervene.

'Deal!' said Defne.

'Deal!' said Madame Margosha, extending her perfectly manicured hand.

For a moment the two women were locked in a handshake while their eyes remained fixed on each other, assessing.

'I can see the fire in your soul,' said Madame Margosha.

'I'm sure you can.' Defne pulled her hand away. 'Can we now focus on Yusuf and Yiorgos?'

Nodding to herself, Madame Margosha twisted and turned the silver ring on her thumb. 'There are five elements that help us in our deepest quests. Four plus one: Fire, Earth, Air, Water and Spirit. Which one would you like me to summon?'

The three of them glanced at each other blankly.

'Unless you think otherwise, I'm going to go with Water,' said Madame Margosha. Closing her eyes, she sat back. Her eyelids were almost translucent, laced with tiny blue capillaries.

For a long minute no one said anything, no one moved. Into the uneasy silence the psychic spoke softly:

'In Cyprus, most of the missing are hidden by a riverbed or a hill overlooking the sea or sometimes inside a well . . . If we can persuade water to help us, we'll find the clues we need.'

Meryem held her breath, inching closer to the edge of her seat.

'I see a tree,' said Madame Margosha. 'What is it – an olive?'

Kostas leaned towards Defne. He didn't have to look at her to sense what she was thinking: that it was a safe bet to mention olive trees in a place like this, where olives were abundant.

'No, not an olive, maybe it's a fig . . . A fig tree, but it's inside, not outside – how strange, a fig inside a room! It's pretty noisy around here – music, laughter, everybody talks over each other . . . What is this place? Is it a restaurant? Food, lots of food. Oh, there they are, your friends! I see them now, they are close, are they dancing? I think they are kissing.'

Despite himself, Kostas felt a shiver at the nape of his neck.

'Yes, they are kissing . . . I'll call out their names and see if they respond. Yusuf . . . Yiorgos . . .' Madame Margosha's breathing slowed down, a rasping sound emanating from her throat. 'Where did they go? They disappeared. I'll try again: Yusuf! Yiorgos! Hey, I'm seeing a baby now. What a lovely little boy! What's his name? Let's see . . . Oh, I get it, he's called Yusuf Yiorgos. He's sitting on a sofa, cushions on four sides. He's chewing on a teether. So cute . . . Oh, no! Oh, poor thing –'

Madame Margosha opened her eyes and stared at Defne. Only at her. 'You sure you want me to continue?'

Fifteen minutes later, the three of them were back on the Avenue by the River. Defne sprinted ahead, her lips pressed tightly into a line, Kostas followed with measured steps and behind them trailed a shaken-looking Meryem. They stopped in front of a jewellery store, now closed. The neon lights from the window, mixed with the glittering reflections of gold bangles, bracelets, necklaces, sharpened their features.

'Why did you do that?' Meryem said, wiping her eyes with the back of her hand. 'You didn't have to upset her. She was going to tell us.'

'No, she wasn't.' Defne pushed her hair out of her face. 'That woman was a charlatan. She was feeding us back the information we gave her. She says, "I see a big, bright kitchen, it could be a house or a restaurant . . ." Then you chip in: "It must be a tavern!" So she says, "Yes, yes, it's a tavern." And you are impressed by that?'

Meryem looked away. 'You know what hurts me the most? The way you treat me as if I don't have any brains of my own. You are clever, right, and I'm not. I'm conventional, traditional. Domestic Meryem! You belittle me and your family. Your own roots! Baba adores you, but he was never good enough for you.'

'That's not true.' Defne placed her hand on her sister's arm. 'Look –'

Meryem stepped back, her chest heaving. 'I don't want to hear it. Not now. I just need to be on my own, please.' She hurried away, the lights along the avenue glancing off her long auburn hair.

Alone with Kostas, Defne peered at him, finding his face half hidden in shadow, his expression one of deep thought. She threw her hands up in the air.

'I feel awful. Why am I always like this? I botched it, didn't I? Meryem is right. After you left, things got tricky at home. I was unhappy all the time and I took it out on my parents. We were always quarrelling. I called them old-fashioned, narrow-minded.'

Kostas shifted on his feet.

'Hey. Let me buy you a drink,' Defne said when she realized he was not going to say anything. 'Let's get gorgeously drunk! I've all this money we didn't pay the psychic.'

Kostas surveyed her face, his concentration absolute. 'Don't you think you should tell me?'

'What?'

'That woman talked about a little boy – Yusuf Yiorgos. I can never imagine a child on this island baptized with a Greek and Turkish name. Impossible. Unless it was you who gave birth to that baby . . .'

She averted her eyes, but only for a second.

'When I learned about the pregnancy, I assumed there had been an abortion. But now I realize maybe I was wrong. Was there or wasn't there? Talk to me, Defne.'

'Why are you asking these things?' she said as she opened her handbag and fished out a cigarette but did not light it. 'Don't tell me you believe in that psychic crap. You are a scientist! How can you take any of this seriously?'

'I don't care about the psychic, I care about what happened to our baby.'

She flinched when he said that, as if she had touched a hot iron.

Kostas said, 'You had no right to hide the pregnancy from me.'

'I had no right? Really?' Defne's stare hardened. 'I was eighteen years old. On my own. Scared out of my wits. I had nowhere to go. If my parents found out, I had no idea what would have happened. I was ashamed. Do you know how it feels to find out you're pregnant and you can't even go out and ask for help? There

238

were soldiers everywhere. In a divided city, at the worst time, the radio blaring, day and night, "Stay at home!", and there are new emergency measures every hour, and you don't know what tomorrow will bring, and there is panic everywhere, people are attacking each other and dying out there, do you know what it's like to try to hide a pregnancy when the world feels like it's collapsing and you have no one to talk to? Where were you? If you weren't there then, you have no right to judge me now.'

'I'm not judging you.'

But she had already walked away.

In the harsh neon light from the store, Kostas stood still, seized by a sense of helplessness so profound that, for a second, he couldn't breathe. Absently, his gaze fell on the window he was standing by, raking the gold and the silver neatly arrayed on glass shelves: rings, bracelets, necklaces bought to mark weddings, birthdays, happy anniversaries – all that they had missed out on this whole time.

She didn't want to talk to him but he needed to learn the truth. Tomorrow morning, first thing, he would call Dr Norman and ask him what had happened in the summer of 1974 when he was miles away.

Not Your Djinni

London, late 2010s

The storm now over, the sky had faded to a pale grey, though still tarnished around the edges like an unwanted photograph tossed into a fire. In the afternoon, Ada and her aunt left the house on the pretext of going shopping, but in reality to visit the exorcist.

'I still can't believe I've agreed to this,' Ada murmured as they headed towards the tube station.

'We're extremely lucky he's agreed to see us,' said Meryem, her wedged heels clacking behind her.

'Well, it's not like the guy had a waiting list.'

'As a matter of fact, he did. The earliest appointment was two and a half months away! I had to use all my charms over the phone.'

They got off at Aldgate East, where they had a brief stopover at a coffee shop and ordered two drinks – a chai latte for Ada, a white chocolate mocha with double cream for Meryem.

'Remember, not a whisper to your father. He'll never forgive me. Promise?'

'Don't worry, I wouldn't tell him about this! Dad will be disappointed in me if he finds out I'm wasting my energy on hocus-pocus. We are bound in shame and secrecy!'

By the time they reached the address it was almost three o'clock, the sun not even a possibility in the leaden sky.

The bustling street was lined with leafless plane trees. There were new-build flats, curry houses, pizza chains, halal restaurants, pashmina and sari stalls, shops that had been owned by successive waves of immigrants, from French Huguenots and Eastern European Jews to Bangladeshi and Pakistani communities. In the kebab shops slabs of meat slowly revolved in the windows, lost in a trance of their own, like the last guests at a party that had gone on for too long. Meryem studied her surroundings with fascination, both puzzled and delighted by this London that she had never known existed.

Walking in the opposite direction to the traffic, they arrived at a semi-detached red-brick house. There was no bell, only a brass knocker in the shape of a scorpion with a raised tail, which they rapped firmly.

'Someone likes to show off,' said Ada, inspecting the fancy knocker with faint distaste.

'Shush, watch your words,' whispered Meryem. 'There is no joking around holy men.'

Before Ada could reply, the door opened. A young woman greeted them. She wore a lime-green headscarf and a dress in a similar shade that reached her ankles.

'*Assalamu alaikum,*' said Meryem.

'*Walaikum salaam,*' said the woman with a curt nod. 'Come on in. We were expecting you earlier.'

'Severe delays on the tube,' said Meryem, omitting to mention the shops she had insisted on visiting along the way.

There were shoes of various sizes tidily lined up at the entrance, all pointing towards the front door. From upstairs came the sound of children quarrelling, the rhythmic thump of a ball. A baby cried somewhere down the corridor. A subtle smell hung in the air – of cooking, old and new.

Meryem's steps halted briefly. Her face fell.

Ada looked up at her aunt curiously. 'What happened?'

'Nothing. I just remembered taking your mum to this famous psychic in Cyprus, long ago. Your dad also came with us.'

'No way! Really – my father agreed to that?'

But there was no time to chat. They were ushered into a room at the back. Inside, rows of plastic chairs faced forward; framed prayers in Arabic hung on the walls. A family of four huddled in a corner, speaking among themselves in hushed tones. Sitting by the door was an elderly woman knitting what looked like a sweater – so tiny it had to be for a doll. Ada and Meryem took the seats beside her.

'First time, right?' the woman said with a knowing smile. 'Is it for the youngster?'

Meryem gave a slight shake of her head. 'How about you?'

'Oh, we've been coming here for years. We tried everything – doctors, pills, therapies. Nothing helped. Then someone recommended us this place. May Allah reward them.'

'So you are saying it works?' Meryem asked.

'It does, but you need to be patient. You are in good hands. This is where all the *majnun* are cured.'

The sound of a scream from the next room cut through the air.

'Don't worry. That's my son,' the woman said, pulling at a strand of yarn. 'He also screams at night in his sleep.'

'Then maybe it's not working,' Ada suggested.

Meryem frowned slightly.

But the woman did not seem offended. 'The problem is there was more than one djinn molesting him. The sheikh removed ten of them, bless his heart, but there is still one more. Then my son will be free.'

'Wow,' said Ada. 'Ten djinn, one more to go. He could have his own football team.'

Meryem's frown deepened.

But once again the woman didn't seem to mind. That's when it occurred to Ada that in the eyes of this stranger, she, too, was one of the *majnun*, and as such she could say crazy things and do even crazier things, and would still be forgiven. What latitude! Perhaps in a world bound with rules and regulations that made little sense, and usually privileged a few over the many, madness was the only true freedom.

In a little while, they were summoned in to see the exorcist.

The room was sparsely furnished – a red settee stretched along one wall, on top of a rug in shades of jade and blue. Strewn here and there were embroidered cushions. A low round coffee table squatted in the centre and, next to it, a basket crammed full of glass bottles and jars.

On the opposite wall was a fireplace that seemed to be a later addition, its tiles chipped, its mantel a slab of cracked marble. A decorative kilim hung above, a woven depiction of a bazaar: stalls piled with spices; a peacock strutting about, displaying the magnificence of his feather fan; men clad in oriental costumes perched on wooden stools, some sipping coffee, others puffing on hookah pipes. The picture looked less like an actual place than someone's imagined likeness of the Middle East.

In the centre of this scene sat, cross-legged, the man who they presumed must be the exorcist. His sunken eyes and angular face were framed by a short, round beard. He did not stand up to greet them. Nor did he shake their hands. Nodding, he gestured to them to take their places on the rug, across from him.

'So who's the patient?'

Meryem cleared her throat. 'My niece, Ada, has been having some problems. The other day at school, she screamed in front of the entire class. She couldn't stop.'

Ada shrugged. 'It was history. Everybody feels like screaming in Mrs Walcott's class.'

If the exorcist got the joke, he did not offer a smile. 'It sounds like the work of the djinn,' he said solemnly. 'They are cunning. First, they seize the body. The weakest link. People do unexpected things – some speak gibberish at a serious meeting, others dance in the middle of a busy road or, like you, they scream . . . If left untreated, it gets worse. The djinn conquer the mind. That's when depression kicks in. Anxiety, panic attacks, suicidal thoughts. Then the djinn go after the soul. That's the last fortress.'

Ada flicked a glance at her aunt and found her listening intently.

'But God is merciful, where there is illness, there is cure,' said the exorcist.

As if on cue, the door opened and the same young woman strode in, carrying a tray loaded with items: a silver bowl of water, a pot of black ink, a piece of paper yellowed around the edges, a pinch of salt, a sprig of rosemary and a quill. She set the tray before the man and retreated to a corner, avoiding eye contact. Was she the exorcist's apprentice, Ada wondered, and what kind of a job was that – like a magician's assistant, minus the glitter and the applause?

'You need to focus,' said the man, surveying Ada. 'I want you to look into the water in this bowl – when you hear me pray, don't move, don't blink, stay still. If we are lucky, you are going to see the face of the djinni that's been pestering you. Try to learn its name. That's important. Once we know the culprit, we can get to the bottom of this problem.'

Ada's eyes narrowed. A part of her wanted to get up and run away. Another part was curious to see what would happen.

Meanwhile, the exorcist dipped the quill in the ink, scribbled a prayer seven times. He folded the paper and dropped it into the bowl before adding the salt and the rosemary. Pulling an amber rosary out of his pocket, he began to thumb the beads as he prayed, his voice rising and falling with each breath.

Ada stared into the water, now murky with swirling ink, and did her best to keep her gaze still, waiting for a sign, for a mystery to unravel. Nothing happened. The sound of the children playing upstairs, the *click-clack* of the rosary beads, the steady sibilant murmur in Arabic . . . It felt meaningless to be sitting here, hoping for a miracle. But more than that, it felt absurd. She closed her mouth, only too late. A loud, nervous chuckle escaped her throat.

The exorcist stopped. 'No use. She can't concentrate. The djinn won't allow.'

Meryem inched closer to Ada. 'Did you see anything?'

'I saw a treasure chest,' Ada whispered. 'I know where the gold is buried. Let's go!'

'As I said, the djinn are clever,' remarked the exorcist. 'They are playing with her mind. They know they can rule over humans only if we fear them. That's why they hide themselves.'

Ada thought about her father then, who always said that knowledge was the antidote to fear. Maybe the exorcist and the scientist could reach an agreement on this one issue.

'We'll have to try a different approach.' The man beckoned to the girl in the corner. 'Jamila, come here.'

He made the two girls sit on cushions opposite one another and dropped a shawl over both their heads, down to their shoulders. On each side, he set smouldering wood chips, soaked in perfumed oil, wafting a pungent smell of oud and musk.

Under the shawl, Ada studied the girl up close as though she were her own reflection in a distorted mirror. She recognized something of herself in Jamila, a trace of her own awkwardness. She could now see the physical resemblance between the exorcist and the girl. They were father and daughter. How had she missed it before? In another universe, they could have been born to each other's families: the daughter of the scientist and the daughter of the exorcist. If she had, would she be a completely different person or would she still be the same?

Did Jamila also suffer from bouts of sadness and feelings of worthlessness, Ada wondered? Did subsequent generations ineluctably start where previous ones had given up, absorbing all of their disappointments and unfulfilled dreams? Was the present moment a mere continuation of the past, every word an afterword to what had already been said or left unsaid? Strangely, the thought was both comforting and unsettling, it took the burden off one's shoulders. Maybe that was why people wanted to believe in destiny.

'All right,' said the exorcist, his voice more commanding now. 'I'm speaking to you, creature of smokeless fire! Leave Ada alone! If you need a prey, take Jamila instead.'

'What?' said Ada. In one swift move, she pulled the shawl off her head, blinking. 'What's going on?'

'Be quiet, child,' said the exorcist. 'Put the shawl back on. Just do as I say.'

'But why did you say "take Jamila"?'

'Because we want this djinni to come to Jamila. Because she knows how to deal with their kind.'

'No way I'm agreeing to that. That's not fair. Why should she have to deal with my problem?'

'Don't worry. Jamila has done this before. She's well trained.'

Ada scrambled to her feet. 'No, thank you. I'm keeping my djinni.'

'It's not *your* djinni,' said the exorcist.

'Well, whatever, I'm not letting you transfer my bad creature to your daughter just because we pay you money. I'm done here!'

As Ada stood up, waving the incense smoke away with a swish of her hand, she thought she caught in the other girl's face the tiniest trace of a smile.

'It is the djinni talking, don't mind her,' the exorcist said.

Meryem sighed. 'I doubt it. It sounds like Ada to me.'

They still had to pay in full. Whether the djinni was exorcized or not, the fee was due.

Outside, a gentle rain fell, the kind that seemed harmless, too slight to wet anyone, though it always did. Puddles of water glistened on the pavements and the lights of passing cars reflected off the asphalt, momentarily making colours brighter, the world more liquid. The musty tang of fallen leaves hung in the air.

'You cold?' asked Meryem.

'I'm fine,' said Ada. 'Sorry, I embarrassed you.'

'Well, I should have known better. It didn't go well that time I took your parents to a psychic either.' Meryem pulled up her coat collar. Her face softened. 'You know . . . for a moment, in that room, I thought I saw your mum in you. You were just like her.'

There was such tenderness in her aunt's voice that Ada felt her heart constrict. No one had said this to her before. For the first time it occurred to her that her father might be seeing the same thing; every day, he might be witnessing in her gestures, in her speeches, in her anger and passion, reflections of her dead mother. If so, he must find it both heart-warming and heartbreaking.

'Aunt Meryem, I don't think I have a djinni hiding inside me.'

'Probably you are right, *canim*. Maybe it's just . . . you know, it's been extremely hard for you. Maybe we give other names to grief because we are too scared to call it by its name.'

Ada's eyes teared. She felt closer to this woman then than she ever thought was possible. Still, when she opened her mouth what came out was different. 'I'll never forgive you for not coming to my mother's funeral, I want you to know that.'

'I understand,' said Meryem. 'I should have; I couldn't.'

They walked in tandem, people rushing by left and right. Every now and then they stepped on a loose paving stone that splashed mud and left stains on their clothes, though neither of them noticed.

Ancient Soul

Cyprus, early 2000s

Back at the Hotel Afrodit, Kostas couldn't sleep, his mind spinning around everything Defne had said . . . and not said. Towards dawn, he dressed and went downstairs, hoping to find a cup of tea. There was no one at the front desk; just the cat curled up in her basket, chasing wild rabbits in her dreams. Unlocking the door, he slipped out. The rich smell of earth came as a relief after the cramped fustiness of his room.

In the distance, by the undulating hills, he saw acacia trees. Sweet-scented, fast growers. An alien and invasive species from Australia. They had been planted widely across the island, with good intentions no doubt, but little understanding of the local ecosystem and its complex groundwater, which they now were quietly changing and destroying. Kostas knew it wasn't only bureaucrats with barely any grasp of ecology who had caused the problem. Acacia trees were also favoured by illegal bird hunters, who kept planting them solely for this purpose.

A slow mist was rising from the ground, thin and fading like unfounded hopes. He felt a headache coming on and walked faster, hoping the fresh air might help. It was only when he got closer to the trees that he saw, looming in front of him, fine-spun nets suspended in the air, and – strung from them like grisly bunting – trapped songbirds.

'Oh, no! Oh God!'

Kostas began to run.

The net was weighted with blackcaps, warblers, chaffinches, pipits, wagtails, wheatears and those brave merry skylarks, fine songsters, the first in every dawn chorus . . . They had been snared in the depths of the night. Kostas stretched up and tugged down hard on the net, but, secured from all four sides, it would not give way. He could only tear one corner. Frantically, he scanned the surrounding trees. Everywhere he looked he saw sticky lime spread on branches high and low. He was surrounded by dead songbirds, their wings spread out, tangled and motionless, their eyes glazed over, as if encased in glass.

About ten feet down the path, he found a robin glued upside down to a twig, its chest a soft ginger, its beak slightly open, lying inert, though still breathing. Gently, he tried to free the bird, but the adhesive was too strong. His gut coiled as he felt helpless, unable to do anything, unwilling to let go. When, a few seconds later, he realized the bird's heart had stopped, he was overcome with a guilty relief.

Back in London, it had always amazed him how hard robins fought to make themselves heard above the urban clamour, trilling their way through the din of traffic, trains and construction machines. Constant effort with little rest. Distracted by the bright lights in the hours of darkness, many birds assumed they should carry on singing. When one began, the others followed, defending their territories. It cost them enormous energy, not being able to tell where the day ended and the night began. He understood how gruelling life could be for birds in the city, so it felt doubly cruel that they had met their deaths here on an idyllic island.

He knew, of course, that it happened all over the place. *Ambelopoulia*, the caviar of Cyprus: cooked songbirds – grilled, fried, pickled, boiled. Considered a delicacy, a popular dish. South. North. The UN territory. The British military zone. Among the islanders, the older generations regarded it as a harmless tradition and the youth saw it as a way to prove their mettle. Kostas remembered his mother's hands, his mother's face, as she neatly arranged the birds on the worktop before pickling them in jars. *Don't do that, Mama. Don't want to eat them any more.*

But what he was witnessing now was more than a local

custom. In the years of his absence, a black market had sprung up – trafficking dead birds had become a profitable business for international gangs and their collaborators. The birds caught in Cyprus were smuggled into other countries where they would be sold for hefty prices. Italy, Romania, Malta, Spain, France, Russia, as far as Asia . . . Some restaurants displayed them on the menu; others served them on the sly at special rates. And the customers cherished the privilege, it was a matter of pride how many they could consume at one sitting. So the birds continued to be slaughtered, poached indiscriminately. More than two million songbirds were slain in Cyprus every year.

It wasn't only passerines: others, too, got caught in the nets – owls, nightingales, even hawks. After sunrise, in no hurry, the poachers came to check on their prizes – one by one, they went through the birds, killing them with a toothpick to the throat. Those that made money were then placed in containers. As for the birds that made nothing, they were tossed away.

The poachers did not need to shoot the birds, they tricked them with their own songs. Hiding speakers behind bushes across open fields, they played pre-recorded avian sounds to lure their prey. And the birds came; looking for one of their own, they flew straight into the traps, the night closing in on them. Between the darkest hour and the earliest light, while they were snagged in the net, many songbirds broke their own wings in their desperation to escape.

Upon returning to the hotel, Kostas made the call he had been planning since the day before. No one picked up so he left a message on an answering machine.

'*Good morning, Dr Norman, it's Kostas here . . . I'm in Cyprus. I decided to travel after we spoke. Thank you for coming to see me that day, it meant a lot to me. I only wish I had known long before what I know now. But there are things I still can't wrap my head around. I met Defne and . . . Dr Norman, can we please talk? It's important. Please call me back.'*

Leaving his number, he hung up. He took a shower, the cold water like balm on his skin. After a cursory late breakfast, he walked to the nearest police headquarters.

'I want to report an incident.'

At first, they thought he was referring to a crime or a theft and took his visit seriously. When they heard his name and realized he was Greek, they became suspicious and wary of his intentions. But upon learning that his complaint was about the killing of songbirds, amusement flooded the policemen's faces. They promised that they would look into 'the matter' and get back to him, but Kostas knew not to expect a reply any time soon.

Later that afternoon, he visited the British Sovereign Base. The clerk there, a man with a compulsive blink, proved more approachable, though equally unhelpful.

'It's one heck of a mess, I'm afraid. It happens under our very noses. Supposed to be illegal, but that doesn't stop the poachers. It's a huge industry. Last month they nabbed a smuggler at the airport. They found 3,529 birds in his suitcases. That fellow was caught but most never will be.'

'So you're not going to do anything about it?' asked Kostas.

'There are sensitivities. Our presence here is delicate, you must understand. We can't upset the locals. I'll be honest with you. People don't appreciate it when you start asking questions about songbirds.'

Kostas stood up; he had heard enough.

'Look, you destroy one net, they'll put up a new one somewhere else,' said the clerk. 'I need to warn you, some of these gangs are dangerous. This is big money we're talking about.'

Back at the hotel, Kostas asked the woman at the front desk if there was a note for him, hoping for a message from Defne. Nothing. He stayed in his room all evening, mostly sitting on the balcony, trying to read but unable to concentrate, watching the island, knowing that she was out there somewhere, slipped away from him perhaps for a few days, perhaps forever. As the night set in, he thought of the nets that were being erected, invisible to the eye, light and gossamer as corn silk, lethal.

After midnight, he went out again, carrying a knife and a batch of paper. Hiding in the shadows, he destroyed every trap he could find, making sure to slash the fibres. He covered the sticky lime spread on the branches with paper and, when he ran out, he used leaves. He moved fast, sweat running in rivulets down his back. When he could find no more nets and could not walk any further, he returned to the hotel, collapsed on his bed and slept a deep, dreamless sleep.

The following night he went out again, only this time he was caught. The poachers were hiding in the bushes, curious to see the person who was destroying the traps.

There were seven of them, one so young he was almost a schoolboy. They did not feel the need to hide their faces. Kostas saw the hardness in their eyes before they started hitting and kicking him.

The next day, lying in bed, gazing at a crack on the ceiling, he might not have answered the phone had he not been expecting to hear from Dr Norman. Moving with difficulty, he picked up the receiver. It was the receptionist.

'Mr Kazantzakis, hi. You have a visitor. There's someone here who wants to see you. She says her name is Defne.'

Kostas tried to sit up, a spear of pain stabbing his ribcage. A groan escaped his lips.

'Are you all right?'

'Yes,' Kostas rasped. 'Can you please tell her to come upstairs?'

'Sorry, we don't allow unmarried couples in our rooms. You have to come downstairs.'

'But . . .' Kostas hesitated. 'Fine. Tell her I'll be there in a few minutes.'

Step by step, he eased himself downstairs, drawing in shallow breaths, every little move shooting a spasm of agony down his side.

When he entered the lobby, the receptionist gasped in shock. Kostas had arrived back so late the previous night he had managed to drag himself to his room without anyone seeing his pitiful state.

'Mr Kazantzakis! What happened to you? Oh, my God. Who did this to you?' She fluttered her hands frantically. 'Shall we call a doctor? Did you put on ice? You have to put on ice!'

'I'm okay, it's not as bad as it seems,' said Kostas, trying to make eye contact with Defne over the woman's head.

Realizing she was obstructing him, the receptionist moved aside.

Kostas walked towards Defne, who was studying him with an expression of pure sadness. She did not seem surprised and he wondered if she had been expecting something like this to happen, for him to get into trouble. Taking a step forward, she touched his lip, split and swollen, tenderly caressing the raw bruise under his left eye, the shade of a plum left out in the sun.

'This colour brings out your eyes,' she said, the tiniest smile twitching at the corners of her mouth.

He laughed, and that hurt, the cut on his lip burning.

'Oh, darling,' she said and kissed him.

So many thoughts crossed his mind in that instant, followed by a sense of stillness and lightness so pure that he let himself drift as she steered. The smell of her hair, the warmth of her skin, still as familiar as if they had never parted ways and time was merely a breath of wind.

Later, as night fell, Defne managed to sneak into his room, the woman at the front desk having mysteriously disappeared, perhaps by coincidence, perhaps out of kindness or sheer pity for them.

That first time they made love, that first touch after years of separation, felt like a curtain of fog lifting to reveal the naked longing beneath. Finally, the mind, with its endless fears and regrets and sorrows, quietened to a whisper. And it was their bodies that remembered what they had long forgotten, pulsing with a force they had thought could belong only to youth, their youth. The flesh had a power of recall of its own, memory tattooed on skin, layer upon layer.

It is a map, the body of an ex-lover, pulling you into its depths and bringing you back to a part of yourself that you thought had been left behind sometime, somewhere. It is a mirror, too, though chipped and cracked, showing all the ways you have changed; and, like every mirror, it dreams of becoming whole again.

Afterwards, as they lay in bed, her face buried in his chest, he told her about the robin with broken wings. He explained that five billion birds flew to Africa and north of the Mediterranean to spend the winter there and, of these, one billion were slaughtered every year. Therefore, every little bird that she saw in the sky was a survivor. Just like her.

He described what was inside the suitcases of the smuggler who had been stopped and searched at the airport – 3,529 birds in total. It was the 3,530th bird he wanted her to think about. Perhaps a Eurasian skylark, swooping into the night, following its companions, but slowing down at the last second and flying at a tangent just above the reach of the net. What had saved it and not others? The cruelty of life rested not only on its injustices, injuries and atrocities, but also in the randomness of it all.

'It's only humans that do this,' said Kostas. 'Animals don't. Plants don't. Yes, trees sometimes overshadow other trees, compete for space, water and nutrients, battle for survival ... Yes,

254

insects eat each other. But mass murder for personal profit, that's peculiar to our species.'

Having listened to every word intently, Defne rose on her elbow and studied his face, her hair falling on to her bare shoulders.

'Kostas Kazantzakis . . .' she said. 'You are a strange one, I've always thought so. I think the Hittites brought you to this island sometime around the late Bronze Age and they forgot to take you back. When I found you, you were already thousands of years old. And you are full of conflicts, my love, like anyone who has lived that long. One minute you are so gentle and patient and calm, I want to cry. The next minute you are out risking your life, getting beaten by mafia gangs. When you make love to me you sing about songbirds. You ancient soul.'

He said nothing. He couldn't. She was pressing on his ribcage now and it was agony, but he didn't want her to move, not even an inch, so he stayed still and held her tight, trying to ride the surge of pain.

'You are either an unsung hero or a glorious fool, I can't decide,' Defne said.

'An unsung fool, I'm sure.'

Smiling, she kissed him, tracing her finger in circular motions across his chest, drawing little lifebuoys for him to hold on to as he floated and swam in the tenderness of this moment. This time when they made love their eyes never left each other, their moves slow and deliberate, rising in steady waves.

He said her name over and over. With each breath, his muscles, his bones, his entire body ached and pulsed like one throbbing wound, and yet he felt more alive than he had in a long, long while.

PART FIVE

Ecosystem

Fig Tree

The next day the butterflies came. They arrived in Cyprus in unparalleled numbers, pouring into our lives, gushing and swirling in a sweep of movement, like a great aerial river tinted the brightest gold. They specked the entire horizon with their yellow-black spots and sandy-orange shades. They settled on moss-laden rocks and orchids, known to the locals as 'The Holy Virgin's Tears'. They fluttered over latticed windows and weather vanes, and crossed the Green Line with its rusty old NO ENTRY sign. They alighted on a divided island, flitting amongst our deepest enmities as if they were flowers from which to draw nectar.

Of all the *Vanessa cardui* that came to rest on my branches, each with a distinct personality, one remained anchored in my memories. Like many others, this particular painted lady had journeyed all the way from North Africa. As she gave me an account of her travels, I listened to her with respect, knowing what resilient migrants they are, seen almost everywhere across the globe. They can fly for an impressive 2,500 miles. I have never understood why humans regard butterflies as fragile. Optimists they may be, but fragile, never!

Our island, with its blossoming trees and lush meadows, was an ideal place to rest and recharge from the butterfly's perspective. Upon leaving Cyprus, she would wing her way to Europe, whence she would never return, although some day her descendants would. Her children would make the journey in reverse, and their children would take the same route back, and thus it would continue, this generational migration, where what mattered was not the final destination but to be on the move, searching, changing, becoming.

The butterfly passed over groves of almond trees with their

bright petals – white ones producing sweet almonds, and pink ones, bitter almonds – and flittered past fields of alfalfa, following the promise of seductive buddleia. Finally, she found a site that seemed well lit, welcoming.

It was a military cemetery, neatly organized with gravel paths running alongside the headstones, so serene and complete in its isolation that it was almost as if nothing existed outside of it. This was the final resting place of British soldiers who had died throughout the Cyprus conflict – except for the Hindu soldiers, · most of whom had been cremated.

The south of the cemetery was overseen by the Greek Cypriot National Guard. The north and west were guarded by the Turkish army. And both sides were monitored by soldiers at the UN observation post. Everyone was constantly watching each other, and perhaps the dead were watching them all. The headstones were dilapidated and decaying, in need of repair. In the past, when a group of Greek Cypriot builders was brought in to mend them, the Turkish army had opposed their presence. And when a group of Turkish Cypriot workers was called, this time it was the Greek side that objected. In the end the graves were left to slowly crumble away.

The sun caressing her wings, the butterfly hopped from one grave marker on to another, glancing at the names carved on them. She noticed their ages. How young they were, all these soldiers who had come from afar to die here. The First Battalion Gordon Highlanders. The First Battalion Royal Norfolk Regiment.

Then she stumbled across a larger grave – Captain Joseph Lane, murdered by two EOKA gunmen in 1956. The inscription said he had kissed his wife and three-month-old baby goodbye to go to work only moments before he was shot in the back.

There were a number of trees growing around here – pines, cedars, cypresses. A eucalyptus spread its blue-grey leaves over a remote corner. 'Widow-makers', they called them. Eucalypti, charming though they are, have the habit of dropping entire branches, injuring, even killing those foolish enough to camp beneath them. Knowing this, the butterfly flew in the opposite direction. And that's when she discovered something unexpected: infants, row upon row. Almost three hundred British babies had perished on this island, snatched from their parents' arms by a mysterious affliction that to this day no one had been able to fully explain.

When the butterfly shared this with me, I was surprised. One doesn't expect to find babies in a military cemetery. I wondered then how many families returned to the Mediterranean to visit these graves. When islanders meet tourists, we assume they must be here for the sun and the sea, never suspecting that sometimes people travel miles away from home just to be able to mourn.

It was in this section of the cemetery that the painted lady came across a group of gardeners. Cautiously, she landed on a hardy geranium, from where she kept a vigilant eye on them. They were planting flowers in the grave beds – crocuses, daffodils, crown daisies – carefully rationing water, which was scarce.

After a while, the gardeners took a break. Spreading a rug under a pine tree, smartly avoiding the eucalyptus, they sat cross-legged on the ground, speaking in whispers out of respect for the dead. One of them took a watermelon from his bag and cut it into thick slices with his knife. Emboldened by the sweet fragrance, the butterfly drew closer and perched on a nearby grave. As she waited for an opportunity to taste that sugary juice, she looked around, noticing the inscription on the tombstone.

OUR BELOVED BABY

IN MEMORY OF YUSUF YIORGOS ROBINSON

JANUARY 1975 NICOSIA – JULY 1976 NICOSIA

When the painted lady recounted this, I made her repeat everything twice. Was there any chance that, distracted by the promise of watermelon, she may not have remembered things correctly? But I knew they were great observers, attentive to every detail. To make up for my rudeness I offered her my ripest fig. Mature and mushy, for a butterfly can only 'eat' liquid.

That was the day thousands of Lepidoptera filled the skies of Cyprus and one of them alighted momentarily on a branch of mine. It was then that I learned a particular fact that forever after cast a shadow over me. I was now beginning to put together various missing elements of the story, acutely aware of who this baby was and why he had been named after Yusuf and Yiorgos. Because in real life, unlike in history books, stories come to us not in their entirety but in bits and pieces, broken segments and partial echoes, a full sentence here, a fragment there, a clue hidden in between. In life, unlike in books, we have to weave our stories out of threads as fine as the gossamer veins that run through a butterfly's wings.

Riddles

Cyprus, early 2000s

When Kostas woke up the next day, it was to the sound of the telephone ringing. By his side, Defne stirred, her nostrils flaring slightly as if she'd caught a scent in her sleep. Carefully reaching over her slumbering body, he picked up the receiver.

'Hello?' Kostas said in a whisper.

'Oh, hello. It's Dr Norman here.'

Instantly, Kostas drew himself upright, now fully awake. He got out of the bed and walked towards the balcony, pulling the cord with him as far from the wall as it would stretch. He sat on the floor, the receiver wedged between his cheek and shoulder.

'Sorry, I missed your call earlier,' Dr Norman said. 'We were down in our place in the country . . . I only received your message today.'

'Thank you, Doctor. When we spoke in London, I wasn't aware of certain things and couldn't ask you the right questions. But now . . .'

He fell quiet, noticing that Defne had rolled on to her side, the sunlight stealing through the curtains to caress her naked back. He took in a quick breath before speaking again. 'When we met, you told me you tried to help Defne, but you didn't elaborate. I'm assuming you meant you performed an abortion. Am I right?'

The silence stretched on before Dr Norman spoke again. 'I'm afraid I cannot answer this question. I'm bound by confidentiality. I don't exactly know what Defne told you, but I'm not at liberty to divulge personal information about my patients. No matter how many years might have passed.'

'But, Doctor –'

'I'm really sorry, I cannot help on this matter. If you'll allow an old man to speak his mind, I'd advise you to leave this matter behind. It was all a long time ago.'

When Kostas hung up, after a minute or so of strained small talk, he stayed still, staring at the sliver of horizon through the balcony rails.

'Who were you talking to?'

Startled, he whipped around. She had got out of bed, her feet bare, her body half covered with a bedsheet. As soon as he saw her face, he knew she had heard everything.

'It was Dr Norman,' he said. 'He refused to tell me.'

She sat on the only chair on the balcony, not caring that the couple at the front desk might spot her from the patio below. 'Do you have a cigarette?'

He shook his head.

'I know you don't smoke,' Defne said vacantly, 'but I kind of hoped you might have a packet tucked at the bottom of your suitcase. Sometimes people do things that run counter to their nature.'

'Please, Defne . . .' He held her hand, tracing the lines on her palm with his thumb as if searching for the warmth he had found there the night before. 'No more riddles. I need to know what happened after I left Cyprus. What happened to our baby?'

In her eyes, he watched one emotion overlay another.

'He died,' Defne said, and her voice was flat like a wall. 'I'm sorry. I thought he would be safe with this family.'

'What family?'

'An English couple. Reliable, decent people. They desperately wanted a child. It seemed the right thing to do. They promised they would take excellent care of him and I know they did. He was a happy baby. They let me come and see him. They told everyone I was the babysitter. I didn't mind, so long as I could be with him.'

Tears started streaming down her cheeks, even as her face remained still, as if she didn't realize she was crying.

264

Kostas put his head on her lap, burying his face into her scent. Defne raked her fingers through his hair. The space between them grew thinner, a tenderness unfurling where pain had been.

'Will you tell me – everything?' he asked.

And this time, she did.

Summer 1974. The roads were dusty and rough, hard to drive on, the sun scorching, the kind of heat that insinuates itself into your pores and never leaves.

She had tried everything. She had lifted every piece of heavy furniture she could find in the house, jumped from high walls, taken scalding-hot baths and drunk cup after cup of slippery elm, the bitter taste burning down her throat. When one method failed, she embarked on the next. Towards the end of the week, exasperated, she used a knitting needle, pushing the sharp edge inside her, the pain so unexpected, she doubled over as her knees buckled under her weight. Afterwards, on the bathroom floor, she lay shaking, sobbing, her voice jagged like a saw, cutting into her very being. She knew there were midwives in the community who could induce miscarriage, but how could she get their help without her parents finding out? And what would happen if they did? That she was pregnant was shameful enough; that it was by a Greek man, beyond conceivable.

When she reeled out of the bathroom, she found her sister glued to the transistor radio. Meryem cast a sideways glance at her.

'You okay? You look like a wreck.'

'My stomach,' Defne said, her face flushed. 'I must have eaten something bad.'

But Meryem wasn't paying attention. 'Have you heard the news? The Turkish army is here! They've landed in Kyrenia, they're coming.'

'What?'

'The Greeks sent two navy torpedo boats to stop them, but they were hit by the Turkish air force. We are in a war!'

Defne could not process the news immediately, her mind spinning with disbelief. But she understood that soon the streets would be teeming with soldiers, paramilitary groups, armoured vehicles. She knew if she were to get an abortion, now was the only chance to still find a way. In a few days, the roads would be closed, maybe a curfew imposed indefinitely. There was no time to think, no time to doubt. Pocketing all the money she found in her father's jacket, emptying the jar of coins in the kitchen, she left the house without a clue as to where she could go. There were Turkish doctors in the area, but she worried that someone might inform her family. With new barriers springing up between entire neighbourhoods, it was almost impossible to get hold of a Greek doctor. Her only chance was a British physician, but all foreign medical staff were leaving the island.

'I cannot treat you,' said Dr Norman.

He had examined her, asking as few questions as possible. He was kind and avuncular, and seemed to understand the predicament she was in. But he would not help.

'I have money,' Defne said, opening her handbag. 'Please, this is all I have. If it's not enough, I'll work and pay you, I promise.'

He took a long, ragged breath. 'Put that back. This is not about money. Our medical practices are closed. We are not authorized to work. Both my nurses have already returned to England and I'm leaving tomorrow morning.'

'Please.' Her eyes filled with tears. 'I have nowhere else to go. My family will never forgive me.'

'I'm sorry, I cannot take your case,' he said again, his voice thickening.

'Doctor –' She started to explain, but then she stopped, something constricting her chest. With a curt nod, she clutched her handbag, turned her back and walked towards the door, the room suddenly too small to contain her.

He watched her for a few seconds, pressure building behind his eyes, pulsating.

'Wait.' Dr Norman gave an inward sigh. 'There's another plane in two days' time. I suppose I could take that one.'

She stopped, her face etched with something like relief, though not quite. She reached for his hands, crying, all the tension she had been storing up inside finally finding its way out.

'My child, calm down.'

He made her sit; gave her a glass of water. A clock down the hall ticked away steadily, each stroke a heartbeat.

'I have a sister who went through a similar ordeal when she was about your age.' His forehead wrinkled as the memory surfaced. 'She was madly in love, planning to get married. It turned out the man had a family already – he had a wife and five children, can you believe? When he heard she was pregnant, he cut off all ties with her. It was the week before the 1950 general election, wintertime. My sister didn't tell me anything, not until later. She visited some kitchen-table surgery on her own. They treated her roughly. She had life-changing complications afterwards. She could never give birth again. I want to help you because I fear that if I don't, you will end up in a backstreet den.'

Listening to his words, Defne felt dizzy.

'There's one issue, though,' Dr Norman said, his voice still gentle but with a new intensity. 'We have been ordered to close all offices. I will hand over the keys this evening. I cannot perform the procedure here.'

She nodded, slowly. 'I think I know of a place.'

The next day, early evening, the back room of The Happy Fig had been transformed into a makeshift clinic. Yiorgos and Yusuf had tidied away the chairs, put three tables side by side and laid newly laundered tablecloths over them, trying to make everything as clean and comfortable as possible. It had been a whole week since the doors of the tavern had closed to customers. Despite the reports of military clashes and civilian casualties, the exodus of populations from each side of the island and rumours of a permanent partition, the two men, partners for long years, had stayed put, unable to leave Nicosia. Given that they did not want to part ways, where would they go – north or south? The faster the chaos around them swirled, the deeper they had sunk into a state of torpor. When Defne told them about her predicament, they instantly offered help.

Standing in the middle of the room, Dr Norman prepared the chloroform he planned to use as an anaesthetic. He wasn't going to give Defne the usual dose, she was too pale and shaken, and he feared that her frail and stressed body might not withstand it. As he sterilized his instruments, she began to cry.

'My child, be brave,' said Dr Norman. 'It's going to be all right. I'm going to sedate you; you won't feel a thing. But please consider one more time, is this really what you want? Is there no way you can talk to your family? Maybe they'll understand.'

She shook her head as the tears kept rolling down her cheeks.

'Oh, darling Defne, don't c-c-cry.' Yusuf, by her side, caressed her hair. 'You d-d-don't have to do this. Look, we can r-r-raise the baby. You'll always be the mother, people don't need to know. It'll be a s-secret. Yiorgos and I will take care. We'll f-find a way. It'll be all right. What do you s-say?'

But his kind words only made her cry harder.

Yiorgos loped off into the kitchen and returned with a glass of carob juice. Defne refused it; the mere sight of it reminded her of Kostas.

They closed the windows, then opened them again, the heat suffocating despite the ceiling fans. The air outside smelled of citronella, planted to get rid of mosquitoes. Meanwhile, Chico, locked in his cage so that he would not disturb anyone, squawked words picked up from happier days.

'Hello, kiss-kiss! Oh la la!'

And that was when they heard the sound of an engine. A car was approaching, its tyres crunching on the gravel. Then, another one. Customers never drove this far as the tavern was nestled between olive groves, they preferred to park in the clearing about a hundred feet away and walk up the hill.

'I'll go and check,' said Yiorgos. 'Probably one of our regulars hoping to sneak in for a tipple on the sly. I'll tell them to come back another time.'

'Wait for me,' said Yusuf as he joined him.

But it wasn't loyal customers craving a drink at their favourite watering hole. It was a group of strangers – young, grubby, sullen men driving around, blowing off steam, spoiling for a fight, alcohol on their breath. They left their cars – all except one. In their hands, they had sticks and clubs, which they held awkwardly, as if they had forgotten why they had taken them.

'We are closed,' said Yiorgos. There was a note of caution in his voice as he tried to work out their intentions. 'Were you looking for something?'

None of the men said a word in response. Their expressions hardened as their eyes raked the tavern, rage unseating levity. That was when Yusuf noticed something he had initially missed. One of the men was also carrying a can of paint with a brush poking out of it.

Yusuf couldn't tear his gaze from the paint. It was bright pink, the colour of the chewing gum that he had once found stuck on the door with a menacing note. The colour of berries that grew on evergreen shrubs clinging precariously to the side of cliffs, gripping the void dangerously.

Fig Tree

Of all the animals in my ecosystem, there were some I admired and others I quietly disliked, but I don't ever remember regretting meeting anyone as I tried to understand and respect every form of life. Except for once, that is. Except her. I wish I had never known her or that I could, at least, find a way to wipe her from my memories. Even though she is long dead, I still hear that high-pitched sound sometimes, an eerie vibration in the air as though she is fast approaching, buzzing in the dark.

Mosquitoes are humankind's nemesis. They've killed half the humans who ever walked the earth. It always amazes me that people are terrified of tigers and crocodiles and sharks, not to mention imaginary vampires and zombies, forgetting that their deadliest foe is none other than the tiny mosquito.

With its swamps, marshes, peatlands and streams, Cyprus used to be their Eden. Famagusta, Larnaca, Limassol . . . they were everywhere once upon a time. An ancient clay tablet found here read, 'the Babylonian mosquito devil is now in my land; he has slain all the men of my country.' Well, it would have been more accurate if it said, 'she has slain . . . ', as it is the female of the species that causes the carnage, but I guess it's not the first time women have been written out of history.

They have been around forever, though not as long as us trees. Across the world you can find mosquitoes from prehistoric times trapped in our resin or petrified sap, sleeping peacefully in their amber wombs. It is remarkable that they still carry the blood of prehistoric reptiles, mammoths, sabre-tooth tigers, woolly rhinoceroses . . .

Malaria. The disease that decimated multitudes of soldiers and civilians alike. That is until Ronald Ross – the Scottish doctor with a lantern jaw and spiked moustache – made the discovery that physicians had overlooked since the days of Hippocrates. In a humble laboratory in India, Ross cut into the stomach of an Anopheles mosquito and there it was, the evidence he had been seeking. It wasn't swamp gas that carried malaria, but a parasite. Armed with this knowledge, he set out to eradicate the disease across the entire British Empire. It was a fateful day in 1913 when Ross visited Cyprus.

Yet the fight against mosquitoes would have to wait until the end of the Second World War, when a Turkish doctor, Mehmet Aziz, launched the campaign in earnest. Having suffered from blackwater fever as a boy, he had seen first-hand how pernicious it was. Supported by the Colonial Development Fund, he dedicated himself to the cause. What I find remarkable about him is that he paid no attention to the ethnic or religious divisions that were tearing the island apart, and focused solely on saving human lives. Starting in the Karpas Peninsula, Aziz had every breeding place sprayed with insecticide, and then again, to wipe out possible larvae. It took him four arduous years, but he would triumph in the end.

Since then Cyprus has been malaria-free. Yet that didn't mean mosquitoes were eradicated completely. They continued breeding in gutters and cesspools. As they loved hanging around fig trees and had a taste for ripe or rotting fruit, I had made the acquaintance of quite a few over the years.

In the tavern they would hover around every night, molesting the customers. Blindingly swift, they whizzed past, zooming up and down their prey in the time between two heartbeats. To keep them at bay, Yusuf and Yiorgos placed pots of basil, rosemary or lemongrass on each table. And when that didn't suffice, they burned coffee grounds. But as the evening carried on and the customers sweated from the booze and the heat, emanating lactic acid, the pestilential bugs swooped in again. Swatting at them was no solution either. A human's clumsy hands are no match for the speed of their wings. Even so, they are no risk takers. They'll remember the scent of the person who tried to kill them and avoid that person for a while, allowing enough time for their prey to forget their presence. They are patient like that, waiting for the right moment to taste blood.

They attack animals too. Cattle, sheep, goats, horses . . . and parrots. Bitten from beak to claw, poor Chico complained all the time. Frankly, none of this bothered me back then. I had accepted mosquitoes the way they were, not giving them further thought – until, that is, I met her in August 1976. By then The Happy Fig had been closed for almost two years and Chico had long gone. It was just me inside the tavern. I was still waiting for Yiorgos and Yusuf to return. I was waiting faithfully. That summer I yielded my best harvest yet. That's the thing about trees, we can grow amidst the rubble, spreading out our roots beneath the detritus of yesterday. My figs, bursting with flavour, remained unplucked from branches, uncollected from the ground, where they attracted all manner of animals and insects.

The mosquito appeared out of nowhere one midnight and found me, lonely and distressed, yearning for the past. She perched on one of my branches, glancing around nervously as she detected the scent of citronella in the air. Instantly, she took off to evade the scent and landed on another branch on the opposite side.

She told me about her children. Whatever one might think of female mosquitoes, there is no denying they are good mothers. They can consume blood up to three times their own body weight and use it as a prenatal supplement. But the mosquito said that lately she could not properly provide for her eggs as she had been infected by the infamous parasite. Desperately trying to nourish her offspring, she ended up feeding the enemy inside.

This is how I came to learn that recently there had been a surge in reports of malaria across the Mediterranean, an uptick in the number of cases due to climate change and international travel. Mosquitoes had developed resistance to DDT, and the parasites to chloroquine. I wasn't too surprised to hear this, though. Humans lose focus easily. Immersed in their politics and conflicts, they get sidetracked, and that is when diseases and pandemics run rampant. But I was taken aback by what the mosquito shared with me next. She talked about a baby she had bitten several times – Yusuf Yiorgos Robinson. I felt a chill spreading from the tip of my branches down to my lateral roots.

Hundreds of British babies died in the 1960s in Cyprus, the cause still unknown. And when Defne's son, adopted by an English couple, succumbed to acute respiratory distress caused by the insect-borne parasite, he would be buried in the same place, next to the other infants who had lost their lives on this island about a decade before.

A wave of sadness washed over me when I found this out. I tried not to hate the mosquito. I reminded myself that she, too, was a casualty of the parasite, and sometimes what you called a perpetrator was just another name for an unacknowledged victim. But I could not see it that way. I failed to overcome the bitterness and anger that rose up in me. To this day, whenever I hear that buzzing sound in the air my trunk stiffens, my limbs tense up and my leaves tremble.

Soldiers and Babies

Cyprus, early 2000s

On the balcony of the hotel, when Defne stopped speaking, Kostas stood up and put his arms around her, feeling her pain surge through him. For a while the two of them gazed silently at the island stretching out before their eyes. A hawk cried overhead, riding the air currents, miles above the earth.

'Shall I go downstairs to find you cigarettes?'

'No, love. I want to finish. I want to tell you everything – just once – and never talk about that day again.'

He settled back down on the floor, put his head on her lap again. She continued to stroke his hair, her fingers tracing circles on his neck.

'I stayed inside the tavern with Dr Norman. At first, we didn't pay attention to what was going on outside. We assumed it would be over in a minute, whatever it was. We heard a scuffle. Angry voices. Shouting. Swearing. Then it got really scary. The doctor asked me to hide under a table, and he did the same. We waited, trying not to make any noise. And don't think I haven't flayed myself for my cowardice all these years. I should have gone out, helped Yiorgos and Yusuf.'

Kostas was about to say something, but she cut him off with a sharp gesture. With an impatient toss of her head, she continued, speaking faster this time.

'As the sounds got louder, Chico panicked. The poor bird became agitated, screaming his head off, banging against his cage. It was awful. I had to leave my hiding place and get him out. Chico had made so much noise, the men outside must have heard him. They tried to come in and check. But Yiorgos and Yusuf blocked the way. There was a tussle. A gun went off. Still we waited quietly, the doctor and I. For how long, I don't know, my legs went numb. When we walked out, the sky was dark and there was this eerie silence all around. I knew in my soul something terrible had occurred and I had done nothing to prevent it.'

'What do you think happened?'

'I believe these thugs had been casing the tavern for some time. They knew Yusuf and Yiorgos were a gay couple and wanted to teach them a lesson. They probably thought the place was closed. They were going to vandalize it, smash the windows, break a few things, write ugly slurs on the walls and leave. With all the chaos across the island, they trusted nobody would bother to investigate such a trivial incident and they would get away with it. But things didn't go according to plan. They didn't expect the owners to be there. Nor did they expect to meet resistance.'

Her hand, tracing his neck, slowed to a halt.

'And neither Yusuf nor Yiorgos would have fought back in this way, they were the gentlest souls. I think they became overprotective because of me; they must have been worried that the men would force their way in and find me with the doctor. How would we explain what we were about to do? What would they do to us then? That's why Yusuf tried to block the entrance and Yiorgos ran inside to get his pistol – things got out of hand.'

'When you went out, they weren't there?'

'No. There was no one. We searched everywhere. The doctor kept saying we had to go, it was dangerous to be out so late. But I didn't care. I just sat there, feeling dazed. My teeth were chattering, I remember, even though I wasn't cold or anything. I had this crazy idea that the fig tree must have witnessed everything. I wished I could find a way to make the tree talk to me, that was the only thing on my mind. I thought I was going mad. I returned the next day, then the next . . . every day that month I walked to the tavern and I waited for Yiorgos and Yusuf to come back.

'I always brought some food for Chico, those biscuits that he loved so much, remember? The bird wasn't doing well. I was planning to take him home with me, but I hadn't been able to talk to my family yet about my own *situation*, I didn't know how they were going to react. One morning I came to the tavern and Chico wasn't there. We never consider how animals are affected by our wars and fights but they suffer just like us.'

He watched her eyes become guarded, her jaw hardening, her cheeks hollowing. He could tell from the tight line around her lips that mentally she was somewhere else, a dark, narrow cave that held her in its thrall, shutting him out.

His throat tight, he asked, 'These men . . . were they Greek or Turkish?'

In reply, she repeated the words she had said to him just the other day, the first time they had met after so many years. 'They were islanders, Kostas, just like us.'

'You never saw Yusuf and Yiorgos again?'

'I never saw them again. I decided to have the baby whatever the consequences. My sister already knew about us. I told her that I was pregnant. Meryem said there was no way we could tell my parents the full truth. We had to keep your name out of this. So between us we came up with a plan. As gently as she could, Meryem conveyed the news to the family. My father was mortified. In his eyes, I had dishonoured our name. I have never seen anyone carry his shame like that, as if it were his skin now, inseparable. This man who was paralysed from the waist down . . . He had lost his job and his friends, and was suffering physically and mentally and financially, but for him honour was everything, and when he found out that I wasn't the daughter he thought he had, it just destroyed him. He wouldn't look at my face, he wouldn't speak to me any more, and my mother . . . I don't know if her reaction was better or worse. She was beside herself with rage – shouting all the time. But I think my father's silence hit me harder in the end.

'And here is something else you can hate me for: Meryem and I decided to tell them the baby was Yusuf's and we were planning to get married, but he had mysteriously disappeared. My mother went to the tavern looking for him, but of course there was no one there. She even called Yusuf's family, asking where he was, accusing them of things they had no knowledge of. And all that time I kept quiet and I despised myself for having smeared the name of a good man – when I didn't even know if he was dead or alive.'

'Oh, Defne . . .'

She made a vague gesture with her hand, not allowing him to say anything else. Quietly, she stood up, went inside and began putting on her clothes.

'Are you leaving?' Kostas asked.

'I'm going for a walk,' she said, without looking at him. 'Why don't you come with me? I'd like to take you to a military cemetery.'

'Why? What's in there?'

'Soldiers,' she said softly. 'And babies.'

Fig Tree

After Yusuf and Yiorgos disappeared and The Happy Fig closed down, Chico fell into a deep depression. He started plucking out his feathers and chewing his skin – a red, raw map of pain spreading across exposed flesh. It happens to parrots, just like humans, they succumb to melancholy, losing all joy and hope, finding each day more excruciating.

The bird wasn't eating properly, even though he had plenty of food. He could easily survive on stores of fruits and nuts, insects and snails, tearing at the sacks in the larder, not to mention the biscuits that Defne brought him. But he had barely any appetite. I tried to help him, only now realizing how little I knew him. All these years we had lived in the same tavern, sharing one space, an exotic parrot and a fig tree, but we had never been close. Our personalities were not exactly aligned. But in times of crisis and despair the most unlikely beings can become friends; that, too, I have learned.

A yellow-headed Amazon parrot, an endangered species native to Mexico, is an unusual sight for Cyprus. You don't find his kind around here. Nor among the thousands of passerine birds that fleetingly grace our skies each year. Chico's presence was an anomaly and I had accepted it as such, never really wondering where Yusuf had got him from.

When I asked him about his past, Chico told me that he used to live in a mansion in Hollywood. I did not believe him, of course. Sounded like a lot of baloney to me. He must have noticed my scepticism, for he got upset. He mentioned the name of an American actress famous for her voluptuous figure and her various roles in classic films. He said she adored exotic birds, had a whole collection of them in her garden. He told me that every time he picked up a new word, the actress rewarded him with a treat. She would clap her hands and say: 'Darling, how clever you are!'

Chico said that after a torrid affair with a mafia leader, during which time she cruised the Mediterranean in a private yacht, the actress had become fond of Cyprus. She especially liked Varosha, the 'French Riviera of the Eastern Mediterranean', where she purchased a spectacular villa. She wasn't the only celebrity who had discovered this heavenly spot. On an ordinary day, you could spot Elizabeth Taylor emerging from a glitzy hotel, Sophia Loren stepping out of her car, her skirt having ridden up above her knees, or Brigitte Bardot strolling along the beach, gazing into the watery depths as if waiting for someone to emerge.

The actress decided to spend more time here. It suited her – the weather, the glamour – but there was one problem: she missed her parrots! So she made arrangements to bring them over. Ten birds in total. Placed in smelly, stuffy containers, loaded from one plane to the next, they were dispatched from LA all the way to Cyprus. And that is how Chico and his clan ended up on our island.

The trip wasn't easy for the birds. Being photosensitive, they found the travel across oceans and continents gruelling. They stopped drinking water and eating properly, homesick in their ornamental brass cages. One died. But the remaining birds, when they finally reached their destination, swiftly adapted to their new home in Varosha, in the southern quarter of Famagusta. Glitzy shops, flashy casinos, exclusive brands, the latest of everything was here . . . Music blasted from brightly coloured convertibles as they glided along the main avenues. Luxury yachts and sightseeing boats bobbed up and down along the harbour. Under the moon, the sea glistened in the dazzle pouring out of the discotheques, its dark waters festooned like carnival floats.

Tourists travelled to Varosha from all over the world to celebrate their honeymoons, graduations, wedding anniversaries . . . They saved money so they could spend a few days in this famous resort. They sipped rum cocktails and dined at exquisite buffets;

they surfed, swam and basked on sandy beaches, bent on getting a perfect tan, the horizon stretching out blue and clear before their eyes. If this was paradise, they knew from news reports there was trouble brewing at its margins, reports of inter-communal tension between Turks and Greeks. But inside the confines of the resort, the spectre of civil war was invisible and life felt fresh, eternally young.

Chico said there were nine of them sharing the same space – four couples plus him. He was the only bird without a partner. He felt hurt, excluded. Parrots are strictly monogamous. Loyal and loving, they mate for life. When they have chicks, they raise their little ones together, males and females sharing the work. They are homemakers like that. None of which worked in Chico's favour. When the others formed pairs, he was left alone. He had no one to love and no one to love him back. And to make things worse, the actress, who now had a new boyfriend and an exciting new film in the works, was busier than ever. She spent solid days and weeks away from home, entrusting her parrots to the housekeeper with long, detailed lists of instructions pinned to the fridge – what to feed the birds, when to give them their drops, how to check their feathers for signs of ectoparasites. Lists that would languish unread.

The housekeeper did not like parrots, finding them noisy, bois-terous and spoiled. She saw them as a burden and made no secret of it. The other birds, busy with their own families, didn't mind this as much. But Chico did, lonely and vulnerable as he was. One morning, he flew out through the open window, leaving behind his kin and the actress and all that gourmet food. Not knowing where to go, he flew without rest, making it all the way to Nicosia, where Yusuf, by a stroke of destiny, found him perched on a wall, squawking in distress, and took him in.

Chico worried that now Yusuf, too, was gone. Humans were all the same, he said. Untrustworthy and selfish to the core.

Protesting with all my might, I tried to explain to him that nei-ther Yusuf nor Yiorgos would just disappear like that, something must have happened to keep them away, but I was increasingly gripped by a pang of anguish myself.

None of us knew then that, in only a few weeks, Varosha's fate would be sealed. In the summer of 1974, after the Turkish army moved in, the entire population of the town, more than 39,000 people, would have to run away, leaving all their belongings behind. Among them must have been the housekeeper. I imagine her packing a bag, rushing out of the door and evacuating with others. Had she remembered to take the parrots with her? Or at least to set them free? To be fair, she probably expected to be back in a few days. That's what everyone thought.

None of them could return. Women in go-go boots, miniskirts, baby-doll dresses, flared jeans; men sporting tie-dye shirts, earth shoes, bell-bottoms, tweed jackets. Film stars, producers, singers, footballers or the paparazzi trailing after them. DJs, bartenders, croupiers, spotlight dancers. And the many, many local families who had been here for generations and had nowhere else to call home. The fishermen who brought their fresh catch to fancy restaurants where they would be sold for ten times the price, the bakers who worked at night to prepare cheese-filled breads and the street vendors who strolled the promenade peddling balloons, candyfloss, ice cream for children and tourists. They all left.

The beaches of Varosha were cordoned off with barbed wire, cement barriers and signs ordering visitors to stay away. Slowly, the hotels disintegrated into webs of steel cables and concrete pylons; the pubs turned dank and deserted, the discotheques crumbled; the houses with flowerpots on their windowsills dissolved into oblivion. This worldwide resort, once opulent and fashionable, became a ghost town.

I have always wondered what happened to those Amazon parrots that a Hollywood actress had brought to Cyprus. I hope they managed to get out of the villa through an open window. Parrots live long lives, and the chances are they might have survived on fruits and insects. Perhaps if you were to pass by the barricades of Varosha today, you might catch a flash of bright green among abandoned buildings and decay, and hear a pair of wings flapping like a sail torn in a storm.

There were many words Chico was able to say. Remarkably talented, he could imitate electronic sounds, mechanical sounds, animal sounds, human sounds . . . He could identify dozens of objects, pulverize cockleshells or even solve puzzles, and if you gave him a pebble, he would use it to crush nuts.

In the empty tavern, as the two of us waited for Yusuf and Yiorgos to return, Chico would display his talents for me.

'Come, birdie, birdie!' he would cry out from the chair behind the till where Yusuf used to sit every evening to greet customers, now covered in an inch of dust.

'*S'agapo*,' Chico would croon in Greek, *I love you*, something he had heard Yiorgos whisper to Yusuf. And then, when the truth sank in and he realized that no one was coming, he would pluck another feather from his bruised flesh and repeat to himself a word he had learned in Turkish: '*Aglama*' – *Don't cry*.

Ammonite

Cyprus, early 2000s

After they visited the military cemetery, and Kostas saw for the first time where his son was buried, they walked in silence, holding hands. They trudged through fields of crown daisies with their pale orange flowers caressed by the wind as thistles and brambles scratched their bare ankles.

In the afternoon they rented a car and drove towards the Castle of Saint Hilarion. It did them good, the long, hard scramble up the steep and twisty hillside, the sheer physicality of the climb. When they reached the top, they surveyed the landscape from a Gothic window carved into the ancient structure, their breaths shallow, their pulses hammering.

That evening, once the castle was closed and both tourists and locals had left, they loitered around, not quite ready to go back and mingle with other people just yet. They sat on a rock where a saint had once rested, worn smooth from centuries of passage.

Steadily, dusk filtered into night. As the darkness around them thickened, it became impossible to walk down the way they had come, so they decided to spend the night there. This being a military zone, they were taking a risk by staying after hours. Next to a patch of meadow saffron, glowing pinkish-white under a pale sliver of moon, they made love. To be naked like that in the open, canopied only by an infinite sky, was a frightening experience, and the closest they had come to freedom in a long time.

They nibbled through a bag of hazelnuts and dried mulberries, the only food they had with them. They drank water from flasks they had brought in their rucksacks, and then whisky. While

Kostas slowed down after a few sips, Defne didn't. Once again, he noticed she was drinking too fast, too much.

'I want you to come with me,' Kostas said, keeping his eyes trained on her as if fearing she might disappear between blinks.

Shaking her head, she gestured at the empty space between them. 'Where?'

'To England.'

Just then the moon darted behind a cloud, giving him barely enough time to detect the change in her expression. A momentary surprise, then withdrawal. He recognized that way she had of closing in on herself defensively.

'We can start all over again, I promise,' Kostas said.

When the cloud edged away, he found her absorbed in thought. Now she was looking at him carefully, surveying his lips, the split still healing, the bruises around his eyes slowly changing colour.

'Is this . . . Wait, are you proposing?'

Kostas swallowed, upset at himself for not being better prepared. He could have brought a ring with him. He remembered the jewellery store they had stopped by after visiting the psychic. He should have gone there the next day, but, busy tracking songbirds, he hadn't had a chance.

'I'm not very good with words,' Kostas said.

'I figured.'

'I love you, Defne. I have always loved you. I know we can't roll back the years – I'm not trying to gloss over what happened, your suffering, our loss – but I want us to give each other a second chance.'

Remembering he still had the fossil in his jacket pocket, he took it out. 'Would it be terribly untoward if I gave you an ammonite instead of a ring?'

She laughed.

'This marine creature lived millions of years ago, imagine. As it got older, it added new chambers to its shell. Ammonites survived three mass extinctions and they weren't even good swimmers. But they had a fascinating ability to adapt, tenacity being their strong suit.'

He handed the fossil to her. 'I want you to come with me to England – will you marry me?'

Her fingers closed around the smooth stone as she felt its delicate pattern. 'Poor Meryem, she was right to be worried when she heard you were back. If we do this, my family will probably never forgive me. My father, my mother, my cousins . . .'

'Let me talk to them.'

'Not a good idea. Meryem already knows about us, but my parents still don't have a clue. I'll tell them everything, I am tired of hiding. They will now learn that I've lied to them all these years about Yusuf being the father of my baby . . . That there was even more reason for them to disown me . . . I'm not sure they will ever absolve me for smearing a Turkish man to protect my Greek lover, what a mess I've made.' She ran her hand through her hair and spoke through a tight jaw. 'But your family won't be happy either. Your younger brother, your uncle, your cousins . . .'

His brow crumpled. 'They'll understand.'

'No, they won't. After all they have gone through, our families will only see this as a betrayal.'

'It's a different world now.'

'Tribal hatreds don't die,' she said, holding the ammonite up. 'They just add new layers to hardened shells.'

The silence stretched thin. A breeze blew through the trees, ruffling the bushes ahead, and she shivered despite herself.

'Without any family support, without a country, we'll be very lonely,' she said.

'Everybody is lonely. We'll just be more aware of it.'

'You were the one who made me read Cavafy – have you forgotten your own poet? You think you can leave your native land because so many people have done it, so why shouldn't you? After all, the world is full of immigrants, runaways, exiles . . . Encouraged, you break free and travel as far as you can, then one day you look back and realize it was coming with you all along, like a shadow. Everywhere we go, it'll follow us, this city, this island.'

He held her hand, kissed her fingertips. She carried the past so

285

close to the surface, pain rushing beneath her skin like blood. 'We can do it if we both believe in it.'

'I'm not very good at believing,' she said.

'I figured,' he said in turn.

He knew, even back then, that she was prone to bouts of melancholy. It came to her in successive waves, an ebb and flow. When the first wave arrived, barely touching her toes, it was so light and translucent a ripple that you might be forgiven for thinking it insignificant, that it would vanish soon, leaving no trace. But then followed another wave, and the next one, rising as far as her ankles, and the one after that covering her knees, and before you knew it she was immersed in liquid pain, up to her neck, drowning. That's how depression sucked her in.

'Are you sure you want to marry me?' said Defne. 'Because I'm not an easy person, as you know, and I have –'

He put his finger on her lips, interrupting her for the first time. 'I have never been more sure of anything in my life. But it's totally fine if you need more time to think – or to turn me down.'

She smiled then, a hint of shyness entering her voice. She leaned over, her breath brushing his skin. 'I don't need to think, darling. I've always dreamed of marrying you.'

And because there was nothing left to say, or that's how they felt, they were silent for a while, listening to the night, alert to every creak and rustle.

'There's one more thing I want to do before we leave the island,' Kostas said at last. 'I want to visit the tavern and see how the old fig tree is doing.'

Fig Tree

Of all the insects, if there is one you cannot possibly ignore when telling the story of an island, it must be the ant. We trees owe a lot to them. So do humans, for that matter. Yet they regard ants as trivial, of no major consequence, as they do so often with things that lie beneath their feet. It is ants who sustain, aerate and improve the soil over which Greeks and Turks have fought so bitterly. Cyprus also belongs to them.

Ants are resilient and hard-working, capable of carrying twenty times their own bodyweight. With a life span that surpasses almost any other insect, they are also the smartest in my opinion. Have you ever watched them drag away a millipede, or gang up on a scorpion, or devour a whole gecko? It is both fascinating and frightening, every step perfectly synchronized. What goes on inside the mind of a single ant in that moment? How does one achieve that kind of inner confidence, the assertiveness to take on an enemy far better equipped for the fight? With their olfactory memory, ants can pick up scent trails, sniff out an intruder from another colony, and, when far from home, they can remember the way back. Should obstacles appear in their path, cracks in the ground or fallen twigs, they can make bridges from their bodies by clinging to each other like skilful acrobats. Everything they learn, they transfer to the next generation. Knowledge is nobody's property. You receive it, you give it back. In this way, a colony remembers what its individual members have long forgotten.

Ants know our island better than anyone. They are familiar with its igneous rocks, recrystallized limestones, ancient coins of Salamis, and they are experts at making use of the resin that drips from tree barks. They also know where the missing lie buried.

The year Kostas Kazantzakis returned to Cyprus, a colony of

ants set up home among my roots. I was expecting this as I had recently been infested by aphids, those smallest of insects that suck sap from leaves and spread viruses, causing trees deep stress. If Yusuf and Yiorgos were here, they would never have allowed this to happen. Every day they checked my branches for pests, spraying my leaves gently with apple cider vinegar, taking good care of me, but now I was on my own, defenceless. Where aphids appear, the ants are sure to follow, fond as they are of harvesting sweet aphid droppings. But that was not the only reason they built an entire colony here. Ants love overripe figs and now that no one was harvesting mine they were all overripe. A fig is not exactly a fruit, you see. It is a syconium – a fascinating structure that hides flowers and seeds in its cavity, with a barely visible opening through which wasps can enter and deposit their pollen. And sometimes, seizing the opportunity, ants, too, crawl through that opening and eat what they can.

So I became used to listening to the pitter-patter of thousands of tiny feet scuttling back and forth. A colony is a strictly class-based society. As long as every member accepts inequality as the norm and agrees to the division of labour, the system operates seamlessly. Workers forage for food, keep living spaces tidy and tend to the queen's endless needs; soldiers protect the community against predators and perils; drones help to propagate the species, and die soon after mating. Then there are the princesses – the future queens. The social stratum must be preserved at all costs.

One night, as I was getting ready to go to sleep, I heard an unusual sound. With only a few attendants in tow, the queen was making her way up the lengthy, rugged path of my trunk.

Still panting from the arduous climb, she began to tell her story. She said she was born by an old well, not far away. She had good memories of growing up there. As a princess she was aware that when the time was ripe, she would be asked to leave her birthplace to start her own kingdom. The colony was thriving, the population growing. In need of more space, they had been enlarging the settlement through subterranean passages and tunnels, connecting chambers to nests. But in a terrible engineering mistake, the workers chewed too far into the wall. One afternoon the east side of the well caved in and collapsed. In the beat of a heart, the water that seeped out drowned hundreds. Some species of ant could swim, but not this one. The survivors scattered in all directions, seeking shelter wherever possible. After this catastrophe, the queen said, she had to leave her home as fast as possible to start a new life.

During the nuptial flight, she held her head high and flew fast, the drones striving to catch up with her. They crossed over a sand track, scrambled up and down tyre marks. They traversed the ruins of the tavern. As soon as she saw me, laden with figs, she knew this was where she would build her kingdom. Here she mated and chewed off her wings as though discarding a wedding dress, so that she could never fly again. She turned herself into a fully fledged egg-laying machine.

Her features contorted in sadness, she then said that when the walls came down, they had found, there at the bottom of the well, two dead men. She didn't know who they were until she met me and learned about the couple who owned this place.

I let my branches drop as the terrible truth behind her words slowly sank in. Seeing my distress, she assured me that they had not touched Yusuf and Yiorgos. They had left them there, undisturbed. Somebody would find them soon, now that they were half in the open.

After the queen and her entourage of loyal courtiers had departed, I drifted into a strange listlessness which grew worse in the days that followed. I was feeling unwell. Like every living thing, a fig tree can suffer from multiple diseases and infections, only this time I had barely any strength to fight back. The tips of my leaves curled into themselves, my bark began to peel off. The flesh on the inside of my figs turned a sickly green and then frighteningly powdery.

As my immunity declined and my strength tapered off, I fell

prey to one of my worst enemies – a fig-tree borer, a large stag-horned beetle, *Phryneta spinator*. Like a nightmare she descended on me and laid her eggs near the base of my trunk. Helpless and filled with fear, I waited, knowing that the grub-like larvae would soon begin to bore into my trunk and start feeding on me, digging tunnels into my branches, destroying me from within, little by little.

The damage from this beetle is often irreparable. Fig trees that are heavily infested need to be destroyed.

I was dying.

Portable Roots

Cyprus, early 2000s

When Defne and Kostas approached The Happy Fig, they found it sunken into undergrowth, broken tiles and building rubble strewn all around, like wreckage after a storm. Knowing it was the first time Kostas would be seeing the place in years, Defne lingered behind, giving him time to take it in.

Kostas pushed open the door, its wood decayed and lifeless, hanging from its hinges. Inside, weeds had forced their way through cracks in the floor, the tiles were stained with lichen and the walls blotched with mildew, black as iron. In a corner, a window screen, its glass splintered long ago, creaked slowly in the breeze. There was a fetid smell in the air, of mould and putrefaction.

The moment he walked in it all came rushing back to him. Evenings redolent with delicious odours of steaming food and warm pastry, the chatter and laughter of the customers, the music and the clapping, the smashing of plates as the night wore on . . . He remembered the afternoons he had trudged up the hill, carrying bottles of carob liquor and those honey-sesame bars that Yiorgos loved so much, and how happy his mother was with the money he brought home . . . His eyes brightened as he recalled Chico flapping his wings, Yiorgos telling jokes to a newly married couple, and Yusuf watching it all with his customary silence and attentive gaze. How proud they were of what they had created together. This tavern was their home, their refuge, their entire world.

'You all right?' Defne said as she put her arms around him.

They stood still for a minute, his breathing slowing to match hers, until his heartbeat grew calmer.

Defne tilted her head and looked about. 'Imagine, the fig has witnessed everything.'

Gently, Kostas disentangled himself from her arms and edged closer to the *Ficus carica*. His brow crumpled. 'Oh, this tree is not in good shape. She's sick.'

'What?'

'She's infested. Look, it has spread everywhere.' He pointed at the branches covered with tiny boreholes, the dry sawdust pulp at the foot of the trunk, the brittle dead leaves littering the ground.

'Can't you help?'

'I'll see what I can do. Let's go and get a few things.'

They returned an hour later, carrying several bags. With the help of a sledgehammer, Kostas knocked down parts of the southern wall of the tavern, crumbled with mould. He wanted to make sure the tree could get more sunshine and oxygen. He then cut off the diseased branches with a pruning saw. Next, he injected insecticide with a syringe into the tunnels that the larvae had burrowed. To prevent the deadly insects from laying their eggs again, he enclosed the lower part of the trunk in wire netting and filled the tree's festering wounds with a sealant.

'Is it going to get better?' asked Defne.

'She – this tree is a female.' Kostas straightened up, wiped his forehead with the back of his hand. 'I don't know if she'll be all right. The grubs are everywhere.'

'I wish she could come with us to England,' Defne said. 'I wish trees were portable.'

Kostas narrowed his eyes as a new thought crossed his mind. 'We could do that.'

She glanced at him, disbelieving.

'You can grow a fig tree from a cutting. If we plant her right away in London, and look after her, there's a chance she'll survive.'

'Are you serious? Can you do that?'

'It can be done,' Kostas said. 'She may not like the English weather but she might be okay. Tomorrow morning I'll come back and check how she's doing. I'll take a cutting from a healthy branch. Then she can travel with us.'

Fig Tree

The next day, as I waited excitedly for Kostas to come back, a honeybee I had known for some time paid me a visit. I had deep respect for her kind. No other species embodies the circle of life quite like the Apidae. If they were to disappear one day, the world would never recover from their loss. Cyprus was their heaven, but heaven did not come easily. Using the sun as their compass, the tireless foragers visited up to three hundred flowers on one flight, which amounted to more than two thousand flowers in a single day.

Such was the bee's life – work, work, work. Sometimes she danced a bit, but that, too, was part of work. When she chanced upon a good source of nectar, she did a waggle dance upon returning to the hive to inform the others where they should be heading next. But sometimes she danced because she felt grateful to be alive. Or because she was high, having accidentally digested too much nectar laced with caffeine.

Humans have hackneyed ideas about bees. Ask them to draw one – and on this infants and adults are surprisingly alike – and they will scrawl a plump, round blob covered in dense yellow-and-black-striped fur. But, in reality, bees come in a wide variety-some are vivid orange, burnt sienna or rich purple, some shimmer in metallic green or blue, while others have bright red or pure white tails that glow in the sun. How can they all look identical to the human eye when they are so mesmerizingly diverse? Sure, it's wonderful that birds are lauded for having a whopping ten thousand species, but why does it often go unnoticed that bees have at least twice that number and just as many personalities?

The honeybee told me that not far from the tavern was a field of ambrosial flowers and lush plants in full bloom. She flew there often, for, as well as daisies and poppies, it had the sweetest cone-flowers, marjoram and, her favourite, sedum, with their pink hues and tiny star-shaped succulent petals all clustered together. At the edge of the site stood a nondescript white block of a building. A sign on the wall read: CMP LABORATORY – UNITED NATIONS PROTECTED AREA.

She had passed by this place countless times on her way back and forth to the hive. Occasionally, on a whim, she diverted from her path and flew straight into the lab through an open window. She liked to buzz around, observe the people working inside and leave the way she came. But today when she entered the building, without a purpose or plan, something unexpected happened. One of the staff members, God knows why, decided it was a good idea to close all the windows. The honeybee found herself trapped!

Trying not to panic, failing all the same, she threw herself at every windowpane, bumbling up and down glassy surfaces, un-able to find an exit. From her vantage point, she could see the flowers outside, so close she could almost taste their nectar, but no matter how hard she tried she could not reach them.

Frustrated and exhausted, the bee settled on top of a cupboard to catch her breath. She turned her attention to the room that had now become her prison cell. Fourteen forensic scientists were employed here – Greek Cypriots and Turkish Cypriots – and by now she knew them all. Every weekday the Greeks travelled from the south and the Turks travelled from the north and they met in this no man's land. This was where all human remains that had been discovered in various exhumations across the island were eventually brought.

Whatever the excavation teams unearthed, the scientists at this lab cleaned and sorted, detaching hard bones from hard bones, separating one set of human remains from another. They worked alone or in small groups, hunched over long, narrow tables on which they arrayed jigsaws of skeletons – vertebral columns, shoulder blades, hip joints, vertebrae, maxillary teeth ... They put them together, piece by missing piece, associating fragments with larger parts. It was painstakingly slow work, and mistakes were not tolerated. The reconstruction of just a single foot, composed of twenty-six individual bones, could take hours. Or one hand – made of twenty-seven bones, a thousand touches and caresses now lost. Eventually, as if rising from murky waters, the identity of the victim surfaced – the sex, the height and the approximate age.

Some of the remains were too fractured to be of any use or no longer contained DNA, destroyed by harmful bacteria. The unidentified pieces were stored away in the hopes that in the not-so-distant future, when science and technology advanced, their mysteries could be solved.

The scientists wrote comprehensive reports on their findings, including elaborate descriptions of clothing and personal belongings, items that, though perishable, could be surprisingly long-lasting. A leather belt with an engraved metal buckle, a silver necklace with a cross or crescent, scuffed leather shoes worn at the heels ... Once, a wallet had been delivered to the lab. Inside, next to some coins and a key to an unknown lock, were photos of Elizabeth Taylor. The victim must have been a fan of the actress. Descriptions of such items were intended as much for the relatives of the missing as for the CMP archives. The families always wanted to know these details. But what they really wanted to know was whether their loved ones had suffered.

At some point the honeybee fell asleep, worn to a frazzle. She was used to crashing out in awkward positions. Sometimes she would take a little siesta inside a flower. She needed this since sleep-deprived foragers have difficulty concentrating or finding their way back home. Even in the hive, they take their nap on the periphery, while the workers, who clean and feed the larvae, occupy the cells closer to the centre. So my friend was a light sleeper by nature.

When she woke up, it was noon. The staff had left for

lunch – all but one. A young Greek woman was still working. Having observed her many times, the bee knew that she liked to be by herself with the bones, and sometimes she talked to them. But this afternoon, alone in the lab, the scientist picked up the phone and dialled a number. As she waited for it to ring, she kept throwing anxious glances at the tables to her left and right, on both of which bones and skulls had been laid out.

'Hello?' the scientist said into the receiver. 'Hi, Defne, hello. It's Eleni here. From the lab, yes. Good, thank you. How is work at the site?'

They chatted a bit, boring human talk, until something Eleni said piqued the bee's attention.

'Look, uhm, the couple you were asking about, your friends . . . We might have found them. We have a DNA match, for both.'

Intrigued, the bee flew closer to listen.

'Oh, no!' Eleni screamed and grabbed a newspaper, waving it wildly about her. Who knew she was terrified of honeybees, this woman who spent her days with cadavers and skeletons?

My poor friend, once again misunderstood and mistaken for something she wasn't, suffered a blow to the head. She tumbled into a coffee mug, thankfully empty save for a few drops of coffee. As she rose to her feet, weak and dizzy, she heard Eleni mutter: 'Where did it go . . . ? Sorry, Defne, there was a bee here. I'm a bit scared of them.'

A bit? my friend thought to herself. If this was what humans did with a bit of fear, imagine what they were capable of doing with loads of it? She managed to scramble up the side of the mug and dry off her wings.

'Yes, of course you may come and see,' Eleni was now saying. 'Oh, really, you're going to England tomorrow? I understand. That's fine. This afternoon is good. Okay, we'll talk when you're here.'

Half an hour later, the other scientists not yet back from lunch, the door opened and a woman rushed in.

'Oh, Eleni, thank you for your call.'

'Hi, Defne.'

'You're sure it's them?'

'I believe so. I checked their DNA results twice with their family references just to be sure and both times they were above the threshold.'

'Where were they found, do you know?'

'In Nicosia.' Eleni paused, hesitating whether to share the next piece of information. 'Inside a well.'

'A well?'

'Yes, I'm afraid so.'

'All this time they were in there?'

'That's right. They had been chained to each other, neither could surface. We were told that the well had collapsed recently and when the builders started working, they found the remains,' said Eleni, her tone subdued. 'I'm so sorry for your loss. I must say, we have never seen anything like this before. Usually it's a Greek Cypriot buried here, a Turkish Cypriot buried there. Killed separately. Buried separately. But never before a Greek and Turk murdered together.'

Defne stood still, her hands hovering above the table before clutching its edge.

'When will you inform their families?'

'Tomorrow, I was thinking. One family is in the north, one in the south.'

'So now they will be separated,' said Defne. Her voice was soft, reedy. 'They can't be buried side by side. How sad – all this time we spent looking for them and maybe it would have been better if they were never found . . . if they could have remained lost together.'

Eleni laid her hand kindly on her shoulder. 'Oh, before I forget . . .' She strode to her desk and took out a plastic case. 'They also found this.'

A pocket watch.

Defne lowered her eyes. 'It belonged to Yiorgos. A birthday present from Yusuf. There should be a poem inside . . . by Cavafy.' She stopped. 'Sorry, Eleni . . . I need some fresh air. Can we open the windows?'

Instantly, the honeybee perked up. This was her chance, perhaps her only one. As soon as they opened a window, my friend gathered her strength and zigzagged her way out. She flew as fast as she could and did not stop until she had reached the safety of the flower fields.

Little Miracles

Cyprus/London, early 2000s

When Kostas returned, he carefully examined the *Ficus carica*. With a pair of secateurs he made one straight cut and one diagonal across a single clean stem. Although he knew it was best to use several shoots in case some did not survive, the tree was in such a poor condition he could only secure one, which he carefully wrapped and then put in his suitcase.

It would be difficult, but not entirely impossible. Little miracles did happen. Just as hope could spring from the depths of despair, or peace germinate among the ruins of war, a tree could grow out of disease and decay. If this cutting from Cyprus were to take root in England, it would be genetically identical but not at all the same.

In London, they planted the cutting in a white ceramic pot and kept it on a table by the window in Kostas's small flat, overlooking a quiet, leafy square. It was here they found out that Defne was pregnant, the two of them sitting cross-legged on the bathroom floor with their heads bent over a home-testing kit. A bulb buzzed and flickered overhead, the wattage fluctuating. Defne would never forget the joy that spread across Kostas's face, his eyes blazing with something akin to gratitude. She, too, was happy, but also apprehensive and slightly frightened. Yet so pure was his joy that it felt like betrayal to tell him about the needles of anxiety that were pricking her skin, splintering her mind. One of her recurrent dreams in those days would be about getting lost in a dense, dark forest with a baby in her arms, crashing through the trees, unable to find a way out, as branches scraped her shoulders and scratched her face.

Only once, about a month later, she asked, 'What if it all goes wrong?'

'Don't even think such things.'

'I'm old to have a baby, we both know that, what if there are complications . . .'

'It'll be okay.'

'But I'm not young any more.'

'Stop saying that.'

'And what if it turns out I'm a terrible mother? What if I fail?'

She could see in the clench of his jaw how hard he was searching for the right words to soothe her, how much he needed her to believe in the future they were building together. And she tried. Some days she was full of confidence and expectation, others she managed just fine, but then there were days, and especially nights, when she would hear, somewhere in the distance, ticking as steady as a metronome, the approaching footsteps of a familiar sense of melancholy. She felt guilty for feeling this way, and she blamed, judged and berated herself endlessly for it. Why couldn't she just appreciate this surprise that life had given her and live fully in the moment? What was the point of stressing this much? Worrying about how good a mother she would be to an unborn baby was like being homesick for a place she had not even visited yet.

Meanwhile, Kostas discovered that the cutting had sprouted new leaves. He was overjoyed. More and more he believed things were coming together for him, for them, his whole life composed of interlocking puzzle pieces that were finally fitting together. His work as a botanist and naturalist was starting to get more attention from people both within and outside the field, he was receiving invitations to give talks and lectures, contribute to journals, and, unobtrusively, he set out to write a new book.

Defne took the resilience of the cutting as a good omen. Pregnancy had made her uncharacteristically superstitious, bringing out a side of her that was surprisingly similar to her sister, though this she would not admit. She stopped drinking. She stopped smoking. She took up painting again. From that moment onwards, the fate of the baby and the fate of the tree merged in her mind. As her belly grew, so did the fig's need for more space. Kostas repotted the plant using a larger pot this time, checking on it daily. They moved to a house in north London. By then the *Ficus carica* was strong enough to be transplanted into the garden, and so they did.

Despite the smoking chimney and the leaking roof, the cracks that ran the length of the walls and the radiators that never fully heated, they were happy in this house, the two of them. Ada was born in early December, two months premature. Her lungs were weak and she had to be kept in an incubator for several weeks. Meanwhile, the little sapling wasn't faring any better, struggling with the new climate. It had to be wrapped in burlap, covered with cardboard, insulated. But by the time summer arrived, they were healthy and growing, the fig tree and the child.

Fig Tree

The last animal in my ecosystem that I remember visiting me before I left the island for good was a mouse. There is a fundamental truth that, although universally relevant and worth recognizing, is never mentioned in history textbooks. Wherever humankind has fought wars, turning fertile lands into battlefields and destroying entire habitats, animals have always moved into the void they left behind. Rodents, for instance. When people lay waste to the buildings that once gave them joy and pride, mice will quietly claim them as their own kingdom.

Over the years I had met plenty of them – female does, male bucks, bright pink little pups, fond as they all are of figs. But this particular mouse was rather unusual for he was born and raised in an iconic place – the Ledra Palace.

'*One of the finest hotels in the Middle East!*' That's how the establishment was advertised when it was built in the second half of the 1940s. Yet the investors were not exactly satisfied with that strapline. The Middle East, they thought, was not an attractive destination for Western tourists. '*One of the finest hotels in Europe!*' That did not sound appealing either; not when the spectre of the Second World War still roamed the European continent. '*One of the finest hotels in the Near East!*' This worked better. 'Near' seemed conveniently within reach, while 'East' added a dash of exoticism. 'Near East' was oriental enough; just enough, not too much.

Designed by a German Jewish architect, a survivor of the Holocaust, the Ledra Palace would require 240,000 Cyprus pounds and two years to complete. The chandeliers were imported from Italy, the marble friezes from Greece. Its location was ideal – close to Nicosia's medieval centre, not far from the surrounding Venetian walls, on a street once named King Edward VII. With 240 bedrooms, it towered over the compact houses and narrow streets in the old town. It even had a toilet and bathroom in every room – the only hotel at the time that offered such luxury. There were bars, lounges, tennis courts, a children's play area, first-rate restaurants, a huge pool to dive into under the merciless sun and a glamorous ballroom that would soon become the talk of the town.

On the day of the opening in October 1949, everyone was there: British colonial officers, local notables, foreign dignitaries, wannabe celebrities . . . Now that the Second World War was over, people needed an assurance that the ground beneath their feet was solid, the buildings they erected strong, and that it would never happen again, the ruins, the horrors. Such a great year for optimism, 1949!

Throughout my long life, I have observed, again and again, this psychological pendulum that drives human nature. Every few decades they sway into a zone of unbridled optimism and insist on seeing everything through a rosy filter, only to be challenged and shaken by events and catapulted back into their habitual apathy and listless indifference.

The good cheer surrounding the birth of the Ledra Palace lasted for as long as it could. Such amazing parties they had back then! The grand ballroom echoed with the clacking of high heels, the popping of corks, the striking of a Ronson lighter before a lady's cigarette, the sound of fingers snapping as the orchestra played 'Smooth Sailing' into the early hours, always ending the night with 'Que Sera Sera'. Scandals broke out under its ornate ceiling, and gossip, like champagne, flowed unceasingly. It was a joyous place. Once they crossed its threshold, visitors felt they had slipped into some other dimension, where they could cast aside the day's worries and forget the violence and ethnic conflict merely a few feet outside the hotel walls.

Although inside the Ledra Palace everyone did their best to shut out the real world, they couldn't always prevent it from trespassing, like the time they found leaflets written in impeccable English scattered across the lobby as if the wind had swept them in: WE HAVE TAKEN UP THE STRUGGLE TO THROW OFF THE ENG-LISH YOKE. DEATH OR VICTORY! Or like that time in November 1955 when EOKA attacked the hotel to assassinate the British governor, Sir John Harding, who was inside having a drink. They hurled in two grenades: the first exploded, causing substantial damage, and the second did not because the attacker had forgotten to pull the pin. An officer picked up the unexploded grenade, put it in his pocket and walked out. And the orchestra played on – Frank Sinatra's 'Learnin' the Blues'. Even when the hotel's entrance was blockaded with sandbags and barrels, and fears of another attack prowled the hallways, the music never stopped.

Over the years, all kinds of personalities frequented the hotel: politicians, diplomats, writers, socialites, call girls, gigolos and spies. Religious leaders too. It was here that Archbishop Makarios met the British governor. And it was here that intercommunal talks were opened in 1968, albeit to fail horribly. As violence escalated, international reporters covering 'the Cyprus story' flocked in with their typewriters and notepads. Then came the soldiers – the United Nations Peacekeeping Force.

Throughout all these manoeuvres, the hotel continued to operate – until the summer of 1974. The guests were lolling on chaises longues, sipping cocktails in the afternoon sun, when they were told to evacuate, and they did so in such fear and panic that they merely grabbed whatever they could and left. Their invoices were posted afterwards, with a note attached:

We hope that you have had a pleasant journey back home and that your stay at the Ledra Palace Hotel was an enjoyable one, up to the unfortunate moment when the Turkish invasion broke out on Saturday, 20th July 1974, for which I'm sure we will all have a memorable experience . . . Enclosed please find your hotel invoice to the amount of . . . for which an early settlement will be much appreciated.*

* From an original letter published in the *Observer*, London, 15 September 1974.

Afterwards, there were mortar shell craters in the walls and bullet holes staring like empty eye sockets. A disturbing silence reigned along the corridors. But underneath the surface, a plethora of sounds swirled: wood-boring beetles carved tunnels inside the balustrades, rust ate through the brass chandeliers and, at night, the floorboards creaked with age, a noise like varnish cracking. Then there was the pattering of cockroaches, the cooing of pigeons roosting in the ceiling and, particularly, the whispers of mice.

They dwelled in the crevices of the lobby, scurried along the expensive oak flooring, skidded up and down the parapets. When the urge hit, they climbed up the chandelier in the ballroom, balanced themselves with their tails, swung from side to side and leaped into the empty space beneath. They were good at jumping from heights.

They never went hungry as there was a lot to munch on in a once-palatial hotel – peeling wallpaper, mouldy carpets, damp plaster. The architect who had designed the building had included a spacious reading room at the back, which was piled with books, magazines and encylopaedias. It was in this library that the mouse passed most of his days, chewing his way through pages, leaving his teeth marks on scores of leather-bound tomes. He nibbled through the twenty-four volumes of the *Encyclopaedia Britannica*, savouring the burgundy buckram binding with its gilt lettering on the spine. He also devoured the classics: Socrates, Plato, Homer, Aristotle . . . *The Histories* by Herodotus, *Antigone* by Sophocles, *Lysistrata* by Aristophanes.

There the mouse would have stayed until the end of its life if it had not been for an unexpected flurry of activity in the premises. Turkish Cypriots and Greek Cypriots had begun to meet on the ground floor of the Ledra Palace under the auspices of the UN contingent located in the hotel. For the first time, the two communities were making headway towards peace and reconciliation.

The members of the CMP sat in designated rooms, listening

to each other, debating who to include in the statistics of violence. Neither side wanted the numbers to rise, for what would that say about them when the world was watching? But then the question remained: would Greek opponents who had been murdered by Greek ultranationalists be counted among the missing? Likewise, would Turkish opponents who had been murdered by Turkish ultranationalists also be included? Could communities that had still not come to terms with their own extremism ever be ready to acknowledge what they had done to their own dissidents?

I learned from the wood mouse that Defne, too, had participated in these meetings, which had been essential groundwork to build intercommunal trust before the excavations could begin in earnest.

After sharing all this with me, and gorging on my figs, the mouse went on his way. I did not see him again. But, before leaving, he mentioned that the last book he had munched his way through had been by someone named Ovid. He had enjoyed his words and, of the thousands of lines he had come across, there was one in particular that had stayed with him:

Some day this pain will be useful to you.

I hoped he was right and that one day, not too far in the future, all this pain would be useful to future generations born on the island, to the grandchildren of those who had lived through the troubles.

If you go to Cyprus today, you can still find tombstones of Greek widows and Turkish widows, engraved in different alphabets but with a similar plea:

If you find my husband, please bury him next to me.

PART SIX

How to Unbury a Tree

Interview

London, late 2010s

On New Year's Eve they had planned a quiet dinner, nothing too complicated, but no dinner could ever be simple when cooked by Meryem. Determined to end a difficult year with a bit of a sweet taste in their mouths, a warm feeling in their bellies, she used every ingredient she could find in the cupboards to prepare a feast for them. As the clocks chimed midnight and fireworks went off outside the windows, Ada let the grown-ups hug her, and she felt their love enfold her, soft but strong like a cloth woven from the fibres of sturdy plants.

The next day, Meryem started packing, though after all the shopping she had done in east London she was struggling to zip up her Marilyn Monroe suitcases. She spent the entire afternoon with Ada in the kitchen, keen as she was to teach her niece basic cooking skills and dole out some 'womanly' advice.

'Look, Adacim, you need a female role model in your life. Now I might not be much of a model in your eyes, but I've been a woman for years and years, all right. You can give me a ring any time. I will also call you often, if that's okay with you.'

'Sure.'

'We can talk about anything. I might not know the answers myself. As they say, if the bald man knew a remedy for hair loss he would rub it on his own head. But I will always be there for you from now on, I will never be away like that again, I promise.'

Ada gave her a long, thoughtful look. She asked, 'What about the interview? Do you want to do it before you go?'

'School homework? Yes, I forgot. Let's do it now!' Meryem

unbraided her hair and swiftly braided it back. 'But first let's make tea, shall we? Otherwise I can't think straight.'

When the samovar began to boil, filling the kitchen with wispy steam, Meryem took out two small glasses. She half filled them with tea, then topped one up with hot water, the other with milk, frowning slightly at this last addition.

'Thank you,' said Ada, though she had never been too fond of tea. 'Ready?'

'Ready.'

Ada pressed the recorder on her phone and opened the notebook on her lap. 'Okay, tell me what life was like when you were a little girl. Did you have a garden? What kind of a house did you live in?'

'Yes, we had a garden,' Meryem said, her face brightening. 'We had mimosas and magnolias. I grew tomatoes in pots . . . We had a mulberry tree in the courtyard. My father was a self-made man. A famous chef, though he rarely cooked at home. That was a woman's job. Baba was not well educated himself, but he always supported his daughters' education. He sent me and Defne to the best schools. We had an English education, we thought we were part of Europe. It turns out the Europeans disagreed.'

'Was it a happy childhood?'

'My childhood was divided into two parts. The first half was happy.'

Ada tilted her head. 'And the other half?'

'Things changed, you could feel it in the air. They used to say, Greeks and Turks are flesh and fingernail. You can't separate your fingernail from your flesh. Seems they were wrong. It could be done. War is a terrible thing. All kinds of wars. But civil wars are the worst perhaps, when old neighbours become new enemies.'

Ada listened intently as Meryem told her about the island – how they would sleep outdoors on the hottest nights of the summer, spreading their mattresses out on the veranda, she and Defne under a diaphanous white net to protect themselves from mosquitoes, counting the stars above; how pleased they were when their

Greek neighbour would offer them candied quince dessert, though their all-time favourite was the New Year's cake, *vasilopita*, with a coin hidden inside; and how their mother, convinced that a neighbour's plate should never be returned empty, would refill it with mastic pudding in rose syrup; how, following the partition, there were sandbags and guard posts in the streets where they once played and hung around; and how the children on the streets would chat with Irish, Canadian, Swedish, Danish soldiers, accepting the UN troops as an inevitable part of daily life . . .

'Imagine, Adacim, some pale-skinned blond soldier who has never seen the sun comes over from miles away and plants himself there, just to make sure you don't kill your old next-door neighbour, or they don't kill you. How sad is that? Why can't we all live in peace without soldiers and machine guns?'

After she stopped talking, her eyes, distant for a few minutes, focused back on her niece. 'Tell me, do they teach you about Cyprus at school?'

'Not really.'

'I thought not. All those tourists who travel to the Mediterranean on holiday, they want the sun and the sea and the fried calamari. But no history, please, it's depressing.' Meryem took a sip from her tea. 'In the past I used to get upset at that. But nowadays I'm thinking, maybe they're right, Adacim. If you weep for all the sorrows in this world, in the end you will have no eyes.'

Thus saying, she sat back with a little smile – one that disappeared completely when she heard what Ada asked next.

'I kind of understand why my older relatives might have found it difficult to accept my parents' marriage. It's a different generation. They all went through a lot, probably. What I don't understand is why my own parents never talked about the past even after they moved to England. Why the silence?'

'I'm not sure I can answer that,' said Meryem, a hint of caution entering her voice.

'Try.' Ada leaned forward and stopped the recorder. 'This is not for school, by the way. It's for me.'

Silences

London, early 2000s

Nine months after Ada was born, Defne decided to go back to working for the Committee on Missing Persons. She might be two thousand miles away from Cyprus, but she believed she could still be of help in the search for the missing. She began to visit immigrant communities from the island settled in various boroughs and suburbs of London. In particular, she wanted to talk to the elderly who had lived through the troubles and who might towards the end of their lives be willing to share some secrets.

Nearly every day that autumn she would put on her blue trench coat and walk around streets with signs in Greek and Turkish, rain pattering on the pavements and running down the gutters. Almost without fail, after a friendly chat, somebody would point her towards this house or that, insinuating that she might find what she was looking for over there. The families she met in this way were usually warm and welcoming, offering her tea and pastries, but a veil of mistrust remained between them, unspoken yet palpable to all in the room.

Occasionally, Defne noticed, a grandfather or a grandmother was keen to talk when there were no other family members around. For they remembered. Memories as elusive and wispy as tufts of wool dispersed in the wind. Quite a number of these men and women, born and raised in mixed villages, spoke Greek and Turkish, and a few, in the throes of Alzheimer's, slipped down the slopes of time into a language they had not used in decades. Some had personally witnessed atrocities, some had heard about them, and then there were others who seemed evasive to her.

It was during these difficult conversations that Defne came to realize that hands were the most honest part of a human's body. Eyes lied. Lips lied. Faces hid themselves behind a thousand masks. But hands rarely ever did. She observed the hands of the elderly, resting demurely on their laps, withered, wrinkled, liver-spotted, bent and blue with veins, creatures with their own minds and consciences. She noticed how, every time she asked an uncomfortable question, the hands answered in their own language, fidgeting, gesturing, picking at their nails.

As she tried to encourage her interviewees to open up, Defne was careful not to demand more than they were ready to provide. She was, however, troubled to observe deep rifts between family members of different ages. Way too often, the first generation of survivors, the ones who had suffered the most, kept their pain close to the surface, memories like splinters lodged under their skin, some protruding, others completely invisible to the eye. Meanwhile, the second generation chose to suppress the past, both what they knew and did not know of it. In contrast, the third generation were eager to dig away and unearth silences. How strange that in families scarred by wars, forced displacements and acts of brutality, it was the youngest who seemed to have the oldest memory.

Behind the many doors she knocked on, Defne came across a plethora of heirlooms brought in from the island. It touched her to see stitched quilt pieces, crocheted doilies, china figurines and mantelpiece clocks, carried lovingly across borders. But then she also became aware of the presence of cultural artefacts that felt completely out of place – stolen church icons, smuggled treasures, broken mosaics, pillaging of history. The international public paid barely any attention to how art and antiques came on to the market. Customers in Western capitals happily acquired them without questioning their provenance. Among the buyers were well-known singers, artists, celebrities.

For the most part, Defne went alone on these house visits, but sometimes she would be accompanied by a colleague from the

CMP. Once they were treated so rudely by the elder son of a ninety-two-year-old survivor – who accused them of unnecessarily probing into the past when bygones should be bygones, acting as the pawn of Western powers and their lobbies and lackeys, and giving their island a terrible image in the international arena – that she and her Greek colleague left the place shaken. They stopped under a street light to catch their breath, their faces shrivelled in the sodium glare.

'There's a pub around the corner,' the other woman said. 'How about a quick drink?'

They found a table at the back, the smell of beer-soaked carpets and damp coats strangely soothing. Defne brought two white wines from the bar. It was the first drink she would have since she had found out she was pregnant. Now she was breastfeeding. Something like relief spreading across her face, she cradled the glass between her palms, feeling its chill slowly turn to warmth. She chuckled nervously, and before they knew it both women were laughing so hard, with tears in their eyes, that the other customers began to look at them disapprovingly, wondering what was so funny, no one imagining it was pain they were setting free.

That night Defne got home late and found Kostas asleep on the sofa with the baby by his side. He startled awake when he heard her footsteps.

'Sorry, darling, I woke you up.'

'It's okay.' He rose slowly, stretching his arms.

'How is Ada? Did you give her the milk I left?'

'Yup, I did, but she woke up two hours later crying. So I tried some formula. Otherwise she wouldn't stop.'

'Oh, I'm sorry,' Defne said again. 'I should have come earlier.'

'That's all right, don't apologize, you needed a break,' Kostas said, surveying her face. 'You okay?'

She didn't answer and he couldn't be sure she had heard him.

She kissed the baby's forehead, smiling at her puckered face, rosebud mouth, and then she said, 'I don't want Ada to be burdened by the things that hurt us. I want you to promise me, Kostas. You won't tell her much about our past. Just a few basic things, but that's it, nothing more.'

'Sweetheart, you can't stop children from asking questions. As she grows up, she's going to be curious.'

Outside, a truck clawed its way down the street, so late an hour, its rumbling filling the void where their voices had been a moment ago.

She frowned, mulling over his words. 'Curiosity is temporary. It comes and it goes. If Ada tries to probe deeper, you can always answer without really answering.'

'Come on, Defne –' He touched her arm.

'No!' She pulled herself away.

'It's late, let's talk tomorrow,' said Kostas, her cold response and the abrupt gesture slicing him like the edge of a blade.

'Please don't patronize me.' Her dark eyes were inscrutable. 'I've thought about this for so long. I've seen how it works. I talk to people all the time. It doesn't go away, Kostas. Once it's inside your head, whether it's your own memory or your parents', or your grandparents', this fucking pain becomes part of your flesh. It stays with you and marks you permanently. It messes up your psychology and shapes how you think of yourself and others.'

The baby stirred just then, and both of them turned towards her, worried that they had made too much noise. But whatever dream she was floating in, Ada had still not left it, her expression glowing calmly as if listening out for something.

Defne sat on the sofa, her arms dangling by her side, a lifeless doll. 'Just promise me, that's all I ask. If we want our child to have a good future we have to cut her off from our past.'

Kostas picked up the smell of alcohol on her breath. A faint, coppery whiff in the air that reminded him of an evening far away, as he had sat still and helpless, looking at songbirds preserved in jars. Had she started drinking again? He told himself she needed an evening out, a little free time for herself after the difficult months of pregnancy and birth and childcare. He told himself not to worry. They were a family now.

Kitchen

London, late 2010s

The day before she was due to leave, Meryem, keen to dispense further advice, ramped up her teachings, firing off a volley of cooking tips and cleaning tricks.

'Now don't forget, always use vinegar to get rid of the limescale on your showerhead. Try scrubbing the bathtub with half a grapefruit. Sprinkle rock salt on it first. It'll be spotless!'

'Right.'

Meryem's eyes panned the kitchen as she spun on her heel. 'Let's see, I descaled the kettle, polished the cutlery. Do you know how to take the rust off? Rub it with onion. And then, what else . . . oh, yes, I removed the coffee stains on the table. It's simple, you just need some toothpaste, like brushing your teeth. Always keep baking soda in the house, it works wonders.'

'Got it.'

'All right, lastly, is there anything special you want me to bake before I go?'

'I don't know.' Ada shrugged. Out of the recesses of her memory came a long-unsampled flavour. 'Maybe *khataifi*.'

Meryem looked both pleased and annoyed to hear this. 'No problem, let's do it, but the name is *kadayif*,' she said, translating the Greek into Turkish.

'*Khataifi*, *kadayif*,' Ada said. 'What difference does it make?'

But it did make a difference to Meryem as she kept correcting names with the zeal of a grammar teacher faced with a split infinitive: not *halloumi* but *hellim*; not *tzatziki* but *cacik*; not *dolmades* but *dolma*; not *kourabiedes* but *kurabiye* . . . and on and on she went. As far as Meryem was concerned, 'Greek baklava' was

'Turkish baklava', and if the Syrians or Lebanese or Egyptians or Jordanians or any others laid claim to her beloved dessert, tough luck, it wasn't theirs either. While the slightest change in her dietary vocabulary could rub her up the wrong way, it was the label 'Greek coffee' that particularly boiled her blood, which to her was, and would always be, 'Turkish coffee'.

By now Ada had long discovered that her aunt was full of contradictions. Although she could be movingly respectful and empathetic towards other cultures, and acutely aware of the dangers of cultural animosities, she automatically transformed into a kind of nationalist in the kitchen, a culinary patriot. Ada found it amusing that a grown woman could be this touchy about words, but she kept her thoughts to herself. She did, however, half jokingly say, 'Jeez, you are so sensitive about food.'

'Food is a sensitive subject,' Meryem said. 'It can cause issues. You know what they say, eat your bread fresh, drink your water clean, and if you have meat on your plate, tell the world it's fish.'

If food was a delicate topic, sex was the next trickiest item on Meryem's list. She could never broach the subject directly, preferring to tread around it in hazy circles.

'Don't you have friends at school?'

'A few. Ed is a good friend.'

'Is that Edwina?'

'It's Edward.'

Meryem's brows snapped together. 'Cotton playing with fire. Boys are not "friends" at your age. Maybe when they are old and feeble and have no teeth left in their mouths . . . But right now they think of only one thing.'

A flash of mischief crossed Ada's face. 'And what thing might that be?'

Meryem waved her hand. 'You know what I'm talking about.'

'I just wanted you to spell it out,' said Ada. 'So boys want sex, but girls don't. Is that it?'

'Women are *different*.'

'Different because we have no sexual desires?'

'Because we are busy! Women have more important things to do. Taking care of our families, our parents, our children, our communities, making sure everything runs smoothly. Women are holding up the world, we don't have time for monkey business!'

Ada pursed her lips, suppressing a smile.

'What's so funny?'

'You! The way you talk. You sound like you've never watched a nature documentary. Why don't you have a chat with my father, he'll tell you about antelopes, honeybees, Komodo dragons . . . You might be surprised to hear that females can be much more interested in sex than males.'

'For babies, *canim*. That's the only reason. Lady animals don't care about sex otherwise.'

'What about bonobos?'

'Never heard of them.'

Taking out her phone, Ada showed her aunt a picture.

But Meryem did not seem impressed. 'That's a monkey, we are human.'

'We share almost ninety-nine per cent of our DNA with bonobos.' Ada put the phone back in her pocket. 'Anyway, I think you're expecting too much of women. You want them to sacrifice themselves for the happiness of others, try to accommodate everyone and conform to beauty standards that aren't based in reality. That's unfair.'

'The world is unfair,' said Meryem. 'If a stone falls on an egg, it is bad for the egg; if an egg falls on a stone, it is still bad for the egg.'

Ada studied her aunt for a moment. 'I don't think we women need to be so hard on ourselves.'

'Well, never say amen to an impossible prayer.'

'It's not impossible! Why can't we be like Canada geese? The males and females look almost alike. And besides, most female birds don't even have gaudy feathers. It's usually the male that looks more colourful.'

Meryem shook her head. 'Sorry, that won't do. For us humans, the rules are different. A woman needs pretty plumage.'

'But why?'

'Because otherwise another female will swoop down and snatch her mate away. And, trust me, when a bird reaches my age, she does not want to be alone in her nest.'

Ada stopped asking questions then, not because she agreed with anything her aunt said but because she had sensed, once again, underneath all the spirited talk and assertive personality, how timid and vulnerable the woman really was.

'I'll keep that in mind,' said Ada. 'So do you have any more cleaning tips?'

Ways of Seeing

London, late 2010s

Kostas sat typing away in his study – a former potting shed – his face thrown into sharp relief by the blue light from the computer screen. He had built a bolthole here for himself, his desk piled with documents, books and academic papers. Every now and then he glanced out of the window, allowing his gaze to settle on the garden. Now that Storm Hera was gone, there was something new in the air, the sense of a delicate peace that comes after a ferocious battle. In a few weeks, spring would arrive and he would unearth the fig tree.

The week Defne died, he had been in Australia on a research trip, leading an international team of scientists. After wildfires had devastated large swathes of forest, he and his colleagues wanted to understand whether trees that had endured drought or extreme heat in the past, or trees with ancestors that might have coped with similar traumas, responded to the present fires any differently to others.

They had carried out numerous experiments on perennial plants in ash-rich soil but were focusing primarily on the common species *Eucalyptus grandis*. When they subjected survivors' seedlings to high-intensity fires in lab conditions, they discovered that trees whose ancestors had experienced hardship reacted more swiftly and produced extra proteins, which they then used to protect and regenerate their cells. Their findings were consistent with earlier studies that showed how genetically identical species of poplars growing in similar conditions responded differently to traumas, such as dry spells, depending on where they came from. Could all this mean that trees not only had some kind of memory but, also, they passed it on to their offspring?

He called Defne, excited to share his findings, but he was not able to reach her. He phoned again later in the day, and then he tried both the landline and Ada's mobile, but each time there was no answer.

He couldn't sleep that night, a tightness in his chest as if a serpent had wound its coils around him. At three in the morning the phone by his bed began to ring. Ada's voice, almost unrecognizable, her gasps between words no less desperate than her sobs. Pushing its way through the heavy curtains, the neon sign outside his hotel room blinked orange and white, and back to pitch-black. In the bathroom as he washed his face, the eyes that stared at him from the mirror were those of a fearful stranger. Abandoning the experiment and the team, he took a cab to the airport and returned to London on the first flight.

Ever since he was a boy, trees had offered him solace, a sanctuary of his own, and he had perceived life through the colours and density of their boughs and foliage. Yet his profound admiration for plants had also afflicted him with a strange sense of guilt, as if by paying this much attention to nature he was neglecting something if not more crucial then at least as urgent and compelling – human suffering. Much as he loved the arboreal world and its complex ecosystem, was he, in some roundabout way, avoiding the day-to-day realities of politics and conflict? A part of him understood that people, especially where he came from, might see it this way, but a bigger part of him fiercely rejected the idea. He had always believed there was no hierarchy – or there should be none – between human pain and animal pain, and no precedence of human rights over animal rights, or indeed of human rights over those of plants, for that matter. He knew many among his fellow countrymen would be deeply offended if he voiced this out loud.

Back in Nicosia, when he observed the work of the Committee on Missing Persons, an unspeakable thought had crossed his mind. It was a peaceful thought, as far as he was concerned. The bodies of the missing, if unearthed, would be taken care of by their loved ones and given the proper burials they deserved. But even those who would never be found were not exactly forsaken. Nature tended to them. Wild thyme and sweet marjoram grew from the same soil, the ground splitting open like a crack in a window to make way for possibilities. Myriad birds, bats and ants carried those seeds far away, where they would grow into fresh vegetation. In the most surprising ways, the victims continued to live, because that is what nature did to death, it transformed abrupt endings into a thousand new beginnings.

Defne had understood how Kostas felt. Over the years they'd had their disagreements, but each time they had come to respect their differences. They were an unlikely couple not because she was Turkish and he was Greek, but because their personalities were strikingly dissimilar. For her, human suffering was paramount and justice the ultimate aim, whereas for him, human existence, though no doubt precious beyond words, had no special priority in the ecological chain.

His throat tightened as he glanced at the framed photo on his desk, taken on a trip to South Africa, just the three of them. With the tip of his index finger, he touched his wife's face, traced his daughter's trusting smile. Defne was gone but Ada was here, and he worried that he was failing her. He had been withdrawn and taciturn this past year, a cloud of lethargy looming over everything he said and couldn't say.

They had been so close once, he and Ada. Like a bard imbuing each tale with suspense, he would tell her about night-blooming chocolate flowers, slow-growing lithops – flowering stones – that strangely resembled pebbles, and *Mimosa pudica*, a plant so shy it would shrink away at the slightest touch. It warmed his heart to see his daughter's endless fascination with nature; he would always patiently answer her questions. Back then, such was the strength of their bond that Defne, only half jokingly, would complain: 'I'm jealous. See how Ada listens to you! She admires you, darling.'

That phase of Ada's life – for it was a phase no matter how many years it might have lasted – was over. Nowadays when his daughter looked at him, she saw his weaknesses, failures and insecurities. Maybe some day in the future, a brighter phase would ensue. But they were not there yet. Kostas closed his eyes, thinking of Defne, her intelligent eyes, her pensive smile, her sudden sparks of anger, her strong sense of justice and equality . . . What would she do if she were in his place now?

'Fight back, ashkim . . . Fight your way out.'

On an impulse, Kostas stood up and left his desk. He walked down the corridor that joined his office to the house, his eyes smarting slightly with the change of light. When he reached Ada's room, he found the door open. Her hair pinned up loosely with a pencil, her head buried in her phone, her face locked in hushed concentration, she bore a nervous thoughtfulness that reminded Kostas of her mother.

'Hi, love.'

She immediately hid her phone. 'Hi, Dad.'

He pretended not to notice. There was no point in launching into a speech against excessive use of gadgets.

'How's the homework going?'

'Fine,' said Ada. 'How's the book going?'

'I'm about to finish it.'

'Oh, wow, that's great – congratulations.'

'Well, I don't know if it's any good . . .' He paused, cleared his throat. 'I was wondering if you'd like to read it and tell me what you think. It'd mean a lot to me.'

'Me? But I know nothing about trees.'

'That's all right, you know so much about everything else.'

She smiled. 'Okay, cool.'

'Cool.' Kostas rapped his knuckles against the door, playing a rhythm he had heard earlier in the day. He mentioned an artist whom he knew Ada loved to listen to, day and night. 'He's not bad. Quite good, actually. A wicked singer with some killer tunes . . .'

Ada suppressed her smile this time, amused at her father's lame attempt to connect with her through emo rap, of which he hadn't got a clue. Maybe she should try speaking his language instead.

'Dad, do you remember, you used to tell me how people look at a tree but don't ever see the same thing? I was thinking about it the other day but couldn't recall exactly. What was that?'

'Right, I think I said it's possible to deduce a person's character based on what they first notice in a tree.'

'Carry on.'

'This is not based on any scientific methodology or empirical research –'

'I know that! Go ahead.'

'What I meant was, some people stand in front of a tree and the first thing they notice is the trunk. These are the ones who prioritize order, safety, rules, continuity. Then there are those who pick out the branches before anything else. They yearn for change, a sense of freedom. And then there are those who are drawn to the roots, though concealed under the ground. They have a deep emotional attachment to their heritage, identity, traditions . . .'

'So which one are you?'

'Don't ask me. I study trees for a living.' He smoothed his hair. 'But for a long time, I think I was in the first group. I longed for a sense of order, security.'

'What about my mother?'

'Second group, definitely. She'd see the branches first and always. She loved freedom.'

'What about Aunt Meryem?'

'Your aunt is probably in the third group. Traditions.'

'How about me?'

Kostas smiled, holding her gaze with his. 'You, my love, are of a different tribe altogether. You spot a tree and you want to connect the trunk and the branches and the roots. You want to hold them all in your vision. And that's a great talent, your inquisitiveness. Don't ever lose it.'

That night in her bedroom, listening to the singer her father was trying hard to like, Ada opened the curtains and stared into the darkness canopying the garden. Invisible as it was, she knew the fig tree was there, biding its time, growing, changing, remembering – trunk and branches and roots all together.

Fig Tree

The ancients believed there was a pole that ran through the universe, joining the underworld to earth and heaven, and at the centre of this pole towered, mighty and magnificent, the great cosmic tree. Its branches held up the sun, the moon, the stars and the constellations, and its roots reached all the way down into the abyss. But when it came to defining exactly what type of plant this might be, humans fell into bitter disagreement. Some said it could only be a balsam poplar. Others argued it must be a tamarind. Yet others insisted it was a cedar or a hickory or a baobab or a sandalwood. This is how humanity divided into hostile nations, warring tribes.

It was a very unwise thing to do in my opinion since all trees are essential and merit attention and commendation. You might even say there is a tree for every mood and every moment. When you have something precious to give to the universe, a song or a poem, you should first share it with a golden oak before anyone else. If you are feeling discouraged and defenceless, look for a Mediterranean cypress or a flowering horse chestnut. Both are strikingly resilient, and they will tell you about all the fires they have survived. And if you want to emerge stronger and kinder from your trials, find an aspen to learn from – a tree so tenacious it can fend off even the flames that aim to destroy it.

If you are hurting and have no one willing to listen to you, it might do you good to spend time beside a sugar maple. If, on the other hand, you are suffering from excessive self-esteem, do pay a visit to a cherry tree and observe its blossoms, which, though undoubtedly pretty, are no less ephemeral than vainglory. By the time you leave, you might feel a bit more humble, more grounded.

To reminisce about the past, seek out a holly to sit under; to dream about the future, choose a magnolia instead. And if it is friends and friendships on your mind, the most suitable companion would be a spruce or a ginkgo. When you arrive at a crossroads and don't know which path to take, contemplating quietly by a sycamore might help.

If you are an artist in need of inspiration, a blue jacaranda or a sweetly scented mimosa could stir your imagination. If it is renewal you are after, seek a wych elm, and if you have too many regrets, a weeping willow will offer solace. When you are in trouble or at your lowest point, and have no one in whom to confide, a hawthorn would be the right choice. There is a reason why hawthorns are home to fairies and known to protect pots of treasure.

For wisdom, try a beech; for intelligence, a pine; for bravery, a rowan; for generosity, a hazel; for joy, a juniper; and for when you need to learn to let go of what you cannot control, a birch with its white-silver bark, peeling and shedding layers like old skins. Then again, if it's love you're after, or love you have lost, come to the fig, always the fig.

The Hidden

London, late 2010s

The evening her aunt left, Ada went to bed early with period cramps. Hugging a hot-water bottle to her stomach, she tried to read a little, but a jumble of thoughts raced through her mind, making it hard to concentrate. Outside the window, she could see the neighbour's Christmas lights still blinking, looking less bright, less festive somehow now the holiday was over. There was a sense in the air of things coming to an end, an exhalation almost.

Cramps were not the only thing bothering her. Her aunt's words about having a female role model around the house had rekindled in her soul a familiar concern: that some day soon her father might marry again. Since her mother's death, this suspicion had become as much a part of her as her heartbeat. But this evening she did not want to be caught yet again in the cobwebs of anxiety that she was all too capable of weaving.

She stepped out into the corridor. A sliver of light was seeping from under her father's door. He must be staying up late – again. In the past her parents would regularly burn the midnight oil together, hunched at each end of the table, their heads buried in their books, the ghost of Duke Ellington singing in the background.

She knocked on the door, pushed it open. She found her father by his computer, his forehead caught up in its glow, his eyes shut, his head cocked to one side, a cup of tea cooling on the table.

'Dad?'

For a moment she feared he might be dead, that crawling terror of losing him, too, and only when she saw his chest rise and fall could she relax a little.

She shifted on her feet, setting the floorboard creaking.

'Ada?' Kostas jolted awake, rubbing his eyes. 'I didn't hear you come in.' Putting on his glasses, he smiled at her. 'Sweetheart, why are you not sleeping? Is everything okay?'

'Yeah, it's just . . . you used to make me toasties, why don't you any more?'

He raised his eyebrows. 'Our fridge is full of your aunt's endless leftovers and you missed my toasties?'

'That's different,' said Ada. 'Like we used to do.'

It was one of their guilty secrets. Despite Defne's objections, the two of them would tuck into toasties in front of the TV late at night, knowing it wasn't the healthiest thing to do but enjoying themselves anyway.

'Actually, I fancy one myself,' said Kostas.

The kitchen, bathed in the light of the moon, smelled vaguely of vinegar and baking soda. Ada grated cheese while Kostas buttered slices of bread and placed them on the pan.

The words tumbled out before Ada could stop them. 'I'm fully aware that one day you might want to date someone . . . and I think I'll be okay with that.'

He turned towards her, his gaze searching.

'It'll happen,' Ada said. 'I just need you to know I'll be fine if you start dating again. I want you to be happy. Mum would have wanted you to be happy. When I go to uni, you're going to be lonely otherwise.'

'How about we make a deal?' said Kostas. 'I keep making you toasties and you stop worrying about me.'

When the food was ready, they sat opposite each other at the kitchen table, the night air condensing itself into droplets of water on the windowpane.

'I loved your mother. She was the love of my life.' His voice didn't sound tired any more. There was a brightness to it, like a golden thread unspooling.

Ada stared down at her hands. 'I never understood why she did that. If she'd cared about me . . . cared about you . . . she wouldn't have.'

They had never talked openly about Defne's death. It was a burning coal in the centre of their lives, impossible to touch.

'Your mother loved you very much.'

'Then why . . . She was drinking a lot, you know that. She took so many pills when you were away, even though she must have realized it could be dangerous. You said it wasn't suicide. The coroner said it wasn't suicide. But what was it, then?'

'It wasn't in her control, Aditsa.'

'I'm sorry, I find that hard to believe. She chose this, didn't she, though she knew what it would do to us? It was totally selfish. I can't forgive her. You weren't here, I was the only one at home with her. All day long she stayed in her room. I thought she must be sleeping or something. I tried not to make any noise. You remember how she could get sometimes . . . so closed off. The whole afternoon went by and still no sign of her. I knocked on the door – not a sound. I walked in and she wasn't in her bed . . . she must have gone, I thought stupidly. Maybe she climbed through the window and left me . . . Then I saw her, lying on the carpet like a broken doll, clasping her knees tightly together.' Ada blinked furiously. 'She must have fallen off the bed.'

Kostas looked down, tracing the lines inside his palm with the edge of his thumb. When he lifted his eyes, they were full of pain, but also something akin to peace.

'When I was a young botanist, an academic in Oxfordshire gave me a call. He was an erudite man, a professor in classical languages and literature, but he had no knowledge of trees and there was this Spanish chestnut in his garden that wasn't doing well. He couldn't understand what was wrong, so he asked me to help. I examined the branches, the leaves. I took samples of the bark, checked the quality of the soil. All the tests came back fine.

But the more I observed, the more I was convinced that the professor was right. The tree was dying. I couldn't understand why. In the end, I grabbed a shovel and I began to dig. That is when I learned a lesson I have never forgotten. You see, the tree's roots were encircling the base of its trunk, choking off the flow of water and nutrients. Nobody had realized because it was invisible, below the soil surface . . .'

'I don't get it,' said Ada.

'It's called girdling. There can be many reasons behind it. In this case, the chestnut was grown in a circular container before being planted out as a sapling. My point is, the tree was being strangled by its own roots. Because it was happening under the earth, it was undetectable. If the encircling roots are not found in time, they start putting pressure on the tree and it just becomes too much to bear.'

Ada was silent.

'Your mother loved you very much, more than anything in this world. Her death has nothing to do with the absence of love. She was blooming and thriving with your love, and I'd like to believe with mine, too, but underneath, something was strangling her – the past, the memories, the roots.'

Ada bit her bottom lip, saying nothing. She remembered how, when she was six years old, she had broken her thumb, and it had swollen to twice its size, the flesh expanding and pushing against itself. That's how words felt in her mouth right now.

Kostas grabbed his plate, realizing she did not wish to talk any more. 'Let's go and see if we can find a film to watch.'

That night, Ada and Kostas ate their toasties in front of the TV. They couldn't agree on a movie, but it felt good to sit there looking for it, and it felt light, too, that moment, for as long as it lasted.

Cynical Hawk

London, late 2010s

On the first day of term, Ada woke up early, too nervous to sleep. She dressed in a hurry, despite having plenty of time, and checked the contents of her rucksack even though she had packed everything carefully the night before. Having barely any appetite, she made do with a glass of milk for breakfast. She covered a few pimples that had appeared overnight with concealer, then worried that she might have made them more visible. She tried putting on a little eyeliner and some mascara, then changed her mind halfway through and spent the next ten minutes scrubbing her face. Seeing her panic, her father insisted on driving her in.

When Kostas pulled over in front of the school, Ada held her breath, still as a marble statue, refusing to get out of the car. Together they watched the students milling about in front of the gates, gathering and breaking apart in groups like shifting pieces in a kaleidoscope. Through the closed windows, they could hear their chatter and peals of laughter.

'Do you want me to walk in with you?' Kostas asked.

Ada shook her head.

Reaching across, Kostas took his daughter's hand. 'It's going to be okay, Ada *mou*. You're going to be fine.'

Ada twisted her lips but said nothing, focusing her gaze on the dry leaves stuck under the windscreen wipers.

Kostas removed his glasses and rubbed his eyes. 'Did I ever tell you about blue jays?'

'No, Dad. Don't think so.'

'Remarkable birds. Highly intelligent. They puzzle ornithologists with their behaviour.'

'Why?'

'Because these small birds, just about ten inches long, are excellent at mimicking hawks. Particularly red-shouldered hawks.'

Ada turned aside, speaking to her own reflection in the window. 'Why do they do that?'

'Well, scientists think the mimicry is intended as a hint to fellow jays, warning them there's a hawk nearby. But some people believe there could be another explanation, that it could be a survival strategy: when the bird is frightened, it helps its nerves to impersonate a hawk. This way, the blue jay scares off its enemies and feels braver.'

Ada flicked a glance at her father. 'Are you telling me to pretend to be someone else?'

'It's not *pretending*. When the blue jay soars into the sky calling out like a red-shouldered hawk, in that moment, it becomes one. Otherwise it couldn't have made the same sound. You see what I mean?'

'All right, Dad, I get the message. I'll go and flap around the classroom like a hawk.'

'A cynical hawk,' said Kostas with a smile. 'I love you. I'm proud of you. And if they give you a hard time, those kids, we'll find a way to sort it out. Please don't worry.'

Ada patted her father's hand. There was something childlike in the way grown-ups had a need for stories. They held a naive belief that by telling an inspiring anecdote – the right fable at the right time – they could lift their children's moods, motivate them to great achievements and simply change reality. There was no point in telling them that life was more complicated than that and words less magical than they presumed.

'Thank you, Dad.'

'I love you,' Kostas said again.

'I love you too.'

Grabbing her school bag and the knitted scarf that her aunt had given her as a present, Ada climbed out of the car. She walked slowly, her legs weighing heavier as she approached the building. A few feet ahead, she spotted Zafaar, leaning against a balustrade, chatting with a group of boys. She felt a sharp stab of hurt as she remembered how he had laughed at her. She quickened her steps.

'Hey, Ada!' He had seen her and left his friends to talk to her.

She stopped, the muscles of her back tensing.

'How you doing?'

'Fine.'

'Look, I felt bad for you when that thing happened.'

'You don't need to feel bad for me.'

Zafaar shifted his weight from one foot to the other. 'No, seriously. I know about your mum, I'm sorry.'

'Thank you.'

Zafaar waited for her to say something else and, when she didn't, buried his hands in the pockets of his blazer. His cheeks flushed.

'Well, see ya,' he said quickly.

She watched him walk away, a new spring in his step as he headed back towards his friends.

In the classroom Ada chatted with Ed a little, half listening to his explanation of how to mix beats using two decks. She then sat in her usual seat by the window, pretending not to notice the curious stares and furtive whispers, the sporadic giggles.

At the next desk, Emma-Rose was watching her with a sort of inquisitive detachment. 'Feeling better?'

'I'm okay, thanks.'

They were distracted by sounds from the opposite side of the room – a group of boys were holding their throats as if they were choking or silently screaming, their mouths wide open, their eyes screwed shut, their faces red with suppressed mischief.

'Ignore them, they're all idiots,' Emma-Rose said with a frown

337

that instantly evolved to a smile. 'Oh, did you hear what happened? Zafaar told Noah he has a crush on someone in our class.'

'Really? . . . So do you know who?' said Ada, trying to sound uninterested.

'Not yet. I need to do a bit more digging.'

Ada felt her cheeks grow hot. She didn't expect it to be her, but then maybe, just maybe, there was a chance.

In a few minutes, Mrs Walcott walked in.

'Hello, everyone. How wonderful to see you all! Hope you had a great break. I'm assuming you have all interviewed an elderly relative and learned a lot about their lives. Please get out your assignments and I will come round and collect them.'

Without waiting to hear their responses, Mrs Walcott moved straight into the lesson. Ada looked back at Emma-Rose and saw her roll her eyes. She couldn't help smiling at the juvenile gesture, remembering her aunt's comments. She skimmed her interview notes and essay, and felt a surge of pride at the thought of Mrs Walcott reading about Auntie Meryem's life.

In the evening, her aunt called.

'Adacim, how was school? Did they give you a hard time?'

'It was all right, actually. It was surprisingly fine.'

'Wonderful.'

'Yeah, I suppose,' said Ada. 'Are you wearing your colourful clothes?'

A giggle. 'Not yet.'

'Start with that pistachio-green skirt,' Ada said and paused. 'You know what, next summer, after the Earth Summit, my father promised to take me to Cyprus.'

'Really?' Meryem's voice rose. 'That's such great news. I've always wanted this to happen. Oh, I can't wait. I'll show you around. I'll take you everywhere . . . But wait, which side will you visit? I mean, there's no harm in seeing both, but which one will be first? North or south?'

'I'll come to the island,' Ada said, a new note in her voice. 'I just want to meet islanders, like myself.'

How to Unbury a Fig Tree in Seven Steps

1. Locate precisely where in your garden you buried your fig all those weeks or months ago.

2. Gently peel away the insulating layers you laid on top.

3. Excavate all soil and leaves, making sure not to harm the tree with your spade or rake while doing so.

4. Inspect your fig tree and check if the cold has done any damage.

5. Carefully stand your tree up and untie the ropes fastened around it. Some branches might break or bend, but the tree will be fine and glad to be upright again.

6. Pack the soil back round the roots to make sure your tree is well supported and ready to face the spring.

7. Say some nice words to your fig tree to welcome her back to the world.

Fig Tree

I can feel the harsh winter beginning to relax its grip, the wheel of seasons revolve once again. Persephone, the goddess of spring, returns to earth, a wreath of silver blossoms about her golden hair. She treads gently above the ground, holding in one hand a bouquet of red poppies and sheaves of wheat, and in the other a broom to brush aside the snow, to remove the mud and the rime. I can hear solid memories dissolving into liquid and water dribbling from the eaves, speaking its own truth, *drip-drip-drip*.

In nature everything talks all the time. Fruit bats, honeybees, wild goats, grass snakes . . . Some screech, others squeak, yet others caw, chatter, croak or chirp. Boulders rumble, grapevines rustle. The salt lakes narrate tales of warfare and homecoming; the field roses chant in unison when the *meltemi* blows; the citrus orchards recite odes to eternal youth.

The voices of our motherlands never stop echoing in our minds. We carry them with us everywhere we go. Still today, here in London, buried in this grave, I can hear those same sounds, and I wake up trembling like a sleepwalker who realizes he has ventured dangerously into the night.

In Cyprus, all creatures, big and small, express themselves – all, that is, except the storks. Although the island is not exactly on their migratory routes, every now and then, a few lonely storks, blown off course by the air currents, will spend several days there before resuming their journey. They are large, graceful and, unlike any other bird, incapable of singing. But Cypriots will tell you this wasn't always so. There was a time when these long-legged wading birds trilled enchanting melodies about far-off kingdoms and destinations unknown, beguiling their audience with tales of overseas odysseys and heroic adventures. Those who heard them were so entranced they forgot to irrigate their crops or shear their sheep or milk their cows or gossip in the shade with their neighbours, and, at night, they even forgot to make love to their sweethearts. Why exhaust yourself with work or engage in tittle-tattle or pledge your heart to someone when all you wanted was to sail away to distant shores? Life came to a halt. In the end, annoyed that the order of things had been disrupted, Aphrodite meddled, as she always does. She put a curse on all the storks passing over Cyprus. From then on the birds remained silent no matter what they saw or heard down there.

Legends, perhaps, but I do not belittle them.

I believe in legends and in the unspoken secrets they try to gently convey.

Even so, take everything I have recounted with a grain of salt, and everything I might have failed to say, too, for I may not be the most impartial narrator. I have my own biases. After all, I have never been too fond of gods and goddesses, and their endless hostilities and rivalries.

I found it touching that Meryem, bless her heart, built a tower of stones in the garden that night, a bridge made of songs and prayers, so that I could leave this world peacefully and move on to the next, if there is one. It was a nice wish, as far as wishes go. But my sister and I have always had our separate views. Whereas she wanted me to migrate to the hereafter, hopefully to be ushered through the gates of paradise, I much preferred to stay where I am, rooted in the earth.

After I died and emptiness swallowed me whole like a huge yawning mouth, I floated about aimlessly for a while. I saw myself lying on the hospital bed where I had remained in a coma, and I knew it was sad but I could not feel what I knew; it was as if a glass wall had been erected between my heart and the sadness surrounding it. But then the door opened and Ada walked in with flowers in her hand, her expectant smile fading with every timid step, and I could not bear watching any more.

I was not ready to leave them. Nor was I able to relocate, yet again. I wanted to continue to be anchored in love, the only thing that humans have yet to destroy. But where could I possibly reside now that I was no longer alive and lacked a body, a shell, a form? And then I knew. The old fig tree! Where else to seek refuge but in its arboreal embrace?

Following the funeral, watching the last of the day slide away and light become dark tranquillity, I drifted above and danced in circles around our *Ficus carica*. I seeped into her vascular tissues, absorbed water from her leaves and breathed life again through her pores.

Poor fig tree. When I metamorphosed into her, she suddenly found herself deeply in love with my husband, but I didn't mind that at all; it made me happy, in fact, to see this, and I wondered what would happen if some day Kostas were to reciprocate – if a human were to fall in love with a tree.

Women, at least where I come from, and for personal reasons of their own, have, time and again, turned themselves into native flora. Defne, Dafne, Daphne . . . Daring to reject Apollo, Daphne became a laurel. Her skin hardened into a protective bark, her arms stretched into slender branches and her hair unfurled into silky foliage while, as Ovid tells us, 'her feet, so swift a moment ago, stuck in slow-growing roots'. Whereas Daphne was transformed into a tree in order to avoid love, I transmuted into a tree in order to hold on to love.

The air is warming up, the sky above London the shyest shade of blue. I can feel a pale ray of sunshine combing the earth, excruciatingly slowly. It will take time, renewal. It will take time, healing.

But I know and I trust that, any moment now, my beloved Kostas Kazantzakis will come out to the garden with a spade in his hand, perhaps wearing his old navy parka again, the one we bought together from a vintage shop on Portobello Road, and he will dig me out and pull me up, holding me gently in his arms, and behind his beautiful eyes, engraved in his soul, they will still be there, the remnants of an island at the far end of the Mediterranean Sea, the remains of our love.

Note to the Reader

Many of the stories of the missing mentioned throughout the novel are based on true accounts. *Beneath the Carob Trees: The Lost Lives of Cyprus* by Nick Danziger and Rory MacLean, launched by the Committee on Missing Persons, UNDP, is a profoundly touching resource for those wishing to read further.

While I was researching this novel the exhumations carried out in Spain and Latin America were of great importance to me. The story about the cab driver is fictional, but inspired by a real account – a chilling remark made to Red Cross representatives by their Francoist guide – that I came across in Layla Renshaw's excellent book *Exhuming Loss: Memory, Materiality and Mass Graves of the Spanish Civil War*.

The story of Kostas's grandfather being shot by soldiers during curfew echoes a similar tragedy that took place and is mentioned in *The British and Cyprus: An Outpost of Empire to Sovereign Bases, 1878–1974* by Mark Simmons. Another insightful book is James Ker-Lindsay's *The Cyprus Problem: What Everyone Needs to Know*.

The article Kostas read in August 1974 was inspired by an article published a year later, on 8 August 1975, in *Science*, 'Are we on the brink of a pronounced global warming?', by the US climate scientist and geochemist Wally Broecker, who was one of the first people to warn us about the connection between human-induced carbon emissions and rising temperatures.

The information on floral farms and wreaths for dead British soldiers, as well as several striking details about the island, are drawn from Tabitha Morgan's wonderful *Sweet and Bitter Island: A History of the British in Cyprus*. Lawrence Durrell's *Bitter Lemons* is an illuminating, personal and perceptive take on Cyprus between 1953 and 1956. Andrekos Varnava's *British Imperialism in Cyprus: The Inconsequential Possession* provides a spectacular account of the period between 1878 and 1915, while the anthology *Nicosia Beyond Borders: Voices from a Divided City*, edited by A. Adil, A. M. Ali, B. Kemal and M. Petrides, brilliantly represents the voices of both Greek Cypriot and Turkish Cypriot writers. For personal anecdotes, myths and history, Colin Thubron's *Journey into Cyprus* offers a compelling narrative.

I came across the letter sent out to guests of Ledra Palace (published in the *Observer* on 15 September 1974) in Kenneth Morrison's *Sarajevo's Holiday Inn on the Frontline of Politics and War*.

In researching mosquitoes, one particular book that stayed with me was Timothy C. Winegard's *The Mosquito: A Human History of Our Deadliest Predator*.

For detailed instructions on how to bury a fig tree, visit https://www.instructables.com/Bury-a-Fig-Tree/

The comment about 'optimism' and 'pessimism' in plants was inspired by an article co-authored by Kouki Hikosaka, Yuko Yasumura, Onno Muller and Riichi Oguchi in *Trees in a Changing Environment: Ecophysiology, Adaptation and Future Survival*, edited by M. Tausz and N. Grulke. On the thought-provoking subject of epigenetic heredity and how memories can be passed down from one generation to the next, not only in plants but also in animals, see *What a Plant Knows: A Field Guide to the Senses* by Daniel Chamovitz.

The section on humans not seeing trees was filmed at the TED Countdown on the climate crisis and ways to build a world with net zero greenhouse emissions.

For further reading on experiments with trees, visit https://www.sciencedaily.com/releases/2011/07/110711164557.htm

For precious insight into the remarkable world of fig trees, see Mike Shanahan's *Gods, Wasps and Stranglers: The Secret History and Redemptive Future of Fig Trees*. *Figs: A Global History* by David Sutton, *The Cabaret of Plants* by Richard Mabey and *The Forest Unseen: A Year's Watch in Nature* by D. G. Haskell also provide great companion pieces. The title of one of Kostas's books in the story was inspired by Merlin Sheldrake's *Entangled Life: How Fungi Make Our Worlds, Change Our Minds and Shape Our Futures*.

So many things in this novel are based on historical facts and events, including the fate of Varosha/Famagusta, the mysterious deaths of British babies and the illegal hunting of songbirds . . . I also wanted to honour local folklore and oral traditions. But everything here is fiction – a mixture of wonder, dreams, love, sorrow and imagination.

Glossary

abla: older sister (Turkish)

agori mou: my boy (Greek)

ambelopoulia: a dish of grilled, fried, pickled or boiled songbirds (Greek)

ashkim: my love (Turkish)

ayip: shame (Turkish)

canim: my dear, my soul (Turkish)

caravanserai: an inn with a central courtyard for travellers (from Persian *karwan-sarai*)

chryso mou: my golden one (Greek)

cigerimin kösesi: the corner of my liver – term of affection (Turkish)

hamam: bath (Turkish)

khataifi: a popular dessert (Greek; *kadayif* in Turkish)

kapnistiri: incense burner (Greek)

kardoula mou: my little heart (Greek)

karidaki glyko: sweet walnut (Greek)

karpuz: watermelon (Turkish)

komboloi: worry beads (Greek)

kourabiedes: a kind of shortbread biscuit (Greek; *kurabiye* in Turkish)

levendi mou: my brave young man (Greek)

lokum: Turkish delight

majnun: a crazy person (Arabic)

mána: mother (Greek)

manti: small dumplings (traditional Turkish dish)

ma'rifah: knowledge / inner knowledge (Arabic)

mati: evil eye (Greek)

melitzanaki glyko: preserve made of baby aubergines (Greek)

meze (mezze, mazza): selection of appetizers served in parts of the Middle East, the Balkans, North Africa, Greece, Turkey and the Levant

moro mou: my baby (Greek)

mou: my (Greek)

mugumo: a fig tree known as sacred to the Kikuyu community in Kenya

nazar: evil eye (Turkish)

paidi mou: my child (Greek)

palikari mou: my strong lad (Greek)

pallikaria: strong young men (Greek)

pastelli: sesame bar, a snack (Greek)

tespih: rosary (Turkish)

xematiasma: ritual to remove the evil eye curse (Greek)

yassou: hello (Greek)

Prickly pear growing through wire fence on the border line in Nicosia, Cyprus.

Acknowledgements

When I left Istanbul for the last time, many years ago now, I didn't know I wouldn't be going back. Had I known this, what would I have taken with me in my suitcase, I have since wondered. Would it have been a book of poems, a ceramic tile glazed in turquoise, a glass ornament, an empty conch shell carried by the waves, the cry of a seagull in the wind . . . Over time, I began to think I would love to have taken a tree with me, a Mediterranean tree with portable roots, and it was that image, that thought, that unlikely possibility, that shaped this story.

My immense gratitude to Mary Mount for her brilliant editorial guidance, sharp attention to detail and unwavering faith in literature. My heartfelt thanks to Isabel Wall, who has the gentlest way of empowering writers. I work with kind, loving and strong women at Viking, and for that I am truly grateful.

Jonny Geller, my wonderful agent, thank you for listening, always being there by my side, even when a story takes me through valleys of anxiety and rivers of depression. To the beautiful, hard-working souls at Curtis Brown, thank you.

Many thanks to Stephen Barber, a dear friend and a Renaissance soul – I learn so much from our conversations, from gardenias to molecular fossils. Much love and a big thank you to Lisa Babalis – how can I express my gratitude, *se efharisto para poli*, Lisa. My affectionate thanks and respect to Gülden Plümer Küçük, and her colleagues at the Committee on Missing Persons, for everything you have done to promote peace, reconciliation and coexistence.

Boundless thanks to Karen Whitlock, for your meticulous care and generosity of heart, what a joy and blessing to work with you. My appreciation to Donna Poppy, Chloe Davis, Elizabeth

Filippouli, Hannah Sawyer, Lorna Owen, Sarah Coward and Ellie Smith, and also Anton Mueller, who, with his words and enthusiasm, continues to inspire me from the other side of the Atlantic.

Thank you to Richard Mabey for your love of nature, Robert Macfarlane for your love of earth, Jonathan Drori for your love of trees, and James Ker-Lindsay for your love of an island close to our hearts.

As ever, to my family, whose love and support inspire me and who never fail to correct my many mispronunciations, *tesekkür ediyorum yürekten*.

Above all, I want to thank the islanders who patiently answered my questions and shared their experiences and feelings with me, especially young Greek Cypriots and Turkish Cypriots whose courage, vision and wisdom will hopefully build a better world than the one we have given them.